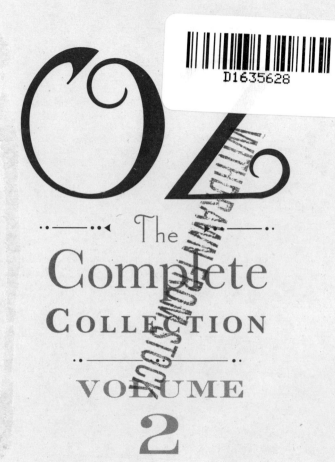

Oz

····──··◄ The ──···

Complete

Collection

··•··────•────··

Volume

2

Follow the yellow brick road to your nearest bookstore
and discover the magic of a land called

OZ

OZ, the COMPLETE COLLECTION, VOLUME 1
The WONDERFUL WIZARD of OZ
The MARVELOUS LAND of OZ
OZMA of OZ

OZ, the COMPLETE COLLECTION, VOLUME 2
DOROTHY and the WIZARD in OZ
The ROAD to OZ
The EMERALD CITY of OZ

OZ, the COMPLETE COLLECTION, VOLUME 3
The PATCHWORK GIRL of OZ
TIK-TOK of OZ
The SCARECROW of OZ

OZ, the COMPLETE COLLECTION, VOLUME 4
RINKITINK in OZ
The LOST PRINCESS of OZ
The TIN WOODMAN of OZ

OZ, the COMPLETE COLLECTION, VOLUME 5
The MAGIC of OZ
GLINDA of OZ
The ROYAL BOOK of OZ

Read them all!

Oz

The Complete Collection

Volume 2

L. Frank Baum

Includes:

DOROTHY and the WIZARD in OZ

The ROAD to OZ

The EMERALD CITY of OZ

SIMON AND SCHUSTER

This edition published in Great Britain by Simon & Schuster UK Ltd, 2013
A CBS COMPANY

Published in the USA by Aladdin,
an imprint of Simon & Schuster Children's Publishing, 2013

Dorothy and the Wizard in Oz originally published in 1908
The Road to Oz originally published in 1909
The Emerald City of Oz originally published in 1910

These titles were previously published individually.

1 3 5 7 9 10 8 6 4 2

Simon & Schuster UK Ltd
1st Floor, 222 Gray's Inn Road
London WC1X 8HB

www.simonandschuster.co.uk

Simon & Schuster Australia, Sydney
Simon & Schuster India, New Delhi

A CIP catalogue record for this book is available from the British Library

PB ISBN 978-1-4711-1702-2
E-Book ISBN 978-1-4711-1703-9

Printed and bound by CPI Group (UK) Ltd, Croydon, CR0 4YY

Contents

DOROTHY and the **WIZARD** in **OZ**

1

The **ROAD** to **OZ**

195

The **EMERALD CITY** of **OZ**

387

Dorothy
and the
Wizard
•••—••◄ in ►•—•••
Oz

Dedicated to Harriet A. B. Neal

To My Readers

It's no use; no use at all. The children won't let me stop telling tales of the Land of Oz. I know lots of other stories, and I hope to tell them, some time or another; but just now my loving tyrants won't allow me. They cry: "Oz—Oz! more about Oz, Mr. Baum!" and what can I do but obey their commands?

This is Our Book—mine and the children's. For they have flooded me with thousands of suggestions in regard to it, and I have honestly tried to adopt as many of these suggestions as could be fitted into one story.

After the wonderful success of *Ozma of Oz* it is evident that Dorothy has become a firm fixture in these Oz stories. The little ones all love Dorothy, and as one of my small friends aptly states: "It isn't a real Oz story without her." So here she is again, as sweet and gentle and innocent as ever, I hope, and the heroine of another strange adventure.

There were many requests from my little correspondents for "more about the Wizard." It seems the jolly old fellow made hosts of friends in the first Oz book, in spite of the fact that he frankly acknowledged himself "a humbug." The children had heard how he mounted into the sky in a balloon and they were all waiting for him to come down again. So what could I do but tell "what happened to the Wizard afterward"? You will find him in these pages, just the same humbug Wizard as before.

There was one thing the children demanded which I found it impossible to do in this present book: they bade me introduce Toto, Dorothy's little black dog, who has many friends among my readers. But you will see, when you begin to read the story, that Toto was in Kansas while Dorothy was in California, and so she had to start on her adventure without him. In this book Dorothy had to take her kitten with her instead of her dog; but in the next Oz book, if I am permitted to write one, I intend to tell a good deal about Toto's further history.

Princess Ozma, whom I love as much as my readers do, is again introduced in this story, and so are several of our old friends of Oz. You will also become acquainted with Jim the cab-horse, the nine tiny piglets, and Eureka, the kitten. I am sorry the kitten was not as well behaved as she ought to have been; but perhaps she wasn't brought up properly. Dorothy found her, you see, and who her parents were nobody knows.

I believe, my dears, that I am the proudest story-teller that ever lived. Many a time tears of pride and joy have stood in my eyes while I read the tender, loving, appealing letters that come to me in almost every mail from my little readers. To have pleased you, to have interested you, to have won your friendship, and perhaps your love, through my stories, is to my mind as great an achievement as to become President of the United States. Indeed, I would much rather be your story-teller, under these conditions, than to be the President. So you have helped me to fulfill my life's ambition, and I am more grateful to you, my dears, than I can express in words.

I try to answer every letter of my young correspondents; yet sometimes there are so many letters that a little time must pass before you get your answer. But be patient, friends, for the answer will surely come, and by writing to me you more than repay me for the pleasant task of preparing these books. Besides, I am proud to acknowledge that the books are partly yours, for your suggestions often guide me in telling the stories, and I am sure they would not be half so good without your clever and thoughtful assistance.

L. Frank Baum

Coronado, 1908

Chapter 1

The EARTHQUAKE

The train from 'Frisco was very late. It should have arrived at Hugson's Siding at midnight, but it was already five o'clock and the grey dawn was breaking in the east when the little train slowly rumbled up to the open shed that served for the station-house. As it came to a stop the conductor called out in a loud voice:

"Hugson's Siding!"

At once a little girl rose from her seat and walked to the door of the car, carrying a wicker suit-case in one hand and a round bird-cage covered up with newspapers in the other, while a parasol was tucked under her arm. The conductor helped her off the car and then the engineer started his train again, so that it puffed and groaned and moved slowly away up the track. The reason he was so late was because all through the night there were times when the solid earth shook and trembled under him, and the engineer was afraid that at any moment the rails might spread apart and an accident happen to his passengers. So he moved the cars slowly and with caution.

The little girl stood still to watch until the train had disappeared around a curve; then she turned to see where she was.

The shed at Hugson's Siding was bare save for an old wooden bench, and did not look very inviting. As she peered through the soft grey light not a house of any sort was visible near the station, nor was any person in sight; but after a while the child discovered a horse and buggy standing near a group of trees a short distance away. She walked toward it and found the horse tied to a tree and standing motionless, with its head hanging down almost to the ground. It was a big horse, tall and bony, with long legs and large knees and feet. She could count his ribs easily where they showed through the skin of his body, and his head was long and seemed altogether too big for him, as if it did not fit. His tail was short and scraggly, and his harness had been broken in many places and fastened together again with cords and bits of wire. The buggy seemed almost new, for it had a shiny top and side curtains. Getting around in front, so that she could look inside, the girl saw a boy curled up on the seat, fast asleep.

She set down the bird-cage and poked the boy with her parasol. Presently he woke up, rose to a sitting position and rubbed his eyes briskly.

"Hello!" he said, seeing her, "are you Dorothy Gale?"

"Yes," she answered, looking gravely at his tousled hair and blinking grey eyes. "Have you come to take me to Hugson's Ranch?"

"Of course," he answered. "Train in?"

"I couldn't be here if it wasn't," she said.

He laughed at that, and his laugh was merry and frank. Jumping out of the buggy he put Dorothy's suit-case under the seat and her bird-cage on the floor in front.

"Canary-birds?" he asked.

"Oh no; it's just Eureka, my kitten. I thought that was the best way to carry her."

The boy nodded.

"Eureka's a funny name for a cat," he remarked.

"I named my kitten that because I found it," she explained. "Uncle Henry says 'Eureka' means 'I have found it.'"

"All right; hop in."

She climbed into the buggy and he followed her. Then the boy picked up the reins, shook them, and said "Gid-dap!"

The horse did not stir. Dorothy thought he just wiggled one of his drooping ears, but that was all.

"Gid-dap!" called the boy, again.

The horse stood still.

"Perhaps," said Dorothy, "if you untied him, he would go."

The boy laughed cheerfully and jumped out.

"Guess I'm half asleep yet," he said, untying the horse. "But Jim knows his business all right—don't you, Jim?" patting the long nose of the animal.

Then he got into the buggy again and took the reins, and the horse at once backed away from the tree, turned slowly around, and began to trot down the sandy road which was just visible in the dim light.

"Thought that train would never come," observed the boy. "I've waited at that station for five hours."

"We had a lot of earthquakes," said Dorothy. "Didn't you feel the ground shake?"

"Yes; but we're used to such things in California," he replied. "They don't scare us much."

"The conductor said it was the worst quake he ever knew."

"Did he? Then it must have happened while I was asleep," he said thoughtfully.

"How is Uncle Henry?" she enquired, after a pause during which the horse continued to trot with long, regular strides.

"He's pretty well. He and Uncle Hugson have been having a fine visit."

"Is Mr. Hugson your uncle?" she asked.

"Yes. Uncle Bill Hugson married your Uncle Henry's wife's sister; so we must be second cousins," said the boy, in an amused tone. "I work for Uncle Bill on his ranch, and he pays me six dollars a month and my board."

"Isn't that a great deal?" she asked, doubtfully.

"Why, it's a great deal for Uncle Hugson, but not for me. I'm a splendid worker. I work as well as I sleep," he added, with a laugh.

"What is your name?" said Dorothy, thinking she liked the boy's manner and the cheery tone of his voice.

"Not a very pretty one," he answered, as if a little ashamed. "My whole name is Zebediah; but folks just call me 'Zeb.' You've been to Australia, haven't you?"

"Yes; with Uncle Henry," she answered. "We got to San Francisco a week ago, and Uncle Henry went right on to Hugson's Ranch for a visit while I stayed a few days in the city with some friends we had met."

"How long will you be with us?" he asked.

"Only a day. Tomorrow Uncle Henry and I must start back for Kansas. We've been away for a long time, you know, and so we're anxious to get home again."

The boy flicked the big, boney horse with his whip and looked thoughtful. Then he started to say something to his little companion, but before he could speak the buggy began to sway dangerously from side to side and the earth seemed to rise up before them. Next minute there was a roar and a sharp crash, and at her side Dorothy saw the ground open in a wide crack and then come together again.

"Goodness!" she cried, grasping the iron rail of the seat. "What was that?"

"That was an awful big quake," replied Zeb, with a white face. "It almost got us that time, Dorothy."

The horse had stopped short, and stood firm as a rock. Zeb shook the reins and urged him to go, but Jim was stubborn. Then the boy cracked his whip and touched the animal's flanks with it, and after a low moan of protest Jim stepped slowly along the road.

Neither the boy nor the girl spoke again for some minutes. There was a breath of danger in the very air, and every few moments the earth would shake violently. Jim's ears were standing erect upon his head and every muscle of his big body was tense as he trotted toward home. He was not going very fast, but on his flanks specks of foam began to appear and at times he would tremble like a leaf.

The sky had grown darker again and the wind made queer sobbing sounds as it swept over the valley.

Suddenly there was a rending, tearing sound, and the earth split into another great crack just beneath the spot where the horse was standing. With a wild neigh of terror the animal fell bodily into the pit, drawing the buggy and its occupants after him.

Dorothy grabbed fast hold of the buggy top and the boy did the same. The sudden rush into space confused them so that they could not think.

Blackness engulfed them on every side, and in breathless silence they waited for the fall to end and crush them against jagged rocks or for the earth to close in on them again and bury them forever in its dreadful depths.

The horrible sensation of falling, the darkness and the terrifying noises, proved more than Dorothy could endure and for a few moments the little girl lost consciousness. Zeb, being a boy, did not faint, but he was badly frightened, and clung to the buggy seat with a tight grip, expecting every moment would be his last.

Chapter 2

The GLASS CITY

When Dorothy recovered her senses they were still falling, but not so fast. The top of the buggy caught the air like a parachute or an umbrella filled with wind, and held them back so that they floated downward with a gentle motion that was not so very disagreeable to bear. The worst thing was their terror of reaching the bottom of this great crack in the earth, and the natural fear that sudden death was about to overtake them at any moment. Crash after crash echoed far above their heads, as the earth came together where it had split, and stones and chunks of clay rattled around them on every side. These they could not see, but they could feel them pelting the buggy top, and Jim screamed almost like a human being when a stone overtook him and struck his boney body. They did not really hurt the poor horse, because everything was falling together; only the stones and rubbish fell faster than the horse and buggy, which were held back by the pressure of the air, so that the terrified animal was actually more frightened than he was injured.

How long this state of things continued Dorothy could not even guess, she was so greatly bewildered. But bye and bye, as she stared ahead into the black chasm with a beating heart, she began to dimly see the form of the horse Jim—his head up in the air, his ears erect and his long legs sprawling in every direction as he tumbled through space. Also, turning her head, she found that she could see the boy beside her, who had until now remained as still and silent as she herself.

Dorothy sighed and commenced to breathe easier. She began to realize that death was not in store for her, after all, but that she had merely started upon another adventure, which promised to be just as queer and unusual as were those she had before encountered.

With this thought in mind the girl took heart and leaned her head over the side of the buggy to see where the strange light was coming from. Far below her she found six great glowing balls suspended in the air. The central and largest one was white, and reminded her of the sun. Around it were arranged, like the five points of a star, the other five brilliant balls; one being rose colored, one violet, one yellow, one blue and one orange. This splendid group of colored suns sent rays darting in every direction, and as the horse and buggy—with Dorothy and Zeb—sank steadily downward and came nearer to the lights, the rays began to take on all the delicate tintings of a rainbow, growing more and more distinct every moment until all the space was brilliantly illuminated.

Dorothy was too dazed to say much, but she watched one of Jim's big ears turn to violet and the other to rose, and wondered that his tail should be yellow and his body striped with blue and orange like the stripes of a zebra. Then she looked at Zeb, whose face was blue and whose hair was pink, and gave a little laugh that sounded a bit nervous.

"Isn't it funny?" she said.

The boy was startled and his eyes were big. Dorothy had a green streak through the center of her face where the blue and yellow lights came together, and her appearance seemed to add to his fright.

"I—I don't s-s-see any-thing funny—'bout it!" he stammered.

Just then the buggy tipped slowly over upon its side, the body of the horse tipping also. But they continued to fall, all together, and the boy and girl had no difficulty in remaining upon the seat, just as they were before. Then they turned bottom side up, and continued to roll slowly over until they were right side up again. During this time Jim struggled frantically, all his legs kicking the air; but on finding himself in his former position the horse said, in a relieved tone of voice:

"Well, that's better!"

Dorothy and Zeb looked at one another in wonder.

"Can your horse talk?" she asked.

"Never knew him to, before," replied the boy.

"Those were the first words I ever said," called out the horse, who had overheard them, "and I can't explain why I happened to speak then. This is a nice scrape you've got me into, isn't it?"

"As for that, we are in the same scrape ourselves," answered Dorothy, cheerfully. "But never mind; something will happen pretty soon."

"Of course," growled the horse; "and then we shall be sorry it happened."

Zeb gave a shiver. All this was so terrible and unreal that he could not understand it at all, and so had good reason to be afraid.

Swiftly they drew near to the flaming colored suns, and passed close beside them. The light was then so bright that it dazzled their eyes, and they covered their faces with their hands to escape being blinded. There was no heat in the colored suns, however, and after they had passed below them the top of the buggy shut out many of the piercing rays so that the boy and girl could open their eyes again.

"We've got to come to the bottom some time," remarked

Zeb, with a deep sigh. "We can't keep falling forever, you know."

"Of course not," said Dorothy. "We are somewhere in the middle of the earth, and the chances are we'll reach the other side of it before long. But it's a big hollow, isn't it?"

"Awful big!" answered the boy.

"We're coming to something now," announced the horse.

At this they both put their heads over the side of the buggy and looked down. Yes; there was land below them; and not so very far away, either. But they were floating very, very slowly—so slowly that it could no longer be called a fall—and the children had ample time to take heart and look about them.

They saw a landscape with mountains and plains, lakes and rivers, very like those upon the earth's surface; but all the scene was splendidly colored by the variegated lights from the six suns. Here and there were groups of houses that seemed made of clear glass, because they sparkled so brightly.

"I'm sure we are in no danger," said Dorothy, in a sober voice. "We are falling so slowly that we can't be dashed to pieces when we land, and this country that we are coming to seems quite pretty."

"We'll never get home again, though!" declared Zeb, with a groan.

"Oh, I'm not so sure of that," replied the girl. "But don't let us worry over such things, Zeb; we can't help ourselves just now, you know, and I've always been told it's foolish to borrow trouble."

The boy became silent, having no reply to so sensible a speech, and soon both were fully occupied in staring at the strange scenes spread out below them. They seemed to be falling right into the middle of a big city which had many tall buildings with glass domes and sharp-pointed spires. These spires were like great spear-points, and if they tumbled upon one of them they were likely to suffer serious injury.

Jim the horse had seen these spires, also, and his ears stood straight up with fear, while Dorothy and Zeb held their breaths in suspense. But no; they floated gently down upon a broad, flat roof, and came to a stop at last.

When Jim felt something firm under his feet the poor beast's legs trembled so much that he could hardly stand; but Zeb at once leaped out of the buggy to the roof, and he was so awkward and hasty that he kicked over Dorothy's bird-cage, which rolled out upon the roof so that the bottom came off. At once a pink kitten crept out of the upset cage, sat down upon the glass roof, and yawned and blinked its round eyes.

"Oh," said Dorothy. "There's Eureka."

"First time I ever saw a pink cat," said Zeb.

"Eureka isn't pink; she's white. It's this queer light that gives her that color."

"Where's my milk?" asked the kitten, looking up into Dorothy's face. "I'm 'most starved to death."

"Oh, Eureka! Can you talk?"

"Talk! Am I talking? Good gracious, I believe I am. Isn't it funny?" asked the kitten.

"It's all wrong," said Zeb, gravely. "Animals ought not to talk. But even old Jim has been saying things since we had our accident."

"I can't see that it's wrong," remarked Jim, in his gruff tones. "At least, it isn't as wrong as some other things. What's going to become of us now?"

"I don't know," answered the boy, looking around him curiously.

The houses of the city were all made of glass, so clear and transparent that one could look through the walls as easily as through a window. Dorothy saw, underneath the roof on which she stood, several rooms used for rest chambers, and even thought she could make out a number of queer forms huddled into the corners of these rooms.

The roof beside them had a great hole smashed through it, and pieces of glass were lying scattered in every direction. A nearby steeple had been broken off short and the fragments lay heaped beside it. Other buildings were cracked in places or had corners chipped off from them; but they must have been very beautiful before these accidents had happened to mar their perfection. The rainbow tints from the colored suns fell upon the glass city softly and gave to the buildings many delicate, shifting hues which were very pretty to see.

But not a sound had broken the stillness since the strangers had arrived, except that of their own voices. They began to wonder if there were no people to inhabit this magnificent city of the inner world.

Suddenly a man appeared through a hole in the roof next to the one they were on and stepped into plain view. He was not a very large man, but was well formed and had a beautiful face—calm and serene as the face of a fine portrait. His clothing fitted his form snugly and was gorgeously colored in brilliant shades of green, which varied as the sunbeams touched them but was not wholly influenced by the solar rays.

The man had taken a step or two across the glass roof before he noticed the presence of the strangers; but then he stopped abruptly. There was no expression of either fear or surprise upon his tranquil face, yet he must have been both astonished and afraid; for after his eyes had rested upon the ungainly form of the horse for a moment he walked rapidly to the furthest edge of the roof, his head turned back over his shoulder to gaze at the strange animal.

"Look out!" cried Dorothy, who noticed that the beautiful man did not look where he was going; "be careful, or you'll fall off!"

But he paid no attention to her warning. He reached the edge of the tall roof, stepped one foot out into the air, and walked into space as calmly as if he were on firm ground.

The girl, greatly astonished, ran to lean over the edge of the roof, and saw the man walking rapidly through the air toward the ground. Soon he reached the street and disappeared through a glass doorway into one of the glass buildings.

"How strange!" she exclaimed, drawing a long breath.

"Yes; but it's lots of fun, if it *is* strange," remarked the small voice of the kitten, and Dorothy turned to find her pet walking in the air a foot or so away from the edge of the roof.

"Come back, Eureka!" she called, in distress, "you'll certainly be killed."

"I have nine lives," said the kitten, purring softly as it walked around in a circle and then came back to the roof; "but I can't lose even one of them by falling in this country, because I really couldn't manage to fall if I wanted to."

"Does the air bear up your weight?" asked the girl.

"Of course; can't you see?" and again the kitten wandered into the air and back to the edge of the roof.

"It's wonderful!" said Dorothy.

"Suppose we let Eureka go down to the street and get some one to help us," suggested Zeb, who had been even more amazed than Dorothy at these strange happenings.

"Perhaps we can walk on the air ourselves," replied the girl.

Zeb drew back with a shiver.

"I wouldn't dare try," he said.

"Maybe Jim will go," continued Dorothy, looking at the horse.

"And maybe he won't!" answered Jim. "I've tumbled through

the air long enough to make me contented on this roof."

"But we didn't tumble to the roof," said the girl; "by the time we reached here we were floating very slowly, and I'm almost sure we could float down to the street without getting hurt. Eureka walks on the air all right."

"Eureka weights only about half a pound," replied the horse, in a scornful tone, "while I weigh about half a ton."

"You don't weigh as much as you ought to, Jim," remarked the girl, shaking her head as she looked at the animal. "You're dreadfully skinny."

"Oh, well; I'm old," said the horse, hanging his head despondently, "and I've had lots of trouble in my day, little one. For a good many years I drew a public cab in Chicago, and that's enough to make anyone skinny."

"He eats enough to get fat, I'm sure," said the boy, gravely.

"Do I? Can you remember any breakfast that I've had today?" growled Jim, as if he resented Zeb's speech.

"None of us has had breakfast," said the boy; "and in a time of danger like this it's foolish to talk about eating."

"Nothing is more dangerous than being without food," declared the horse, with a sniff at the rebuke of his young master; "and just at present no one can tell whether there are any oats in this queer country or not. If there are, they are liable to be glass oats!"

"Oh, no!" exclaimed Dorothy. "I can see plenty of nice gardens and fields down below us, at the edge of this city.

But I wish we could find a way to get to the ground."

"Why don't you walk down?" asked Eureka. "I'm as hungry as the horse is, and I want my milk."

"Will you try it, Zeb?" asked the girl, turning to her companion.

Zeb hesitated. He was still pale and frightened, for this dreadful adventure had upset him and made him nervous and worried. But he did not wish the little girl to think him a coward, so he advanced slowly to the edge of the roof.

Dorothy stretched out a hand to him and Zeb put one foot out and let it rest in the air a little over the edge of the roof. It seemed firm enough to walk upon, so he took courage and put out the other foot. Dorothy kept hold of his hand and followed him, and soon they were both walking through the air, with the kitten frisking beside them.

"Come on, Jim!" called the boy. "It's all right."

Jim had crept to the edge of the roof to look over, and being a sensible horse and quite experienced, he made up his mind that he could go where the others did. So, with a snort and a neigh and a whisk of his short tail he trotted off the roof into the air and at once began floating downward to the street. His great weight made him fall faster than the children walked, and he passed them on the way down; but when he came to the glass pavement he alighted upon it so softly that he was not even jarred.

"Well, well!" said Dorothy, drawing a long breath, "What a strange country this is."

People began to come out of the glass doors to look at the new arrivals, and pretty soon quite a crowd had assembled. There were men and women, but no children at all, and the folks were all beautifully formed and attractively dressed and had wonderfully handsome faces. There was not an ugly person in all the throng, yet Dorothy was not especially pleased by the appearance of these people because their features had no more expression than the faces of dolls. They did not smile nor did they frown, or show either fear or surprise or curiosity or friendliness. They simply stared at the strangers, paying most attention to Jim and Eureka, for they had never before seen either a horse or a cat and the children bore an outward resemblance to themselves.

Pretty soon a man joined the group who wore a glistening star in the dark hair just over his forehead. He seemed to be a person of authority, for the others pressed back to give him room. After turning his composed eyes first upon the animals and then upon the children he said to Zeb, who was a little taller than Dorothy:

"Tell me, intruder, was it you who caused the Rain of Stones?"

For a moment the boy did not know what he meant by this question. Then, remembering the stones that had fallen with them and passed them long before they had reached this place, he answered:

"No, sir; we didn't cause anything. It was the earthquake."

The man with the star stood for a time quietly thinking over this speech. Then he asked:

"What is an earthquake?"

"I don't know," said Zeb, who was still confused. But Dorothy, seeing his perplexity, answered:

"It's a shaking of the earth. In this quake a big crack opened and we fell through—horse and buggy, and all—and the stones got loose and came down with us."

The man with the star regarded her with his calm, expressionless eyes.

"The Rain of Stones has done much damage to our city," he said; "and we shall hold you responsible for it unless you can prove your innocence."

"How can we do that?" asked the girl.

"That I am not prepared to say. It is your affair, not mine. You must go to the House of the Sorcerer, who will soon discover the truth."

"Where is the House of the Sorcerer?" the girl enquired.

"I will lead you to it. Come!"

He turned and walked down the street, and after a moment's hesitation Dorothy caught Eureka in her arms and climbed into the buggy. The boy took his seat beside her and said: "Gid-dap Jim."

As the horse ambled along, drawing the buggy, the people of the glass city made way for them and formed a procession in their rear. Slowly they moved down one street and up another, turning first this way and then that, until they came to an open square in the center of which was a big glass palace having a central dome and four tall spires on each corner.

Chapter 3

The ARRIVAL of the WIZARD

The doorway of the glass palace was quite big enough for the horse and buggy to enter, so Zeb drove straight through it and the children found themselves in a lofty hall that was very beautiful. The people at once followed and formed a circle around the sides of the spacious room, leaving the horse and buggy and the man with the star to occupy the center of the hall.

"Come to us, oh, Gwig!" called the man, in a loud voice.

Instantly a cloud of smoke appeared and rolled over the floor; then it slowly spread and ascended into the dome, disclosing a strange personage seated upon a glass throne just before Jim's nose. He was formed just as were the other inhabitants of this land and his clothing only differed from theirs in being bright yellow. But he had no hair at all, and all over his bald head and face and upon the backs of his hands grew sharp thorns like those found on the branches of rose-bushes. There was even a thorn upon the tip of his nose and he looked so funny that Dorothy laughed when she saw him.

The Sorcerer, hearing the laugh, looked toward the little girl with cold, cruel eyes, and his glance made her grow sober in an instant.

"Why have you dared to intrude your unwelcome persons into the secluded Land of the Mangaboos?" he asked, sternly.

"'Cause we couldn't help it," said Dorothy.

"Why did you wickedly and viciously send the Rain of Stones to crack and break our houses?" he continued.

"We didn't," declared the girl.

"Prove it!" cried the Sorcerer.

"We don't have to prove it," answered Dorothy, indignantly. "If you had any sense at all you'd known it was the earthquake."

"We only know that yesterday came a Rain of Stones upon us, which did much damage and injured some of our people. Today came another Rain of Stones, and soon after it you appeared among us."

"By the way," said the man with the star, looking steadily at the Sorcerer, "you told us yesterday that there would not be a second Rain of Stones. Yet one has just occurred that was even worse than the first. What is your sorcery good for if it cannot tell us the truth?"

"My sorcery does tell the truth!" declared the thorn-covered man. "I said there would be but one Rain of Stones. This second one was a Rain of People-and-Horse-and-Buggy. And some stones came with them."

"Will there be any more Rains?" asked the man with the star.

"No, my Prince."

"Neither stones nor people?"

"No, my Prince."

"Are you sure?"

"Quite sure, my Prince. My sorcery tells me so."

Just then a man came running into the hall and addressed the Prince after making a low bow.

"More wonders in the air, my Lord," said he.

Immediately the Prince and all of his people flocked out of the hall into the street, that they might see what was about to happen. Dorothy and Zeb jumped out of the buggy and ran after them, but the Sorcerer remained calmly in his throne.

Far up in the air was an object that looked like a balloon. It was not so high as the glowing star of the six colored suns, but was descending slowly through the air—so slowly that at first it scarcely seemed to move.

The throng stood still and waited. It was all they could do, for to go away and leave that strange sight was impossible; nor could they hurry its fall in any way. The earth children were not noticed, being so near the average size of the Mangaboos, and the horse had remained in the House of the Sorcerer, with Eureka curled up asleep on the seat of the buggy.

Gradually the balloon grew bigger, which was proof that it was settling down upon the Land of the Mangaboos. Dorothy was surprised to find how patient the people were, for her own little heart was beating rapidly with excitement. A balloon meant to her some other arrival from the surface of the earth, and she hoped it would be some one able to assist her and Zeb out of their difficulties.

In an hour the balloon had come near enough for her to see a basket suspended below it; in two hours she could see a head looking over the side of the basket; in three hours the big balloon settled slowly into the great square in which they stood and came to rest on the glass pavement.

Then a little man jumped out of the basket, took off his tall hat, and bowed very gracefully to the crowd of Mangaboos around him. He was quite an old little man and his head was long and entirely bald.

"Why," cried Dorothy, in amazement, "it's Oz!"

The little man looked toward her and seemed as much surprised as she was. But he smiled and bowed as he answered:

"Yes, my dear; I am Oz, the Great and Terrible. Eh? And you are little Dorothy, from Kansas. I remember you very well."

"Who did you say it was?" whispered Zeb to the girl.

"It's the wonderful Wizard of Oz. Haven't you heard of him?"

Just then the man with the star came and stood before the Wizard.

"Sir," said he, "why are you here, in the Land of the Mangaboos?"

"Didn't know what land it was, my son," returned the other, with a pleasant smile; "and, to be honest, I didn't mean to visit you when I started out. I live on top of the earth, your honor, which is far better than living inside it; but yesterday I went up in a balloon, and when I came down I fell into a big crack in the earth, caused by an earthquake. I had let so much gas out of my balloon that I could not rise again, and in a few minutes the earth closed over my head. So I continued to descend until I reached this place, and if you will show me a way to get out of it, I'll go with pleasure. Sorry to have troubled you; but it couldn't be helped."

The Prince had listened with attention. Said he:

"This child, who is from the crust of the earth, like yourself, called you a Wizard. Is not a Wizard something like a Sorcerer?"

"It's better," replied Oz, promptly. "One Wizard is worth three Sorcerers."

"Ah, you shall prove that," said the Prince. "We Mangaboos have, at the present time, one of the most wonderful Sorcerers that ever was picked from a bush; but he sometimes makes mistakes. Do you ever make mistakes?"

"Never!" declared the Wizard, boldly.

"Oh, Oz!" said Dorothy; "you made a lot of mistakes when you were in the marvelous Land of Oz."

"Nonsense!" said the little man, turning red—although just then a ray of violet sunlight was on his round face.

"Come with me," said the Prince to him. "I wish you to meet our Sorcerer."

The Wizard did not like this invitation, but he could not refuse to accept it. So he followed the Prince into the great domed hall, and Dorothy and Zeb came after them, while the throng of people trooped in also.

There sat the thorny Sorcerer in his chair of state, and when the Wizard saw him he began to laugh, uttering comical little chuckles.

"What an absurd creature!" he exclaimed.

"He may look absurd," said the Prince, in his quiet voice; "but he is an excellent Sorcerer. The only fault I find with him is that he is so often wrong."

"I am never wrong," answered the Sorcerer.

"Only a short time ago you told me there would be no more Rain of Stones or of People," said the Prince.

"Well, what then?"

"Here is another person descended from the air to prove you were wrong."

"One person cannot be called 'people,'" said the Sorcerer. "If two should come out of the sky you might with justice say I was wrong; but unless more than this one appears I will hold that I was right."

"Very clever," said the Wizard, nodding his head as if pleased. "I am delighted to find humbugs inside the earth, just the same as on top of it. Were you ever with a circus, brother?"

"No," said the Sorcerer.

"You ought to join one," declared the little man seriously. "I belong to Bailum & Barney's Great Consolidated Shows— three rings in one tent and a menagerie on the side. It's a fine aggregation, I assure you."

"What do you do?" asked the Sorcerer.

"I go up in a balloon, usually, to draw the crowds to the circus. But I've just had the bad luck to come out of the sky, skip the solid earth, and land lower down than I intended. But never mind. It isn't everybody who gets a chance to see your Land of the Gabazoos."

"Mangaboos," said the Sorcerer, correcting him. "If you are a Wizard you ought to be able to call people by their right names."

"Oh, I'm a Wizard; you may be sure of that. Just as good a Wizard as you are a Sorcerer."

"That remains to be seen," said the other.

"If you are able to prove that you are better," said the

Prince to the little man, "I will make you the Chief Wizard of this domain. Otherwise—"

"What will happen otherwise?" asked the Wizard.

"I will stop you from living and forbid you to be planted," returned the Prince.

"That does not sound especially pleasant," said the little man, looking at the one with the star uneasily. "But never mind. I'll beat Old Prickly, all right."

"My name is Gwig," said the Sorcerer, turning his heartless, cruel eyes upon his rival. "Let me see you equal the sorcery I am about to perform."

He waved a thorny hand and at once the tinkling of bells was heard, playing sweet music. Yet, look where she would, Dorothy could discover no bells at all in the great glass hall.

The Mangaboo people listened, but showed no great interest. It was one of the things Gwig usually did to prove he was a sorcerer.

Now was the Wizard's turn, so he smiled upon the assemblage and asked:

"Will somebody kindly loan me a hat?"

No one did, because the Mangaboos did not wear hats, and Zeb had lost his, somehow, in his flight through the air.

"Ahem!" said the Wizard, "will somebody please loan me a handkerchief?"

But they had no handkerchiefs, either.

"Very good," remarked the Wizard. "I'll use my own hat,

if you please. Now, good people, observe me carefully. You see, there is nothing up my sleeve and nothing concealed about my person. Also, my hat is quite empty." He took off his hat and held it upside down, shaking it briskly.

"Let me see it," said the Sorcerer.

He took the hat and examined it carefully, returning it afterward to the Wizard.

"Now," said the little man, "I will create something out of nothing."

He placed the hat upon the glass floor, made a pass with his hand, and then removed the hat, displaying a little white piglet no bigger than a mouse, which began to run around here and there and to grunt and squeal in a tiny, shrill voice.

The people watched it intently, for they had never seen a pig before, big or little. The Wizard reached out, caught the wee creature in his hand, and holding its head between one thumb and finger and its tail between the other thumb and finger he pulled it apart, each of the two parts becoming a whole and separate piglet in an instant.

He placed one upon the floor, so that it could run around, and pulled apart the other, making three piglets in all; and then one of these was pulled apart, making four piglets. The Wizard continued this surprising performance until nine tiny piglets were running about at his feet, all squealing and grunting in a very comical way.

"Now," said the Wizard of Oz, "having created something

from nothing, I will make something nothing again."

With this he caught up two of the piglets and pushed them together, so that the two were one. Then he caught up another piglet and pushed it into the first, where it disappeared. And so, one by one, the nine tiny piglets were pushed together until but a single one of the creatures remained. This the Wizard placed underneath his hat and made a mystic sign above it. When he removed his hat the last piglet had disappeared entirely.

The little man gave a bow to the silent throng that had watched him, and then the Prince said, in his cold, calm voice:

"You are indeed a wonderful Wizard, and your powers are greater than those of my Sorcerer."

"He will not be a wonderful Wizard long," remarked Gwig.

"Why not?" enquired the Wizard.

"Because I am going to stop your breath," was the reply. "I perceive that you are curiously constructed, and that if you cannot breathe you cannot keep alive."

The little man looked troubled.

"How long will it take you to stop my breath?" he asked.

"About five minutes. I'm going to begin now. Watch me carefully."

He began making queer signs and passes toward the Wizard; but the little man did not watch him long. Instead, he drew a leathern case from his pocket and took from it several sharp knives, which he joined together, one after another, until they made a long sword. By the time he had attached a handle to this sword he was having much trouble to breathe, as the charm of the Sorcerer was beginning to take effect.

So the Wizard lost no more time, but leaping forward he raised the sharp sword, whirled it once or twice around his head, and then gave a mighty stroke that cut the body of the Sorcerer exactly in two.

Dorothy screamed and expected to see a terrible sight; but as the two halves of the Sorcerer fell apart on the floor she saw that he had no bones or blood inside of him at all, and that the place where he was cut looked much like a sliced turnip or potato.

"Why, he's vegetable!" cried the Wizard, astonished.

"Of course," said the Prince. "We are all vegetable, in this country. Are you not vegetable, also?"

"No," answered the Wizard. "People on top of the earth are all meat. Will your Sorcerer die?"

"Certainly, sir. He is really dead now, and will wither very quickly. So we must plant him at once, that other Sorcerers may grow upon his bush," continued the Prince.

"What do you mean by that?" asked the little Wizard, greatly puzzled.

"If you will accompany me to our public gardens," replied the Prince, "I will explain to you much better than I can here the mysteries of our Vegetable Kingdom."

Chapter 4

The VEGETABLE KINGDOM

fter the Wizard had wiped the dampness from his sword and taken it apart and put the pieces into their leathern case again, the man with the star ordered some of his people to carry the two halves of the Sorcerer to the public gardens.

Jim pricked up his ears when he heard they were going to the gardens, and wanted to join the party, thinking he might find something proper to eat; so Zeb put down the top of the buggy and invited the Wizard to ride with them. The seat was amply wide enough for the little man and the two children, and when Jim started to leave the hall the kitten jumped upon his back and sat there quite contentedly.

So the procession moved through the streets, the bearers of the Sorcerer first, the Prince next, then Jim drawing the buggy with the strangers inside of it, and last the crowd of vegetable people who had no hearts and could neither smile nor frown.

The glass city had several fine streets, for a good many people lived there; but when the procession had passed through these it came upon a broad plain covered with gardens and watered by many pretty brooks that flowed through it. There were paths through these gardens, and over some of the brooks were ornamental glass bridges.

Dorothy and Zeb now got out of the buggy and walked beside the Prince, so that they might see and examine the flowers and plants better.

"Who built these lovely bridges?" asked the little girl.

"No one built them," answered the man with the star. "They grow."

"That's queer," said she. "Did the glass houses in your city grow, too?"

"Of course," he replied. "But it took a good many years for them to grow as large and fine as they are now. That is why we are so angry when a Rain of Stones comes to break our towers and crack our roofs."

"Can't you mend them?" she enquired.

"No; but they will grow together again, in time, and we must wait until they do."

They first passed through many beautiful gardens of flowers, which grew nearest the city; but Dorothy could hardly tell what kind of flowers they were, because the colors were constantly changing under the shifting lights of the six suns. A flower would be pink one second, white the next, then blue or yellow; and it was the same way when they came to the plants, which had broad leaves and grew close to the ground.

When they passed over a field of grass Jim immediately stretched down his head and began to nibble.

"A nice country this is," he grumbled, "where a respectable horse has to eat pink grass!"

"It's violet," said the Wizard, who was in the buggy.

"Now it's blue," complained the horse. "As a matter of fact, I'm eating rainbow grass."

"How does it taste?" asked the Wizard.

"Not bad at all," said Jim. "If they give me plenty of it I'll not complain about its color."

By this time the party had reached a freshly plowed field, and the Prince said to Dorothy:

"This is our planting-ground."

Several Mangaboos came forward with glass spades and dug a hole in the ground. Then they put the two halves of the Sorcerer into it and covered him up. After that other people brought water from a brook and sprinkled the earth.

"He will sprout very soon," said the Prince, "and grow

into a large bush, from which we shall in time be able to pick several very good sorcerers."

"Do all your people grow on bushes?" asked the boy.

"Certainly," was the reply. "Do not all people grow upon bushes where you came from, on the outside of the earth?"

"Not that I ever heard of."

"How strange! But if you will come with me to one of our folk gardens I will show you the way we grow in the Land of the Mangaboos."

It appeared that these odd people, while they were able to walk through the air with ease, usually moved upon the ground in the ordinary way. There were no stairs in their houses, because they did not need them, but on a level surface they generally walked just as we do.

The little party of strangers now followed the Prince across a few more of the glass bridges and along several paths until they came to a garden enclosed by a high hedge. Jim had refused to leave the field of grass, where he was engaged in busily eating; so the Wizard got out of the buggy and joined Zeb and Dorothy, and the kitten followed demurely at their heels.

Inside the hedge they came upon row after row of large and handsome plants with broad leaves gracefully curving until their points nearly reached the ground. In the center of each plant grew a daintily dressed Mangaboo, for the clothing of all these creatures grew upon them and was attached to their bodies.

The growing Mangaboos were of all sizes, from the blossom that had just turned into a wee baby to the full-grown and almost ripe man or woman. On some of the bushes might be seen a bud, a blossom, a baby, a half-grown person and a ripe one; but even those ready to pluck were motionless and silent, as if devoid of life. This sight explained to Dorothy why she had seen no children among the Mangaboos, a thing she had until now been unable to account for.

"Our people do not acquire their real life until they leave their bushes," said the Prince. "You will notice they are all attached to the plants by the soles of their feet, and when they are quite ripe they are easily separated from the stems and at once attain the powers of motion and speech. So while they grow they cannot be said to really live, and they must be picked before they can become good citizens."

"How long do you live, after you are picked?" asked Dorothy.

"That depends upon the care we take of ourselves," he replied. "If we keep cool and moist, and meet with no accidents, we often live for five years. I've been picked over six years, but our family is known to be especially long lived."

"Do you eat?" asked the boy.

"Eat! No, indeed. We are quite solid inside our bodies, and have no need to eat, any more than does a potato."

"But the potatoes sometimes sprout," said Zeb.

"And sometimes we do," answered the Prince; "but that is considered a great misfortune, for then we must be planted at once."

"Where did you grow?" asked the Wizard.

"I will show you," was the reply. "Step this way, please."

He led them within another but smaller circle of hedge, where grew one large and beautiful bush.

"This," said he, "is the Royal Bush of the Mangaboos. All of our Princes and Rulers have grown upon this one bush from time immemorial."

They stood before it in silent admiration. On the central stalk stood poised the figure of a girl so exquisitely formed and colored and so lovely in the expression of her delicate features that Dorothy thought she had never seen so sweet and adorable a creature in all her life. The maiden's gown was soft as satin and fell about her in ample folds, while dainty lace-like traceries trimmed the bodice and sleeves. Her flesh was fine and smooth as polished ivory, and her poise expressed both dignity and grace.

"Who is this?" asked the Wizard, curiously.

The Prince had been staring hard at the girl on the bush. Now he answered, with a touch of uneasiness in his cold tones:

"She is the Ruler destined to be my successor, for she is a Royal Princess. When she becomes fully ripe I must abandon the sovereignty of the Mangaboos to her."

"Isn't she ripe now?" asked Dorothy.

He hesitated.

"Not quite," said he, finally. "It will be several days before she needs to be picked, or at least that is my judgment. I am in no hurry to resign my office and be planted, you may be sure."

"Probably not," declared the Wizard, nodding.

"This is one of the most unpleasant things about our vege-table lives," continued the Prince, with a sigh, "that while we are in our full prime we must give way to another, and be covered up in the ground to sprout and grow and give birth to other people."

"I'm sure the Princess is ready to be picked," asserted Dorothy, gazing hard at the beautiful girl on the bush. "She's as perfect as she can be."

"Never mind," answered the Prince, hastily, "she will be all right for a few days longer, and it is best for me to rule until I can dispose of you strangers, who have come to our land uninvited and must be attended to at once."

"What are you going to do with us?" asked Zeb.

"That is a matter I have not quite decided upon," was the reply. "I think I shall keep this Wizard until a new Sorcerer is ready to pick, for he seems quite skillful and may be of use to us. But the rest of you must be destroyed in some way, and you cannot be planted, because I do not wish horses and cats and meat people growing all over our country."

"You needn't worry," said Dorothy. "We wouldn't grow under ground, I'm sure."

"But why destroy my friends?" asked the little Wizard. "Why not let them live?"

"They do not belong here," returned the Prince. "They have no right to be inside the earth at all."

"We didn't ask to come down here; we fell," said Dorothy.

"That is no excuse," declared the Prince, coldly.

The children looked at each other in perplexity, and the Wizard sighed. Eureka rubbed her paw on her face and said in her soft, purring voice:

"He won't need to destroy *me*, for if I don't get something to eat pretty soon I shall starve to death, and so save him the trouble."

"If he planted you, he might grow some cat-tails," suggested the Wizard.

"Oh, Eureka! perhaps we can find you some milk-weeds to eat," said the boy.

"Phoo!" snarled the kitten; "I wouldn't touch the nasty things!"

"You don't need milk, Eureka," remarked Dorothy; "you are big enough now to eat any kind of food."

"If I can get it," added Eureka.

"I'm hungry myself," said Zeb. "But I noticed some strawberries growing in one of the gardens, and some melons in another place. These people don't eat such things, so perhaps on our way back they will let us get them."

"Never mind your hunger," interrupted the Prince. "I shall order you destroyed in a few minutes, so you will have no need to ruin our pretty melon vines and berry bushes. Follow me, please, to meet your doom."

·——·◄ Chapter 5 ►·——··

DOROTHY PICKS the PRINCESS

The words of the cold and moist vegetable Prince were not very comforting, and as he spoke them he turned away and left the enclosure. The children, feeling sad and despondent, were about to follow him when the Wizard touched Dorothy softly on her shoulder.

"Wait!" he whispered.

"What for?" asked the girl.

"Suppose we pick the Royal Princess," said the Wizard. "I'm quite sure she's ripe, and as soon as she comes to life she will be the Ruler, and may treat us better than that heartless Prince intends to."

"All right!" exclaimed Dorothy, eagerly. "Let's pick her while we have the chance, before the man with the star comes back."

So together they leaned over the great bush and each of them seized one hand of the lovely Princess.

"Pull!" cried Dorothy, and as they did so the royal lady leaned toward them and the stems snapped and separated from her feet. She was not at all heavy, so the Wizard and Dorothy managed to lift her gently to the ground.

The beautiful creature passed her hands over her eyes an instant, tucked in a stray lock of hair that had become disarranged, and after a look around the garden made those present a gracious bow and said, in a sweet but even toned voice:

"I thank you very much."

"We salute your Royal Highness!" cried the Wizard, kneeling and kissing her hand.

Just then the voice of the Prince was heard calling upon them to hasten, and a moment later he returned to the enclosure, followed by a number of his people.

Instantly the Princess turned and faced him, and when he saw that she was picked the Prince stood still and began to tremble.

"Sir," said the Royal Lady, with much dignity, "you have wronged me greatly, and would have wronged me still more had not these strangers come to my rescue. I have been ready for picking all the past week, but because you were selfish and desired to continue your unlawful rule, you left me to stand silent upon my bush."

"I did not know that you were ripe," answered the Prince, in a low voice.

"Give me the Star of Royalty!" she commanded.

Slowly he took the shining star from his own brow and placed it upon that of the Princess. Then all the people bowed low to her, and the Prince turned and walked away alone. What became of him afterward our friends never knew.

The people of Mangaboo now formed themselves into a procession and marched toward the glass city to escort their new ruler to her palace and to perform those ceremonies proper to the occasion. But while the people in the procession walked upon the ground the Princess walked in the air just above their heads, to show that she was a superior being and more exalted than her subjects.

No one now seemed to pay any attention to the strangers, so Dorothy and Zeb and the Wizard let the train pass on and then wandered by themselves into the vegetable gardens. They did not bother to cross the bridges over the brooks, but when they came to a stream they stepped high and walked in the air to the other side. This was a very interesting experience to them, and Dorothy said:

"I wonder why it is that we can walk so easily in the air."

"Perhaps," answered the Wizard, "it is because we are close

to the center of the earth, where the attraction of gravitation is very slight. But I've noticed that many queer things happen in fairy countries."

"Is this a fairy country?" asked the boy.

"Of course it is," returned Dorothy promptly. "Only a fairy country could have veg'table people; and only in a fairy country could Eureka and Jim talk as we do."

"That's true," said Zeb, thoughtfully.

In the vegetable gardens they found the strawberries and melons, and several other unknown but delicious fruits, of which they ate heartily. But the kitten bothered them constantly by demanding milk or meat, and called the Wizard names because he could not bring her a dish of milk by means of his magical arts.

As they sat upon the grass watching Jim, who was still busily eating, Eureka said:

"I don't believe you are a Wizard at all!"

"No," answered the little man, "you are quite right. In the strict sense of the word I am not a Wizard, but only a humbug."

"The Wizard of Oz has always been a humbug," agreed Dorothy. "I've known him for a long time."

"If that is so," said the boy, "how could he do that wonderful trick with the nine tiny piglets?"

"Don't know," said Dorothy, "but it must have been humbug."

"Very true," declared the Wizard, nodding at her. "It was

necessary to deceive that ugly Sorcerer and the Prince, as well as their stupid people; but I don't mind telling you, who are my friends, that the thing was only a trick."

"But I saw the little pigs with my own eyes!" exclaimed Zeb.

"So did I," purred the kitten.

"To be sure," answered the Wizard. "You saw them because they were there. They are in my inside pocket now. But the pulling of them apart and pushing them together again was only a sleight-of-hand trick."

"Let's see the pigs," said Eureka, eagerly.

The little man felt carefully in his pocket and pulled out the tiny piglets, setting them upon the grass one by one, where they ran around and nibbled the tender blades.

"They're hungry, too," he said.

"Oh, what cunning things!" cried Dorothy, catching up one and petting it.

"Be careful!" said the piglet, with a squeal, "you're squeezing me!"

"Dear me!" murmured the Wizard, looking at his pets in astonishment. "They can actually talk!"

"May I eat one of them?" asked the kitten, in a pleading voice. "I'm awfully hungry."

"Why, Eureka," said Dorothy, reproachfully, "what a cruel question! It would be dreadful to eat these dear little things."

"I should say so!" grunted another of the piglets, looking uneasily at the kitten; "cats are cruel things."

"I'm not cruel," replied the kitten, yawning. "I'm just hungry."

"You cannot eat my piglets, even if you are starving," declared the little man, in a stern voice. "They are the only things I have to prove I'm a wizard."

"How did they happen to be so little?" asked Dorothy. "I never saw such small pigs before."

"They are from the Island of Teenty-Weent," said the Wizard, "where everything is small because it's a small island. A sailor brought them to Los Angeles and I gave him nine tickets to the circus for them."

"But what am I going to eat?" wailed the kitten, sitting in front of Dorothy and looking pleadingly into her face. "There are no cows here to give milk; or any mice, or even grasshoppers. And if I can't eat the piglets you may as well plant me at once and raise catsup."

"I have an idea," said the Wizard, "that there are fishes in these brooks. Do you like fish?"

"Fish!" cried the kitten. "Do I like fish? Why, they're better than piglets—or even milk!"

"Then I'll try to catch you some," said he.

"But won't they be veg'table, like everything else here?" asked the kitten.

"I think not. Fishes are not animals, and they are as cold

and moist as the vegetables themselves. There is no reason, that I can see, why they may not exist in the waters of this strange country."

Then the Wizard bent a pin for a hook and took a long piece of string from his pocket for a fish-line. The only bait he could find was a bright red blossom from a flower; but he knew fishes are easy to fool if anything bright attracts their attention, so he decided to try the blossom. Having thrown the end of his line in the water of a nearby brook he soon felt a sharp tug that told him a fish had bitten and was caught on the bent pin; so the little man drew in the string and, sure enough, the fish came with it and was landed safely on the shore, where it began to flop around in great excitement.

The fish was fat and round, and its scales glistened like beautifully cut jewels set close together; but there was no time to examine it closely, for Eureka made a jump and caught it between her claws, and in a few moments it had entirely disappeared.

"Oh, Eureka!" cried Dorothy, "did you eat the bones?"

"If it had any bones, I ate them," replied the kitten, composedly, as it washed its face after the meal. "But I don't think that fish had any bones, because I didn't feel them scratch my throat."

"You were very greedy," said the girl.

"I was very hungry," replied the kitten.

The little pigs had stood huddled in a group, watching this scene with frightened eyes.

"Cats are dreadful creatures!" said one of them.

"I'm glad we are not fishes!" said another.

"Don't worry," Dorothy murmured, soothingly, "I'll not let the kitten hurt you."

Then she happened to remember that in a corner of her suit-case were one or two crackers that were left over from her luncheon on the train, and she went to the buggy and brought them. Eureka stuck up her nose at such food, but the tiny piglets squealed delightedly at the sight of the crackers and ate them up in a jiffy.

"Now let us go back to the city," suggested the Wizard. "That is, if Jim has had enough of the pink grass."

The cab-horse, who was browsing near, lifted his head with a sigh.

"I've tried to eat a lot while I had the chance," said he, "for it's likely to be a long while between meals in this strange country. But I'm ready to go, now, at any time you wish."

So, after the Wizard had put the piglets back into his inside pocket, where they cuddled up and went to sleep, the three climbed into the buggy and Jim started back to the town.

"Where shall we stay?" asked the girl.

"I think I shall take possession of the House of the Sorcerer," replied the Wizard; "for the Prince said in the presence of his people that he would keep me until they picked another Sorcerer, and the new Princess won't know but that we belong there."

They agreed to this plan, and when they reached the great square Jim drew the buggy into the big door of the domed hall.

"It doesn't look very homelike," said Dorothy, gazing around at the bare room. "But it's a place to stay, anyhow."

"What are those holes up there?" enquired the boy, pointing to some openings that appeared near the top of the dome.

"They look like doorways," said Dorothy; "only there are no stairs to get to them."

"You forget that stairs are unnecessary," observed the Wizard. "Let us walk up, and see where the doors lead to."

With this he began walking in the air toward the high openings, and Dorothy and Zeb followed him. It was the same sort of climb one experiences when walking up a hill, and they were nearly out of breath when they came to the row of openings, which they perceived to be doorways leading into halls in the upper part of the house. Following these halls they discovered many small rooms opening from them, and some were furnished with glass benches, tables and chairs. But there were no beds at all.

"I wonder if these people never sleep," said the girl.

"Why, there seems to be no night at all in this country," Zeb replied. "Those colored suns are exactly in the same place they were when we came, and if there is no sunset there can be no night."

"Very true," agreed the Wizard. "But it is a long time since I have had any sleep, and I'm tired. So I think I shall lie down upon one of these hard glass benches and take a nap."

"I will, too," said Dorothy, and chose a little room at the end of the hall.

Zeb walked down again to unharness Jim, who, when he found himself free, rolled over a few times and then settled down to sleep, with Eureka nestling comfortably beside his big, boney body. Then the boy returned to one of the upper rooms, and in spite of the hardness of the glass bench was soon deep in slumberland.

Chapter 6

The MANGABOOS PROVE DANGEROUS

When the Wizard awoke the six colored suns were shining down upon the Land of the Mangaboos just as they had done ever since his arrival. The little man, having had a good sleep, felt rested and refreshed, and looking through the glass partition of the room he saw Zeb sitting up on his bench and yawning. So the Wizard went in to him.

"Zeb," said he, "my balloon is of no further use in this strange country, so I may as well leave it on the square where it fell. But in the basket-car are some things I would like to keep with me. I wish you would go and fetch my satchel, two lanterns, and a can of kerosene oil that is under the seat. There is nothing else that I care about."

So the boy went willingly upon the errand, and by the time he had returned Dorothy was awake. Then the three held a counsel to decide what they should do next, but could think of no way to better their condition.

"I don't like these veg'table people," said the little girl. "They're cold and flabby, like cabbages, in spite of their prettiness."

"I agree with you. It is because there is no warm blood in them," remarked the Wizard.

"And they have no hearts; so they can't love anyone—not even themselves," declared the boy.

"The Princess is lovely to look at," continued Dorothy, thoughtfully; "but I don't care much for her, after all. If there was any other place to go, I'd like to go there."

"But *is* there any other place?" asked the Wizard.

"I don't know," she answered.

Just then they heard the big voice of Jim the cab-horse calling to them, and going to the doorway leading to the dome they found the Princess and a throng of her people had entered the House of the Sorcerer.

So they went down to greet the beautiful vegetable lady, who said to them:

"I have been talking with my advisors about you meat people, and we have decided that you do not belong in the

Land of the Mangaboos and must not remain here."

"How can we go away?" asked Dorothy.

"Oh, you cannot go away, of course; so you must be destroyed," was the answer.

"In what way?" enquired the Wizard.

"We shall throw you three people into the Garden of the Twining Vines," said the Princess, "and they will soon crush you and devour your bodies to make themselves grow bigger. The animals you have with you we will drive to the mountains and put into the Black Pit. Then our country will be rid of all its unwelcome visitors."

"But you are in need of a Sorcerer," said the Wizard, "and not one of those growing is yet ripe enough to pick. I am greater than any thorn-covered sorcerer that ever grew in your garden. Why destroy me?"

"It is true we need a Sorcerer," acknowledged the Princess, "but I am informed that one of our own will be ready to pick in a few days, to take the place of Gwig, whom you cut in two before it was time for him to be planted. Let us see your arts, and the sorceries you are able to perform. Then I will decide whether to destroy you with the others or not."

At this the Wizard made a bow to the people and repeated his trick of producing the nine tiny piglets and making them disappear again. He did it very cleverly, indeed, and the Princess looked at the strange piglets as if she were as truly astonished as any vegetable person could be. But afterward she said:

"I have heard of this wonderful magic. But it accomplishes nothing of value. What else can you do?"

The Wizard tried to think. Then he jointed together the blades of his sword and balanced it very skillfully upon the end of his nose. But even that did not satisfy the Princess.

Just then his eye fell upon the lanterns and the can of kerosene oil which Zeb had brought from the car of his balloon, and he got a clever idea from those commonplace things.

"Your Highness," said he, "I will now proceed to prove my magic by creating two suns that you have never seen before; also I will exhibit a Destroyer much more dreadful than your Clinging Vines."

So he placed Dorothy upon one side of him and the boy upon the other and set a lantern upon each of their heads.

"Don't laugh," he whispered to them, "or you will spoil the effect of my magic."

Then, with much dignity and a look of vast importance upon his wrinkled face, the Wizard got out his match-box and lighted the two lanterns. The glare they made was very small when compared with the radiance of the six great colored suns; but still they gleamed steadily and clearly. The Mangaboos were much impressed because they had never before seen any light that did not come directly from their suns.

Next the Wizard poured a pool of oil from the can upon the glass floor, where it covered quite a broad surface. When he lighted the oil a hundred tongues of flame shot up, and the effect was really imposing.

"Now, Princess," exclaimed the Wizard, "those of your advisors who wished to throw us into the Garden of Clinging Vines must step within this circle of light. If they advised you well, and were in the right, they will not be injured in any way. But if any advised you wrongly, the light will wither him."

The advisors of the Princess did not like this test; but she commanded them to step into the flame and one by one they did so, and were scorched so badly that the air was soon filled with an odor like that of baked potatoes. Some of the Mangaboos fell down and had to be dragged from the fire, and all were so withered that it would be necessary to plant them at once.

"Sir," said the Princess to the Wizard, "you are greater than any Sorcerer we have ever known. As it is evident that my people have advised me wrongly, I will not cast you three people into the dreadful Garden of the Clinging Vines; but your animals must be driven into the Black Pit in the mountain, for my subjects cannot bear to have them around."

The Wizard was so pleased to have saved the two children and himself that he said nothing against this decree; but when the Princess had gone both Jim and Eureka protested they did not want to go to the Black Pit, and Dorothy promised she would do all that she could to save them from such a fate.

For two or three days after this—if we call days the periods between sleep, there being no night to divide the hours into days—our friends were not disturbed in any way. They were even permitted to occupy the House of the Sorcerer in peace, as if it had been their own, and to wander in the gardens in search of food.

Once they came near to the enclosed Garden of the Clinging Vines, and walking high into the air looked down upon it with much interest. They saw a mass of tough green vines all matted together and writhing and twisting around like a nest of great snakes. Everything the vines touched they crushed, and our adventurers were indeed thankful to have escaped being cast among them.

Whenever the Wizard went to sleep he would take the nine tiny piglets from his pocket and let them run around on the floor of his room to amuse themselves and get some exercise; and one time they found his glass door ajar and wandered into the hall and then into the bottom part of the great dome, walking through the air as easily as Eureka could. They knew the kitten, by this time, so they scampered over to where she lay beside Jim and commenced to frisk and play with her.

The cab-horse, who never slept long at a time, sat upon his haunches and watched the tiny piglets and the kitten with much approval.

"Don't be rough!" he would call out, if Eureka knocked over one of the round, fat piglets with her paw; but the pigs never minded, and enjoyed the sport very greatly.

Suddenly they looked up to find the room filled with the silent, solemn-eyed Mangaboos. Each of the vegetable folks bore a branch covered with sharp thorns, which was thrust defiantly toward the horse, the kitten and the piglets.

"Here—stop this foolishness!" Jim roared, angrily; but after being pricked once or twice he got upon his four legs and kept out of the way of the thorns.

The Mangaboos surrounded them in solid ranks, but left an opening to the doorway of the hall; so the animals slowly retreated until they were driven from the room and out upon the street. Here were more of the vegetable people with thorns, and silently they urged the now frightened creatures down the street. Jim had to be careful not to step upon the tiny piglets, who scampered under his feet grunting and squealing, while Eureka, snarling and biting at the thorns pushed toward her, also tried to protect the pretty little things from injury. Slowly but steadily the heartless Mangaboos drove them on, until they had passed through the city and the gardens and come to the broad plains leading to the mountain.

"What does all this mean, anyhow?" asked the horse, jumping to escape a thorn.

"Why, they are driving us toward the Black Pit, into which they threatened to cast us," replied the kitten. "If I were as big as you are, Jim, I'd fight these miserable turnip-roots!"

"What would you do?" enquired Jim.

"I'd kick out with those long legs and iron-shod hoofs."

"All right," said the horse; "I'll do it."

An instant later he suddenly backed toward the crowd of Mangaboos and kicked out his hind legs as hard as he could. A dozen of them smashed together and tumbled to the ground, and seeing his success Jim kicked again and again, charging into the vegetable crowd, knocking them in all directions and sending the others scattering to escape his iron heels. Eureka helped him by flying into the faces of the enemy and scratching and biting furiously, and the kitten ruined so many vegetable complexions that the Mangaboos feared her as much as they did the horse.

But the foes were too many to be repulsed for long. They tired Jim and Eureka out, and although the field of battle was thickly covered with mashed and disabled Mangaboos, our animal friends had to give up at last and allow themselves to be driven to the mountain.

Chapter 7

INTO the BLACK PIT and OUT AGAIN

When they came to the mountain it proved to be a rugged, towering chunk of deep green glass, and looked dismal and forbidding in the extreme. Half way up the steep was a yawning cave, black as night beyond the point where the rainbow rays of the colored suns reached into it.

The Mangaboos drove the horse and the kitten and the piglets into this dark hole and then, having pushed the buggy in after them—for it seemed some of them had dragged it all the way from the domed hall—they began to pile big glass rocks within the entrance, so that the prisoners could not get out again.

"This is dreadful!" groaned Jim. "It will be about the end of our adventures, I guess."

"If the Wizard was here," said one of the piglets, sobbing bitterly, "he would not see us suffer so."

"We ought to have called him and Dorothy when we were first attacked," added Eureka. "But never mind; be brave, my friends, and I will go and tell our masters where you are, and get them to come to your rescue."

The mouth of the hole was nearly filled up now, but the kitten gave a leap through the remaining opening and at once scampered up into the air. The Mangaboos saw her escape, and several of them caught up their thorns and gave chase, mounting through the air after her. Eureka, however, was lighter than the Mangaboos, and while they could mount only about a hundred feet above the earth the kitten found she could go nearly two hundred feet. So she ran along over their heads until she had left them far behind and below and had come to the city and the House of the Sorcerer. There she entered in at Dorothy's window in the dome and aroused her from her sleep.

As soon as the little girl knew what had happened she awakened the Wizard and Zeb, and at once preparations were made to go to the rescue of Jim and the piglets. The Wizard carried his satchel, which was quite heavy, and Zeb carried the two lanterns and the oil can. Dorothy's wicker suit-case was still under the seat of the buggy, and by good fortune the boy had also placed the harness in the buggy when he had taken it off from Jim to let the horse lie down and rest. So there was nothing for the girl to carry but the kitten, which she held close to her bosom and tried to comfort, for its little heart was still beating rapidly.

Some of the Mangaboos discovered them as soon as they left the House of the Sorcerer; but when they started toward the mountain the vegetable people allowed them to proceed without interference, yet followed in a crowd behind them so that they could not go back again.

Before long they neared the Black Pit, where a busy swarm of Mangaboos, headed by their Princess, was engaged in piling up glass rocks before the entrance.

"Stop, I command you!" cried the Wizard, in an angry tone, and at once began pulling down the rocks to liberate Jim and the piglets. Instead of opposing him in this they stood back in silence until he had made a good-sized hole in the barrier, when by order of the Princess they all sprang forward and thrust out their sharp thorns.

Dorothy hopped inside the opening to escape being pricked, and Zeb and the Wizard, after enduring a few stabs from the thorns, were glad to follow her. At once the Mangaboos began piling up the rocks of glass again, and as the little man realized that they were all about to be entombed in the mountain he said to the children:

"My dears, what shall we do? Jump out and fight?"

"What's the use?" replied Dorothy. "I'd as soon die here as live much longer among these cruel and heartless people."

"That's the way I feel about it," remarked Zeb, rubbing his wounds. "I've had enough of the Mangaboos."

"All right," said the Wizard; "I'm with you, whatever you decide. But we can't live long in this cavern, that's certain."

Noticing that the light was growing dim he picked up his nine piglets, patted each one lovingly on its fat little head, and placed them carefully in his inside pocket.

Zeb struck a match and lighted one of the lanterns. The rays of the colored suns were now shut out from them forever, for the last chinks had been filled up in the wall that separated their prison from the Land of the Mangaboos.

"How big is this hole?" asked Dorothy.

"I'll explore it and see," replied the boy.

So he carried the lantern back for quite a distance, while Dorothy and the Wizard followed at his side. The cavern did not come to an end, as they had expected it would, but slanted upward through the great glass mountain, running in a direction that promised to lead them to the side opposite the Mangaboo country.

"It isn't a bad road," observed the Wizard, "and if we followed it it might lead us to some place that is more comfortable than this black pocket we are now in. I suppose the vegetable folk were always afraid to enter this cavern because it is dark; but we have our lanterns to light the way, so I propose that we start out and discover where this tunnel in the mountain leads to."

The others agreed readily to this sensible suggestion, and at once the boy began to harness Jim to the buggy. When all was in readiness the three took their seats in the buggy and Jim started cautiously along the way, Zeb driving while the Wizard and Dorothy each held a lighted lantern so the horse could see where to go.

Sometimes the tunnel was so narrow that the wheels of the buggy grazed the sides; then it would broaden out as wide as a street; but the floor was usually smooth, and for a long time they traveled on without any accident. Jim stopped sometimes to rest, for the climb was rather steep and tiresome.

"We must be nearly as high as the six colored suns, by this time," said Dorothy. "I didn't know this mountain was so tall."

"We are certainly a good distance away from the Land of the Mangaboos," added Zeb; "for we have slanted away from it ever since we started."

But they kept steadily moving, and just as Jim was about tired out with his long journey the way suddenly grew lighter, and Zeb put out the lanterns to save the oil.

To their joy they found it was a white light that now greeted them, for all were weary of the colored rainbow lights which, after a time, had made their eyes ache with their constantly shifting rays. The sides of the tunnel showed before them like the inside of a long spy-glass, and the floor became more level. Jim hastened his lagging steps at this assurance of a quick relief from the dark passage, and in a few moments more they had emerged from the mountain and found themselves face to face with a new and charming country.

Chapter 8

The VALLEY of VOICES

By journeying through the glass mountain they had reached a delightful valley that was shaped like the hollow of a great cup, with another rugged mountain showing on the other side of it, and soft and pretty green hills at the ends. It was all laid out into lovely lawns and gardens, with pebble paths leading through them and groves of beautiful and stately trees dotting the landscape here and there. There were orchards, too, bearing luscious fruits that are all unknown in our world. Alluring brooks of crystal water flowed sparkling between their flower-strewn banks, while scattered over the valley were dozens of the quaintest and most picturesque cottages our travelers had ever beheld. None of them were in clusters, such as villages or towns, but each had ample grounds of its own, with orchards and gardens surrounding it.

As the new arrivals gazed upon this exquisite scene they were enraptured by its beauties and the fragrance that permeated the soft air, which they breathed so gratefully after the confined atmosphere of the tunnel. Several minutes were consumed in silent admiration before they noticed two very singular and unusual facts about this valley. One was that it was lighted from some unseen source; for no sun or moon was in the arched blue sky, although every object was flooded with a clear and perfect light. The second and even more singular fact was the absence of any inhabitant of this splendid place. From their elevated position they could overlook the entire valley, but not a single moving object could they see. All appeared mysteriously deserted.

The mountain on this side was not glass, but made of a stone similar to granite. With some difficulty and danger Jim drew the buggy over the loose rocks until he reached the green lawns below, where the paths and orchards and gardens began. The nearest cottage was still some distance away.

"Isn't it fine?" cried Dorothy, in a joyous voice, as she sprang out of the buggy and let Eureka run frolicking over the velvety grass.

"Yes, indeed!" answered Zeb. "We were lucky to get away from those dreadful vegetable people."

"It wouldn't be so bad," remarked the Wizard, gazing around him, "if we were obliged to live here always. We couldn't find a prettier place, I'm sure."

He took the piglets from his pocket and let them run on the grass, and Jim tasted a mouthful of the green blades and declared he was very contented in his new surroundings.

"We can't walk in the air here, though," called Eureka, who had tried it and failed; but the others were satisfied to walk on the ground, and the Wizard said they must be nearer the surface of the earth then they had been in the Mangaboo country, for everything was more homelike and natural.

"But where are the people?" asked Dorothy.

The little man shook his bald head.

"Can't imagine, my dear," he replied.

They heard the sudden twittering of a bird, but could not find the creature anywhere. Slowly they walked along the path toward the nearest cottage, the piglets racing and gambolling beside them and Jim pausing at every step for another mouthful of grass.

Presently they came to a low plant which had broad, spreading leaves, in the center of which grew a single fruit about as large as a peach. The fruit was so daintily colored and so fragrant, and looked so appetizing and delicious that Dorothy stopped and exclaimed:

"What is it, do you s'pose?"

The piglets had smelled the fruit quickly, and before the

girl could reach out her hand to pluck it every one of the nine tiny ones had rushed in and commenced to devour it with great eagerness.

"It's good, anyway," said Zeb, "or those little rascals wouldn't have gobbled it up so greedily."

"Where are they?" asked Dorothy, in astonishment.

They all looked around, but the piglets had disappeared.

"Dear me!" cried the Wizard; "they must have run away. But I didn't see them go; did you?"

"No!" replied the boy and the girl, together.

"Here,—piggy, piggy, piggy!" called their master, anxiously.

Several squeals and grunts were instantly heard at his feet, but the Wizard could not discover a single piglet.

"Where are you?" he asked.

"Why, right beside you," spoke a tiny voice. "Can't you see us?"

"No," answered the little man, in a puzzled tone.

"We can see you," said another of the piglets.

The Wizard stooped down and put out his hand, and at once felt the small fat body of one of his pets. He picked it up, but could not see what he held.

"It is very strange," said he, soberly. "The piglets have become invisible, in some curious way."

"I'll bet it's because they ate that peach!" cried the kitten.

"It wasn't a peach, Eureka," said Dorothy. "I only hope it wasn't poison."

"It was fine, Dorothy," called one of the piglets.

"We'll eat all we can find of them," said another.

"But *we* mus'n't eat them," the Wizard warned the children, "or we too may become invisible, and lose each other. If we come across another of the strange fruit we must avoid it."

Calling the piglets to him he picked them all up, one by one, and put them away in his pocket; for although he could not see them he could feel them, and when he had buttoned his coat he knew they were safe for the present.

The travelers now resumed their walk toward the cottage, which they presently reached. It was a pretty place, with vines growing thickly over the broad front porch. The door stood open and a table was set in the front room, with four chairs drawn up to it. On the table were plates, knives and forks, and dishes of bread, meat and fruits. The meat was smoking hot and the knives and forks were performing strange antics and jumping here and there in quite a puzzling way. But not a single person appeared to be in the room.

"How funny!" exclaimed Dorothy, who with Zeb and the Wizard now stood in the doorway.

A peal of merry laughter answered her, and the knives and forks fell to the plates with a clatter. One of the chairs pushed back from the table, and this was so astonishing and mysterious that Dorothy was almost tempted to run away in fright.

"Here are strangers, mama!" cried the shrill and childish voice of some unseen person.

"So I see, my dear," answered another voice, soft and womanly.

"What do you want?" demanded a third voice, in a stern, gruff accent.

"Well, well!" said the Wizard; "are there really people in this room?"

"Of course," replied the man's voice.

"And—pardon me for the foolish question—but, are you all invisible?"

"Surely," the woman answered, repeating her low, rippling laughter. "Are you surprised that you are unable to see the people of Voe?"

"Why, yes," stammered the Wizard. "All the people I have ever met before were very plain to see."

"Where do you come from, then?" asked the woman, in a curious tone.

"We belong upon the face of the earth," explained the Wizard, "but recently, during an earthquake, we fell down a crack and landed in the Country of the Mangaboos."

"Dreadful creatures!" exclaimed the woman's voice. "I've heard of them."

"They walled us up in a mountain," continued the Wizard; "but we found there was a tunnel through to this side, so we came here. It is a beautiful place. What do you call it?"

"It is the Valley of Voe."

"Thank you. We have seen no people since we arrived, so we came to this house to enquire our way."

"Are you hungry?" asked the woman's voice.

"I could eat something," said Dorothy.

"So could I," added Zeb.

"But we do not wish to intrude, I assure you," the Wizard hastened to say.

"That's all right," returned the man's voice, more pleasantly than before. "You are welcome to what we have."

As he spoke the voice came so near to Zeb that he jumped back in alarm. Two childish voices laughed merrily at this action, and Dorothy was sure they were in no danger among such light-hearted folks, even if those folks couldn't be seen.

"What curious animal is that which is eating the grass on my lawn?" enquired the man's voice.

"That's Jim," said the girl. "He's a horse."

"What is he good for?" was the next question.

"He draws the buggy you see fastened to him, and we ride in the buggy instead of walking," she explained.

"Can he fight?" asked the man's voice.

"No! he can kick pretty hard with his heels, and bite a little; but Jim can't 'zactly fight," she replied.

"Then the bears will get him," said one of the children's voices.

"Bears!" exclaimed Dorothy. "Are there bears here?"

"That is the one evil of our country," answered the invisible man. "Many large and fierce bears roam in the Valley of Voe, and when they can catch any of us they eat us up; but as they cannot see us, we seldom get caught."

"Are the bears invis'ble, too?" asked the girl.

"Yes; for they eat of the dama-fruit, as we all do, and that keeps them from being seen by any eye, whether human or animal."

"Does the dama-fruit grow on a low bush, and look something like a peach?" asked the Wizard.

"Yes," was the reply.

"If it makes you invis'ble, why do you eat it?" Dorothy enquired.

"For two reasons, my dear," the woman's voice answered. "The dama-fruit is the most delicious thing that grows, and when it makes us invisible the bears cannot find us to eat us up. But now, good wanderers, your luncheon is on the table, so please sit down and eat as much as you like."

·····◄ Chapter 9 ►·····

They Fight the Invisible Bears

The strangers took their seats at the table willingly enough, for they were all hungry and the platters were now heaped with good things to eat. In front of each place was a plate bearing one of the delicious dama-fruit, and the perfume that rose from these was so enticing and sweet that they were sorely tempted to eat of them and become invisible.

But Dorothy satisfied her hunger with other things, and her companions did likewise, resisting the temptation.

"Why do you not eat the damas?" asked the woman's voice.

"We don't want to get invis'ble," answered the girl.

"But if you remain visible the bears will see you and devour you," said a girlish young voice, that belonged to one of the children. "We who live here much prefer to be invisible; for we can still hug and kiss one another, and are quite safe from the bears."

"And we do not have to be so particular about our dress," remarked the man.

"And mama can't tell whether my face is dirty or not!" added the other childish voice, gleefully.

"But I make you wash it, every time I think of it," said the mother; "for it stands to reason your face is dirty, Ianu, whether I can see it or not."

Dorothy laughed and stretched out her hands.

"Come here, please—Ianu and your sister—and let me feel of you," she requested.

They came to her willingly, and Dorothy passed her hands over their faces and forms and decided one was a girl of about her own age and the other a boy somewhat smaller. The girl's hair was soft and fluffy and her skin as smooth as satin. When Dorothy gently touched her nose and ears and lips they seemed to be well and delicately formed.

"If I could see you I am sure you would be beautiful," she declared.

The girl laughed, and her mother said:

"We are not vain in the Valley of Voe, because we can not display our beauty, and good actions and pleasant ways are what make us lovely to our companions. Yet we can see and appreciate the beauties of nature, the dainty flowers and trees, the green fields and the clear blue of the sky."

"How about the birds and beasts and fishes?" asked Zeb.

"The birds we cannot see, because they love to eat of the damas as much as we do; yet we hear their sweet songs and enjoy them. Neither can we see the cruel bears, for they also eat the fruit. But the fishes that swim in our brooks we can see, and often we catch them to eat."

"It occurs to me you have a great deal to make you happy, even while invisible," remarked the Wizard. "Nevertheless, we prefer to remain visible while we are in your valley."

Just then Eureka came in, for she had been until now wandering outside with Jim; and when the kitten saw the table set with food she cried out:

"Now you must feed me, Dorothy, for I'm half starved."

The children were inclined to be frightened by the sight of the small animal, which reminded them of the bears; but Dorothy reassured them by explaining that Eureka was a pet and could do no harm even if she wished to. Then, as the others had by this time moved away from the table, the kitten sprang upon the chair and put her paws upon the cloth to see what there was to eat. To her surprise an unseen hand clutched her and held her suspended in the air. Eureka was frantic with terror, and tried to scratch and bite, so the next moment she was dropped to the floor.

"Did you see that, Dorothy?" she gasped.

"Yes, dear," her mistress replied; "there are people living in this house, although we cannot see them. And you must have better manners, Eureka, or something worse will happen to you."

She placed a plate of food upon the floor and the kitten ate greedily.

"Give me that nice-smelling fruit I saw on the table," she begged, when she had cleaned the plate.

"Those are damas," said Dorothy, "and you must never even taste them, Eureka, or you'll get invis'ble, and then we can't see you at all."

The kitten gazed wistfully at the forbidden fruit.

"Does it hurt to be invis'ble?" she asked.

"I don't know," Dorothy answered; "but it would hurt me dre'fully to lose you."

"Very well, I won't touch it," decided the kitten; "but you must keep it away from me, for the smell is very tempting."

"Can you tell us, sir or ma'am," said the Wizard, addressing the air because he did not quite know where the unseen people stood, "if there is any way we can get out of your beautiful Valley, and on top of the earth again."

"Oh, one can leave the Valley easily enough," answered the man's voice; "but to do so you must enter a far less pleasant country. As for reaching the top of the earth, I have never heard that it is possible to do that, and if you succeeded in getting there you would probably fall off."

"Oh, no," said Dorothy, "we've been there, and we know."

"The Valley of Voe is certainly a charming place," resumed the Wizard; "but we cannot be contented in any other land than our own, for long. Even if we should come to unpleasant places on our way it is necessary, in order to reach the earth's surface, to keep moving on toward it."

"In that case," said the man, "it will be best for you to cross our Valley and mount the spiral staircase inside the Pyramid Mountain. The top of that mountain is lost in the clouds, and when you reach it you will be in the awful Land of Naught, where the Gargoyles live."

"What are Gargoyles?" asked Zeb.

"I do not know, young sir. Our greatest Champion, Overman-Anu, once climbed the spiral stairway and fought nine days with the Gargoyles before he could escape them and come back; but he could never be induced to describe the dreadful creatures, and soon afterward a bear caught him and ate him up."

The wanderers were rather discouraged by this gloomy report, but Dorothy said with a sigh:

"If the only way to get home is to meet the Gurgles, then we've got to meet 'em. They can't be worse than the Wicked Witch or the Nome King."

"But you must remember you had the Scarecrow and the Tin Woodman to help you conquer those enemies," suggested the Wizard. "Just now, my dear, there is not a single warrior in your company."

"Oh, I guess Zeb could fight if he had to. Couldn't you, Zeb?" asked the little girl.

"Perhaps; if I had to," answered Zeb, doubtfully.

"And you have the jointed sword that you chopped the veg'table Sorcerer in two with," the girl said to the little man.

"True," he replied; "and in my satchel are other useful things to fight with."

"What the Gargoyles most dread is a noise," said the man's voice. "Our Champion told me that when he shouted his battle-cry the creatures shuddered and drew back, hesitating to continue the combat. But they were in great numbers, and the Champion could not shout much because he had to save his breath for fighting."

"Very good," said the Wizard; "we can all yell better than we can fight, so we ought to defeat the Gargoyles."

"But tell me," said Dorothy, "how did such a brave Champion happen to let the bears eat him? And if he was invis'ble, and the bears invis'ble, who knows that they really ate him up?"

"The Champion had killed eleven bears in his time," returned the unseen man; "and we know this is true because when any creature is dead the invisible charm of the dama-fruit ceases to be active, and the slain one can be plainly seen by all eyes. When the Champion killed a bear everyone could see it; and when the bears killed the Champion we all saw several pieces of him scattered about, which of course disappeared again when the bears devoured them."

They now bade farewell to the kind but unseen people of the cottage, and after the man had called their attention to a high, pyramid-shaped mountain on the opposite side of the Valley, and told them how to travel in order to reach it, they again started upon their journey.

They followed the course of a broad stream and passed several more pretty cottages; but of course they saw no one, nor did any one speak to them. Fruits and flowers grew plentifully all about, and there were many of the delicious damas that the people of Voe were so fond of.

About noon they stopped to allow Jim to rest in the shade of a pretty orchard, and while they plucked and ate some of the cherries and plums that grew there a soft voice suddenly said to them:

"There are bears near by. Be careful."

The Wizard got out his sword at once, and Zeb grabbed the horse-whip. Dorothy climbed into the buggy, although Jim had been unharnessed from it and was grazing some distance away.

The owner of the unseen voice laughed lightly and said:

"You cannot escape the bears that way."

"How *can* we 'scape?" asked Dorothy, nervously, for an unseen danger is always the hardest to face.

"You must take to the river," was the reply. "The bears will not venture upon the water."

"But we would be drowned!" exclaimed the girl.

"Oh, there is no need of that," said the voice, which from its gentle tones seemed to belong to a young girl. "You are strangers in the Valley of Voe, and do not seem to know our ways; so I will try to save you."

The next moment a broad-leaved plant was jerked from the ground where it grew and held suspended in the air before the Wizard.

"Sir," said the voice, "you must rub these leaves upon the soles of all your feet, and then you will be able to walk upon the water without sinking below the surface. It is a secret the bears do not know, and we people of Voe usually walk upon the water when we travel, and so escape our enemies."

"Thank you!" cried the Wizard, joyfully, and at once rubbed a leaf upon the soles of Dorothy's shoes and then upon his own. The girl took a leaf and rubbed it upon the kitten's paws, and the rest of the plant was handed to Zeb, who, after applying it to his own feet, carefully rubbed it upon all four of Jim's hoofs and then upon the tires of the buggy-wheels. He had nearly finished this last task when a low growling was suddenly heard and the horse began to jump around and kick viciously with his heels.

"Quick! To the water, or you are lost!" cried their unseen friend, and without hesitation the Wizard drew the buggy down the bank and out upon the broad river, for Dorothy was still seated in it with Eureka in her arms. They did not sink at all, owing to the virtues of the strange plant they had used, and when the buggy was in the middle of the stream the Wizard returned to the bank to assist Zeb and Jim.

The horse was plunging madly about, and two or three deep gashes appeared upon its flanks, from which the blood flowed freely.

"Run for the river!" shouted the Wizard, and Jim quickly freed himself from his unseen tormenters by a few vicious kicks and then obeyed. As soon as he trotted out upon the surface of the river he found himself safe from pursuit, and Zeb was already running across the water toward Dorothy.

As the little Wizard turned to follow them he felt a hot breath against his cheek and heard a low, fierce growl. At once he began stabbing at the air with his sword, and he knew that he had struck some substance because when he drew back the blade it was dripping with blood. The third time that he thrust out the weapon there was a loud roar and a fall, and suddenly at his feet appeared the form of a great red bear, which was nearly as big as the horse and much stronger and fiercer. The beast was quite dead from the sword thrusts, and after a glance at its terrible claws and sharp teeth the little man turned in a panic and rushed out upon the water, for other menacing growls told him more bears were near.

On the river, however, the adventurers seemed to be perfectly safe. Dorothy and the buggy had floated slowly down stream with the current of the water, and the others made haste to join her. The Wizard opened his satchel and got out some sticking-plaster with which he mended the cuts Jim had received from the claws of the bears.

"I think we'd better stick to the river, after this," said Dorothy. "If our unknown friend hadn't warned us, and told us what to do, we would all be dead by this time."

"That is true," agreed the Wizard, "and as the river seems to be flowing in the direction of the Pyramid Mountain it will be the easiest way for us to travel."

Zeb hitched Jim to the buggy again, and the horse trotted along and drew them rapidly over the smooth water. The kitten was at first dreadfully afraid of getting wet, but Dorothy let her down and soon Eureka was frisking along beside the buggy without being scared a bit. Once a little fish swam too near the surface, and the kitten grabbed it in her mouth and ate it up as quick as a wink; but Dorothy cautioned her to be careful what she ate in this valley of enchantments, and no more fishes were careless enough to swim within reach.

After a journey of several hours they came to a point where the river curved, and they found they must cross a mile or so of the Valley before they came to the Pyramid Mountain. There were few houses in this part, and few orchards or flowers; so our friends feared they might encounter more of the savage bears, which they had learned to dread with all their hearts.

"You'll have to make a dash, Jim," said the Wizard, "and run as fast as you can go."

"All right," answered the horse; "I'll do my best. But you must remember I'm old, and my dashing days are past and gone."

All three got into the buggy and Zeb picked up the reins, though Jim needed no guidance of any sort. The horse was still smarting from the sharp claws of the invisible bears, and as soon as he was on land and headed toward the mountain the thought that more of those fearsome creatures might be near acted as a spur and sent him galloping along in a way that made Dorothy catch her breath.

Then Zeb, in a spirit of mischief, uttered a growl like that of the bears, and Jim pricked up his ears and fairly flew. His boney legs moved so fast they could scarcely be seen, and the Wizard clung fast to the seat and yelled "Whoa!" at the top of his voice.

"I—I'm 'fraid he's—he's running away!" gasped Dorothy.

"I *know* he is," said Zeb; "but no bear can catch him if he keeps up that gait—and the harness or the buggy don't break."

Jim did not make a mile a minute; but almost before they were aware of it he drew up at the foot of the mountain, so suddenly that the Wizard and Zeb both sailed over the dashboard and landed in the soft grass—where they rolled over several times before they stopped. Dorothy nearly went with them, but she was holding fast to the iron rail of the seat, and that saved her. She squeezed the kitten, though, until it screeched; and then the old cab-horse made several curious sounds that led the little girl to suspect he was laughing at them all.

Chapter 10

The BRAIDED MAN of PYRAMID MOUNTAIN

The mountain before them was shaped like a cone and was so tall that its point was lost in the clouds. Directly facing the place where Jim had stopped was an arched opening leading to a broad stairway. The stairs were cut in the rock inside the mountain, and they were broad and not very steep, because they circled around like a cork-screw, and at the arched opening where the flight began the circle was quite big. At the foot of the stairs was a sign reading:

WARNING.
These steps lead to the Land of the Gargoyles.
DANGER! KEEP OUT.

"I wonder how Jim is ever going to draw the buggy up so many stairs," said Dorothy, gravely.

"No trouble at all," declared the horse, with a contemptuous neigh. "Still, I don't care to drag any passengers. You'll all have to walk."

"Suppose the stairs get steeper?" suggested Zeb, doubtfully.

"Then you'll have to boost the buggy-wheels, that's all," answered Jim.

"We'll try it, anyway," said the Wizard. "It's the only way to get out of the Valley of Voe."

So they began to ascend the stairs, Dorothy and the Wizard first, Jim next, drawing the buggy, and then Zeb to watch that nothing happened to the harness.

The light was dim, and soon they mounted into total darkness, so that the Wizard was obliged to get out his lanterns to light the way. But this enabled them to proceed steadily until they came to a landing where there was a rift in the side of the mountain that let in both light and air. Looking through this opening they could see the Valley of Voe lying far below them, the cottages seeming like toy houses from that distance.

After resting a few moments they resumed their climb, and still the stairs were broad and low enough for Jim to draw the buggy easily after him. The old horse panted a little, and had to stop often to get his breath. At such times they were all glad to wait for him, for continually climbing up stairs is sure to make one's legs ache.

They wound about, always going upward, for some time. The lights from the lanterns dimly showed the way, but it was a gloomy journey, and they were pleased when a broad streak of light ahead assured them they were coming to a second landing.

Here one side of the mountain had a great hole in it, like the mouth of a cavern, and the stairs stopped at the near edge of the floor and commenced ascending again at the opposite edge.

The opening in the mountain was on the side opposite to the Valley of Voe, and our travelers looked out upon a strange scene. Below them was a vast space, at the bottom of which was a black sea with rolling billows, through which little tongues of flame constantly shot up. Just above them, and almost on a level with their platform, were banks of rolling clouds which constantly shifted position and changed color. The blues and greys were very beautiful, and Dorothy noticed that on the cloud banks sat or reclined fleecy, shadowy forms of beautiful beings who must have been the Cloud Fairies. Mortals who stand upon the earth and look up at the sky cannot often distinguish these forms, but our friends were now so near to the clouds that they observed the dainty fairies very clearly.

"Are they real?" asked Zeb, in an awed voice.

"Of course," replied Dorothy, softly. "They are the Cloud Fairies."

"They seem like open-work," remarked the boy, gazing

intently. "If I should squeeze one, there wouldn't be anything left of it."

In the open space between the clouds and the black, bubbling sea far beneath, could be seen an occasional strange bird winging its way swiftly through the air. These birds were of enormous size, and reminded Zeb of the rocs he had read about in the Arabian Nights. They had fierce eyes and sharp talons and beaks, and the children hoped none of them would venture into the cavern.

"Well, I declare!" suddenly exclaimed the little Wizard. "What in the world is this?"

They turned around and found a man standing on the floor in the center of the cave, who bowed very politely when he saw he had attracted their attention. He was a very old man, bent nearly double; but the queerest thing about him was his white hair and beard. These were so long that they reached to his feet, and both the hair and the beard were carefully plaited into many braids, and the end of each braid fastened with a bow of colored ribbon.

"Where did you come from?" asked Dorothy, wonderingly.

"No place at all," answered the man with the braids; "that is, not recently. Once I lived on top the earth, but for many years I have had my factory in this spot—half way up Pyramid Mountain."

"Are we only half way up?" enquired the boy, in a discouraged tone.

"I believe so, my lad," replied the braided man. "But as I have never been in either direction, down or up, since I arrived, I cannot be positive whether it is exactly half way or not."

"Have you a factory in this place?" asked the Wizard, who had been examining the strange personage carefully.

"To be sure," said the other. "I am a great inventor, you must know, and I manufacture my products in this lonely spot."

"What are your products?" enquired the Wizard.

"Well, I make Assorted Flutters for flags and bunting, and a superior grade of Rustles for ladies' silk gowns."

"I thought so," said the Wizard, with a sigh. "May we examine some of these articles?"

"Yes, indeed; come into my shop, please," and the braided man turned and led the way into a smaller cave, where he evidently lived. Here, on a broad shelf, were several cardboard boxes of various sizes, each tied with cotton cord.

"This," said the man, taking up a box and handling it gently, "contains twelve dozen rustles—enough to last any lady a year. Will you buy it, my dear?" he asked, addressing Dorothy.

"My gown isn't silk," she said, smiling.

"Never mind. When you open the box the rustles will escape, whether you are wearing a silk dress or not," said the man, seriously. Then he picked up another box. "In this," he continued, "are many assorted flutters. They are invaluable to make flags flutter on a still day, when there is no wind. You, sir," turning to the Wizard, "ought to have this assortment. Once you have tried my goods I am sure you will never be without them."

"I have no money with me," said the Wizard, evasively.

"I do not want money," returned the braided man, "for I could not spend it in this deserted place if I had it. But I would like very much a blue hair-ribbon. You will notice my braids are tied with yellow, pink, brown, red, green, white and black; but I have no blue ribbons."

"I'll get you one!" cried Dorothy, who was sorry for the poor man; so she ran back to the buggy and took from her suit-case a pretty blue ribbon. It did her good to see how the braided man's eyes sparkled when he received this treasure.

"You have made me very, very happy, my dear!" he exclaimed; and then he insisted on the Wizard taking the box of flutters and the little girl accepting the box of rustles.

"You may need them, some time," he said, "and there is really no use in my manufacturing these things unless somebody uses them."

"Why did you leave the surface of the earth?" enquired the Wizard.

"I could not help it. It is a sad story, but if you will try to restrain your tears I will tell you about it. On earth I was a manufacturer of Imported Holes for American Swiss Cheese, and I will acknowledge that I supplied a superior article, which was in great demand. Also I made pores for porous plasters and high-grade holes for doughnuts and buttons. Finally I invented a new Adjustable Post-hole, which I thought would make my fortune. I manufactured a large quantity of these post-holes, and having no room in which to store them I set them all end to end and put the top one in the ground. That made an extraordinary long hole, as you may imagine, and reached far down into the earth; and, as I leaned over it to try to see to the bottom, I lost my balance and tumbled in. Unfortunately, the hole led directly into the vast space you see outside this mountain; but I managed to catch a point of rock that projected from this cavern, and so saved myself from tumbling headlong into the black waves beneath, where the tongues of flame that dart out would certainly have consumed me. Here, then, I made my home; and although it is a lonely place I amuse myself making rustles and flutters, and so get along very nicely."

When the braided man had completed this strange tale Dorothy nearly laughed, because it was all so absurd; but the Wizard tapped his forehead significantly, to indicate that he thought the poor man was crazy. So they politely bade him good day, and went back to the outer cavern to resume their journey.

Chapter 11

THEY MEET the WOODEN
GARGOYLES

nother breathless climb brought our
adventurers to a third landing where
there was a rift in the mountain. On
peering out all they could see was rolling
banks of clouds, so thick that they obscured all else.

But the travelers were obliged to rest, and while they
were sitting on the rocky floor the Wizard felt in his pocket
and brought out the nine tiny piglets. To his delight they
were now plainly visible, which proved that they had passed
beyond the influence of the magical Valley of Voe.

"Why, we can see each other again!" cried one, joyfully.

"Yes," sighed Eureka; "and I also can see you again, and

the sight makes me dreadfully hungry. Please, Mr. Wizard, may I eat just one of the fat little piglets? You'd never miss *one* of them, I'm sure!"

"What a horrid, savage beast!" exclaimed a piglet; "and after we've been such good friends, too, and played with one another!"

"When I'm not hungry, I love to play with you all," said the kitten, demurely; "but when my stomach is empty it seems that nothing would fill it so nicely as a fat piglet."

"And we trusted you so!" said another of the nine, reproachfully.

"And thought you were respectable!" said another.

"It seems we were mistaken," declared a third, looking at the kitten timorously, "no one with such murderous desires should belong to our party, I'm sure."

"You see, Eureka," remarked Dorothy, reprovingly, "you are making yourself disliked. There are certain things proper for a kitten to eat; but I never heard of a kitten eating a pig, under *any* cir'stances."

"Did you ever see such little pigs before?" asked the kitten. "They are no bigger than mice, and I'm sure mice are proper for me to eat."

"It isn't the bigness, dear; it's the variety," replied the girl. "These are Mr. Wizard's pets, just as you are my pet, and it wouldn't be any more proper for you to eat them than it would be for Jim to eat you."

"And that's just what I shall do if you don't let those little balls of pork alone," said Jim, glaring at the kitten with his round, big eyes. "If you injure any one of them I'll chew you up instantly."

The kitten looked at the horse thoughtfully, as if trying to decide whether he meant it or not.

"In that case," she said, "I'll leave them alone. You haven't many teeth left, Jim, but the few you have are sharp enough to make me shudder. So the piglets will be perfectly safe, hereafter, as far as I am concerned."

"That is right, Eureka," remarked the Wizard, earnestly. "Let us all be a happy family and love one another."

Eureka yawned and stretched herself.

"I've always loved the piglets," she said; "but they don't love me."

"No one can love a person he's afraid of," asserted Dorothy. "If you behave, and don't scare the little pigs, I'm sure they'll grow very fond of you."

The Wizard now put the nine tiny ones back into his pocket and the journey was resumed.

"We must be pretty near the top, now," said the boy, as they climbed wearily up the dark, winding stairway.

"The Country of the Gurgles can't be far from the top of the earth," remarked Dorothy. "It isn't very nice down here. I'd like to get home again, I'm sure."

No one replied to this, because they found they needed all

their breath for the climb. The stairs had become narrower and Zeb and the Wizard often had to help Jim pull the buggy from one step to another, or keep it from jamming against the rocky walls.

At last, however, a dim light appeared ahead of them, which grew clearer and stronger as they advanced.

"Thank goodness we're nearly there!" panted the little Wizard.

Jim, who was in advance, saw the last stair before him and stuck his head above the rocky sides of the stairway. Then he halted, ducked down and began to back up, so that he nearly fell with the buggy onto the others.

"Let's go down again!" he said, in his hoarse voice.

"Nonsense!" snapped the tired Wizard. "What's the matter with you, old man?"

"Everything," grumbled the horse. "I've taken a look at this place, and it's no fit country for real creatures to go to. Everything's dead, up there—no flesh or blood or growing thing anywhere."

"Never mind; we can't turn back," said Dorothy; "and we don't intend to stay there, anyhow."

"It's dangerous," growled Jim, in a stubborn tone.

"See here, my good steed," broke in the Wizard, "little Dorothy and I have been in many queer countries in our travels, and always escaped without harm. We've even been to the marvelous Land of Oz—haven't we, Dorothy?—so we don't much care what the Country of the Gargoyles is like. Go ahead, Jim, and whatever happens we'll make the best of it."

"All right," answered the horse; "this is your excursion, and not mine; so if you get into trouble don't blame me."

With this speech he bent forward and dragged the buggy up the remaining steps. The others followed and soon they were all standing upon a broad platform and gazing at the most curious and startling sight their eyes had ever beheld.

"The Country of the Gargoyles is all wooden!" exclaimed Zeb; and so it was. The ground was sawdust and the pebbles scattered around were hard knots from trees, worn smooth in course of time. There were odd wooden houses, with carved wooden flowers in the front yards. The tree-trunks were of coarse wood, but the leaves of the trees were shavings. The patches of grass were splinters of wood, and where neither grass nor sawdust showed was a solid wooden flooring. Wooden birds fluttered among the trees and wooden cows were browsing upon the wooden grass; but the most amazing things of all were the wooden people—the creatures known as Gargoyles.

These were very numerous, for the place was thickly inhabited, and a large group of the queer people clustered near, gazing sharply upon the strangers who had emerged from the long spiral stairway.

The Gargoyles were very small of stature, being less than three feet in height. Their bodies were round, their legs short and thick and their arms extraordinarily long and stout. Their heads were too big for their bodies and their faces were decidedly ugly to look upon. Some had long, curved noses and chins, small eyes and wide, grinning mouths. Others had flat noses, protruding eyes, and ears that were shaped like those of an elephant. There were many types, indeed, scarcely two being alike; but all were equally disagreeable in appearance. The tops of their heads had no hair, but were carved into a variety of fantastic shapes, some having a row of points or balls around the top, other designs resembling flowers or vegetables, and still others having squares that looked like waffles cut criss-cross on their heads. They all wore short wooden wings which were fastened to their wooden bodies by means of wooden hinges with wooden screws, and with these wings they flew swiftly and noiselessly here and there, their legs being of little use to them.

This noiseless motion was one of the most peculiar things about the Gargoyles. They made no sounds at all, either in flying or trying to speak, and they conversed mainly by means of quick signals made with their wooden fingers or lips. Neither was there any sound to be heard anywhere throughout the wooden country. The birds did not sing, nor did the cows moo; yet there was more than ordinary activity everywhere.

The group of these queer creatures which was discovered clustered near the stairs at first remained staring and motionless, glaring with evil eyes at the intruders who had so suddenly appeared in their land. In turn the Wizard and the children, the horse and the kitten, examined the Gargoyles with the same silent attention.

"There's going to be trouble, I'm sure," remarked the horse. "Unhitch those tugs, Zeb, and set me free from the buggy, so I can fight comfortably."

"Jim's right," sighed the Wizard. "There's going to be trouble, and my sword isn't stout enough to cut up those wooden bodies—so I shall have to get out my revolvers."

He got his satchel from the buggy and, opening it, took out two deadly looking revolvers that made the children shrink back in alarm just to look at.

"What harm can the Gurgles do?" asked Dorothy. "They have no weapons to hurt us with."

"Each of their arms is a wooden club," answered the little man, "and I'm sure the creatures mean mischief, by the looks of their eyes. Even these revolvers can merely succeed in damaging a few of their wooden bodies, and after that we will be at their mercy."

"But why fight at all, in that case?" asked the girl.

"So I may die with a clear conscience," returned the Wizard, gravely. "It's every man's duty to do the best he knows how; and I'm going to do it."

"Wish I had an axe," said Zeb, who by now had unhitched the horse.

"If we had known we were coming we might have brought

along several other useful things," responded the Wizard. "But we dropped into this adventure rather unexpectedly."

The Gargoyles had backed away a distance when they heard the sound of talking, for although our friends had spoken in low tones their words seemed loud in the silence surrounding them. But as soon as the conversation ceased, the grinning, ugly creatures arose in a flock and flew swiftly toward the strangers, their long arms stretched out before them like the bowsprits of a fleet of sail-boats. The horse had especially attracted their notice, because it was the biggest and strangest creature they had ever seen; so it became the center of their first attack.

But Jim was ready for them, and when he saw them coming he turned his heels toward them and began kicking out as hard as he could. Crack! crash! bang! went his iron-shod hoofs against the wooden bodies of the Gargoyles, and they were battered right and left with such force that they scattered like straws in the wind. But the noise and clatter seemed as dreadful to them as Jim's heels, for all who were able swiftly turned and flew away to a great distance. The others picked themselves up from the ground one by one and quickly rejoined their fellows, so for a moment the horse thought he had won the fight with ease.

But the Wizard was not so confident.

"Those wooden things are impossible to hurt," he said, "and all the damage Jim has done to them is to knock a few splinters from their noses and ears. That cannot make them look any uglier, I'm sure, and it is my opinion they will soon renew the attack."

"What made them fly away?" asked Dorothy.

"The noise, of course. Don't you remember how the Champion escaped them by shouting his battle-cry?"

"Suppose we escape down the stairs, too," suggested the boy. "We have time, just now, and I'd rather face the invis'ble bears than those wooden imps."

"No," returned Dorothy, stoutly, "it won't do to go back, for then we would never get home. Let's fight it out."

"That is what I advise," said the Wizard. "They haven't defeated us yet, and Jim is worth a whole army."

But the Gargoyles were clever enough not to attack the horse the next time. They advanced in a great swarm, having been joined by many more of their kind, and they flew straight over Jim's head to where the others were standing.

The Wizard raised one of his revolvers and fired into the throng of his enemies, and the shot resounded like a clap of thunder in that silent place.

Some of the wooden beings fell flat upon the ground, where they quivered and trembled in every limb; but most of them managed to wheel and escape again to a distance.

Zeb ran and picked up one of the Gargoyles that lay nearest to him. The top of its head was carved into a crown and the Wizard's bullet had struck it exactly in the left eye, which was a hard wooden knot. Half of the bullet stuck in the wood and half stuck out, so it had been the jar and the sudden noise that had knocked the creature down, more than the fact that it was really hurt. Before this crowned Gargoyle had recovered himself Zeb had wound a strap several times around its body, confining its wings and arms so that it could not move. Then, having tied the wooden creature securely, the boy buckled the strap and tossed his prisoner into the buggy. By that time the others had all retired.

·····◄ Chapter 12 ►·····

A WONDERFUL ESCAPE

For a while the enemy hesitated to renew the attack. Then a few of them advanced until another shot from the Wizard's revolver made them retreat.

"That's fine," said Zeb. "We've got 'em on the run now, sure enough."

"But only for a time," replied the Wizard, shaking his head gloomily. "These revolvers are good for six shots each, but when those are gone we shall be helpless."

The Gargoyles seemed to realize this, for they sent a few of their band time after time to attack the strangers and draw the fire from the little man's revolvers. In this way none of them was shocked by the dreadful report more than once, for the main band kept far away and each time a new company was sent into the battle. When the Wizard had fired all of his twelve bullets he had caused no damage to the enemy except to stun a few by the noise, and so he was no nearer to victory than in the beginning of the fray.

"What shall we do now?" asked Dorothy, anxiously.

"Let's yell—all together," said Zeb.

"And fight at the same time," added the Wizard. "We will get near Jim, so that he can help us, and each one must take some weapon and do the best he can. I'll use my sword, although it isn't much account in this affair. Dorothy must take her parasol and open it suddenly when the wooden folks attack her. I haven't anything for you, Zeb."

"I'll use the king," said the boy, and pulled his prisoner out of the buggy. The bound Gargoyle's arms extended far out beyond its head, so by grasping its wrists Zeb found the king made a very good club. The boy was strong for one of his years, having always worked upon a farm; so he was likely to prove more dangerous to the enemy than the Wizard.

When the next company of Gargoyles advanced, our adventurers began yelling as if they had gone mad. Even the kitten gave a dreadfully shrill scream and at the same time Jim the cab-horse neighed loudly. This daunted the enemy for a time, but the defenders were soon out of breath. Perceiving this, as well as the fact that there were no more of the awful "bangs" to come from the revolvers, the Gargoyles advanced in a swarm as thick as bees, so that the air was filled with them.

Dorothy squatted upon the ground and put up her parasol, which nearly covered her and proved a great protection. The Wizard's sword-blade snapped into a dozen pieces at the first blow he struck against the wooden people. Zeb pounded away with the Gargoyle he was using as a club until he had knocked down dozens of foes; but at the last they clustered so thickly about him that he no longer had room in which to swing his arms. The horse performed some wonderful kicking and even Eureka assisted when she leaped bodily upon the Gargoyles and scratched and bit at them like a wild-cat.

But all this bravery amounted to nothing at all. The wooden things wound their long arms around Zeb and the Wizard and held them fast. Dorothy was captured in the same way, and numbers of the Gargoyles clung to Jim's legs, so weighting him down that the poor beast was helpless. Eureka made a desperate dash to escape and scampered along the ground like a streak; but a grinning Gargoyle flew after her and grabbed her before she had gone very far.

All of them expected nothing less than instant death; but to their surprise the wooden creatures flew into the air with them and bore them far away, over miles and miles of wooden country, until they came to a wooden city. The houses of this city had many corners, being square and six-sided and eight-sided. They were tower-like in shape and the best of them seemed old and weather-worn; yet all were strong and substantial.

To one of these houses which had neither doors nor windows, but only one broad opening far up underneath the roof, the prisoners were brought by their captors. The Gargoyles roughly pushed them into the opening, where there was a platform, and then flew away and left them. As they had no wings the strangers could not fly away, and if they jumped down from such a height they would surely be killed. The creatures had sense enough to reason that way, and the only mistake they made was in supposing the earth people were unable to overcome such ordinary difficulties.

Jim was brought with the others, although it took a good many Gargoyles to carry the big beast through the air and land him on the high platform, and the buggy was thrust in after him because it belonged to the party and the wooden folks had no idea what it was used for or whether it was alive or not. When Eureka's captor had thrown the kitten after the others the last Gargoyle silently disappeared, leaving our friends to breathe freely once more.

"What an awful fight!" said Dorothy, catching her breath in little gasps.

"Oh, I don't know," purred Eureka, smoothing her ruffled fur with her paw; "we didn't manage to hurt anybody, and nobody managed to hurt us."

"Thank goodness we are together again, even if we are prisoners," sighed the little girl.

"I wonder why they didn't kill us on the spot," remarked Zeb, who had lost his king in the struggle.

"They are probably keeping us for some ceremony," the Wizard answered, reflectively; "but there is no doubt they intend to kill us as dead as possible in a short time."

"As dead as poss'ble would be pretty dead, wouldn't it?" asked Dorothy.

"Yes, my dear. But we have no need to worry about that just now. Let us examine our prison and see what it is like."

The space underneath the roof, where they stood, permitted them to see on all sides of the tall building, and they looked with much curiosity at the city spread out beneath them. Everything visible was made of wood, and the scene seemed stiff and extremely unnatural.

From their platform a stair descended into the house, and the children and the Wizard explored it after lighting a lantern to show them the way. Several stories of empty rooms rewarded their search, but nothing more; so after a time they came back to the platform again. Had there been any doors or windows in the lower rooms, or had not the boards of the house been so thick and stout, escape could have been easy; but to remain down below was like being in a cellar or the hold of a ship, and they did not like the darkness or the damp smell.

In this country, as in all others they had visited underneath the earth's surface, there was no night, a constant and strong light coming from some unknown source. Looking out, they could see into some of the houses near them, where there were open windows in abundance, and were able to mark the forms of the wooden Gargoyles moving about in their dwellings.

"This seems to be their time of rest," observed the Wizard. "All people need rest, even if they are made of wood, and as there is no night here they select a certain time of the day in which to sleep or doze."

"I feel sleepy myself," remarked Zeb, yawning.

"Why, where's Eureka?" cried Dorothy, suddenly.

They all looked around, but the kitten was no place to be seen.

"She's gone out for a walk," said Jim, gruffly.

"Where? On the roof?" asked the girl.

"No; she just dug her claws into the wood and climbed down the sides of this house to the ground."

"She couldn't climb *down*, Jim," said Dorothy. "To climb means to go up."

"Who said so?" demanded the horse.

"My school-teacher said so; and she knows a lot, Jim."

"To 'climb down' is sometimes used as a figure of speech," remarked the Wizard.

"Well, this was a figure of a cat," said Jim, "and she *went* down, anyhow, whether she climbed or crept."

"Dear me! how careless Eureka is," exclaimed the girl, much distressed. "The Gurgles will get her, sure!"

"Ha, ha!" chuckled the old cab-horse; "they're not 'Gurgles,' little maid; they're Gargoyles."

"Never mind; they'll get Eureka, whatever they're called."

"No they won't," said the voice of the kitten, and Eureka herself crawled over the edge of the platform and sat down quietly upon the floor.

"Wherever have you been, Eureka?" asked Dorothy, sternly.

"Watching the wooden folks. They're too funny for any-thing, Dorothy. Just now they are all going to bed, and—what do you think?—they unhook the hinges of their wings and put them in a corner until they wake up again."

"What, the hinges?"

"No; the wings."

"That," said Zeb, "explains why this house is used by them for a prison. If any of the Gargoyles act badly, and have to be put in jail, they are brought here and their wings unhooked and taken away from them until they promise to be good."

The Wizard had listened intently to what Eureka had said.

"I wish we had some of those loose wings," he said.

"Could we fly with them?" asked Dorothy.

"I think so. If the Gargoyles can unhook the wings then the power to fly lies in the wings themselves, and not in the wooden bodies of the people who wear them. So, if we had the wings, we could probably fly as well as they do—as least while we are in their country and under the spell of its magic."

"But how would it help us to be able to fly?" questioned the girl.

"Come here," said the little man, and took her to one of the corners of the building. "Do you see that big rock standing on the hillside yonder?" he continued, pointing with his finger.

"Yes; it's a good way off, but I can see it," she replied.

"Well, inside that rock, which reaches up into the clouds, is an archway very much like the one we entered when we climbed the spiral stairway from the Valley of Voe. I'll get my spy-glass, and then you can see it more plainly."

He fetched a small but powerful telescope, which had been in his satchel, and by its aid the little girl clearly saw the opening.

"Where does it lead to?" she asked.

"That I cannot tell," said the Wizard; "but we cannot now be far below the earth's surface, and that entrance may lead to another stairway that will bring us on top of our world again, where we belong. So, if we had the wings, and could escape the Gargoyles, we might fly to that rock and be saved."

"I'll get you the wings," said Zeb, who had thoughtfully listened to all this. "That is, if the kitten will show me where they are."

"But how can you get down?" enquired the girl, wonderingly.

For answer Zeb began to unfasten Jim's harness, strap by strap, and to buckle one piece to another until he had made a long leather strip that would reach to the ground.

"I can climb down that, all right," he said.

"No you can't," remarked Jim, with a twinkle in his round eyes. "You may *go* down, but you can only *climb* up."

"Well, I'll climb up when I get back, then," said the boy, with a laugh. "Now, Eureka, you'll have to show me the way to those wings."

"You must be very quiet," warned the kitten; "for if you make the least noise the Gargoyles will wake up. They can hear a pin drop."

"I'm not going to drop a pin," said Zeb.

He had fastened one end of the strap to a wheel of the buggy, and now he let the line dangle over the side of the house.

"Be careful," cautioned Dorothy, earnestly.

"I will," said the boy, and let himself slide over the edge.

The girl and the Wizard leaned over and watched Zeb work his way carefully downward, hand over hand, until he stood upon the ground below. Eureka clung with her claws to the wooden side of the house and let herself down easily. Then together they crept away to enter the low doorway of a neighboring dwelling.

The watchers waited in breathless suspense until the boy

again appeared, his arms now full of the wooden wings.

When he came to where the strap was hanging he tied the wings all in a bunch to the end of the line, and the Wizard drew them up. Then the line was let down again for Zeb to climb up by. Eureka quickly followed him, and soon they were all standing together upon the platform, with eight of the much prized wooden wings beside them.

The boy was no longer sleepy, but full of energy and excitement. He put the harness together again and hitched Jim to the buggy. Then, with the Wizard's help, he tried to fasten some of the wings to the old cab-horse.

This was no easy task, because half of each one of the hinges of the wings was missing, it being still fastened to the body of the Gargoyle who had used it. However, the Wizard went once more to his satchel—which seemed to contain a surprising variety of odds and ends—and brought out a spool of strong wire, by means of which they managed to fasten four of the wings to Jim's harness, two near his head and two near his tail. They were a bit wiggley, but secure enough if only the harness held together.

The other four wings were then fastened to the buggy, two on each side, for the buggy must bear the weight of the children and the Wizard as it flew through the air.

These preparations had not consumed a great deal of time, but the sleeping Gargoyles were beginning to wake up and move around, and soon some of them would be hunting for their missing wings. So the prisoners resolved to leave their prison at once.

They mounted into the buggy, Dorothy holding Eureka safe in her lap. The girl sat in the middle of the seat, with Zeb and the Wizard on each side of her. When all was ready the boy shook the reins and said:

"Fly away, Jim!"

"Which wings must I flop first?" asked the cab-horse, undecidedly.

"Flop them all together," suggested the Wizard.

"Some of them are crooked," objected the horse.

"Never mind; we will steer with the wings on the buggy," said Zeb. "Just you light out and make for that rock, Jim; and don't waste any time about it, either."

So the horse gave a groan, flopped its four wings all together, and flew away from the platform. Dorothy was a little anxious about the success of their trip, for the way Jim arched his long neck and spread out his bony legs as he fluttered and floundered through the air was enough to make anybody nervous. He groaned, too, as if frightened, and the wings creaked dreadfully because the Wizard had forgotten to oil them; but they kept fairly good time with the wings of the buggy, so that they made excellent progress from the start. The only thing that anyone could complain of with justice was the fact that they wobbled first up and then down, as if the road were rocky instead of being as smooth as the air could make it.

The main point, however, was that they flew, and flew swiftly, if a bit unevenly, toward the rock for which they had headed.

Some of the Gargoyles saw them, presently, and lost no time in collecting a band to pursue the escaping prisoners; so that when Dorothy happened to look back she saw them coming in a great cloud that almost darkened the sky.

Chapter 13

The DEN of the DRAGONETTES

Our friends had a good start and were able to maintain it, for with their eight wings they could go just as fast as could the Gargoyles. All the way to the great rock the wooden people followed them, and when Jim finally alighted at the mouth of the cavern the pursuers were still some distance away.

"But, I'm afraid they'll catch us yet," said Dorothy, greatly excited.

"No; we must stop them," declared the Wizard. "Quick Zeb, help me pull off these wooden wings!"

They tore off the wings, for which they had no further use,

and the Wizard piled them in a heap just outside the entrance to the cavern. Then he poured over them all the kerosene oil that was left in his oil-can, and lighting a match set fire to the pile.

The flames leaped up at once and the bonfire began to smoke and roar and crackle just as the great army of wooden Gargoyles arrived. The creatures drew back at once, being filled with fear and horror; for such a dreadful thing as a fire they had never before known in all the history of their wooden land.

Inside the archway were several doors, leading to different rooms built into the mountain, and Zeb and the Wizard lifted these wooden doors from their hinges and tossed them all on the flames.

"That will prove a barrier for some time to come," said the little man, smiling pleasantly all over his wrinkled face at the success of their stratagem. "Perhaps the flames will set fire to all that miserable wooden country, and if it does the loss will be very small and the Gargoyles never will be missed. But come, my children; let us explore the mountain and discover which way we must go in order to escape from this cavern, which is getting to be almost as hot as a bake-oven."

To their disappointment there was within this mountain no regular flight of steps by means of which they could mount to the earth's surface. A sort of inclined tunnel led upward for a way, and they found the floor of it both rough and steep. Then a sudden turn brought them to a narrow gallery where the buggy could not pass. This delayed and bothered them for a while, because they did not wish to leave the buggy behind them. It carried their baggage and was useful to ride in wherever there were good roads, and since it had accompanied them so far in their travels they felt it their duty to preserve it. So Zeb and the Wizard set to work and took off the wheels and the top, and then they put the buggy edgewise, so it would take up the smallest space. In this position they managed, with the aid of the patient cab-horse, to drag the vehicle through the narrow part of the passage. It was not a great distance, fortunately, and when the path grew broader they put the buggy together again and proceeded more comfortably. But the road was nothing more than a series of rifts or cracks in the mountain, and it went zig-zag in every direction, slanting first up and then down until they were puzzled as to whether they were any nearer to the top of the earth than when they had started, hours before.

"Anyhow," said Dorothy, "we've 'scaped those awful Gurgles, and that's *one* comfort!"

"Probably the Gargoyles are still busy trying to put out the fire," returned the Wizard. "But even if they succeeded in doing that it would be very difficult for them to fly amongst these rocks; so I am sure we need fear them no longer."

Once in a while they would come to a deep crack in the floor, which made the way quite dangerous; but there was still enough oil in the lanterns to give them light, and the cracks were not so wide but that they were able to jump over them.

Sometimes they had to climb over heaps of loose rock, where Jim could scarcely drag the buggy. At such times Dorothy, Zeb and the Wizard all pushed behind, and lifted the wheels over the roughest places; so they managed, by dint of hard work, to keep going. But the little party was both weary and discouraged when at last, on turning a sharp corner, the wanderers found themselves in a vast cave arching high over their heads and having a smooth, level floor.

The cave was circular in shape, and all around its edge, near to the ground, appeared groups of dull yellow lights, two of them being always side by side. These were motionless at first, but soon began to flicker more brightly and to sway slowly from side to side and then up and down.

"What sort of place is this?" asked the boy, trying to see more clearly through the gloom.

"I cannot imagine, I'm sure," answered the Wizard, also peering about.

"Woogh!" snarled Eureka, arching her back until her hair stood straight on end; "it's a den of alligators, or crocodiles, or some other dreadful creatures! Don't you see their terrible eyes?"

"Eureka sees better in the dark than we can," whispered Dorothy. "Tell us, dear, what do the creatures look like?" she asked, addressing her pet.

"I simply can't describe 'em," answered the kitten, shuddering. "Their eyes are like pie-plates and their mouths like coal-scuttles. But their bodies don't seem very big."

"Where are they?" enquired the girl.

"They are in little pockets all around the edge of this cavern. Oh, Dorothy—you can't imagine what horrid things they are! They're uglier than the Gargoyles."

"Tut-tut! be careful how you criticise your neighbors," spoke a rasping voice near by. "As a matter of fact you are rather ugly-looking creatures yourselves, and I'm sure mother has often told us we were the loveliest and prettiest things in all the world."

Hearing these words our friends turned in the direction of the sound, and the Wizard held his lanterns so that their light would flood one of the little pockets in the rock.

"Why, it's a dragon!" he exclaimed.

"No," answered the owner of the big yellow eyes which were blinking at them so steadily; "you are wrong about that. We hope to grow to be dragons some day, but just now we're only dragonettes."

"What's that?" asked Dorothy, gazing fearfully at the great scaley head, the yawning mouth and the big eyes.

"Young dragons, of course; but we are not allowed to call ourselves real dragons until we get our full growth," was the reply. "The big dragons are very proud, and don't think children amount to much; but mother says that some day we will all be very powerful and important."

"Where is your mother?" asked the Wizard, anxiously looking around.

"She has gone up to the top of the earth to hunt for our dinner. If she has good luck she will bring us an elephant, or a brace of rhinoceri, or perhaps a few dozen people to stay our hunger."

"Oh; are you hungry?" enquired Dorothy, drawing back.

"Very," said the dragonette, snapping its jaws.

"And—and—do you eat people?"

"To be sure, when we can get them. But they've been very scarce for a few years and we usually have to be content with elephants or buffaloes," answered the creature, in a regretful tone.

"How old are you?" enquired Zeb, who stared at the yellow eyes as if fascinated.

"Quite young, I grieve to say; and all of my brothers and sisters that you see here are practically my own age. If I remember rightly, we were sixty-six years old the day before yesterday."

"But that isn't young!" cried Dorothy, in amazement.

"No?" drawled the dragonette; "it seems to me very babyish."

"How old is your mother?" asked the girl.

"Mother's about two thousand years old; but she carelessly lost track of her age a few centuries ago and skipped several hundreds. She's a little fussy, you know, and afraid of growing old, being a widow and still in her prime."

"I should think she would be," agreed Dorothy. Then, after

a moment's thought, she asked: "Are we friends or enemies? I mean, will you be good to us, or do you intend to eat us?"

"As for that, we dragonettes would love to eat you, my child; but unfortunately mother has tied all our tails around the rocks at the back of our individual caves, so that we can not crawl out to get you. If you choose to come nearer we will make a mouthful of you in a wink; but unless you do you will remain quite safe."

There was a regretful accent in the creature's voice, and at the words all the other dragonettes sighed dismally.

Dorothy felt relieved. Presently she asked:

"Why did your mother tie your tails?"

"Oh, she is sometimes gone for several weeks on her hunting trips, and if we were not tied we would crawl all over the mountain and fight with each other and get into a lot of mischief. Mother usually knows what she is about, but she made a mistake this time; for you are sure to escape us unless you come too near, and you probably won't do that."

"No, indeed!" said the little girl. "We don't wish to be eaten by such awful beasts."

"Permit me to say," returned the dragonette, "that you are rather impolite to call us names, knowing that we cannot resent your insults. We consider ourselves very beautiful in appearance, for mother has told us so, and she knows. And we are of an excellent family and have a pedigree that I challenge any humans to equal, as it extends back about twenty thousand years, to the time of the famous Green Dragon of Atlantis, who lived in a time when humans had not yet been created. Can you match that pedigree, little girl?"

"Well," said Dorothy, "I was born on a farm in Kansas, and I guess that's being just as 'spectable and haughty as living in a cave with your tail tied to a rock. If it isn't I'll have to stand it, that's all."

"Tastes differ," murmured the dragonette, slowly drooping its scaley eyelids over its yellow eyes, until they looked like half-moons.

Being reassured by the fact that the creatures could not crawl out of their rock-pockets, the children and the Wizard now took time to examine them more closely. The heads of the dragonettes were as big as barrels and covered with hard, greenish scales that glittered brightly under the light of the lanterns. Their front legs, which grew just back of their heads, were also strong and big; but their bodies were smaller around than their heads, and dwindled away in a long line until their tails were slim as a shoe-string. Dorothy thought, if it had taken them sixty-six years to grow to this size, that it would be fully a hundred years more before they could hope to call themselves dragons, and that seemed like a good while to wait to grow up.

"It occurs to me," said the Wizard, "that we ought to get out of this place before the mother dragon comes back."

"Don't hurry," called one of the dragonettes; "mother will be glad to meet you, I'm sure."

"You may be right," replied the Wizard, "but we're a little particular about associating with strangers. Will you kindly tell us which way your mother went to get on top the earth?"

"That is not a fair question to ask us," declared another dragonette. "For, if we told you truly, you might escape us altogether; and if we told you an untruth we would be naughty and deserve to be punished."

"Then," decided Dorothy, "we must find our way out the best we can."

They circled all around the cavern, keeping a good distance away from the blinking yellow eyes of the dragonettes, and presently discovered that there were two paths leading from the wall opposite to the place where they had entered. They selected one of these at a venture and hurried along it as fast as they could go, for they had no idea when the mother dragon would be back and were very anxious not to make her acquaintance.

Chapter 14

OZMA USES the MAGIC BELT

For a considerable distance the way led straight upward in a gentle incline, and the wanderers made such good progress that they grew hopeful and eager, thinking they might see sunshine at any minute. But at length they came unexpectedly upon a huge rock that shut off the passage and blocked them from proceeding a single step farther.

This rock was separate from the rest of the mountain and was in motion, turning slowly around and around as if upon a pivot. When first they came to it there was a solid wall before them; but presently it revolved until there was exposed a wide, smooth path across it to the other side. This appeared so unexpectedly that they were unprepared to take advantage of it at first, and allowed the rocky wall to swing around again before they had decided to pass over. But they knew now that there was a means of escape and so waited patiently until the path appeared for the second time.

The children and the Wizard rushed across the moving rock and sprang into the passage beyond, landing safely though a little out of breath. Jim the cab-horse came last, and the rocky wall almost caught him; for just as he leaped to the floor of the further passage the wall swung across it and a loose stone that the buggy wheels knocked against fell into the narrow crack where the rock turned, and became wedged there.

They heard a crunching, grinding sound, a loud snap, and the turn-table came to a stop with its broadest surface shutting off the path from which they had come.

"Never mind," said Zeb, "we don't want to get back, anyhow."

"I'm not so sure of that," returned Dorothy. "The mother dragon may come down and catch us here."

"It is possible," agreed the Wizard, "if this proves to be the path she usually takes. But I have been examining this tunnel, and I do not see any signs of so large a beast having passed through it."

"Then we're all right," said the girl, "for if the dragon went the other way she can't poss'bly get to us now."

"Of course not, my dear. But there is another thing to consider. The mother dragon probably knows the road to the earth's surface, and if she went the other way then we have come the wrong way," said the Wizard, thoughtfully.

"Dear me!" cried Dorothy. "That would be unlucky, wouldn't it?"

"Very. Unless this passage also leads to the top of the earth," said Zeb. "For my part, if we manage to get out of here I'll be glad it isn't the way the dragon goes."

"So will I," returned Dorothy. "It's enough to have your pedigree flung in your face by those saucy dragonettes. No one knows what the mother might do."

They now moved on again, creeping slowly up another steep incline. The lanterns were beginning to grow dim, and the Wizard poured the remaining oil from one into the other, so that the one light would last longer. But their journey was almost over, for in a short time they reached a small cave from which there was no further outlet.

They did not realize their ill fortune at first, for their hearts were gladdened by the sight of a ray of sunshine coming through a small crack in the roof of the cave, far overhead. That meant that their world—the real world—was not very far away, and that the succession of perilous adventures they had encountered had at last brought them near the earth's surface, which meant home to them. But when the adventurers looked more carefully around them they discovered that they were in a strong prison from which there was no hope of escape.

"But we're *almost* on earth again," cried Dorothy, "for there is the sun—the most *beau'ful* sun that shines!" and she pointed eagerly at the crack in the distant roof.

"Almost on earth isn't being there," said the kitten, in a discontented tone. "It wouldn't be possible for even me to get up to that crack—or through it if I got there."

"It appears that the path ends here," announced the Wizard, gloomily.

"And there is no way to go back," added Zeb, with a low whistle of perplexity.

"I was sure it would come to this, in the end," remarked the old cab-horse. "Folks don't fall into the middle of the earth and then get back again to tell of their adventures—not in real life. And the whole thing has been unnatural because that cat and I are both able to talk your language, and to understand the words you say."

"And so can the nine tiny piglets," added Eureka. "Don't forget them, for I may have to eat them, after all."

"I've heard animals talk before," said Dorothy, "and no harm came of it."

"Were you ever before shut up in a cave, far under the earth, with no way of getting out?" enquired the horse, seriously.

"No," answered Dorothy. "But don't you lose heart, Jim, for I'm sure this isn't the end of our story, by any means."

The reference to the piglets reminded the Wizard that his pets had not enjoyed much exercise lately, and must be tired of their prison in his pocket. So he sat down upon the floor of the cave, brought the piglets out one by one, and allowed them to run around as much as they pleased.

"My dears," he said to them, "I'm afraid I've got you into a lot of trouble, and that you will never again be able to leave this gloomy cave."

"What's wrong?" asked a piglet. "We've been in the dark quite a while, and you may as well explain what has happened."

The Wizard told them of the misfortune that had over-taken the wanderers.

"Well," said another piglet, "you are a wizard, are you not?"

"I am," replied the little man.

"Then you can do a few wizzes and get us out of this hole," declared the tiny one, with much confidence.

"I could if I happened to be a real wizard," returned the master sadly. "But I'm not, my piggy-wees; I'm a humbug wizard."

"Nonsense!" cried several of the piglets, together.

"You can ask Dorothy," said the little man, in an injured tone.

"It's true enough," returned the girl, earnestly. "Our friend Oz is merely a humbug wizard, for he once proved it to me. He can do several very wonderful things—if he knows how. But he can't wiz a single thing if he hasn't the tools and machinery to work with."

"Thank you, my dear, for doing me justice," responded the Wizard, gratefully. "To be accused of being a real wizard, when I'm not, is a slander I will not tamely submit to. But I am one of the greatest humbug wizards that ever lived, and you will realize this when we have all starved together and our bones are scattered over the floor of this lonely cave."

"I don't believe we'll realize anything, when it comes to that," remarked Dorothy, who had been deep in thought. "But I'm not going to scatter my bones just yet, because I need them, and you prob'ly need yours, too."

"We are helpless to escape," sighed the Wizard.

"*We* may be helpless," answered Dorothy, smiling at him, "but there are others who can do more than we can. Cheer up, friends. I'm sure Ozma will help us."

"Ozma!" exclaimed the Wizard. "Who is Ozma?"

"The girl that rules the marvelous Land of Oz," was the reply. "She's a friend of mine, for I met her in the Land of Ev, not long ago, and went to Oz with her."

"For the second time?" asked the Wizard, with great interest.

"Yes. The first time I went to Oz I found you there, ruling the Emerald City. After you went up in a balloon, and escaped us, I got back to Kansas by means of a pair of magical silver shoes."

"I remember those shoes," said the little man, nodding. "They once belonged to the Wicked Witch. Have you them here with you?"

"No; I lost them somewhere in the air," explained the child. "But the second time I went to the Land of Oz I owned the Nome King's Magic Belt, which is much more powerful than were the Silver Shoes."

"Where is that Magic Belt?" enquired the Wizard, who had listened with great interest.

"Ozma has it; for its powers won't work in a common, ordinary country like the United States. Anyone in a fairy country like the Land of Oz can do anything with it; so I left it with my friend the Princess Ozma, who used it to wish me in Australia with Uncle Henry."

"And were you?" asked Zeb, astonished at what he heard.

"Of course; in just a jiffy. And Ozma has an enchanted picture hanging in her room that shows her the exact scene where any of her friends may be, at any time she chooses. All she has to do is to say: 'I wonder what So-and-so is doing,' and at once the picture shows where her friend is and what the friend is doing. That's *real* magic, Mr. Wizard; isn't it? Well, every day at four o'clock Ozma has promised to look at me in that picture, and if I am in need of help I am to make her a certain sign and she will put on the Nome King's Magic Belt and wish me to be with her in Oz."

"Do you mean that Princess Ozma will see this cave in her enchanted picture, and see all of us here, and what we are doing?" demanded Zeb.

"Of course; when it is four o'clock," she replied, with a laugh at his startled expression.

"And when you make a sign she will bring you to her in the Land of Oz?" continued the boy.

"That's it, exactly; by means of the Magic Belt."

"Then," said the Wizard, "you will be saved, little Dorothy; and I am very glad of it. The rest of us will die much more cheerfully when we know you have escaped our sad fate."

"*I* won't die cheerfully!" protested the kitten. "There's nothing cheerful about dying that I could ever see, although they say a cat has nine lives, and so must die nine times."

"Have you ever died yet?" enquired the boy.

"No, and I'm not anxious to begin," said Eureka.

"Don't worry, dear," Dorothy exclaimed, "I'll hold you in my arms, and take you with me."

"Take us, too!" cried the nine tiny piglets, all in one breath.

"Perhaps I can," answered Dorothy. "I'll try."

"Couldn't you manage to hold me in your arms?" asked the cab-horse.

Dorothy laughed.

"I'll do better than that," she promised, "for I can easily save you all, once I am myself in the Land of Oz."

"How?" they asked.

"By using the Magic Belt. All I need do is to wish you with me, and there you'll be—safe in the royal palace!"

"Good!" cried Zeb.

"I built that palace, and the Emerald City, too," remarked the Wizard, in a thoughtful tone, "and I'd like to see them again, for I was very happy among the Munchkins and Winkies and Quadlings and Gillikins."

"Who are they?" asked the boy.

"The four nations that inhabit the Land of Oz," was the reply. "I wonder if they would treat me nicely if I went there again."

"Of course they would!" declared Dorothy. "They are still proud of their former Wizard, and often speak of you kindly."

"Do you happen to know whatever became of the Tin Woodman and the Scarecrow?" he enquired.

"They live in Oz yet," said the girl, "and are very important people."

"And the Cowardly Lion?"

"Oh, he lives there too, with his friend the Hungry Tiger; and Billina is there, because she liked the place better than Kansas, and wouldn't go with me to Australia."

"I'm afraid I don't know the Hungry Tiger and Billina," said the Wizard, shaking his head. "Is Billina a girl?"

"No; she's a yellow hen, and a great friend of mine. You're sure to like Billina, when you know her," asserted Dorothy.

"Your friends sound like a menagerie," remarked Zeb,

uneasily. "Couldn't you wish me in some safer place than Oz."

"Don't worry," replied the girl. "You'll just love the folks in Oz, when you get acquainted. What time is it, Mr. Wizard?"

The little man looked at his watch—a big silver one that he carried in his vest pocket.

"Half-past three," he said.

"Then we must wait for half an hour," she continued; "but it won't take long, after that, to carry us all to the Emerald City."

They sat silently thinking for a time. Then Jim suddenly asked:

"Are there any horses in Oz?"

"Only one," replied Dorothy, "and he's a sawhorse."

"A what?"

"A sawhorse. Princess Ozma once brought him to life with a witch-powder, when she was a boy."

"Was Ozma once a boy?" asked Zeb, wonderingly.

"Yes; a wicked witch enchanted her, so she could not rule her kingdom. But she's a girl now, and the sweetest, loveliest girl in all the world."

"A sawhorse is a thing they saw boards on," remarked Jim, with a sniff.

"It is when it's not alive," acknowledged the girl. "But this sawhorse can trot as fast as you can, Jim; and he's very wise, too."

"Pah! I'll race the miserable wooden donkey any day in the week!" cried the cab-horse.

Dorothy did not reply to that. She felt that Jim would know more about the Sawhorse later on.

The time dragged wearily enough to the eager watchers, but finally the Wizard announced that four o'clock had arrived, and Dorothy caught up the kitten and began to make the signal that had been agreed upon to the far-away invisible Ozma.

"Nothing seems to happen," said Zeb, doubtfully.

"Oh, we must give Ozma time to put on the Magic Belt," replied the girl.

She had scarcely spoken the words when she suddenly disappeared from the cave, and with her went the kitten. There had been no sound of any kind and no warning. One moment Dorothy sat beside them with the kitten in her lap, and a moment later the horse, the piglets, the Wizard and the boy were all that remained in the underground prison.

"I believe we will soon follow her," announced the Wizard, in a tone of great relief; "for I know something about the magic of the fairyland that is called the Land of Oz. Let us be ready, for we may be sent for any minute."

He put the piglets safely away in his pocket again and then he and Zeb got into the buggy and sat expectantly upon the seat.

"Will it hurt?" asked the boy, in a voice that trembled a little.

"Not at all," replied the Wizard. "It will all happen as quick as a wink."

And that was the way it did happen.

The cab-horse gave a nervous start and Zeb began to rub his eyes to make sure he was not asleep. For they were in the streets of a beautiful emerald-green city, bathed in a grateful green •light that was especially pleasing to their eyes, and surrounded by merry faced people in gorgeous green-and-gold costumes of many extraordinary designs.

Before them were the jewel-studded gates of a magnificent palace, and now the gates opened slowly as if inviting them to enter the courtyard, where splendid flowers were blooming and pretty fountains shot their silvery sprays into the air.

Zeb shook the reins to rouse the cab-horse from his stupor of amazement, for the people were beginning to gather around and stare at the strangers.

"Gid-dap!" cried the boy, and at the word Jim slowly trotted into the courtyard and drew the buggy along the jewelled driveway to the great entrance of the royal palace.

·····◄ Chapter 15 ►·····

OLD FRIENDS ARE REUNITED

Many servants dressed in handsome uniforms stood ready to welcome the new arrivals, and when the Wizard got out of the buggy a pretty girl in a green gown cried out in surprise:

"Why, it's Oz, the Wonderful Wizard, come back again!"

The little man looked at her closely and then took both the maiden's hands in his and shook them cordially.

"On my word," he exclaimed, "it's little Jellia Jamb—as pert and pretty as ever!"

"Why not, Mr. Wizard?" asked Jellia, bowing low. "But I'm afraid you cannot rule the Emerald City, as you used to, because we now have a beautiful Princess whom everyone loves dearly."

"And the people will not willingly part with her," added a tall soldier in a Captain-General's uniform.

The Wizard turned to look at him.

"Did you not wear green whiskers at one time?" he asked.

"Yes," said the soldier; "but I shaved them off long ago, and since then I have risen from a private to be the Chief General of the Royal Armies."

"That's nice," said the little man. "But I assure you, my good people, that I do not wish to rule the Emerald City," he added, earnestly.

"In that case you are very welcome!" cried all the servants, and it pleased the Wizard to note the respect with which the royal retainers bowed before him. His fame had not been forgotten in the Land of Oz, by any means.

"Where is Dorothy?" enquired Zeb, anxiously, as he left the buggy and stood beside his friend the little Wizard.

"She is with the Princess Ozma, in the private rooms of the palace," replied Jellia Jamb. "But she has ordered me to make you welcome and to show you to your apartments."

The boy looked around him with wondering eyes. Such magnificence and wealth as was displayed in this palace was more than he had ever dreamed of, and he could scarcely believe that all the gorgeous glitter was real and not tinsel.

"What's to become of me?" asked the horse, uneasily. He

had seen considerable of life in the cities in his younger days, and knew that this regal palace was no place for him.

It perplexed even Jellia Jamb, for a time, to know what to do with the animal. The green maiden was much astonished at the sight of so unusual a creature, for horses were unknown in this Land; but those who lived in the Emerald City were apt to be astonished by queer sights, so after inspecting the cab-horse and noting the mild look in his big eyes the girl decided not to be afraid of him.

"There are no stables here," said the Wizard, "unless some have been built since I went away."

"We have never needed them before," answered Jellia; "for the Sawhorse lives in a room of the palace, being much smaller and more natural in appearance than this great beast you have brought with you."

"Do you mean that I'm a freak?" asked Jim, angrily.

"Oh, no," she hastened to say, "there may be many more like you in the place you came from, but in Oz any horse but a Sawhorse is unusual."

This mollified Jim a little, and after some thought the green maiden decided to give the cab-horse a room in the palace, such a big building having many rooms that were seldom in use.

So Zeb unharnessed Jim, and several of the servants then led the horse around to the rear, where they selected a nice large apartment that he could have all to himself.

Then Jellia said to the Wizard:

"Your own room—which was back of the great Throne Room—has been vacant ever since you left us. Would you like it again?"

"Yes, indeed!" returned the little man. "It will seem like being at home again, for I lived in that room for many, many years."

He knew the way to it, and a servant followed him, carrying his satchel. Zeb was also escorted to a room—so grand and beautiful that he almost feared to sit in the chairs or lie upon the bed, lest he might dim their splendor. In the closets he discovered many fancy costumes of rich velvets and brocades, and one of the attendants told him to dress himself in any of the clothes that pleased him and to be prepared to dine with the Princess and Dorothy in an hour's time.

Opening from the chamber was a fine bath-room having a marble tub with perfumed water; so the boy, still dazed by the novelty of his surroundings, indulged in a good bath and then selected a maroon velvet costume with silver buttons to replace his own soiled and much worn clothing. There were silk stockings and soft leather slippers with diamond buckles to accompany his new costume, and when he was fully dressed Zeb looked much more dignified and imposing than ever before in his life.

He was all ready when an attendant came to escort him to the presence of the Princess; he followed bashfully and was ushered into a room more dainty and attractive than it was

DOROTHY and the WIZARD in OZ

splendid. Here he found Dorothy seated beside a young girl so marvelously beautiful that the boy stopped suddenly with a gasp of admiration.

But Dorothy sprang up and ran to seize her friend's hand, drawing him impulsively toward the lovely Princess, who smiled most graciously upon her guest. Then the Wizard entered, and his presence relieved the boy's embarrassment. The little man was clothed in black velvet, with many sparkling emerald ornaments decorating his breast; but his bald head and wrinkled features made him appear more amusing than impressive.

Ozma had been quite curious to meet the famous man who had built the Emerald City and united the Munchkins, Gillikins, Quadlings and Winkies into one people; so when they were all four seated at the dinner table the Princess said:

"Please tell me, Mr. Wizard, whether you called yourself Oz after this great country, or whether you believe my country is called Oz after you. It is a matter that I have long wished to enquire about, because you are of a strange race and my own name is Ozma. No one, I am sure, is better able to explain this mystery than you."

"That is true," answered the little Wizard; "therefore it will give me pleasure to explain my connection with your country. In the first place, I must tell you that I was born in Omaha, and my father, who was a politician, named me Oscar Zoroaster Phadrig Isaac Norman Henkle Emmannuel Ambroise Diggs,

Diggs being the last name because he could think of no more to go before it. Taken altogether, it was a dreadfully long name to weigh down a poor innocent child, and one of the hardest lessons I ever learned was to remember my own name. When I grew up I just called myself O. Z., because the other initials were P-I-N-H-E-A-D; and that spelled 'pinhead,' which was a reflection on my intelligence."

"Surely no one could blame you for cutting your name short," said Ozma, sympathetically. "But didn't you cut it almost too short?"

"Perhaps so," replied the Wizard. "When a young man I ran away from home and joined a circus. I used to call myself a Wizard, and do tricks of ventriloquism."

"What does that mean?" asked the Princess.

"Throwing my voice into any object I pleased, to make it appear that the object was speaking instead of me. Also I began to make balloon ascensions. On my balloon and on all the other articles I used in the circus I painted the two initials: 'O. Z.,' to show that those things belonged to me.

"One day my balloon ran away with me and brought me across the deserts to this beautiful country. When the people saw me come from the sky they naturally thought me some superior creature, and bowed down before me. I told them I was a Wizard, and showed them some easy tricks that amazed them; and when they saw the initials painted on the balloon they called me Oz."

"Now I begin to understand," said the Princess, smiling.

"At that time," continued the Wizard, busily eating his soup while talking, "there were four separate countries in this Land, each one of the four being ruled by a Witch. But the people thought my power was greater than that of the Witches; and perhaps the Witches thought so too, for they never dared oppose me. I ordered the Emerald City to be built just where the four countries cornered together, and when it was completed I announced myself the Ruler of the Land of Oz, which included all the four countries of the Munchkins, the Gillikins, the Winkies and the Quadlings. Over this Land I ruled in peace for many years, until I grew old and longed to see my native city once again. So when Dorothy was first blown to this place by a cyclone I arranged to go away with her in a balloon; but the balloon escaped too soon and carried me back alone. After many adventures I reached Omaha, only to find that all my old friends were dead or had moved away. So, having nothing else to do, I joined a circus again, and made my balloon ascensions until the earthquake caught me."

"That is quite a history," said Ozma; "but there is a little more history about the Land of Oz that you do not seem to understand—perhaps for the reason that no one ever told it you. Many years before you came here this Land was united under one Ruler, as it is now, and the Ruler's name was always 'Oz,' which means in our language 'Great and Good'; or, if the Ruler happened to be a woman, her name was always 'Ozma.'

But once upon a time four Witches leagued together to depose the king and rule the four parts of the kingdom themselves; so when the Ruler, my grandfather, was hunting one day, one Wicked Witch named Mombi stole him and carried him away, keeping him a close prisoner. Then the Witches divided up the kingdom, and ruled the four parts of it until you came here. That was why the people were so glad to see you, and why they thought from your initials that you were their rightful ruler."

"But, at that time," said the Wizard, thoughtfully, "there were two Good Witches and two Wicked Witches ruling in the land."

"Yes," replied Ozma, "because a good Witch had conquered Mombi in the North and Glinda the Good had conquered the evil Witch in the South. But Mombi was still my grandfather's jailor, and afterward my father's jailor. When I was born she transformed me into a boy, hoping that no one would ever recognize me and know that I was the rightful Princess of the Land of Oz. But I escaped from her and am now the Ruler of my people."

"I am very glad of that," said the Wizard, "and hope you will consider me one of your most faithful and devoted subjects."

"We owe a great deal to the Wonderful Wizard," continued the Princess, "for it was you who built this splendid Emerald City."

"Your people built it," he answered. "I only bossed the job, as we say in Omaha."

"But you ruled it wisely and well for many years," said she, "and made the people proud of your magical art. So, as you are now too old to wander abroad and work in a circus, I offer you a home here as long as you live. You shall be the Official Wizard of my kingdom, and be treated with every respect and consideration."

"I accept your kind offer with gratitude, gracious Princess," the little man said, in a soft voice, and they could all see that tear-drops were standing in his keen old eyes. It meant a good deal to him to secure a home like this.

"He's only a humbug Wizard, though," said Dorothy, smiling at him.

"And that is the safest kind of a Wizard to have," replied Ozma, promptly.

"Oz can do some good tricks, humbug or no humbug," announced Zeb, who was now feeling more at ease.

"He shall amuse us with his tricks tomorrow," said the Princess. "I have sent messengers to summon all of Dorothy's old friends to meet her and give her welcome, and they ought to arrive very soon, now."

Indeed, the dinner was no sooner finished than in rushed the Scarecrow, to hug Dorothy in his padded arms and tell her how glad he was to see her again. The Wizard was also most heartily welcomed by the straw man, who was an important personage in the Land of Oz.

"How are your brains?" enquired the little humbug, as he grasped the soft, stuffed hands of his old friend.

"Working finely," answered the Scarecrow. "I'm very certain, Oz, that you gave me the best brains in the world, for I can think with them day and night, when all other brains are fast asleep."

"How long did you rule the Emerald City, after I left here?" was the next question.

"Quite awhile, until I was conquered by a girl named General Jinjur. But Ozma soon conquered her, with the help of Glinda the Good, and after that I went to live with Nick Chopper, the Tin Woodman."

Just then a loud cackling was heard outside; and, when a servant threw open the door with a low bow, a yellow hen strutted in. Dorothy sprang forward and caught the fluffy fowl in her arms, uttering at the same time a glad cry.

"Oh, Billina!" she said; "how fat and sleek you've grown."

"Why shouldn't I?" asked the hen, in a sharp, clear voice. "I live on the fat of the land—don't I, Ozma?"

"You have everything you wish for," said the Princess.

Around Billina's neck was a string of beautiful pearls, and on her legs were bracelets of emeralds. She nestled herself comfortably in Dorothy's lap until the kitten gave a snarl of jealous anger and leaped up with a sharp claw fiercely bared to strike Billina a blow. But the little girl gave the angry kitten such a severe cuff that it jumped down again without daring to scratch.

"How horrid of you, Eureka!" cried Dorothy. "Is that the way to treat my friends?"

"You have queer friends, seems to me," replied the kitten, in a surly tone.

"Seems to me the same way," said Billina, scornfully, "if that beastly cat is one of them."

"Look here!" said Dorothy, sternly. "I won't have any quarrelling in the Land of Oz, I can tell you! Everybody lives in peace here, and loves everybody else; and unless you two, Billina and Eureka, make up and be friends, I'll take my Magic Belt and wish you both home again, *immejitly*. So, there!"

They were both much frightened at the threat, and promised meekly to be good. But it was never noticed that they became very warm friends, for all of that.

And now the Tin Woodman arrived, his body most beautifully nickel-plated, so that it shone splendidly in the brilliant light of the room. The Tin Woodman loved Dorothy most tenderly, and welcomed with joy the return of the little old Wizard.

"Sir," said he to the latter, "I never can thank you enough for the excellent heart you once gave me. It has made me many friends, I assure you, and it beats as kindly and lovingly today as it ever did."

"I'm glad to hear that," said the Wizard. "I was afraid it would get moldy in that tin body of yours."

"Not at all," returned Nick Chopper. "It keeps finely, being preserved in my air-tight chest."

Zeb was a little shy when first introduced to these queer

people; but they were so friendly and sincere that he soon grew to admire them very much, even finding some good qualities in the yellow hen. But he became nervous again when the next visitor was announced.

"This," said Princess Ozma, "is my friend Mr. H. M. Woggle-Bug, T.E., who assisted me one time when I was in great distress, and is now the Dean of the Royal College of Athletic Science."

"Ah," said the Wizard; "I'm pleased to meet so distinguished a personage."

"H. M.," said the Woggle-Bug, pompously, "means Highly Magnified; and T.E. means Thoroughly Educated. I am, in reality, a very big bug, and doubtless the most intelligent being in all this broad domain."

"How well you disguise it," said the Wizard. "But I don't doubt your word in the least."

"Nobody doubts it, sir," replied the Woggle-Bug, and drawing a book from its pocket the strange insect turned its back on the company and sat down in a corner to read.

Nobody minded this rudeness, which might have seemed more impolite in one less thoroughly educated; so they straightway forgot him and joined in a merry conversation that kept them well amused until bed-time arrived.

····•·‹ Chapter 16 ›·•·····

JIM, the CAB-HORSE

Jim the cab-horse found himself in possession of a large room with a green marble floor and carved marble wainscoting, which was so stately in its appearance that it would have awed anyone else. Jim accepted it as a mere detail, and at his command the attendants gave his coat a good rubbing, combed his mane and tail, and washed his hoofs and fetlocks. Then they told him dinner would be served directly and he replied that they could not serve it too quickly to suit his convenience. First they brought him a steaming bowl of soup, which the horse eyed in dismay.

"Take that stuff away!" he commanded. "Do you take me for a salamander?"

They obeyed at once, and next served a fine large turbot on a silver platter, with drawn gravy poured over it.

"Fish!" cried Jim, with a sniff. "Do you take me for a tom-cat? Away with it!"

The servants were a little discouraged, but soon they brought in a great tray containing two dozen nicely roasted quail on toast.

"Well, well!" said the horse, now thoroughly provoked. "Do you take me for a weasel? How stupid and ignorant you are, in the Land of Oz, and what dreadful things you feed upon! Is there nothing that is decent to eat in this palace?"

The trembling servants sent for the Royal Steward, who came in haste and said:

"What would your Highness like for dinner?"

"Highness!" repeated Jim, who was unused to such titles.

"You are at least six feet high, and that is higher than any other animal in this country," said the Steward.

"Well, my Highness would like some oats," declared the horse.

"Oats? We have no whole oats," the Steward replied, with much deference. "But there is any quantity of oatmeal, which we often cook for breakfast. Oatmeal is a breakfast dish," added the Steward, humbly.

"I'll make it a dinner dish," said Jim. "Fetch it on, but don't cook it, as you value your life."

You see, the respect shown the worn-out old cab-horse

made him a little arrogant, and he forgot he was a guest, never having been treated otherwise than as a servant since the day he was born, until his arrival in the Land of Oz. But the royal attendants did not heed the animal's ill temper. They soon mixed a tub of oatmeal with a little water, and Jim ate it with much relish.

Then the servants heaped a lot of rugs upon the floor and the old horse slept on the softest bed he had ever known in his life.

In the morning, as soon as it was daylight, he resolved to take a walk and try to find some grass for breakfast; so he ambled calmly through the handsome arch of the doorway, turned the corner of the palace, wherein all seemed asleep, and came face to face with the Sawhorse.

Jim stopped abruptly, being startled and amazed. The Sawhorse stopped at the same time and stared at the other with its queer protruding eyes, which were mere knots in the log that formed its body. The legs of the Sawhorse were four sticks driven into holes bored in the log; its tail was a small branch that had been left by accident and its mouth a place chopped in one end of the body which projected a little and served as a head. The ends of the wooden legs were shod with plates of solid gold, and the saddle of the Princess Ozma, which was of red leather set with sparkling diamonds, was strapped to the clumsy body.

Jim's eyes stuck out as much as those of the Sawhorse, and

he stared at the creature with his ears erect and his long head drawn back until it rested against his arched neck.

In this comical position the two horses circled slowly around each other for a while, each being unable to realize what the singular thing might be which it now beheld for the first time. Then Jim exclaimed:

"For goodness sake, what sort of a being are you?"

"I'm a Sawhorse," replied the other.

"Oh; I believe I've heard of you," said the cab-horse; "but you are unlike anything that I expected to see."

"I do not doubt it," the Sawhorse observed, with a tone of pride. "I am considered quite unusual."

"You are, indeed. But a rickety wooden thing like you has no right to be alive."

"I couldn't help it," returned the other, rather crestfallen. "Ozma sprinkled me with a magic powder, and I just had to live. I know I'm not much account; but I'm the only horse in all the Land of Oz, so they treat me with great respect."

"You, a horse!"

"Oh, not a real one, of course. There are no real horses here at all. But I'm a splendid imitation of one."

Jim gave an indignant neigh.

"Look at me!" he cried. "Behold a real horse!"

The wooden animal gave a start, and then examined the other intently.

"Is it possible that you are a Real Horse?" he murmured.

"Not only possible, but true," replied Jim, who was gratified by the impression he had created. "It is proved by my fine points. For example, look at the long hairs on my tail, with which I can whisk away the flies."

"The flies never trouble me," said the Sawhorse.

"And notice my great strong teeth, with which I nibble the grass."

"It is not necessary for me to eat," observed the Sawhorse.

"Also examine my broad chest, which enables me to draw deep, full breaths," said Jim, proudly.

"I have no need to breathe," returned the other.

"No; you miss many pleasures," remarked the cab-horse, pityingly. "You do not know the relief of brushing away a fly that has bitten you, nor the delight of eating delicious food, nor the satisfaction of drawing a long breath of fresh, pure air. You may be an imitation of a horse, but you're a mighty poor one."

"Oh, I cannot hope ever to be like you," sighed the Sawhorse. "But I am glad to meet at last a Real Horse. You are certainly the most beautiful creature I ever beheld."

This praise won Jim completely. To be called beautiful was a novelty in his experience. Said he:

"Your chief fault, my friend, is in being made of wood, and that I suppose you cannot help. Real Horses, like myself, are made of flesh and blood and bones."

"I can see the bones all right," replied the Sawhorse, "and

they are admirable and distinct. Also I can see the flesh. But the blood, I suppose is tucked away inside."

"Exactly," said Jim.

"What good is it?" asked the Sawhorse.

Jim did not know, but he would not tell the Sawhorse that.

"If anything cuts me," he replied, "the blood runs out to show where I am cut. You, poor thing! cannot even bleed when you are hurt."

"But I am never hurt," said the Sawhorse. "Once in a while I get broken up some, but I am easily repaired and put in good order again. And I never feel a break or a splinter in the least."

Jim was almost tempted to envy the wooden horse for being unable to feel pain; but the creature was so absurdly unnatural that he decided he would not change places with it under any circumstances.

"How did you happen to be shod with gold?" he asked.

"Princess Ozma did that," was the reply; "and it saves my legs from wearing out. We've had a good many adventures together, Ozma and I, and she likes me."

The cab-horse was about to reply when suddenly he gave a start and a neigh of terror and stood trembling like a leaf. For around the corner had come two enormous savage beasts, treading so lightly that they were upon him before he was aware of their presence. Jim was in the act of plunging down the path to escape when the Sawhorse cried out:

"Stop, my brother! Stop, Real Horse! These are friends, and will do you no harm."

Jim hesitated, eyeing the beasts fearfully. One was an enormous Lion with clear, intelligent eyes, a tawney mane bushy and well kept, and a body like yellow plush. The other was a great Tiger with purple stripes around his lithe body, powerful limbs, and eyes that showed through the half closed lids like coals of fire. The huge forms of these monarchs of the forest and jungle were enough to strike terror to the stoutest heart, and it is no wonder Jim was afraid to face them.

But the Sawhorse introduced the stranger in a calm tone, saying:

"This, noble Horse, is my friend the Cowardly Lion, who is the valiant King of the Forest, but at the same time a faithful vassal of Princess Ozma. And this is the Hungry Tiger, the terror of the jungle, who longs to devour fat babies but is prevented by his Conscience from doing so. These royal beasts are both warm friends of little Dorothy and have come to the Emerald City this morning to welcome her to our fairyland."

Hearing these words Jim resolved to conquer his alarm. He bowed his head with as much dignity as he could muster toward the savage looking beasts, who in return nodded in a friendly way.

"Is not the Real Horse a beautiful animal?" asked the Sawhorse admiringly.

"That is doubtless a matter of taste," returned the Lion.

"In the forest he would be thought ungainly, because his face is stretched out and his neck is uselessly long. His joints, I notice, are swollen and overgrown, and he lacks flesh and is old in years."

"And dreadfully tough," added the Hungry Tiger, in a sad voice. "My Conscience would never permit me to eat so tough a morsel as the Real Horse."

"I'm glad of that," said Jim; "for I, also, have a Conscience, and it tells me not to crush in your skull with a blow of my powerful hoof."

If he thought to frighten the striped beast by such language he was mistaken. The Tiger seemed to smile, and winked one eye slowly.

"You have a good Conscience, friend Horse," it said, "and if you attend to its teachings it will do much to protect you from harm. Some day I will let you try to crush in my skull, and afterward you will know more about tigers than you do now."

"Any friend of Dorothy," remarked the Cowardly Lion, "must be our friend, as well. So let us cease this talk of skull crushing and converse upon more pleasant subjects. Have you breakfasted, Sir Horse?"

"Not yet," replied Jim. "But here is plenty of excellent clover, so if you will excuse me I will eat now."

"He's a vegetarian," remarked the Tiger, as the horse began to munch the clover. "If I could eat grass I would not need a Conscience, for nothing could then tempt me to devour babies and lambs."

Just then Dorothy, who had risen early and heard the voices of the animals, ran out to greet her old friends. She hugged both the Lion and the Tiger with eager delight, but seemed to love the King of Beasts a little better than she did his hungry friend, having known him longer.

By the time they had indulged in a good talk and Dorothy had told them all about the awful earthquake and her recent adventures, the breakfast bell rang from the palace and the little girl went inside to join her human comrades. As she entered the great hall a voice called out, in a rather harsh tone:

"What! are *you* here again?"

"Yes, I am," she answered, looking all around to see where the voice came from.

"What brought you back?" was the next question, and Dorothy's eye rested on an antlered head hanging on the wall just over the fireplace, and caught its lips in the act of moving.

"Good gracious!" she exclaimed. "I thought you were stuffed."

"So I am," replied the head. "But once on a time I was part of the Gump, which Ozma sprinkled with the Powder of Life. I was then for a time the Head of the finest Flying Machine that was ever known to exist, and we did many wonderful things. Afterward the Gump was taken apart and I was put back on this wall; but I can still talk when I feel in the mood, which is not often."

"It's very strange," said the girl. "What were you when you were first alive?"

"That I have forgotten," replied the Gump's Head, "and I do not think it is of much importance. But here comes Ozma; so I'd better hush up, for the Princess doesn't like me to chatter since she changed her name from Tip to Ozma."

Just then the girlish Ruler of Oz opened the door and greeted Dorothy with a good-morning kiss. The little Princess seemed fresh and rosy and in good spirits.

"Breakfast is served, dear," she said, "and I am hungry. So don't let us keep it waiting a single minute."

Chapter 17

The NINE TINY PIGLETS

fter breakfast Ozma announced that she had ordered a holiday to be observed throughout the Emerald City, in honor of her visitors. The people had learned that their old Wizard had returned to them and all were anxious to see him again, for he had always been a rare favorite. So first there was to be a grand procession through the streets, after which the little old man was requested to perform some of his wizardries in the great Throne Room of the palace. In the afternoon there were to be games and races.

The procession was very imposing. First came the Imperial Cornet Band of Oz, dressed in emerald velvet uniforms with slashes of pea-green satin and buttons of immense cut emeralds. They played the National air called "The Oz Spangled Banner," and behind them were the standard bearers with the Royal flag. This flag was divided into four quarters, one being colored sky-blue, another pink, a third lavender and a fourth white. In the center was a large emerald-green star, and all over the four quarters were sewn spangles that glittered beautifully in the sunshine. The colors represented the four countries of Oz, and the green star the Emerald City.

Just behind the royal standard-bearers came the Princess Ozma in her royal chariot, which was of gold encrusted with emeralds and diamonds set in exquisite designs. The chariot was drawn on this occasion by the Cowardly Lion and the Hungry Tiger, who were decorated with immense pink and blue bows. In the chariot rode Ozma and Dorothy, the former in splendid raiment and wearing her royal coronet, while the little Kansas girl wore around her waist the Magic Belt she had once captured from the Nome King.

Following the chariot came the Scarecrow mounted on the Sawhorse, and the people cheered him almost as loudly as they did their lovely Ruler. Behind him stalked with regular, jerky steps, the famous machine-man called Tik-Tok, who had been wound up by Dorothy for the occasion. Tik-Tok moved by clockwork, and was made all of burnished copper. He really belonged to the Kansas girl, who had much respect for his thoughts after they had been properly wound and set going;

but as the copper man would be useless in any place but a fairy country Dorothy had left him in charge of Ozma, who saw that he was suitably cared for.

There followed another band after this, which was called the Royal Court Band, because the members all lived in the palace. They wore white uniforms with real diamond buttons and played "What is Oz without Ozma" very sweetly.

Then came Professor Woggle-Bug, with a group of students from the Royal College of Scientific Athletics. The boys wore long hair and striped sweaters and yelled their college yell every other step they took, to the great satisfaction of the populace, which was glad to have this evidence that their lungs were in good condition.

The brilliantly polished Tin Woodman marched next, at the head of the Royal Army of Oz which consisted of twenty-eight officers, from Generals down to Captains. There were no privates in the army because all were so courageous and skillful that they had been promoted one by one until there were no privates left. Jim and the buggy followed, the old cab-horse being driven by Zeb while the Wizard stood up on the seat and bowed his bald head right and left in answer to the cheers of the people, who crowded thick about him.

Taken altogether the procession was a grand success, and when it had returned to the palace the citizens crowded into the great Throne Room to see the Wizard perform his tricks.

The first thing the little humbug did was to produce a tiny

white piglet from underneath his hat and pretend to pull it apart, making two. This act he repeated until all of the nine tiny piglets were visible, and they were so glad to get out of his pocket that they ran around in a very lively manner. The pretty little creatures would have been a novelty anywhere, so the people were as amazed and delighted at their appearance as even the Wizard could have desired. When he had made them all disappear again Ozma declared she was sorry they were gone, for she wanted one of them to pet and play with. So the Wizard pretended to take one of the piglets out of the hair of the Princess (while really he slyly took it from his inside pocket) and Ozma smiled joyously as the creature nestled in her arms, and she promised to have an emerald collar made for its fat neck and to keep the little squealer always at hand to amuse her.

Afterward it was noticed that the Wizard always performed his famous trick with eight piglets, but it seemed to please the people just as well as if there had been nine of them.

In his little room back of the Throne Room the Wizard had found a lot of things he had left behind him when he went away in the balloon, for no one had occupied the apartment in his absence. There was enough material there to enable him to prepare several new tricks which he had learned from some of the jugglers in the circus, and he had passed part of the night in getting them ready. So he followed the trick of the nine tiny piglets with several other wonderful feats that greatly delighted his audience and the people did not seem to care a bit whether the little man was a humbug Wizard or not, so long as he succeeded in amusing them. They applauded all his tricks and at the end of the performance begged him earnestly not to go away again and leave them.

"In that case," said the little man, gravely, "I will cancel all of my engagements before the crowned heads of Europe and America and devote myself to the people of Oz, for I love you all so well that I can deny you nothing."

After the people had been dismissed with this promise our friends joined Princess Ozma at an elaborate luncheon in the palace, where even the Tiger and the Lion were sumptuously fed and Jim the cab-horse ate his oatmeal out of a golden bowl with seven rows of rubies, sapphires and diamonds set around the rim of it.

In the afternoon they all went to a great field outside the city gates where the games were to be held. There was a beautiful canopy for Ozma and her guests to sit under and watch the people run races and jump and wrestle. You may be sure the folks of Oz did their best with such a distinguished company watching them, and finally Zeb offered to wrestle with a little Munchkin who seemed to be the champion. In appearance he was twice as old as Zeb, for he had long pointed whiskers and wore a peaked hat with little bells all around the brim of it, which tinkled gaily as he moved. But although the

Munchkin was hardly tall enough to come to Zeb's shoulder he was so strong and clever that he laid the boy three times on his back with apparent ease.

Zeb was greatly astonished at his defeat, and when the pretty Princess joined her people in laughing at him he proposed a boxing-match with the Munchkin, to which the little Ozite readily agreed. But the first time that Zeb managed to give him a sharp box on the ears the Munchkin sat down upon the ground and cried until the tears ran down his whiskers, because he had been hurt. This made Zeb laugh, in turn, and the boy felt comforted to find that Ozma laughed as merrily at her weeping subject as she had at him.

Just then the Scarecrow proposed a race between the Sawhorse and the cab-horse; and although all the others were delighted at the suggestion the Sawhorse drew back, saying:

"Such a race would not be fair."

"Of course not," added Jim, with a touch of scorn; "those little wooden legs of yours are not half as long as my own."

"It isn't that," said the Sawhorse, modestly; "but I never tire, and you do."

"Bah!" cried Jim, looking with great disdain at the other; "do you imagine for an instant that such a shabby imitation of a horse as you are can run as fast as I?"

"I don't know, I'm sure," replied the Sawhorse.

"That is what we are trying to find out," remarked the

Scarecrow. "The object of a race is to see who can win it—or at least that is what my excellent brains think."

"Once, when I was young," said Jim, "I was a race horse, and defeated all who dared run against me. I was born in Kentucky, you know, where all the best and most aristocratic horses come from."

"But you're old, now, Jim," suggested Zeb.

"Old! Why, I feel like a colt today," replied Jim. "I only wish there was a real horse here for me to race with. I'd show the people a fine sight, I can tell you."

"Then why not race with the Sawhorse?" enquired the Scarecrow.

"He's afraid," said Jim.

"Oh, no," answered the Sawhorse. "I merely said it wasn't fair. But if my friend the Real Horse is willing to undertake the race I am quite ready."

So they unharnessed Jim and took the saddle off the Sawhorse, and the two queerly matched animals were stood side by side for the start.

"When I say 'Go!'" Zeb called to them, "you must dig out and race until you reach those three trees you see over yonder. Then circle 'round them and come back again. The first one that passes the place where the Princess sits shall be named the winner. Are you ready?"

"I suppose I ought to give the wooden dummy a good start of me," growled Jim.

"Never mind that," said the Sawhorse. "I'll do the best I can."

"Go!" cried Zeb; and at the word the two horses leaped forward and the race was begun.

Jim's big hoofs pounded away at a great rate, and although he did not look very graceful he ran in a way to do credit to his Kentucky breeding. But the Sawhorse was swifter than the wind. Its wooden legs moved so fast that their twinkling could scarcely be seen, and although so much smaller than the cab-horse it covered the ground much faster. Before they had reached the trees the Sawhorse was far ahead, and the wooden animal returned to the starting place and was being lustily cheered by the Ozites before Jim came panting up to the canopy where the Princess and her friends were seated.

I am sorry to record the fact that Jim was not only ashamed of his defeat but for a moment lost control of his temper. As he looked at the comical face of the Sawhorse he imagined that the creature was laughing at him; so in a fit of unreasonable anger he turned around and made a vicious kick that sent his rival tumbling head over heels upon the ground, and broke off one of its legs and its left ear.

An instant later the Tiger crouched and launched its huge body through the air swift and resistless as a ball from a cannon. The beast struck Jim full on his shoulder and sent the astonished cab-horse rolling over and over, amid shouts

of delight from the spectators, who had been horrified by the
ungracious act he had been guilty of.

When Jim came to himself and sat upon his haunches he
found the Cowardly Lion crouched on one side of him and the
Hungry Tiger on the other, and their eyes were glowing like
balls of fire.

"I beg your pardon, I'm sure," said Jim, meekly. "I was
wrong to kick the Sawhorse, and I am sorry I became angry
at him. He has won the race, and won it fairly; but what can a
horse of flesh do against a tireless beast of wood?"

Hearing this apology the Tiger and the Lion stopped lash-
ing their tails and retreated with dignified steps to the side of
the Princess.

"No one must injure one of our friends in our presence,"
growled the Lion; and Zeb ran to Jim and whispered that unless
he controlled his temper in the future he would probably be
torn to pieces.

Then the Tin Woodman cut a straight and strong limb from
a tree with his gleaming axe and made a new leg and a new ear
for the Sawhorse; and when they had been securely fastened in
place Princess Ozma took the coronet from her own head and
placed it upon that of the winner of the race. Said she:

"My friend, I reward you for your swiftness by proclaiming
you Prince of Horses, whether of wood or of flesh; and hereafter all other horses—in the Land of Oz, at least—must be

considered imitations, and you the real Champion of your race."

There was more applause at this, and then Ozma had the jewelled saddle replaced upon the Sawhorse and herself rode the victor back to the city at the head of the grand procession.

"I ought to be a fairy," grumbled Jim, as he slowly drew the buggy home; "for to be just an ordinary horse in a fairy country is to be of no account whatever. It's no place for us, Zeb."

"It's lucky we got here, though," said the boy; and Jim thought of the dark cave, and agreed with him.

····─·◄ Chapter 18 ►·····─·

The TRIAL of EUREKA the KITTEN

Several days of festivity and merry-making followed, for such old friends did not often meet and
there was much to be told and talked over between
them, and many amusements to be enjoyed in this
delightful country.

Ozma was happy to have Dorothy beside her, for girls
of her own age with whom it was proper for the Princess to
associate were very few, and often the youthful Ruler of Oz
was lonely for lack of companionship.

It was the third morning after Dorothy's arrival, and she
was sitting with Ozma and their friends in a reception room,
talking over old times, when the Princess said to her maid:

"Please go to my boudoir, Jellia, and get the white piglet I left on the dressing-table. I want to play with it."

Jellia at once departed on the errand, and she was gone so long that they had almost forgotten her mission when the green robed maiden returned with a troubled face.

"The piglet is not there, your Highness," said she.

"Not there!" exclaimed Ozma. "Are you sure?"

"I have hunted in every part of the room," the maid replied.

"Was not the door closed?" asked the Princess.

"Yes, your Highness; I am sure it was; for when I opened it Dorothy's white kitten crept out and ran up the stairs."

Hearing this, Dorothy and the Wizard exchanged startled glances, for they remembered how often Eureka had longed to eat a piglet. The little girl jumped up at once.

"Come, Ozma," she said, anxiously; "let us go ourselves to search for the piglet."

So the two went to the dressing-room of the Princess and searched carefully in every corner and among the vases and baskets and ornaments that stood about the pretty boudoir. But not a trace could they find of the tiny creature they sought.

Dorothy was nearly weeping, by this time, while Ozma was angry and indignant. When they returned to the others the Princess said:

"There is little doubt that my pretty piglet has been eaten

by that horrid kitten, and if that is true the offender must be punished."

"I don't b'lieve Eureka would do such a dreadful thing!" cried Dorothy, much distressed. "Go and get my kitten, please, Jellia, and we'll hear what she has to say about it."

The green maiden hastened away, but presently returned and said:

"The kitten will not come. She threatened to scratch my eyes out if I touched her."

"Where is she?" asked Dorothy.

"Under the bed in your own room," was the reply.

So Dorothy ran to her room and found the kitten under the bed.

"Come here, Eureka!" she said.

"I won't," answered the kitten, in a surly voice.

"Oh, Eureka! Why are you so bad?"

The kitten did not reply.

"If you don't come to me, right away," continued Dorothy, getting provoked, "I'll take my Magic Belt and wish you in the Country of the Gurgles."

"Why do you want me?" asked Eureka, disturbed by this threat.

"You must go to Princess Ozma. She wants to talk to you."

"All right," returned the kitten, creeping out. "I'm not afraid of Ozma—or anyone else."

Dorothy carried her in her arms back to where the others sat in grieved and thoughtful silence.

"Tell me, Eureka," said the Princess, gently: "did you eat my pretty piglet?"

"I won't answer such a foolish question," asserted Eureka, with a snarl.

"Oh, yes you will, dear," Dorothy declared. "The piglet is gone, and you ran out of the room when Jellia opened the door. So, if you are innocent, Eureka, you must tell the Princess how you came to be in her room, and what has become of the piglet."

"Who accuses me?" asked the kitten, defiantly.

"No one," answered Ozma. "Your actions alone accuse you. The fact is that I left my little pet in my dressing-room lying asleep upon the table; and you must have stolen in without my knowing it. When next the door was opened you ran out and hid yourself—and the piglet was gone."

"That's none of my business," growled the kitten.

"Don't be impudent, Eureka," admonished Dorothy.

"It is you who are impudent," said Eureka, "for accusing me of such a crime when you can't prove it except by guessing."

Ozma was now greatly incensed by the kitten's conduct. She summoned her Captain-General, and when the long, lean officer appeared she said:

"Carry this cat away to prison, and keep her in safe confinement until she is tried by law for the crime of murder."

So the Captain-General took Eureka from the arms of the now weeping Dorothy and in spite of the kitten's snarls and scratches carried it away to prison.

"What shall we do now?" asked the Scarecrow, with a sigh, for such a crime had cast a gloom over all the company.

"I will summon the Court to meet in the Throne Room at three o'clock," replied Ozma. "I myself will be the judge, and the kitten shall have a fair trial."

"What will happen if she is guilty?" asked Dorothy.

"She must die," answered the Princess.

"Nine times?" enquired the Scarecrow.

"As many times as is necessary," was the reply. "I will ask the Tin Woodman to defend the prisoner, because he has such a kind heart I am sure he will do his best to save her. And the Woggle-Bug shall be the Public Accuser, because he is so learned that no one can deceive him."

"Who will be the jury?" asked the Tin Woodman.

"There ought to be several animals on the jury," said Ozma, "because animals understand each other better than we people understand them. So the jury shall consist of the Cowardly Lion, the Hungry Tiger, Jim the cab-horse, the Yellow Hen, the Scarecrow, the Wizard, Tik-Tok the Machine Man, the Sawhorse and Zeb of Hugson's Ranch. That makes the nine which the law requires, and all my people shall be admitted to hear the testimony."

They now separated to prepare for the sad ceremony; for

whenever an appeal is made to law sorrow is almost certain to follow—even in a fairyland like Oz. But it must be stated that the people of that Land were generally so well-behaved that there was not a single lawyer amongst them, and it had been years since any Ruler had sat in judgment upon an offender of the law. The crime of murder being the most dreadful crime of all, tremendous excitement prevailed in the Emerald City when the news of Eureka's arrest and trial became known.

The Wizard, when he returned to his own room, was exceedingly thoughtful. He had no doubt Eureka had eaten his piglet, but he realized that a kitten cannot be depended upon at all times to act properly, since its nature is to destroy small animals and even birds for food, and the tame cat that we keep in our houses today is descended from the wild cat of the jungle—a very ferocious creature, indeed. The Wizard knew that if Dorothy's pet was found guilty and condemned to death the little girl would be made very unhappy; so, although he grieved over the piglet's sad fate as much as any of them, he resolved to save Eureka's life.

Sending for the Tin Woodman the Wizard took him into a corner and whispered:

"My friend, it is your duty to defend the white kitten and try to save her, but I fear you will fail because Eureka has long wished to eat a piglet, to my certain knowledge, and my opinion is that she has been unable to resist the temptation. Yet her disgrace and death would not bring back the piglet, but only serve to make Dorothy unhappy. So I intend to prove the kitten's innocence by a trick."

He drew from his inside pocket one of the eight tiny piglets that were remaining and continued:

"This creature you must hide in some safe place, and if the jury decides that Eureka is guilty you may then produce this piglet and claim it is the one that was lost. All the piglets are exactly alike, so no one can dispute your word. This deception will save Eureka's life, and then we may all be happy again."

"I do not like to deceive my friends," replied the Tin Woodman; "still, my kind heart urges me to save Eureka's life, and I can usually trust my heart to do the right thing. So I will do as you say, friend Wizard."

After some thought he placed the little pig inside his funnel-shaped hat, and then put the hat upon his head and went back to his room to think over his speech to the jury.

Chapter 19

The WIZARD PERFORMS ANOTHER TRICK

t three o'clock the Throne Room was crowded with citizens, men, women and children being eager to witness the great trial.

Princess Ozma, dressed in her most splendid robes of state, sat in the magnificent emerald throne, with her jewelled sceptre in her hand and her sparkling coronet upon her fair brow. Behind her throne stood the twenty-eight officers of her army and many officials of the royal household. At her right sat the queerly assorted jury—animals, animated dummies and people—all gravely prepared to listen to what was said. The kitten had been placed in a large cage just before the throne, where she sat upon her haunches and gazed through the bars at the crowds around her, with seeming unconcern.

And now, at a signal from Ozma, the Woggle-Bug arose and addressed the jury. His tone was pompous and he strutted up and down in an absurd attempt to appear dignified.

"Your Royal Highness and Fellow Citizens," he began; "the small cat you see a prisoner before you is accused of the crime of first murdering and then eating our esteemed Ruler's fat piglet—or else first eating and then murdering it. In either case a grave crime has been committed which deserves a grave punishment."

"Do you mean my kitten must be put in a grave?" asked Dorothy.

"Don't interrupt, little girl," said the Woggle-Bug. "When I get my thoughts arranged in good order I do not like to have anything upset them or throw them into confusion."

"If your thoughts were any good they wouldn't become confused," remarked the Scarecrow, earnestly. "My thoughts are always—"

"Is this a trial of thoughts, or of kittens?" demanded the Woggle-Bug.

"It's a trial of one kitten," replied the Scarecrow; "but your manner is a trial to us all."

"Let the Public Accuser continue," called Ozma from her throne, "and I pray you do not interrupt him."

"The criminal who now sits before the court licking her

paws," resumed the Woggle-Bug, "has long desired to unlaw-fully eat the fat piglet, which was no bigger than a mouse. And finally she made a wicked plan to satisfy her depraved appe-tite for pork. I can see her, in my mind's eye—"

"What's that?" asked the Scarecrow.

"I say I can see her in my mind's eye—"

"The mind has no eye," declared the Scarecrow. "It's blind."

"Your Highness," cried the Woggle-Bug, appealing to Ozma, "have I a mind's eye, or haven't I?"

"If you have, it is invisible," said the Princess.

"Very true," returned the Woggle-Bug, bowing. "I say I see the criminal, in my mind's eye, creeping stealthily into the room of our Ozma and secreting herself, when no one was looking, until the Princess had gone away and the door was closed. Then the murderer was alone with her helpless victim, the fat piglet, and I see her pounce upon the innocent creature and eat it up—"

"Are you still seeing with your mind's eye?" enquired the Scarecrow.

"Of course; how else could I see it? And we know the thing is true, because since the time of that interview there is no piglet to be found anywhere."

"I suppose, if the cat had been gone, instead of the piglet, your mind's eye would see the piglet eating the cat," suggested the Scarecrow.

"Very likely," acknowledged the Woggle-Bug. "And now, Fellow Citizens and Creatures of the Jury, I assert that so awful a crime deserves death, and in the case of the ferocious criminal before you—who is now washing her face—the death penalty should be inflicted nine times."

There was great applause when the speaker sat down. Then the Princess spoke in a stern voice:

"Prisoner, what have you to say for yourself? Are you guilty, or not guilty?"

"Why, that's for you to find out," replied Eureka. "If you can prove I'm guilty, I'll be willing to die nine times, but a mind's eye is no proof, because the Woggle-Bug has no mind to see with."

"Never mind, dear," said Dorothy.

Then the Tin Woodman arose and said:

"Respected Jury and dearly beloved Ozma, I pray you not to judge this feline prisoner unfeelingly. I do not think the innocent kitten can be guilty, and surely it is unkind to accuse a luncheon of being a murder. Eureka is the sweet pet of a lovely little girl whom we all admire, and gentleness and innocence are her chief virtues. Look at the kitten's intelligent eyes;" (here Eureka closed her eyes sleepily) "gaze at her smiling countenance!" (here Eureka snarled and showed her teeth) "mark the tender pose of her soft, padded little hands!" (Here Eureka bared her sharp claws and scratched at the bars of the cage.) "Would such a gentle animal be guilty of eating a fellow creature? No; a thousand times, no!"

"Oh, cut it short," said Eureka; "you've talked long enough."

"I'm trying to defend you," remonstrated the Tin Woodman.

"Then say something sensible," retorted the kitten. "Tell them it would be foolish for me to eat the piglet, because I had sense enough to know it would raise a row if I did. But don't try to make out I'm too innocent to eat a fat piglet if I could do it and not be found out. I imagine it would taste mighty good."

"Perhaps it would, to those who eat," remarked the Tin Woodman. "I myself, not being built to eat, have no personal experience in such matters. But I remember that our great poet once said:

> 'To eat is sweet
> When hunger's seat
> Demands a treat
> Of savory meat.'

"Take this into consideration, friends of the jury, and you will readily decide that the kitten is wrongfully accused and should be set at liberty."

When the Tin Woodman sat down no one applauded him, for his arguments had not been very convincing and few believed that he had proved Eureka's innocence. As for the jury, the members whispered to each other for a few minutes and then they appointed the Hungry Tiger their spokesman. The huge beast slowly arose and said:

"Kittens have no consciences, so they eat whatever pleases them. The jury believes the white kitten known as Eureka is guilty of having eaten the piglet owned by Princess Ozma, and recommends that she be put to death in punishment of the crime."

The judgment of the jury was received with great applause, although Dorothy was sobbing miserably at the fate of her pet. The Princess was just about to order Eureka's head chopped off with the Tin Woodman's axe when that brilliant personage once more arose and addressed her.

"Your Highness," said he, "see how easy it is for a jury to be mistaken. The kitten could not have eaten your piglet—for here it is!"

He took off his funnel hat and from beneath it produced a tiny white piglet, which he held aloft that all might see it clearly.

Ozma was delighted and exclaimed, eagerly:

"Give me my pet, Nick Chopper!"

And all the people cheered and clapped their hands, rejoicing that the prisoner had escaped death and been proved to be innocent.

As the Princess held the white piglet in her arms and stroked its soft hair she said: "Let Eureka out of the cage, for she is no longer a prisoner, but our good friend. Where did you find my missing pet, Nick Chopper?"

"In a room of the palace," he answered.

"Justice," remarked the Scarecrow, with a sigh, "is a dangerous thing to meddle with. If you hadn't happened to find the piglet, Eureka would surely have been executed."

"But justice prevailed at the last," said Ozma, "for here is my pet, and Eureka is once more free."

"I refuse to be free," cried the kitten, in a sharp voice, "unless the Wizard can do his trick with eight piglets. If he can produce but seven, then this is not the piglet that was lost, but another one."

"Hush, Eureka!" warned the Wizard.

"Don't be foolish," advised the Tin Woodman, "or you may be sorry for it."

"The piglet that belonged to the Princess wore an emerald collar," said Eureka, loudly enough for all to hear.

"So it did!" exclaimed Ozma. "This cannot be the one the Wizard gave me."

"Of course not; he had nine of them, altogether," declared Eureka; "and I must say it was very stingy of him not to let me eat just a few. But now that this foolish trial is ended, I will tell you what really became of your pet piglet."

At this everyone in the Throne Room suddenly became quiet, and the kitten continued, in a calm, mocking tone of voice:

"I will confess that I intended to eat the little pig for my breakfast; so I crept into the room where it was kept while the Princess was dressing and hid myself under a chair. When Ozma went away she closed the door and left her pet on the table. At once I jumped up and told the piglet not to make a fuss, for he would be inside of me in half a second; but no one can teach one of these creatures to be reasonable. Instead of keeping still, so I could eat him comfortably, he trembled so with fear that he fell off the table into a big vase that was standing on the floor. The vase had a very small neck, and spread out at the top like a bowl. At first the piglet stuck in the neck of the vase and I thought I should get him, after all, but he wriggled himself through and fell down into the deep bottom part—and I suppose he's there yet."

All were astonished at this confession, and Ozma at once sent an officer to her room to fetch the vase. When he returned the Princess looked down the narrow neck of the big ornament and discovered her lost piglet, just as Eureka had said she would.

There was no way to get the creature out without breaking the vase, so the Tin Woodman smashed it with his axe and set the little prisoner free.

Then the crowd cheered lustily and Dorothy hugged the kitten in her arms and told her how delighted she was to know that she was innocent.

"But why didn't you tell us at first?" she asked.

"It would have spoiled the fun," replied the kitten, yawning.

Ozma gave the Wizard back the piglet he had so kindly

allowed Nick Chopper to substitute for the lost one, and then she carried her own into the apartments of the palace where she lived. And now, the trial being over, the good citizens of the Emerald City scattered to their homes, well content with the day's amusement.

Chapter 20

ZEB RETURNS to the RANCH

Eureka was much surprised to find herself in disgrace; but she was, in spite of the fact that she had not eaten the piglet. For the folks of Oz knew the kitten had tried to commit the crime, and that only an accident had prevented her from doing so; therefore even the Hungry Tiger preferred not to associate with her. Eureka was forbidden to wander around the palace and was made to stay in confinement in Dorothy's room; so she began to beg her mistress to send her to some other place where she could enjoy herself better.

Dorothy was herself anxious to get home, so she promised Eureka they would not stay in the Land of Oz much longer.

The next evening after the trial the little girl begged Ozma to allow her to look in the enchanted picture, and the Princess readily consented. She took the child to her room and said: "Make your wish, dear, and the picture will show the scene you desire to behold."

Then Dorothy found, with the aid of the enchanted picture, that Uncle Henry had returned to the farm in Kansas, and she also saw that both he and Aunt Em were dressed in mourning, because they thought their little niece had been killed by the earthquake.

"Really," said the girl, anxiously, "I must get back as soon as poss'ble to my own folks."

Zeb also wanted to see his home, and although he did not find anyone mourning for him, the sight of Hugson's Ranch in the picture made him long to get back there.

"This is a fine country, and I like all the people that live in it," he told Dorothy. "But the fact is, Jim and I don't seem to fit into a fairyland, and the old horse has been begging me to go home again ever since he lost the race. So, if you can find a way to fix it, we'll be much obliged to you."

"Ozma can do it, easily," replied Dorothy. "Tomorrow morning I'll go to Kansas and you can go to Californy."

That last evening was so delightful that the boy will never forget it as long as he lives. They were all together (except Eureka) in the pretty rooms of the Princess, and the Wizard did some new tricks, and the Scarecrow told stories, and the

Tin Woodman sang a love song in a sonorous, metallic voice, and everybody laughed and had a good time. Then Dorothy wound up Tik-Tok and he danced a jig to amuse the company, after which the Yellow Hen related some of her adventures with the Nome King in the Land of Ev.

The Princess served delicious refreshments to those who were in the habit of eating, and when Dorothy's bed time arrived the company separated after exchanging many friendly sentiments.

Next morning they all assembled for the final parting, and many of the officials and courtiers came to look upon the impressive ceremonies.

Dorothy held Eureka in her arms and bade her friends a fond good-bye.

"You must come again, some time," said the little Wizard; and she promised she would if she found it possible to do so.

"But Uncle Henry and Aunt Em need me to help them," she added, "so I can't ever be very long away from the farm in Kansas."

Ozma wore the Magic Belt; and, when she had kissed Dorothy farewell and had made her wish, the little girl and her kitten disappeared in a twinkling.

"Where is she?" asked Zeb, rather bewildered by the suddenness of it.

"Greeting her uncle and aunt in Kansas, by this time," returned Ozma, with a smile.

Then Zeb brought out Jim, all harnessed to the buggy, and took his seat.

"I'm much obliged for all your kindness," said the boy, "and very grateful to you for saving my life and sending me home again after all the good times I've had. I think this is the loveliest country in the world; but not being fairies Jim and I feel we ought to be where we belong—and that's at the ranch. Good-bye, everybody!"

He gave a start and rubbed his eyes. Jim was trotting along the well-known road, shaking his ears and whisking his tail with a contented motion. Just ahead of them were the gates of Hugson's Ranch, and Uncle Hugson now came out and stood with uplifted arms and wide open mouth, staring in amazement.

"Goodness gracious! It's Zeb—and Jim, too!" he exclaimed. "Where in the world have you been, my lad?"

"Why, in the world, Uncle," answered Zeb, with a laugh.

The
Road
·····─····· to ·····─·····
Oz

To my first grandson, Joslyn Stanton Baum

To My Readers

W ell, my dears, here is what you have asked for: another "Oz Book" about Dorothy's strange adventures. Toto is in this story, because you wanted him to be there, and many other characters which you will recognize are in the story, too. Indeed, the wishes of my little correspondents have been considered as carefully as possible, and if the story is not exactly as you would have written it yourselves, you must remember that a story has to be a story before it can be written down, and the writer cannot change it much without spoiling it.

In the preface to *Dorothy and the Wizard in Oz* I said I would love to write some stories that were not "Oz" stories, because I thought I had written about Oz long enough; but since that volume was published I have been fairly deluged with letters from children imploring me to "write more about Dorothy," and "more about Oz," and since I write only to please the children I shall try to respect their wishes.

There are some new characters in this book that ought to win your live. I'm very fond of the shaggy man myself, and I think you will like him, too. As for Polychrome—the Rainbow's Daughter—and stupid little Button-Bright, they seem to have brought a new element of fun into these Oz stories, and I am glad I discovered them. Yet I am anxious to have you write and tell me how you like them.

Since this book was written I have received some very remarkable news from The Land of Oz, which has greatly astonished me. I believe it will astonish you, too, my dears, when you hear it. But it is such a long and exciting story that it must be saved for another book—and perhaps that book will be the last story that will ever be told about the Land of Oz.

L. Frank Baum

Coronado, 1909

Chapter 1

The WAY to BUTTERFIELD

"Please, miss," said the shaggy man, "can you tell me the road to Butterfield?"

Dorothy looked him over. Yes, he was shaggy, all right, but there was a twinkle in his eye that seemed pleasant.

"Oh yes," she replied; "I can tell you. But it isn't this road at all."

"No?"

"You cross the ten-acre lot, follow the lane to the highway, go north to the five branches, and take—let me see—"

"To be sure, miss; see as far as Butterfield, if you like," said the shaggy man.

"You take the branch next the willow stump, I b'lieve; or else the branch by the gopher holes; or else—"

"Won't any of 'em do, miss?"

"'Course not, Shaggy Man. You must take the right road to get to Butterfield."

"And is that the one by the gopher stump, or—"

"Dear me!" cried Dorothy. "I shall have to show you the way; you're so stupid. Wait a minute till I run in the house and get my sunbonnet."

The shaggy man waited. He had an oat-straw in his mouth, which he chewed slowly as if it tasted good; but it didn't. There was an apple-tree beside the house, and some apples had fallen to the ground. The shaggy man thought they would taste better than the oat-straw, so he walked over to get some. A little black dog with bright brown eyes dashed out of the farm-house and ran madly toward the shaggy man, who had already picked up three apples and put them in one of the big wide pockets of his shaggy coat. The little dog barked, and made a dive for the shaggy man's leg; but he grabbed the dog by the neck and put it in his big pocket along with the apples. He took more apples, afterward, for many were on the ground; and each one that he tossed into his pocket hit the little dog somewhere upon the head or back, and made him growl. The little dog's name was Toto, and he was sorry he had been put in the shaggy man's pocket.

Pretty soon Dorothy came out of the house with her sunbonnet, and she called out:

"Come on, Shaggy Man, if you want me to show you the road to Butterfield." She climbed the fence into the ten-acre lot and he followed her, walking slowly and stumbling over the little hillocks in the pasture as if he was thinking of something else and did not notice them.

"My, but you're clumsy!" said the little girl. "Are your feet tired?"

"No, miss; it's my whiskers; they tire very easily in this warm weather," said he. "I wish it would snow; don't you?"

"'Course not, Shaggy Man," replied Dorothy, giving him a severe look. "If it snowed in August it would spoil the corn and the oats and the wheat; and then Uncle Henry wouldn't have any crops; and that would make him poor; and—"

"Never mind," said the shaggy man. "It won't snow, I guess. Is this the lane?"

"Yes," replied Dorothy, climbing another fence; "I'll go as far as the highway with you."

"Thankee, miss; you're very kind for your size, I'm sure," said he gratefully.

"It isn't everyone who knows the road to Butterfield," Dorothy remarked as she tripped along the lane; "but I've driven there many a time with Uncle Henry, and so I b'lieve I could find it blindfolded."

"Don't do that, miss," said the shaggy man earnestly; "you might make a mistake."

"I won't," she answered, laughing. "Here's the highway.

Now it's the second—no, the third turn to the left—or else it's the fourth. Let's see. The first one is by the elm tree, and the second is by the gopher holes; and then—"

"Then what?" he inquired, putting his hands in his coat pockets. Toto grabbed a finger and bit it; the shaggy man took his hand out of that pocket quickly, and said "Oh!"

Dorothy did not notice. She was shading her eyes from the sun with her arm, looking anxiously down the road.

"Come on," she commanded. "It's only a little way farther, so I may as well show you."

After a while they came to the place where five roads branched in different directions; Dorothy pointed to one, and said:

"That's it, Shaggy Man."

"I'm much obliged, miss," he said, and started along another road.

"Not that one!" she cried; "you're going wrong."

He stopped.

"I thought you said that other was the road to Butterfield," said he, running his fingers through his shaggy whiskers in a puzzled way.

"So it is."

"But I don't want to go to Butterfield, miss."

"You don't?"

"Of course not. I wanted you to show me the road, so I shouldn't go there by mistake."

"Oh! Where *do* you want to go, then?"

"I'm not particular, miss."

This answer astonished the little girl; and it made her provoked, too, to think she had taken all this trouble for nothing.

"There are a good many roads here," observed the shaggy man, turning slowly around, like a human windmill. "Seems to me a person could go 'most anywhere, from this place."

Dorothy turned around too, and gazed in surprise. There *were* a good many roads; more than she had ever seen before. She tried to count them, knowing there ought to be five; but when she had counted seventeen she grew bewildered and stopped, for the roads were as many as the spokes of a wheel and ran in every direction from the place where they stood; so if she kept on counting she was likely to count some of the roads twice.

"Dear me!" she exclaimed. "There used to be only five roads, highway and all. And now—why, where's the highway, Shaggy Man?"

"Can't say, miss," he responded, sitting down upon the ground as if tired with standing. "Wasn't it here a minute ago?"

"I thought so," she answered, greatly perplexed. "And I saw the gopher holes, too, and the dead stump; but they're not here now. These roads are all strange—and what a lot of them there are! Where do you suppose they all go to?"

"Roads," observed the shaggy man, "don't go anywhere. They stay in one place, so folks can walk on them."

He put his hand in his side-pocket and drew out an apple— quick, before Toto could bite him again. The little dog got his head out this time and said "Bow-wow!" so loudly that it made Dorothy jump.

"O, Toto!" she cried; "where did you come from?"

"I brought him along," said the shaggy man.

"What for?" she asked.

"To guard these apples in my pocket, miss, so no one would steal them."

With one hand the shaggy man held the apple, which he began eating, while with the other hand he pulled Toto out of his pocket and dropped him to the ground. Of course Toto made for Dorothy at once, barking joyfully at his release from the dark pocket. When the child had patted his head lovingly, he sat down before her, his red tongue hanging out one side of his mouth, and looked up into her face with his bright brown eyes, as if asking her what they should do next.

Dorothy didn't know. She looked around her anxiously for some familiar landmark; but everything was strange. Between the branches of the many roads were green meadows and a few shrubs and trees, but she couldn't see anywhere the farm-house from which she had just come, or anything she had ever seen before—except the shaggy man and Toto.

Besides this, she had turned around and around so many

times trying to find out where she was, that now she couldn't even tell which direction the farm-house ought to be in; and this began to worry her and make her feel anxious.

"I'm 'fraid, Shaggy Man," she said, with a sigh, "that we're lost!"

"That's nothing to be afraid of," he replied, throwing away the core of his apple and beginning to eat another one. "Each of these roads must lead somewhere, or it wouldn't be here. So what does it matter?"

"I want to go home again," she said.

"Well, why don't you?" said he.

"I don't know which road to take."

"That is too bad," he said, shaking his shaggy head gravely. "I wish I could help you; but I can't. I'm a stranger in these parts."

"Seems as if I were, too," she said, sitting down beside him. "It's funny. A few minutes ago I was home, and I just came to show you the way to Butterfield—"

"So I shouldn't make a mistake and go there—"

"And now I'm lost myself and don't know how to get home!"

"Have an apple," suggested the shaggy man, handing her one with pretty red cheeks.

"I'm not hungry," said Dorothy, pushing it away.

"But you may be, to-morrow; then you'll be sorry you didn't eat the apple," said he.

"If I am, I'll eat the apple then," promised Dorothy.

"Perhaps there won't be any apple then," he returned, beginning to eat the red-cheeked one himself. "Dogs sometimes can find their way home better than people," he went on; "perhaps your dog can lead you back to the farm."

"Will you, Toto?" asked Dorothy.

Toto wagged his tail vigorously.

"All right," said the girl; "let's go home."

Toto looked around a minute and dashed up one of the roads.

"Good-bye, Shaggy Man," called Dorothy, and ran after Toto. The little dog pranced briskly along for some distance, when he turned around and looked at his mistress questioningly.

"Oh, don't 'spect *me* to tell you anything; I don't know the way," she said. "You'll have to find it yourself."

But Toto couldn't. He wagged his tail, and sneezed, and shook his ears, and trotted back where they had left the shaggy man. From here he started along another road; then came back and tried another; but each time he found the way strange and decided it would not take them to the farm-house. Finally, when Dorothy had begun to tire with chasing after him, Toto sat down panting beside the shaggy man and gave up.

Dorothy sat down, too, very thoughtful. The little girl had encountered some queer adventures since she came to live at the farm; but this was the queerest of them all. To get lost in fifteen minutes, so near to her home and in the unromantic

State of Kansas, was an experience that fairly bewildered her.

"Will your folks worry?" asked the shaggy man, his eyes twinkling in a pleasant way.

"I s'pose so," answered Dorothy with a sigh. "Uncle Henry says there's *always* something happening to me; but I've always come home safe at the last. So perhaps he'll take comfort and think I'll come home safe this time."

"I'm sure you will," said the shaggy man, smilingly nodding at her. "Good little girls never come to any harm, you know. For my part, I'm good, too; so nothing ever hurts me."

Dorothy looked at him curiously. His clothes were shaggy, his boots were shaggy and full of holes, and his hair and whiskers were shaggy. But his smile was sweet and his eyes were kind.

"Why didn't you want to go to Butterfield?" she asked.

"Because a man lives there who owes me fifteen cents, and if I went to Butterfield and he saw me he'd want to pay me the money. I don't want money, my dear."

"Why not?" she inquired.

"Money," declared the shaggy man, "makes people proud and haughty; I don't want to be proud and haughty. All I want is to have people love me; and as long as I own the Love Magnet, everyone I meet is sure to love me dearly."

"The Love Magnet! Why, what's that?"

"I'll show you, if you won't tell any one," he answered, in a low, mysterious voice.

"There isn't any one to tell, 'cept Toto," said the girl.

The shaggy man searched in one pocket, carefully; and in another pocket; and in a third. At last he drew out a small parcel wrapped in crumpled paper and tied with a cotton string. He unwound the string, opened the parcel, and took out a bit of metal shaped like a horseshoe. It was dull and brown, and not very pretty.

"This, my dear," said he, impressively, "is the wonderful Love Magnet. It was given me by an Eskimo in the Sandwich Islands—where there are no sandwiches at all—and as long as I carry it every living thing I meet will love me dearly."

"Why didn't the Eskimo keep it?" she asked, looking at the Magnet with interest.

"He got tired of being loved and longed for some one to hate him. So he gave me the Magnet and the very next day a grizzly bear ate him."

"Wasn't he sorry then?" she inquired.

"He didn't say," replied the shaggy man, wrapping and tying the Love Magnet with great care and putting it away in another pocket. "But the bear didn't seem sorry a bit," he added.

"Did you know the bear?" asked Dorothy.

"Yes; we used to play ball together in the Caviar Islands. The bear loved me because I had the Love Magnet. I couldn't blame him for eating the Eskimo, because it was his nature to do so."

"Once," said Dorothy, "I knew a Hungry Tiger who longed to eat fat babies, because it was his nature to; but he never ate any because he had a Conscience."

"This bear," replied the shaggy man, with a sigh, "had no Conscience, you see."

The shaggy man sat silent for several minutes, apparently considering the cases of the bear and the tiger, while Toto watched him with an air of great interest. The little dog was doubtless thinking of his ride in the shaggy man's pocket and planning to keep out of reach in the future.

At last the shaggy man turned and inquired, "What's your name, little girl?"

"My name's Dorothy," said she, jumping up again, "but what are we going to do? We can't stay here forever, you know."

"Let's take the seventh road," he suggested. "Seven is a lucky number for little girls named Dorothy."

"The seventh from where?"

"From where you begin to count."

So she counted seven roads, and the seventh looked just like all the others; but the shaggy man got up from the ground where he had been sitting and started down this road as if sure it was the best way to go; and Dorothy and Toto followed him.

Chapter 2

DOROTHY MEETS BUTTON-BRIGHT

The seventh road was a good road, and curved this way and that—winding through green meadows and fields covered with daisies and buttercups and past groups of shady trees. There were no houses of any sort to be seen, and for some distance they met with no living creature at all.

Dorothy began to fear they were getting a good way from the farm-house, since here everything was strange to her; but it would do no good at all to go back where the other roads all met, because the next one they chose might lead her just as far from home.

She kept on beside the shaggy man, who whistled cheerful

tunes to beguile the journey, until by-and-by they followed a turn in the road and saw before them a big chestnut tree making a shady spot over the highway. In the shade sat a little boy dressed in sailor clothes, who was digging a hole in the earth with a bit of wood. He must have been digging some time, because the hole was already big enough to drop a football into.

Dorothy and Toto and the shaggy man came to a halt before the little boy, who kept on digging in a sober and persistent fashion.

"Who are you?" asked the girl.

He looked up at her calmly. His face was round and chubby and his eyes were big, blue, and earnest.

"I'm Button-Bright," said he.

"But what's your real name?" she inquired.

"Button-Bright."

"That isn't a really-truly name!" she exclaimed.

"Isn't it?" he asked, still digging.

"'Course not. It's just a—a thing to call you by. You must have a name."

"Must I?"

"To be sure. What does your mama call you?"

He paused in his digging and tried to think.

"Papa always said I was bright as a button; so mama always called me Button-Bright," he said.

"What is your papa's name?"

"Just Papa."

"What else?"

"Don't know."

"Never mind," said the shaggy man, smiling. "We'll call the boy Button-Bright, as his mama does. That name is as good as any, and better than some."

Dorothy watched the boy dig.

"Where do you live?" she asked.

"Don't know," was the reply.

"How did you come here?"

"Don't know," he said again.

"Don't you know where you came from?"

"No," said he.

"Why, he must be lost," she said to the shaggy man. She turned to the boy once more.

"What are you going to do?" she inquired.

"Dig," said he.

"But you can't dig forever; and what are you going to do then?" she persisted.

"Don't know," said the boy.

"But you *must* know *something*," declared Dorothy, getting provoked.

"Must I?" he asked, looking up in surprise.

"Of course you must."

"What must I know?"

"What's going to become of you, for one thing," she answered.

"Do *you* know what's going to become of me?" he asked.

"Not—not 'zactly," she admitted.

"Do you know what's going to become of *you*?" he continued, earnestly.

"I can't say I do," replied Dorothy, remembering her present difficulties.

The shaggy man laughed.

"No one knows everything, Dorothy," he said.

"But Button-Bright doesn't seem to know *any*thing," she declared. "Do you, Button-Bright?"

He shook his head, which had pretty curls all over it, and replied with perfect calmness:

"Don't know."

Never before had Dorothy met with anyone who could give her so little information. The boy was evidently lost, and his people would be sure to worry about him. He seemed two or three years younger than Dorothy, and was prettily dressed, as if someone loved him dearly and took much pains to make him look well. How, then, did he come to be in this lonely road? she wondered.

Near Button-Bright, on the ground, lay a sailor hat with a gilt anchor on the band. His sailor trousers were long and wide at the bottom, and the broad collar of his blouse had gold anchors sewed on its corners. The boy was still digging at his hole.

"Have you ever been to sea?" asked Dorothy.

"To see what?" answered Button-Bright.

"I mean, have you ever been where there's water?"

"Yes," said Button-Bright; "there's a well in our back yard."

"You don't understand," cried Dorothy. "I mean, have you ever been on a big ship floating on a big ocean?"

"Don't know," said he.

"Then why do you wear sailor clothes?"

"Don't know," he answered, again.

Dorothy was in despair.

"You're just *awful* stupid, Button-Bright," she said.

"Am I?" he asked.

"Yes, you are."

"Why?" looking up at her with big eyes.

She was going to say: "Don't know," but stopped herself in time.

"That's for you to answer," she replied.

"It's no use asking Button-Bright questions," said the shaggy man, who had been eating another apple; "but someone ought to take care of the poor little chap, don't you think? So he'd better come along with us."

Toto had been looking with great curiosity in the hole which the boy was digging, and growing more and more excited every minute, perhaps thinking that Button-Bright was after some wild animal. The little dog began barking loudly and jumped into the hole himself, where he began to dig with his tiny paws, making the earth fly in all directions. It spattered over the boy. Dorothy seized him and raised him to his feet, brushing his clothes with her hand.

"Stop that, Toto!" she called. "There aren't any mice or woodchucks in that hole, so don't be foolish."

Toto stopped, sniffed at the hole suspiciously, and jumped out of it, wagging his tail as if he had done something important.

"Well," said the shaggy man, "let's start on, or we won't get anywhere before night comes."

"Where do you expect to get to?" asked Dorothy.

"I'm like Button-Bright; I don't know," answered the shaggy man, with a laugh. "But I've learned from long experience that every road leads somewhere, or there wouldn't be any road; so it's likely that if we travel long enough, my dear, we will come to some place or another in the end. What place it will be we can't even guess at this moment, but we're sure to find out when we get there."

"Why, yes," said Dorothy; "that seems reas'n'ble, Shaggy Man."

·——·< Chapter 3 >·——·

A QUEER VILLAGE

Button-Bright took the shaggy man's hand willingly; for the shaggy man had the Love Magnet, you know, which was the reason Button-Bright had loved him at once. They started on, with Dorothy on one side, and Toto on the other, the little party trudging along more cheerfully than you might have supposed. The girl was getting used to queer adventures, which interested her very much. Wherever Dorothy went Toto was sure to go, like Mary's little lamb. Button-Bright didn't seem a bit afraid or worried because he was lost, and the shaggy man had no home, perhaps, and was as happy in one place as in another.

Before long they saw ahead of them a fine big arch spanning the road, and when they came nearer they found that the arch was beautifully carved and decorated with rich colors. A row of peacocks with spread tails ran along the top of it, and all the feathers were gorgeously painted. In the center was a large fox's head, and the fox wore a shrewd and knowing expression and had large spectacles over its eyes and a small golden crown with shiny points on top of its head.

While the travelers were looking with curiosity at this beautiful arch there suddenly marched out of it a company of soldiers—only the soldiers were all foxes dressed in uniforms. They wore green jackets and yellow pantaloons, and their little round caps and their high boots were a bright red color. Also, there was a big red bow tied about the middle of each long, bushy tail. Each soldier was armed with a wooden sword having an edge of sharp teeth set in a row, and the sight of these teeth at first caused Dorothy to shudder.

A captain marched in front of the company of fox-soldiers, his uniform embroidered with gold braid to make it hand-somer than the others.

Almost before our friends realized it the soldiers had surrounded them on all sides, and the captain was calling out in a harsh voice:

"Surrender! You are our prisoners."

"What's a pris'ner?" asked Button-Bright.

"A prisoner is a captive," replied the fox-captain, strutting up and down with much dignity.

"What's a captive?" asked Button-Bright.

"You're one," said the captain.

That made the shaggy man laugh.

"Good afternoon, captain," he said, bowing politely to all the foxes and very low to their commander. "I trust you are in good health, and that your families are all well?"

The fox-captain looked at the shaggy man, and his sharp features grew pleasant and smiling.

"We're pretty well, thank you, Shaggy Man," said he; and Dorothy knew that the Love Magnet was working and that all the foxes now loved the shaggy man because of it. But Toto didn't know this, for he began barking angrily and tried to bite the captain's hairy leg where it showed between his red boots and his yellow pantaloons.

"Stop, Toto!" cried the little girl, seizing the dog in her arms. "These are our friends."

"Why, so we are!" remarked the captain in tones of astonishment. "I thought at first we were enemies, but it seems you are friends instead. You must come with me to see King Dox."

"Who's he?" asked Button-Bright, with earnest eyes.

"King Dox of Foxville; the great and wise sovereign who rules over our community."

"What's sov'rin, and what's c'u'nity?" inquired Button-Bright.

"Don't ask so many questions, little boy."

"Why?"

"Ah, why indeed?" exclaimed the captain, looking at Button-Bright admiringly. "If you don't ask questions you will learn nothing. True enough. I was wrong. You're a very clever little boy, come to think of it—very clever indeed. But now, friends, please come with me, for it is my duty to escort you at once to the royal palace."

The soldiers marched back through the arch again, and with them marched the shaggy man, Dorothy, Toto, and Button-Bright. Once through the opening they found a fine, big city spread out before them, all the houses of carved marble in beautiful colors. The decorations were mostly birds and other fowl, such as peacocks, pheasants, turkeys, prairie-chickens, ducks, and geese. Over each doorway was carved a head representing the fox who lived in that house, this effect being quite pretty and unusual.

As our friends marched along, some of the foxes came out on the porches and balconies to get a view of the strangers. These foxes were all handsomely dressed, the girl-foxes and women-foxes wearing gowns of feathers woven together effectively and colored in bright hues which Dorothy thought were quite artistic and decidedly attractive.

Button-Bright stared until his eyes were big and round, and he would have stumbled and fallen more than once had not the shaggy man grasped his hand tightly. They were all interested, and Toto was so excited he wanted to bark every minute and to chase and fight every fox he caught sight of;

but Dorothy held his little wiggling body fast in her arms and commanded him to be good and behave himself. So he finally quieted down, like a wise doggy, deciding there were too many foxes in Foxville to fight at one time.

By-and-by they came to a big square, and in the center of the square stood the royal palace. Dorothy knew it at once because it had over its great door the carved head of a fox just like the one she had seen on the arch, and this fox was the only one who wore a golden crown.

There were many fox-soldiers guarding the door, but they bowed to the captain and admitted him without question. The captain led them through many rooms, where richly dressed foxes were sitting on beautiful chairs or sipping tea, which was being passed around by fox-servants in white aprons. They came to a big doorway covered with heavy curtains of cloth of gold.

Beside this doorway stood a huge drum. The fox-captain went to this drum and knocked his knees against it—first one knee and then the other—so that the drum said: "Boom-boom."

"You must all do exactly what I do," ordered the captain; so the shaggy man pounded the drum with his knees, and so did Dorothy and so did Button-Bright. The boy wanted to keep on pounding it with his little fat knees, because he liked the sound of it; but the captain stopped him. Toto couldn't pound the drum with his knees and he didn't know enough to wag his tail against it, so Dorothy pounded the drum for him and that made him bark, and when the little dog barked the fox-captain scowled.

The golden curtains drew back far enough to make an opening, through which marched the captain with the others.

The broad, long room they entered was decorated in gold with stained-glass windows of splendid colors. In the corner of the room upon a richly carved golden throne, sat the fox-king, surrounded by a group of other foxes, all of whom wore great spectacles over their eyes, making them look solemn and important.

Dorothy knew the King at once, because she had seen his head carved on the arch and over the doorway of the palace. Having met with several other kings in her travels, she knew what to do, and at once made a low bow before the throne. The shaggy man bowed, too, and Button-Bright bobbed his head and said "Hello."

"Most wise and noble Potentate of Foxville," said the captain, addressing the King in a pompous voice, "I humbly beg to report that I found these strangers on the road leading to your Foxy Majesty's dominions, and have therefore brought them before you, as is my duty."

"So—so," said the King, looking at them keenly. "What brought you here, strangers?"

"Our legs, may it please your Royal Hairiness," replied the shaggy man.

"What is your business here?" was the next question.

"To get away as soon as possible," said the shaggy man.

The King didn't know about the Magnet, of course; but it made him love the shaggy man at once.

"Do just as you please about going away," he said; "but I'd like to show you the sights of my city and to entertain your party while you are here. We feel highly honored to have little Dorothy with us, I assure you, and we appreciate her kindness in making us a visit. For whatever country Dorothy visits is sure to become famous."

This speech greatly surprised the little girl, who asked:

"How did your Majesty know my name?"

"Why, everybody knows you, my dear," said the Fox-King. "Don't you realize that? You are quite an important personage since Princess Ozma of Oz made you her friend."

"Do you know Ozma?" she asked, wondering.

"I regret to say that I do not," he answered, sadly; "but I hope to meet her soon. You know the Princess Ozma is to celebrate her birthday on the twenty-first of this month."

"Is she?" said Dorothy. "I didn't know that."

"Yes; it is to be the most brilliant royal ceremony ever held in any city in fairyland, and I hope you will try to get me an invitation."

Dorothy thought a moment.

"I'm sure Ozma would invite you if I asked her," she said; "but how could you get to the Land of Oz and the Emerald City? It's a good way from Kansas."

"Kansas!" he exclaimed, surprised.

"Why, yes; we are in Kansas now, aren't we?" she returned.

"What a queer notion!" cried the Fox-King, beginning to laugh. "Whatever made you think this is Kansas?"

"I left Uncle Henry's farm only about two hours ago; that's the reason," she said, rather perplexed.

"But, tell me, my dear, did you ever see so wonderful a city as Foxville in Kansas?" he questioned.

"No, your Majesty."

"And haven't you traveled from Oz to Kansas in less than half a jiffy, by means of the Silver Shoes and the Magic Belt?"

"Yes, your Majesty," she acknowledged.

"Then why do you wonder that an hour or two could bring you to Foxville, which is nearer to Oz than it is to Kansas?"

"Dear me!" exclaimed Dorothy; "is this another fairy adventure?"

"It seems to be," said the Fox-King, smiling.

Dorothy turned to the shaggy man, and her face was grave and reproachful.

"Are you a magician? or a fairy in disguise?" she asked. "Did you enchant me when you asked the way to Butterfield?"

The shaggy man shook his head.

"Who ever heard of a shaggy fairy?" he replied. "No, Dorothy, my dear; I'm not to blame for this journey in any way, I assure you. There's been something strange about me ever since I owned the Love Magnet; but I don't know what it is any more than you do. I didn't try to get you away from home, at all. If you want to find your way back to the farm I'll go with you willingly, and do my best to help you."

"Never mind," said the little girl, thoughtfully. "There isn't so much to see in Kansas as there is here, and I guess Aunt Em won't be *very* much worried; that is, if I don't stay away too long."

"That's right," declared the Fox-King, nodding approval. "Be contented with your lot, whatever it happens to be, if you are wise. Which reminds me that you have a new companion on this adventure—he looks very clever and bright."

"He is," said Dorothy; and the shaggy man added:

"That's his name, your Royal Foxiness—Button-Bright."

Chapter 4

KING DOX

It was amusing to note the expression on the face of King Dox as he looked the boy over, from his sailor hat to his stubby shoes; and it was equally diverting to watch Button-Bright stare at the King in return. No fox ever beheld a fresher, fairer child's face, and no child had ever before heard a fox talk, or met with one who dressed so handsomely and ruled so big a city. I am sorry to say that no one had ever told the little boy much about fairies of any kind; this being the case, it is easy to understand how much this strange experience startled and astonished him.

"How do you like us?" asked the King.

"Don't know," said Button-Bright.

"Of course you don't. It's too short an acquaintance," returned his Majesty. "What do you suppose my name is?"

"Don't know," said Button-Bright.

"How should you? Well, I'll tell you. My private name is Dox, but a King can't be called by his private name; he has to take one that is official. Therefore my official name is King Renard the Fourth. Ren-ard with the accent on the 'Ren.'"

"What's 'ren'?" asked Button-Bright.

"How clever!" exclaimed the King, turning a pleased face toward his counselors. "This boy is indeed remarkably bright. 'What's "ren"?' he asks; and of course 'ren' is nothing at all, all by itself. Yes; he's very bright indeed."

"That question is what your Majesty might call foxy," said one of the counselors, an old grey fox.

"So it is," declared the King. Turning again to Button-Bright, he asked:

"Having told you my name, what would you call me?"

"King Dox," said the boy.

"Why?"

"'Cause 'ren''s nothing at all," was the reply.

"Good! Very good indeed! You certainly have a brilliant mind. Do you know why two and two make four?"

"No," said Button-Bright.

"Clever! clever indeed! Of course you don't know. Nobody knows why; we only know it's so, and can't tell why it's so. Button-Bright, those curls and blue eyes do not go well with so much wisdom. They make you look too youthful, and hide your real cleverness. Therefore, I will do you a great favor. I will confer upon you the head of a fox, so that you may hereafter look as bright as you really are."

As he spoke the King waved his paw toward the boy, and at once the pretty curls and fresh round face and big blue eyes were gone, while in their place a fox's head appeared upon Button-Bright's shoulders—a hairy head with a sharp nose, pointed ears, and keen little eyes.

"Oh, don't do that!" cried Dorothy, shrinking back from her transformed companion with a shocked and dismayed face.

"Too late, my dear; it's done. But you also shall have a fox's head if you can prove you're as clever as Button-Bright."

"I don't want it; it's dreadful!" she exclaimed; and, hearing this verdict, Button-Bright began to boo-hoo just as if he were still a little boy.

"How can you call that lovely head dreadful?" asked the King. "It's a much prettier face than he had before, to my notion, and my wife says I'm a good judge of beauty. Don't cry, little fox-boy. Laugh and be proud, because you are so highly favored. How do you like the new head, Button-Bright?"

"D-d-don't n-n-n-know!" sobbed the child.

"Please, please change him back again, your Majesty!" begged Dorothy.

King Renard IV shook his head.

"I can't do that," he said; "I haven't the power, even if I

wanted to. No, Button-Bright must wear his fox head, and he'll be sure to love it dearly as soon as he gets used to it."

Both the shaggy man and Dorothy looked grave and anxious, for they were sorrowful that such a misfortune had overtaken their little companion. Toto barked at the fox-boy once or twice, not realizing it was his former friend who now wore the animal head; but Dorothy cuffed the dog and made him stop. As for the foxes, they all seemed to think Button-Bright's new head very becoming and that their King had conferred a great honor on this little stranger.

It was funny to see the boy reach up to feel of his sharp nose and wide mouth, and wail afresh with grief. He wagged his ears in a comical manner and tears were in his little black eyes. But Dorothy couldn't laugh at her friend just yet, because she felt so sorry.

Just then three little fox-princesses, daughters of the King, entered the room, and when they saw Button-Bright one exclaimed: "How lovely he is!" and the next one cried in delight: "How sweet he is!" and the third princess clapped her hands with pleasure and said, "How beautiful he is!"

Button-Bright stopped crying and asked timidly:

"Am I?"

"In all the world there is not another face so pretty," declared the biggest fox-princess.

"You must live with us always, and be our brother," said the next.

"We shall all love you dearly," the third said.

This praise did much to comfort the boy, and he looked around and tried to smile. It was a pitiful attempt, because the fox face was new and stiff, and Dorothy thought his expression more stupid than before the transformation.

"I think we ought to be going now," said the shaggy man, uneasily, for he didn't know what the King might take into his head to do next.

"Don't leave us yet, I beg of you," pleaded King Renard. "I intend to have several days of feasting and merry-making in honor of your visit."

"Have it after we're gone, for we can't wait," said Dorothy, decidedly. But seeing this displeased the King, she added: "If I'm going to get Ozma to invite you to her party I'll have to find her as soon as poss'ble, you know."

In spite of all the beauty of Foxville and the gorgeous dresses of its inhabitants, both the girl and the shaggy man felt they were not quite safe there, and would be glad to see the last of it.

"But it is now evening," the King reminded them, "and you must stay with us until morning, anyhow. Therefore, I invite you to be my guests at dinner, and to attend the theater afterward and sit in the royal box. To-morrow morning, if you really insist upon it, you may resume your journey."

They consented to this, and some of the fox-servants led them to a suite of lovely rooms in the big palace.

Button-Bright was afraid to be left alone, so Dorothy took him into her own room. While a maid-fox dressed the little girl's hair—which was a bit tangled—and put some bright, fresh ribbons in it, another maid-fox combed the hair on poor Button-Bright's face and head and brushed it carefully, tying a pink bow to each of his pointed ears. The maids wanted to dress the children in fine costumes of woven feathers, such as all the foxes wore; but neither of them consented to that.

"A sailor suit and a fox head do not go well together," said one of the maids, "for no fox was ever a sailor that I can remember."

"I'm not a fox!" cried Button-Bright.

"Alas, no," agreed the maid. "But you've got a lovely fox head on your skinny shoulders, and that's *almost* as good as being a fox."

The boy, reminded of his misfortune, began to cry again. Dorothy petted and comforted him and promised to find some way to restore him his own head.

"If we can manage to get to Ozma," she said, "the Princess will change you back to yourself in half a second; so you just wear that fox head as comf't'bly as you can, dear, and don't worry about it at all. It isn't nearly as pretty as your own head, no matter what the foxes say; but you can get along with it for a little while longer, can't you?"

"Don't know," said Button-Bright, doubtfully; but he didn't cry any more after that.

Dorothy let the maids pin ribbons to her shoulders, after which they were ready for the King's dinner. When they met the shaggy man in the splendid drawing room of the palace they found him just the same as before. He had refused to give up his shaggy clothes for new ones, because if he did that he would no longer be the shaggy man, he said, and he might have to get acquainted with himself all over again.

He told Dorothy he had brushed his shaggy hair and whiskers; but she thought he must have brushed them the wrong way, for they were quite as shaggy as before.

As for the company of foxes assembled to dine with the strangers, they were most beautifully costumed, and their rich dresses made Dorothy's simple gown and Button-Bright's sailor suit and the shaggy man's shaggy clothes look commonplace. But they treated their guests with great respect and the King's dinner was a very good dinner indeed.

Foxes, as you know, are fond of chicken and other fowl; so they served chicken soup and roasted turkey and stewed duck and fried grouse and broiled quail and goose pie, and as the cooking was excellent the King's guests enjoyed the meal and ate heartily of the various dishes.

The party went to the theater, where they saw a play acted by foxes dressed in costumes of brilliantly colored feathers. The play was about a fox-girl who was stolen by some wicked wolves and carried to their cave; and just as they were about to kill her and eat her a company of fox-soldiers marched up, saved the girl, and put all the wicked wolves to death.

"How do you like it?" the King asked Dorothy.

"Pretty well," she answered. "It reminds me of one of Mr. Aesop's fables."

"Don't mention Aesop to me, I beg of you!" exclaimed King Dox. "I hate that man's name. He wrote a good deal about foxes, but always made them out cruel and wicked, whereas we are gentle and kind, as you may see."

"But his fables showed you to be wise and clever, and more shrewd than other animals," said the shaggy man, thoughtfully.

"So we are. There is no question about our knowing more than men do," replied the King, proudly. "But we employ our wisdom to do good, instead of harm; so that horrid Aesop did not know what he was talking about."

They did not like to contradict him, because they felt he ought to know the nature of foxes better than men did; so they sat still and watched the play, and Button-Bright became so interested that for the time he forgot he wore a fox head.

Afterward they went back to the palace and slept in soft beds stuffed with feathers; for the foxes raised many fowl for food, and used their feathers for clothing and to sleep upon.

Dorothy wondered why the animals living in Foxville did not wear just their own hairy skins as wild foxes do; when she mentioned it to King Dox he said they clothed themselves because they were civilized.

"But you were born without clothes," she observed, "and you don't seem to me to need them."

"So were human beings born without clothes," he replied; "and until they became civilized they wore only their natural skins. But to become civilized means to dress as elaborately and prettily as possible, and to make a show of your clothes so your neighbors will envy you, and for that reason both civilized foxes and civilized humans spend most of their time dressing themselves."

"I don't," declared the shaggy man.

"That is true," said the King, looking at him carefully; "but perhaps you are not civilized."

After a sound sleep and a good night's rest they had their breakfast with the King and then bade his Majesty good-bye.

"You've been kind to us—'cept poor Button-Bright," said Dorothy, "and we've had a nice time in Foxville."

"Then," said King Dox, "perhaps you'll be good enough to get me an invitation to Princess Ozma's birthday celebration."

"I'll try," she promised; "if I see her in time."

"It's on the twenty-first, remember," he continued; "and if you'll just see that I'm invited I'll find a way to cross the Dreadful Desert into the marvelous Land of Oz. I've always wanted to visit the Emerald City, so I'm sure it was fortunate you arrived here just when you did, you being Princess Ozma's friend and able to assist me in getting the invitation."

"If I see Ozma I'll ask her to invite you," she replied.

The Fox-King had a delightful luncheon put up for them, which the shaggy man shoved in his pocket, and the fox-captain escorted them to an arch at the side of the village opposite the one by which they had entered. Here they found more soldiers guarding the road.

"Are you afraid of enemies?" asked Dorothy.

"No; because we are watchful and able to protect ourselves," answered the captain. "But this road leads to another village peopled by big, stupid beasts who might cause us trouble if they thought we were afraid of them."

"What beasts are they?" asked the shaggy man.

The captain hesitated to answer. Finally, he said:

"You will learn all about them when you arrive at their city. But do not be afraid of them. Button-Bright is so wonderfully clever and has now such an intelligent face that I'm sure he will manage to find a way to protect you."

This made Dorothy and the shaggy man rather uneasy, for they had not so much confidence in the fox-boy's wisdom as the captain seemed to have. But as their escort would say no more about the beasts, they bade him good-bye and proceeded on their journey.

Chapter 5

The RAINBOW'S DAUGHTER

Toto, now allowed to run about as he pleased, was glad to be free again and able to bark at the birds and chase the butterflies. The country around them was charming, yet in the pretty fields of wild-flowers and groves of leafy trees were no houses whatever, or sign of any inhabitants. Birds flew through the air and cunning white rabbits darted amongst the tall grasses and green bushes; Dorothy noticed even the ants toiling busily along the roadway, bearing gigantic loads of clover seed; but of people there were none at all.

They walked briskly on for an hour or two, for even little Button-Bright was a good walker and did not tire easily. At length as they turned a curve in the road they beheld just before them a curious sight.

A little girl, radiant and beautiful, shapely as a fairy and exquisitely dressed, was dancing gracefully in the middle of the lonely road, whirling slowly this way and that, her dainty feet twinkling in sprightly fashion. She was clad in flowing, fluffy robes of soft material that reminded Dorothy of woven cobwebs, only it was colored in soft tintings of violet, rose, topaz, olive, azure, and white, mingled together most harmoniously in stripes which melted one into the other with soft blendings. Her hair was like spun gold and flowed around her in a cloud, no strand being fastened or confined by either pin or ornament or ribbon.

Filled with wonder and admiration our friends approached and stood watching this fascinating dance. The girl was no taller than Dorothy, although more slender; nor did she seem any older than our little heroine.

Suddenly she paused and abandoned the dance, as if for the first time observing the presence of strangers. As she faced them, shy as a frightened fawn, poised upon one foot as if to fly the next instant, Dorothy was astonished to see tears flowing from her violet eyes and trickling down her lovely rose-hued cheeks. That the dainty maiden should dance and weep at the same time was indeed surprising; so Dorothy asked in a soft, sympathetic voice:

"Are you unhappy, little girl?"

"Very!" was the reply; "I am lost."

"Why, so are we," said Dorothy, smiling; "but we don't cry about it."

"Don't you? Why not?"

"'Cause I've been lost before, and always got found again," answered Dorothy, simply.

"But I've never been lost before," murmured the dainty maiden, "and I'm worried and afraid."

"You were dancing," remarked Dorothy, in a puzzled tone of voice.

"Oh, that was just to keep warm," explained the maiden, quickly. "It was not because I felt happy or gay, I assure you."

Dorothy looked at her closely. Her gauzy flowing robes might not be very warm, yet the weather wasn't at all chilly, but rather mild and balmy, like a spring day.

"Who are you, dear?" she asked, gently.

"I'm Polychrome," was the reply.

"Polly whom?"

"Polychrome. I'm the Daughter of the Rainbow."

"Oh!" said Dorothy with a gasp; "I didn't know the Rainbow had children. But I *might* have known it, before you spoke. You couldn't really be anything else."

"Why not?" inquired Polychrome, as if surprised.

"Because you're so lovely and sweet."

The little maiden smiled through her tears, came up to

Dorothy, and placed her slender fingers in the Kansas girl's chubby hand.

"You'll be my friend—won't you?" she said, pleadingly.

"Of course."

"And what is your name?"

"I'm Dorothy; and this is my friend Shaggy Man, who owns the Love Magnet; and this is Button-Bright—only you don't see him as he really is because the Fox-King carelessly changed his head into a fox head. But the real Button-Bright is good to look at, and I hope to get him changed back to himself, some time."

The Rainbow's Daughter nodded cheerfully, no longer afraid of her new companions.

"But who is this?" she asked, pointing to Toto, who was sitting before her wagging his tail in the most friendly manner and admiring the pretty maid with his bright eyes. "Is this, also, some enchanted person?"

"Oh no, Polly—I may call you Polly, mayn't I? Your whole name's awful hard to say."

"Call me Polly if you wish, Dorothy."

"Well, Polly, Toto's just a dog; but he has more sense than Button-Bright, to tell the truth; and I'm very fond of him."

"So am I," said Polychrome, bending gracefully to pat Toto's head.

"But how did the Rainbow's Daughter ever get on this lonely road, and become lost?" asked the shaggy man, who had listened wonderingly to all this.

"Why, my father stretched his rainbow over here this morning, so that one end of it touched this road," was the reply; "and I was dancing upon the pretty rays, as I love to do, and never noticed I was getting too far over the bend in the circle. Suddenly I began to slide, and I went faster and faster until at last I bumped on the ground, at the very end. Just then father lifted the rainbow again, without noticing me at all, and though I tried to seize the end of it and hold fast, it melted away entirely and I was left alone and helpless on the cold, hard earth!"

"It doesn't seem cold to me, Polly," said Dorothy; "but perhaps you're not warmly dressed."

"I'm so used to living nearer the sun," replied the Rainbow's Daughter, "that at first I feared I would freeze down here. But my dance has warmed me some, and now I wonder how I am ever to get home again."

"Won't your father miss you, and look for you, and let down another rainbow for you?"

"Perhaps so, but he's busy just now because it rains in so many parts of the world at this season, and he has to set his rainbow in a lot of different places. What would you advise me to do, Dorothy?"

"Come with us," was the answer. "I'm going to try to find my way to the Emerald City, which is in the fairy Land of Oz. The Emerald City is ruled by a friend of mine, the Princess Ozma, and if we can manage to get there I'm sure she will know a way to send you home to your father again."

"Do you really think so?" asked Polychrome, anxiously.

"I'm pretty sure."

"Then I'll go with you," said the little maid; "for travel will help keep me warm, and father can find me in one part of the world as well as another—if he gets time to look for me."

"Come along, then," said the shaggy man, cheerfully; and they started on once more. Polly walked beside Dorothy a while, holding her new friend's hand as if she feared to let it go; but her nature seemed as light and buoyant as her fleecy robes, for suddenly she darted ahead and whirled round in a giddy dance. Then she tripped back to them with sparkling eyes and smiling cheeks, having regained her usual happy mood and forgotten all her worry about being lost.

They found her a charming companion, and her dancing and laughter—for she laughed at times like the tinkling of a silver bell—did much to enliven their journey and keep them contented.

——◃ Chapter 6 ▹——

The CITY of BEASTS

When noon came they opened the Fox-King's basket of luncheon, and found a nice roasted turkey with cranberry sauce and some slices of bread and butter. As they sat on the grass by the roadside the shaggy man cut up the turkey with his pocket-knife and passed slices of it around.

"Haven't you any dewdrops, or mist-cakes, or cloudbuns?" asked Polychrome, longingly.

"'Course not," replied Dorothy. "We eat solid things, down here on the earth. But there's a bottle of cold tea. Try some, won't you?"

The Rainbow's Daughter watched Button-Bright devour one leg of the turkey.

"Is it good?" she asked.

He nodded.

"Do you think I could eat it?"

"Not this," said Button-Bright.

"But I mean another piece?"

"Don't know," he replied.

"Well, I'm going to try, for I'm very hungry," she decided, and took a thin slice of the white breast of turkey which the shaggy man cut for her, as well as a bit of bread and butter. When she tasted it Polychrome thought the turkey was good—better even than mist-cakes; but a little satisfied her hunger and she finished with a tiny sip of cold tea.

"That's about as much as a fly would eat," said Dorothy, who was making a good meal herself. "But I know some people in Oz who eat nothing at all."

"Who are they?" inquired the shaggy man.

"One is a scarecrow who's stuffed with straw, and the other a woodman made out of tin. They haven't any appetites inside of 'em, you see; so they never eat anything at all."

"Are they alive?" asked Button-Bright.

"Oh yes," replied Dorothy; "and they're very clever and very nice, too. If we get to Oz I'll introduce them to you."

"Do you really expect to get to Oz?" inquired the shaggy man, taking a drink of cold tea.

"I don't know just what to 'spect," answered the child, seriously; "but I've noticed if I happen to get lost I'm almost sure to come to the Land of Oz in the end, somehow 'r other; so I may get there this time. But I can't promise, you know; all I can do is wait and see."

"Will the Scarecrow scare me?" asked Button-Bright.

"No; 'cause you're not a crow," she returned. "He has the loveliest smile you ever saw—only it's painted on and he can't help it."

Luncheon being over they started again upon their journey, the shaggy man, Dorothy and Button-Bright walking soberly along, side by side, and the Rainbow's Daughter dancing merrily before them.

Sometimes she darted along the road so swiftly that she was nearly out of sight, then she came tripping back to greet them with her silvery laughter. But once she came back more sedately, to say:

"There's a city a little way off."

"I 'spected that," returned Dorothy; "for the fox-people warned us there was one on this road. It's filled with stupid beasts of some sort, but we musn't be afraid of 'em 'cause they won't hurt us."

"All right," said Button-Bright; but Polychrome didn't know whether it was all right or not.

"It's a big city," she said, "and the road runs straight through it."

"Never mind," said the shaggy man; "as long as I carry the Love Magnet every living thing will love me, and you may be sure I shan't allow any of my friends to be harmed in any way."

This comforted them somewhat, and they moved on again. Pretty soon they came to a sign-post that read:

HAF A MYLE TO DUNKITON

"Oh," said the shaggy man, "if they're donkeys, we've nothing to fear at all."

"They may kick," said Dorothy, doubtfully.

"Then we will cut some switches, and make them behave," he replied. At the first tree he cut himself a long, slender switch from one of the branches, and shorter switches for the others.

"Don't be afraid to order the beasts around," he said; "they're used to it."

Before long the road brought them to the gates of the city. There was a high wall all around, which had been whitewashed, and the gate just before our travelers was a mere opening in the wall, with no bars across it. No towers or steeples or domes showed above the enclosure, nor was any living thing to be seen as our friends drew near.

Suddenly, as they were about to boldly enter through the opening, there arose a harsh clamor of sound that swelled and echoed on every side, until they were nearly deafened by the racket and had to put their fingers to their ears to keep the noise out.

It was like the firing of many cannon, only there were no cannon-balls or other missiles to be seen; it was like the rolling of mighty thunder, only not a cloud was in the sky; it was like the roar of countless breakers on a rugged seashore, only there was no sea or other water anywhere about.

They hesitated to advance; but, as the noise did no harm, they entered through the whitewashed wall and quickly discovered the cause of the turmoil. Inside were suspended many sheets of tin or thin iron, and against these metal sheets a row of donkeys were pounding their heels with vicious kicks.

The shaggy man ran up to the nearest donkey and gave the beast a sharp blow with his switch.

"Stop that noise!" he shouted; and the donkey stopped kicking the metal sheet and turned its head to look with surprise at the shaggy man. He switched the next donkey, and made him stop, and then the next, so that gradually the rattling of heels ceased and the awful noise subsided. The donkeys stood in a group and eyed the strangers with fear and trembling.

"What do you mean by making such a racket?" asked the shaggy man, sternly.

"We were scaring away the foxes," said one of the donkeys,

meekly. "Usually they run fast enough when they hear the noise, which makes them afraid."

"There are no foxes here," said the shaggy man.

"I beg to differ with you. There's one, anyhow," replied the donkey, sitting upright on its haunches and waving a hoof toward Button-Bright. "We saw him coming and thought the whole army of foxes was marching to attack us."

"Button-Bright isn't a fox," explained the shaggy man. "He's only wearing a fox head for a time, until he can get his own head back."

"Oh, I see," remarked the donkey, waving its left ear reflectively. "I'm sorry we made such a mistake, and had all our work and worry for nothing."

The other donkeys by this time were sitting up and examining the strangers with big, glassy eyes. They made a queer picture, indeed; for they wore wide, white collars around their necks and the collars had many scallops and points. The gentlemen-donkeys wore high pointed caps set between their great ears, and the lady-donkeys wore sunbonnets with holes cut in the top for the ears to stick through. But they had no other clothing except their hairy skins, although many wore gold and silver bangles on their front wrists and bands of different metals on their rear ankles. When they were kicking they had braced themselves with their front legs, but now they all stood or sat upright on their hind legs and used their front ones as arms. Having no fingers or hands the beasts were rather clumsy, as you may guess; but Dorothy was surprised to observe how many things they could do with their stiff, heavy hoofs.

Some of the donkeys were white, some were brown, or grey, or black, or spotted; but their hair was sleek and smooth and their broad collars and caps gave them a neat, if whimsical, appearance.

"This is a nice way to welcome visitors, I must say!" remarked the shaggy man, in a reproachful tone.

"Oh, we did not mean to be impolite," replied a grey donkey which had not spoken before. "But you were not expected, nor did you send in your visiting cards, as it is proper to do."

"There is some truth in that," admitted the shaggy man; "but, now you are informed that we are important and distinguished travelers, I trust you will accord us proper consideration."

These big words delighted the donkeys, and made them bow to the shaggy man with great respect. Said the grey one:

"You shall be taken before his great and glorious Majesty King Kik-a-bray, who will greet you as becomes your exalted stations."

"That's right," answered Dorothy. "Take us to some one who knows something."

"Oh, we all know something, my child, or we shouldn't be donkeys," asserted the grey one, with dignity. "The word 'donkey' means 'clever,' you know."

"I didn't know it," she replied. "I thought it meant 'stupid.'"

"Not at all, my child. If you will look in the Encyclopedia Donkaniara you will find I'm correct. But come; I will myself lead you before our splendid, exalted, and most intellectual ruler."

All donkeys love big words, so it is no wonder the grey one used so many of them.

Chapter 7

The SHAGGY MAN'S TRANSFORMATION

They found the houses of the town all low and square and built of bricks, neatly whitewashed inside and out. The houses were not set in rows, forming regular streets, but placed here and there in a haphazard manner which made it puzzling for a stranger to find his way.

"Stupid people must have streets and numbered houses in their cities, to guide them where to go," observed the grey donkey, as he walked before the visitors on his hind legs, in an awkward but comical manner; "but clever donkeys know their way about without such absurd marks. Moreover, a mixed city is much prettier than one with straight streets."

Dorothy did not agree with this, but she said nothing to contradict it. Presently she saw a sign on a house that read: "Madam de Fayke, Hoofist," and she asked their conductor:

"What's a 'hoofist,' please?"

"One who reads your fortune in your hoofs," replied the grey donkey.

"Oh, I see," said the little girl. "You are quite civilized here."

"Dunkiton," he replied, "is the center of the world's highest civilization."

They came to a house where two youthful donkeys were whitewashing the wall, and Dorothy stopped a moment to watch them. They dipped the ends of their tails, which were much like paint-brushes, into a pail of whitewash, backed up against the house, and wagged their tails right and left until the whitewash was rubbed on the wall, after which they dipped these funny brushes in the pail again and repeated the performance.

"That must be fun," said Button-Bright.

"No, it's work," replied the old donkey; "but we make our youngsters do all the whitewashing, to keep them out of mischief."

"Don't they go to school?" asked Dorothy.

"All donkeys are born wise," was the reply, "so the only school we need is the school of experience. Books are only for those who know nothing, and so are obliged to learn things from other people."

"In other words, the more stupid one is, the more he thinks he knows," observed the shaggy man. The grey donkey paid no attention to this speech because he had just stopped before a house which had painted over the doorway a pair of hoofs, with a donkey tail between them and a rude crown and sceptre above.

"I'll see if his magnificent Majesty King Kik-a-bray is at home," said he. He lifted his head and called "Whee-haw! whee-haw! whee-haw!" three times, in a shocking voice, turning about and kicking with his heels against the panel of the door. For a time there was no reply; then the door opened far enough to permit a donkey's head to stick out and look at them.

It was a white head, with big, awful ears and round, solemn eyes.

"Have the foxes gone?" it asked, in a trembling voice.

"They haven't been here, most stupendous Majesty," replied the grey one. "The new arrivals prove to be travelers of distinction."

"Oh," said the King, in a relieved tone of voice. "Let them come in."

He opened the door wide, and the party marched into a big room, which, Dorothy thought, looked quite unlike a king's palace. There were mats of woven grasses on the floor and the place was clean and neat; but his Majesty had no other furniture at all—perhaps because he didn't need it. He squatted down in the center of the room and a little brown donkey ran and brought a big gold crown which it placed on the monarch's head, and a golden staff with a jeweled ball at the end of it, which the King held between his front hoofs as he sat upright.

"Now, then," said his Majesty, waving his long ears gently to and fro, "tell me why you are here, and what you expect me to do for you." He eyed Button-Bright rather sharply, as if afraid of the little boy's queer head, though it was the shaggy man who undertook to reply.

"Most noble and supreme ruler of Dunkiton," he said, trying not to laugh in the solemn King's face, "we are strangers traveling through your dominions and have entered your magnificent city because the road led through it, and there was no way to go around. All we desire is to pay our respects to your Majesty—the cleverest king in all the world, I'm sure—and then to continue on our way."

This polite speech pleased the King very much; indeed, it pleased him so much that it proved an unlucky speech for the shaggy man. Perhaps the Love Magnet helped to win his Majesty's affections as well as the flattery, but however this may be, the white donkey looked kindly upon the speaker and said:

"Only a donkey should be able to use such fine, big words, and you are too wise and admirable in all ways to be a mere man. Also I feel that I love you as well as I do my own favored people, so I will bestow upon you the greatest gift within my power—a donkey's head."

As he spoke he waved his jeweled staff. Although the shaggy man cried out and tried to leap backward and escape, it proved of no use. Suddenly his own head was gone and a donkey head appeared in its place—a brown, shaggy head so absurd and droll that Dorothy and Polly both broke into merry laughter, and even Button-Bright's fox face wore a smile.

"Dear me! dear me!" cried the shaggy man, feeling of his shaggy new head and his long ears. "What a misfortune—what a great misfortune! Give me back my own head, you stupid king—if you love me at all!"

"Don't you like it?" asked the King, surprised.

"Hee-haw! I hate it! Take it away—quick!" said the shaggy man.

"But I can't do that," was the reply. "My magic works only one way. I can *do* things, but I can't *un*do them. You'll have to find the Truth Pond, and bathe in its water, in order to get back your own head. But I advise you not to do that. This head is much more beautiful than the old one."

"That's a matter of taste," said Dorothy.

"Where is the Truth Pond?" asked the shaggy man, earnestly.

"Somewhere in the Land of Oz; but just the exact location of it I can not tell," was the answer.

"Don't worry, Shaggy Man," said Dorothy, smiling because

her friend wagged his new ears so comically. "If the Truth Pond is in Oz we'll be sure to find it when we get there."

"Oh! Are you going to the Land of Oz?" asked King Kik-a-bray.

"I don't know," she replied, "but we've been told we are nearer the Land of Oz than to Kansas, and if that's so the quickest way for me to get home is to find Ozma."

"Haw-haw! Do you know the mighty Princess Ozma?" asked the King, his tone both surprised and eager.

"'Course I do; she's my friend," said Dorothy.

"Then perhaps you'll do me a favor," continued the white donkey, much excited.

"What is it?" she asked.

"Perhaps you can get me an invitation to Princess Ozma's birthday celebration, which will be the grandest royal function ever held in fairyland. I'd love to go."

"Hee-haw! You deserve punishment, rather than reward, for giving me this dreadful head," said the shaggy man, sorrowfully.

"I wish you wouldn't say 'hee-haw' so much," Polychrome begged him; "it makes cold chills run down my back."

"But I can't help it, my dear; my donkey head wants to bray continually," he replied. "Doesn't your fox head want to yelp every minute?" he asked Button-Bright.

"Don't know," said the boy, still staring at the shaggy man's ears. These seemed to interest him greatly, and the sight also made him forget his own fox head, which was a comfort.

"What do you think, Polly? Shall I promise the donkey king an invitation to Ozma's party?" asked Dorothy of the Rainbow's Daughter, who was flitting about the room like a sunbeam because she could never keep still.

"Do as you please, dear," answered Polychrome. "He might help to amuse the guests of the Princess."

"Then, if you will give us some supper and a place to sleep to-night, and let us get started on our journey early to-morrow morning," said Dorothy to the King, "I'll ask Ozma to invite you—if I happen to get to Oz."

"Good! Hee-haw! Excellent!" cried Kik-a-bray, much pleased. "You shall all have fine suppers and good beds. What food would you prefer, a bran mash or ripe oats in the shell?"

"Neither one," replied Dorothy, promptly.

"Perhaps plain hay, or some sweet juicy grass would suit you better," suggested Kik-a-bray, musingly.

"Is that all you have to eat?" asked the girl.

"What more do you desire?"

"Well, you see we're not donkeys," she explained, "and so we're used to other food. The foxes gave us a nice supper in Foxville."

"We'd like some dewdrops and mist-cakes," said Polychrome.

"I'd prefer apples and a ham sandwich," declared the

shaggy man, "for although I've a donkey head, I still have my own particular stomach."

"I want pie," said Button-Bright.

"I think some beefsteak and chocolate layer-cake would taste best," said Dorothy.

"Hee-haw! I declare!" exclaimed the King. "It seems each one of you wants a different food. How queer all living creatures are, except donkeys!"

"And donkeys like you are queerest of all," laughed Polychrome.

"Well," decided the King, "I suppose my Magic Staff will produce the things you crave; if you are lacking in good taste it is not my fault."

With this, he waved his staff with the jeweled ball, and before them instantly appeared a tea-table, set with linen and pretty dishes, and on the table were the very things each had wished for. Dorothy's beefsteak was smoking hot, and the shaggy man's apples were plump and rosy-cheeked. The King had not thought to provide chairs, so they all stood in their places around the table and ate with good appetite, being hungry. The Rainbow's Daughter found three tiny dewdrops on a crystal plate, and Button-Bright had a big slice of apple-pie, which he devoured eagerly.

Afterward the King called the brown donkey, which was his favorite servant, and bade it lead his guests to the vacant house where they were to pass the night. It had only one room and no furniture except beds of clean straw and a few mats of woven grasses; but our travelers were contented with these simple things because they realized it was the best the Donkey-King had to offer them. As soon as it was dark they lay down on the mats and slept comfortably until morning.

At daybreak there was a dreadful noise throughout the city. Every donkey in the place brayed. When he heard this the shaggy man woke up and called out "Hee-haw!" as loud as he could.

"Stop that!" said Button-Bright, in a cross voice. Both Dorothy and Polly looked at the shaggy man reproachfully.

"I couldn't help it, my dears," he said, as if ashamed of his bray; "but I'll try not to do it again."

Of course they forgave him, for as he still had the Love Magnet in his pocket they were all obliged to love him as much as ever.

They did not see the King again, but Kik-a-bray remembered them; for a table appeared again in their room with the same food upon it as on the night before.

"Don't want pie for breakfus'," said Button-Bright.

"I'll give you some of my beefsteak," proposed Dorothy; "there's plenty for us all."

That suited the boy better, but the shaggy man said he was content with his apples and sandwiches, although he ended the meal by eating Button-Bright's pie. Polly liked her dewdrops and mist-cakes better than any other food, so they all enjoyed an excellent breakfast. Toto had the scraps left from the beefsteak, and he stood up nicely on his hind legs while Dorothy fed them to him.

Breakfast ended, they passed through the village to the side opposite that by which they had entered, the brown servant-donkey guiding them through the maze of scattered houses. There was the road again, leading far away into the unknown country beyond.

"King Kik-a-bray says you must not forget his invitation," said the brown donkey, as they passed through the opening in the wall.

"I shan't," promised Dorothy.

Perhaps no one ever beheld a more strangely assorted group than the one which now walked along the road, through pretty green fields and past groves of feathery pepper-trees and fragrant mimosa. Polychrome, her beautiful gauzy robes floating around her like a rainbow cloud, went first, dancing back and forth and darting now here to pluck a wild-flower or there to watch a beetle crawl across the path. Toto ran after her at times, barking joyously the while, only to become sober again and trot along at Dorothy's heels. The little Kansas girl walked holding Button-Bright's hand clasped in her own, and the wee boy with his fox head covered by the sailor hat presented an odd appearance. Strangest of all, perhaps, was the shaggy man, with his shaggy donkey head, who shuffled along in the rear with his hands thrust deep in his big pockets.

None of the party was really unhappy. All were straying in an unknown land and had suffered more or less annoyance and discomfort; but they realized they were having a fairy adventure in a fairy country, and were much interested in finding out what would happen next.

···—·‹ Chapter 8 ›·—···

The MUSICKER

bout the middle of the forenoon they began to go up a long hill. By-and-by this hill suddenly dropped down into a pretty valley, where the travelers saw to their surprise, a small house standing by the road-side.

It was the first house they had seen, and they hastened into the valley to discover who lived there. No one was in sight as they approached, but when they began to get nearer the house they heard queer sounds coming from it. They could not make these out at first, but as they became louder our friends thought they heard a sort of music like that made by a wheezy hand-organ; the music fell upon their ears in this way:

Tiddle-widdle-iddle, oom pom-pom!
Oom, pom-pom! oom, pom-pom!
Tiddle-tiddle-tiddle, oom pom-pom!
Oom, pom-pom—pah!

"What is it, a band or a mouth-organ?" asked Dorothy.

"Don't know," said Button-Bright.

"Sounds to me like a played-out phonograph," said the shaggy man, lifting his enormous ears to listen.

"Oh, there just *couldn't* be a funnygraf in fairyland!" cried Dorothy.

"It's rather pretty, isn't it?" asked Polychrome, trying to dance to the strains.

Tiddle-widdle-iddle, oom pom-pom,
Oom pom-pom; oom pom-pom!

came the music to their ears, more distinctly as they drew nearer the house. Presently, they saw a little fat man sitting on a bench before the door. He wore a red, braided jacket that reached to his waist, a blue waistcoat, and white trousers with gold stripes down the sides. On his bald head was perched a little, round, red cap held in place by a rubber elastic underneath his chin. His face was round, his eyes a faded blue, and he wore white cotton gloves. The man leaned on a stout gold-headed cane, bending forward on his seat to watch his visitors approach.

Singularly enough, the musical sounds they had heard seemed to come from the inside of the fat man himself; for he was playing no instrument nor was any to be seen near him.

They came up and stood in a row, staring at him, and he stared back while the queer sounds came from him as before:

> *Tiddle-iddle-iddle, oom pom-pom,*
> *Oom, pom-pom; oom pom-pom!*
> *Tiddle-widdle-iddle, oom pom-pom,*
> *Oom, pom-pom—pah!*

"Why, he's a reg'lar musicker!" said Button-Bright.

"What's a musicker?" asked Dorothy.

"Him!" said the boy.

Hearing this, the fat man sat up a little stiffer than before, as if he had received a compliment, and still came the sounds:

> *Tiddle-widdle-iddle, oom pom-pom,*
> *Oom pom-pom, oom—*

"Stop it!" cried the shaggy man, earnestly. "Stop that dreadful noise."

The fat man looked at him sadly and began his reply. When he spoke the music changed and the words seemed to accompany the notes. He said—or rather sang:

It isn't a noise that you hear,
But Music, harmonic and clear.
My breath makes me play
Like an organ, all day—
That bass note is in my left ear.

"How funny!" exclaimed Dorothy; "he says his breath makes the music."

"That's all nonsense," declared the shaggy man; but now the music began again, and they all listened carefully.

My lungs are full of reeds like those
In organs, therefore I suppose,
If I breathe in or out my nose,
The reeds are bound to play.

So, as I breathe to live, you know,
I squeeze out music as I go;
I'm very sorry this is so—
Forgive my piping, pray!

"Poor man," said Polychrome; "he can't help it. What a great misfortune it is!"

"Yes," replied the shaggy man; "we are only obliged to hear this music a short time, until we leave him and go away; but the poor fellow must listen to himself as long as he lives, and that is enough to drive him crazy. Don't you think so?"

"Don't know," said Button-Bright. Toto said, "Bow-wow!" and the others laughed.

"Perhaps that's why he lives all alone," suggested Dorothy.

"Yes; if he had neighbors, they might do him an injury," responded the shaggy man.

All this while the little fat musicker was breathing the notes:

Tiddle-tiddle-iddle, oom, pom-pom,

and they had to speak loud in order to hear themselves. The shaggy man said:

"Who are you, sir?"

The reply came in the shape of this sing-song:

I'm Allegro da Capo, a very famous man;
Just find another, high or low, to match me if you can.
Some people try, but can't, to play
And have to practice every day;
But I've been musical alway, since first my life began.

"Why, I b'lieve he's proud of it," exclaimed Dorothy; "and seems to me I've heard worse music than he makes."

"Where?" asked Button-Bright.

"I've forgotten, just now. But Mr. Da Capo is certainly a

strange person—isn't he?—and p'r'aps he's the only one of his kind in all the world."

This praise seemed to please the little fat musicker, for he swelled out his chest, looked important and sang as follows:

I wear no band around me,
And yet I am a band!
I do not strain to make my strains
But, on the other hand,
My toot is always destitute
Of flats or other errors;
To see sharp and be natural are
For me but minor terrors.

"I don't quite understand that," said Polychrome, with a puzzled look; "but perhaps it's because I'm accustomed only to the music of the spheres."

"What's that?" asked Button-Bright.

"Oh, Polly means the atmosphere and hemisphere, I s'pose," explained Dorothy.

"Oh," said Button-Bright.

"Bow-wow!" said Toto.

But the musicker was still breathing his constant

Oom, pom-pom; oom, pom-pom—

and it seemed to jar on the shaggy man's nerves.

"Stop it, can't you?" he cried angrily; "or breathe in a whisper; or put a clothes-pin on your nose. Do something, anyhow!"

But the fat one, with a sad look, sang this answer:

> *Music hath charms, and it may*
> *Soothe even the savage, they say;*
> *So if savage you feel*
> *Just list to my reel,*
> *For sooth to say that's the real way.*

The shaggy man had to laugh at this, and when he laughed he stretched his donkey mouth wide open. Said Dorothy:

"I don't know how good his poetry is, but it seems to fit the notes, so that's all that can be 'xpected."

"I like it," said Button-Bright, who was staring hard at the musicker, his little legs spread wide apart. To the surprise of his companions, the boy asked this long question:

"If I swallowed a mouth-organ, what would I be?"

"An organette," said the shaggy man. "But come, my dears; I think the best thing we can do is to continue on our journey before Button-Bright swallows anything. We must try to find that Land of Oz, you know."

Hearing this speech the musicker sang, quickly:

If you go to the Land of Oz
Please take me along, because
On Ozma's birthday
I'm anxious to play
The loveliest song ever was.

"No thank you," said Dorothy; "we prefer to travel alone. But if I see Ozma I'll tell her you want to come to her birthday party."

"Let's be going," urged the shaggy man, anxiously.

Polly was already dancing along the road, far in advance, and the others turned to follow her. Toto did not like the fat musicker and made a grab for his chubby leg. Dorothy quickly caught up the growling little dog and hurried after her companions, who were walking faster than usual in order to get out of hearing. They had to climb a hill, and until they got to the top they could not escape the musicker's monotonous piping:

Oom, pom-pom; oom, pom-pom;
Tiddle-iddle-widdle, oom, pom-pom;
Oom, pom-pom—pah!

As they passed the brow of the hill, however, and descended on the other side, the sounds gradually died away, whereat they all felt much relieved.

"I'm glad I don't have to live with the organ-man; aren't you, Polly?" said Dorothy.

"Yes, indeed," answered the Rainbow's Daughter.

"He's nice," declared Button-Bright, soberly.

"I hope your Princess Ozma won't invite him to her birth-day celebration," remarked the shaggy man; "for the fellow's music would drive her guests all crazy. You've given me an idea, Button-Bright; I believe the musicker must have swal-lowed an accordeon in his youth."

"What's 'cordeon?" asked the boy.

"It's a kind of pleating," explained Dorothy, putting down the dog.

"Bow-wow!" said Toto, and ran away at a mad gallop to chase a bumble-bee.

Chapter 9

FACING the SCOODLERS

The country wasn't so pretty now. Before the travelers appeared a rocky plain covered with hills on which grew nothing green. They were nearing some low mountains, too, and the road, which before had been smooth and pleasant to walk upon, grew rough and uneven.

Button-Bright's little feet stumbled more than once, and Polychrome ceased her dancing because the walking was now so difficult that she had no trouble to keep warm.

It had become afternoon, yet there wasn't a thing for their luncheon except two apples which the shaggy man had taken from the breakfast table. He divided these into four pieces and gave a portion to each of his companions. Dorothy and Button-Bright were glad to get theirs; but Polly was satisfied with a small bite, and Toto did not like apples.

"Do you know," asked the Rainbow's Daughter, "if this is the right road to the Emerald City?"

"No, I don't," replied Dorothy, "but it's the only road in this part of the country, so we may as well go to the end of it."

"It looks now as if it might end pretty soon," remarked the shaggy man; "and what shall we do if it does?"

"Don't know," said Button-Bright.

"If I had my Magic Belt," replied Dorothy, thoughtfully, "it could do us a lot of good just now."

"What is your Magic Belt?" asked Polychrome.

"It's a thing I captured from the Nome King one day, and it can do 'most any wonderful thing. But I left it with Ozma, you know; 'cause magic won't work in Kansas, but only in fairy countries."

"Is this a fairy country?" asked Button-Bright.

"I should think you'd know," said the little girl, gravely. "If it wasn't a fairy country you couldn't have a fox head and the shaggy man couldn't have a donkey head, and the Rainbow's Daughter would be invis'ble."

"What's that?" asked the boy.

"You don't seem to know anything, Button-Bright. Invis'ble is a thing you can't see."

"Then Toto's invis'ble," declared the boy, and Dorothy

found he was right. Toto had disappeared from view, but they could hear him barking furiously among the heaps of grey rock ahead of them.

They moved forward a little faster to see what the dog was barking at, and found perched upon a point of rock by the roadside a curious creature. It had the form of a man, middle-sized and rather slender and graceful; but as it sat silent and motionless upon the peak they could see that its face was black as ink, and it wore a black cloth costume made like a union suit and fitting tight to its skin. Its hands were black, too, and its toes curled down, like a bird's. The creature was black all over except its hair, which was fine, and yellow, banged in front across the black forehead and cut close at the sides. The eyes, which were fixed steadily upon the barking dog, were small and sparkling and looked like the eyes of a weasel.

"What in the world do you s'pose that is?" asked Dorothy in a hushed voice, as the little group of travelers stood watching the strange creature.

"Don't know," said Button-Bright.

The thing gave a jump and turned half around, sitting in the same place but with the other side of its body facing them. Instead of being black, it was now pure white, with a face like that of a clown in a circus and hair of a brilliant purple. The creature could bend either way, and its white toes now curled the same way the black ones on the other side had done.

"It has a face both front and back," whispered Dorothy, wonderingly; "only there's no back at all, but two fronts."

Having made the turn, the being sat motionless as before, while Toto barked louder at the white man than he had done at the black one.

"Once," said the shaggy man, "I had a jumping-jack like that, with two faces."

"Was it alive?" asked Button-Bright.

"No," replied the shaggy man; "it worked on strings, and was made of wood."

"Wonder if this works with strings," said Dorothy; but Polychrome cried "Look!" for another creature just like the first had suddenly appeared sitting on another rock, its black side toward them. The two twisted their heads around and showed a black face on the white side of one and a white face on the black side of the other.

"How curious," said Polychrome; "and how loose their heads seem to be! Are they friendly to us, do you think?"

"Can't tell, Polly," replied Dorothy. "Let's ask 'em."

The creatures flopped first one way and then the other, showing black or white by turns; and now another joined them, appearing on another rock. Our friends had come to a little hollow in the hills, and the place where they now stood was surrounded by jagged peaks of rock, except where the road ran through.

"Now there are four of them," said the shaggy man.

"Five," declared Polychrome.

"Six," said Dorothy.

"Lots of 'em!" cried Button-Bright; and so there were—quite a row of the two-sided black and white creatures sitting on the rocks all around.

Toto stopped barking and ran between Dorothy's feet, where he crouched down as if afraid. The creatures did not look pleasant or friendly, to be sure, and the shaggy man's donkey face became solemn, indeed.

"Ask 'em who they are, and what they want," whispered Dorothy; so the shaggy man called out in a loud voice:

"Who are you?"

"Scoodlers!" they yelled in chorus, their voices sharp and shrill.

"What do you want?" called the shaggy man.

"You!" they yelled, pointing their thin fingers at the group; and they all flopped around, so they were white, and then all flopped back again, so they were black.

"But what do you want us for?" asked the shaggy man, uneasily.

"Soup!" they all shouted, as if with one voice.

"Goodness me!" said Dorothy, trembling a little; "the Scoodlers must be reg'lar cannibals."

"Don't want to be soup," protested Button-Bright, beginning to cry.

"Hush, dear," said the little girl, trying to comfort him; "we don't any of us want to be soup. But don't worry; the shaggy man will take care of us."

"Will he?" asked Polychrome, who did not like the Scoodlers at all, and kept close to Dorothy.

"I'll try," promised the shaggy man; but he looked worried.

Happening just then to feel the Love Magnet in his pocket, he said to the creatures, with more confidence:

"Don't you love me?"

"Yes!" they shouted, all together.

"Then you mustn't harm me, or my friends," said the shaggy man, firmly.

"We love you in soup!" they yelled, and in a flash turned their white sides to the front.

"How dreadful!" said Dorothy. "This is a time, Shaggy Man, when you get loved too much."

"Don't want to be soup!" wailed Button-Bright again; and Toto began to whine dismally, as if he didn't want to be soup, either.

"The only thing to do," said the shaggy man to his friends, in a low tone, "is to get out of this pocket in the rocks as soon as we can, and leave the Scoodlers behind us. Follow me, my dears, and don't pay any attention to what they do or say."

With this, he began to march along the road to the opening in the rocks ahead, and the others kept close behind him. But the Scoodlers closed up in front, as if to bar their way, and so the shaggy man stooped down and picked up a loose stone, which he threw at the creatures to scare them from the path.

At this the Scoodlers raised a howl. Two of them picked their heads from their shoulders and hurled them at the shaggy man with such force that he fell over in a heap, greatly astonished. The two now ran forward with swift leaps, caught up their heads, and put them on again, after which they sprang back to their positions on the rocks.

Chapter 10

ESCAPING the SOUP-KETTLE

The shaggy man got up and felt of himself to see if he was hurt; but he was not. One of the heads had struck his breast and the other his left shoulder; yet though they had knocked him down, the heads were not hard enough to bruise him.

"Come on," he said firmly; "we've got to get out of here some way," and forward he started again.

The Scoodlers began yelling and throwing their heads in great numbers at our frightened friends. The shaggy man was knocked over again, and so was Button-Bright, who kicked his heels against the ground and howled as loud as he could, although he was not hurt a bit. One head struck Toto, who first

yelped and then grabbed the head by an ear and started running away with it.

The Scoodlers who had thrown their heads began to scram-
ble down and run to pick them up, with wonderful quickness;
but the one whose head Toto had stolen found it hard to get
it back again. The head couldn't see the body with either pair
of its eyes, because the dog was in the way, so the headless
Scoodler stumbled around over the rocks and tripped on them
more than once in its effort to regain its top. Toto was trying
to get outside the rocks and roll the head down the hill; but
some of the other Scoodlers came to the rescue of their unfortunate comrade and pelted the dog with their own heads until
he was obliged to drop his burden and hurry back to Dorothy.

The little girl and the Rainbow's Daughter had both
escaped the shower of heads, but they saw now that it would
be useless to try to run away from the dreadful Scoodlers.

"We may as well submit," declared the shaggy man, in a
rueful voice, as he got upon his feet again. He turned toward
their foes and asked:

"What do you want us to do?"

"Come!" they cried, in a triumphant chorus, and at once
sprang from the rocks and surrounded their captives on all sides.
One funny thing about the Scoodlers was they could walk in either
direction, coming or going, without turning around; because
they had two faces and, as Dorothy said, "two front sides," and
their feet were shaped like the letter T upside down (⊥). They

moved with great rapidity and there was something about their glittering eyes and contrasting colors and removable heads that inspired the poor prisoners with horror, and made them long to escape.

But the creatures led their captives away from the rocks and the road, down the hill by a side path until they came before a low mountain of rock that looked like a huge bowl turned upside down. At the edge of this mountain was a deep gulf—so deep that when you looked into it there was nothing but blackness below. Across the gulf was a narrow bridge of rock, and at the other end of the bridge was an arched opening that led into the mountain.

Over this bridge the Scoodlers led their prisoners, through the opening into the mountain, which they found to be an immense hollow dome lighted by several holes in the roof. All around the circular space were built rock houses, set close together, each with a door in the front wall. None of these houses was more than six feet wide, but the Scoodlers were thin people sidewise and did not need much room. So vast was the dome that there was a large space in the middle of the cave, in front of all these houses, where the creatures might congregate as in a great hall.

It made Dorothy shudder to see a huge iron kettle suspended by a stout chain in the middle of the place, and underneath the kettle a great heap of kindling wood and shavings, ready to light.

"What's that?" asked the shaggy man, drawing back as they approached this place, so that they were forced to push him forward.

"The Soup Kettle!" yelled the Scoodlers; and then they shouted in the next breath:

"We're hungry!"

Button-Bright, holding Dorothy's hand in one chubby fist and Polly's hand in the other, was so affected by this shout that he began to cry again, repeating the protest:

"Don't want to be soup, I don't!"

"Never mind," said the shaggy man, consolingly; "I ought to make enough soup to feed them all, I'm so big; so I'll ask them to put me in the kettle first."

"All right," said Button-Bright, more cheerfully.

But the Scoodlers were not ready to make soup yet. They led the captives into a house at the farthest side of the cave—a house somewhat wider than the others.

"Who lives here?" asked the Rainbow's Daughter. The Scoodlers nearest her replied:

"The Queen."

It made Dorothy hopeful to learn that a woman ruled over these fierce creatures, but a moment later they were ushered by two or three of the escort into a gloomy, bare room—and her hope died away.

For the Queen of the Scoodlers proved to be much more dreadful in appearance than any of her people. One side of her was fiery red, with jet-black hair and green eyes and the other side of her was bright yellow, with crimson hair and black eyes. She wore a short skirt of red and yellow and her hair, instead of being banged, was a tangle of short curls upon which rested a circular crown of silver—much dented and twisted because the Queen had thrown her head at so many things so many times. Her form was lean and bony and both her faces were deeply wrinkled.

"What have we here?" asked the Queen sharply, as our friends were made to stand before her.

"Soup!" cried the guard of Scoodlers, speaking together.

"We're not!" said Dorothy, indignantly; "we're nothing of the sort."

"Ah, but you will be soon," retorted the Queen, a grim smile making her look more dreadful than before.

"Pardon me, most beautiful vision," said the shaggy man, bowing before the queen politely. "I must request your Serene Highness to let us go our way without being made into soup. For I own the Love Magnet, and whoever meets me must love me and all my friends."

"True," replied the Queen. "We love you very much; so much that we intend to eat your broth with real pleasure. But tell me, do you think I am so beautiful?"

"You won't be at all beautiful if you eat me," he said, shaking his head sadly. "Handsome is as handsome does, you know."

The Queen turned to Button-Bright.

"Do *you* think I'm beautiful?" she asked.

"No," said the boy; "you're ugly."

"*I* think you're a fright," said Dorothy.

"If you could see yourself you'd be terribly scared," added Polly.

The Queen scowled at them and flopped from her red side to her yellow side.

"Take them away," she commanded the guard, "and at six o'clock run them through the meat chopper and start the soup kettle boiling. And put plenty of salt in the broth this time, or I'll punish the cooks severely."

"Any onions, your Majesty?" asked one of the guard.

"Plenty of onions and garlic and a dash of red pepper. Now, go!"

The Scoodlers led the captives away and shut them up in one of the houses, leaving only a single Scoodler to keep guard.

The place was a sort of store-house; containing bags of potatoes and baskets of carrots, onions, and turnips.

"These," said their guard, pointing to the vegetables, "we use to flavor our soups with."

The prisoners were rather disheartened by this time, for they saw no way to escape and did not know how soon it would be six o'clock and time for the meat-chopper to begin work. But the shaggy man was brave and did not intend to submit to such a horrid fate without a struggle.

"I'm going to fight for our lives," he whispered to the children, "for if I fail we will be no worse off than before, and to sit here quietly until we are made into soup would be foolish and cowardly."

The Scoodler on guard stood near the doorway, turning first his white side toward them and then his black side, as if he wanted to show to all of his greedy four eyes the sight of so many fat prisoners. The captives sat in a sorrowful group at the other end of the room—except Polychrome, who danced back and forth in the little place to keep herself warm, for she felt the chill of the cave. Whenever she approached the shaggy man he would whisper something in her ear, and Polly would nod her pretty head as if she understood.

The shaggy man told Dorothy and Button-Bright to stand before him while he emptied the potatoes out of one of the sacks. When this had been secretly done, little Polychrome, dancing near to the guard, suddenly reached out her hand and slapped his face, the next instant whirling away from him quickly to rejoin her friends.

The angry Scoodler at once picked off his head and hurled it at the Rainbow's Daughter; but the shaggy man was expecting that, and caught the head very neatly, putting it in the sack, which he tied at the mouth. The body of the guard, not having the eyes of its head to guide it, ran here and there in an aimless manner, and the shaggy man easily dodged it and opened the door. Fortunately there was no one in the big cave at that moment, so he told Dorothy and Polly to run as fast as they could for the entrance, and out across the narrow bridge.

"I'll carry Button-Bright," he said, for he knew the little boy's legs were too short to run fast.

Dorothy picked up Toto and then seized Polly's hand and ran swiftly toward the entrance to the cave. The shaggy man perched Button-Bright on his shoulders and ran after them. They moved so quickly and their escape was so wholly unexpected that they had almost reached the bridge when one of the Scoodlers looked out of his house and saw them.

The creature raised a shrill cry that brought all of its fellows bounding out of the numerous doors, and at once they started in chase. Dorothy and Polly had reached the bridge and crossed it when the Scoodlers began throwing their heads. One of the queer missiles struck the shaggy man on his back and nearly knocked him over; but he was at the mouth of the cave now, so he set down Button-Bright and told the boy to run across the bridge to Dorothy.

Then the shaggy man turned around and faced his enemies, standing just outside the opening, and as fast as they threw their heads at him he caught them and tossed them into the black gulf below. The headless bodies of the foremost Scoodlers kept the others from running close up, but they also threw their heads in an effort to stop the escaping prisoners. The shaggy man caught them all and sent them whirling down into the black gulf. Among them he noticed the crimson and yellow head of the Queen, and this he tossed after the others with right good will.

Presently every Scoodler of the lot had thrown its head, and every head was down in the deep gulf, and now the helpless bodies of the creatures were mixed together in the cave and wriggling around in a vain attempt to discover what had become of their heads. The shaggy man laughed and walked across the bridge to rejoin his companions.

"It's lucky I learned to play base-ball when I was young," he remarked, "for I caught all those heads easily and never missed one. But come along, little ones; the Scoodlers will never bother us or anyone else any more."

Button-Bright was still frightened and kept insisting, "I don't want to be soup!" for the victory had been gained so suddenly that the boy could not realize they were free and safe. But the shaggy man assured him that all danger of their being made into soup was now past, as the Scoodlers would be unable to eat soup for some time to come.

So now, anxious to get away from the horrid gloomy cave as soon as possible, they hastened up the hillside and regained the road just beyond the place where they had first met the Scoodlers; and you may be sure they were glad to find their feet on the old familiar path again.

Chapter 11

JOHNNY DOOIT DOES IT

I t's getting awful rough walking," said Dorothy, as they trudged along. Button-Bright gave a deep sigh and said he was hungry. Indeed, all were hungry, and thirsty, too; for they had eaten nothing but the apples since breakfast; so their steps lagged and they grew silent and weary. At last they slowly passed over the crest of a barren hill and saw before them a line of green trees with a strip of grass at their feet. An agreeable fragrance was wafted toward them.

Our travelers, hot and tired, ran forward on beholding this refreshing sight and were not long in coming to the trees. Here they found a spring of pure bubbling water, around which the grass was full of wild strawberry plants, their pretty red berries ripe and ready to eat. Some of the trees bore yellow oranges and some russet pears, so the hungry adventurers suddenly found themselves provided with plenty to eat and to drink.

They lost no time in picking the biggest strawberries and ripest oranges and soon had feasted to their hearts' content. Walking beyond the line of trees they saw before them a fearful, dismal desert, everywhere grey sand. At the edge of this awful waste was a large, white sign with black letters neatly painted upon it and the letters made these words:

ALL PERSONS ARE WARNED NOT TO
VENTURE UPON THIS DESERT
For the Deadly Sands will Turn Any Living
Flesh to Dust in an Instant. Beyond This
Barrier is the LAND OF OZ.
But no one can Reach that Beautiful Country
because of these Destroying Sands.

"Oh," said Dorothy, when the shaggy man had read the sign aloud; "I've seen this desert before, and it's true no one can live who tries to walk upon the sands."

"Then we musn't try it," answered the shaggy man thoughtfully. "But as we can't go ahead and there's no use going back, what shall we do next?"

"Don't know," said Button-Bright.

"I'm sure I don't know, either," added Dorothy, despondently.

"I wish father would come for me," sighed the pretty Rainbow's Daughter, "I would take you all to live upon the rainbow, where you could dance along its rays from morning till night, without a care or worry of any sort. But I suppose father's too busy just now to search the world for me."

"Don't want to dance," said Button-Bright, sitting down wearily upon the soft grass.

"It's very good of you, Polly," said Dorothy; "but there are other things that would suit me better than dancing on rainbows. I'm 'fraid they'd be kind of soft an' squnshy under foot, anyhow, although they're so pretty to look at."

This didn't help to solve the problem, and they all fell silent and looked at one another questioningly.

"Really, I don't know what to do," muttered the shaggy man, gazing hard at Toto; and the little dog wagged his tail and said "Bow-wow!" just as if he could not tell, either, what to do. Button-Bright got a stick and began to dig in the earth, and the others watched him for a while in deep thought. Finally, the shaggy man said:

"It's nearly evening, now; so we may as well sleep in this pretty place and get rested; perhaps by morning we can decide what is best to be done."

There was little chance to make beds for the children, but the leaves of the trees grew thickly and would serve to keep off the night dews, so the shaggy man piled soft grasses in the thickest shade and when it was dark they lay down and slept peacefully until morning.

Long after the others were asleep, however, the shaggy man sat in the starlight by the spring, gazing thoughtfully into its bubbling waters. Suddenly he smiled and nodded to himself as if he had found a good thought, after which he, too, laid himself down under a tree and was soon lost in slumber.

In the bright morning sunshine, as they ate of the strawberries and sweet juicy pears, Dorothy said:

"Polly, can you do any magic?"

"No, dear," answered Polychrome, shaking her dainty head.

"You ought to know *some* magic, being the Rainbow's Daughter," continued Dorothy, earnestly.

"But we who live on the rainbow among the fleecy clouds have no use for magic," replied Polychrome.

"What I'd like," said Dorothy, "is to find some way to cross the desert to the Land of Oz and its Emerald City. I've crossed it already, you know, more than once. First a cyclone carried my house over, and some Silver Shoes brought me back again—in half a second. Then Ozma took me over on her Magic Carpet, and the Nome King's Magic Belt took me home that time. You see it was magic that did it every time 'cept the first, and we can't 'spect a cyclone to happen along and take us to the Emerald City now."

"No, indeed," returned Polly, with a shudder, "I hate cyclones, anyway."

"That's why I wanted to find out if you could do any magic," said the little Kansas girl. "I'm sure I can't; and I'm sure Button-Bright can't; and the only magic the shaggy man has is the Love Magnet, which won't help us much."

"Don't be too sure of that, my dear," spoke the shaggy man, a smile on his donkey face. "I may not be able to do magic myself, but I can call to us a powerful friend who loves me because I own the Love Magnet, and this friend surely will be able to help us."

"Who is your friend?" asked Dorothy.

"Johnny Dooit."

"What can Johnny do?"

"Anything," answered the shaggy man, with confidence.

"Ask him to come," she exclaimed, eagerly.

The shaggy man took the Love Magnet from his pocket and unwrapped the paper that surrounded it. Holding the charm in the palm of his hand he looked at it steadily and said these words:

> *"Dear Johnny Dooit, come to me.*
> *I need you bad as bad can be."*

"Well, here I am," said a cheery little voice; "but you shouldn't say you need me bad, 'cause I'm always, *always*, good."

At this they quickly whirled around to find a funny little man sitting on a big copper chest, puffing smoke from a long pipe. His hair was grey, his whiskers were grey; and these whiskers were so long that he had wound the ends of them around his waist and tied them in a hard knot underneath the leather apron that reached from his chin nearly to his feet, and which was soiled and scratched as if it had been used a long time. His nose was broad, and stuck up a little; but his eyes were twinkling and merry. The little man's hands and arms were as hard and tough as the leather in his apron, and Dorothy thought Johnny Dooit looked as if he had done a lot of hard work in his lifetime.

"Good morning, Johnny," said the shaggy man. "Thank you for coming to me so quickly."

"I never waste time," said the newcomer, promptly. "But what's happened to you? Where did you get that donkey head? Really, I wouldn't have known you at all, Shaggy Man, if I hadn't looked at your feet."

The shaggy man introduced Johnny Dooit to Dorothy and Toto and Button-Bright and the Rainbow's Daughter, and told him the story of their adventures, adding that they were anxious now to reach the Emerald City in the Land of Oz, where Dorothy had friends who would take care of them and send them safe home again.

"But," said he, "we find that we can't cross this desert, which turns all living flesh that touches it into dust; so I have asked you to come and help us."

Johnny Dooit puffed his pipe and looked carefully at the dreadful desert in front of them—stretching so far away they could not see its end.

"You must ride," he said, briskly.

"What in?" asked the shaggy man.

"In a sand-boat, which has runners like a sled and sails like a ship. The wind will blow you swiftly across the desert and the sand cannot touch your flesh to turn it into dust."

"Good!" cried Dorothy, clapping her hands delightedly. "That was the way the Magic Carpet took us across. We didn't have to touch the horrid sand at all."

"But where is the sand-boat?" asked the shaggy man, looking all around him.

"I'll make you one," said Johnny Dooit.

As he spoke, he knocked the ashes from his pipe and put it in his pocket. Then he unlocked the copper chest and lifted the lid, and Dorothy saw it was full of shining tools of all sorts and shapes.

Johnny Dooit moved quickly now—so quickly that they were astonished at the work he was able to accomplish. He had in his chest a tool for everything he wanted to do, and these must have been magic tools because they did their work so fast and so well.

The man hummed a little song as he worked, and Dorothy tried to listen to it. She thought the words were something like these:

> *The only way to do a thing*
> *Is do it when you can,*
> *And do it cheerfully, and sing*
> *And work and think and plan.*
> *The only real unhappy one*
> *Is he who dares to shirk;*
> *The only really happy one*
> *Is he who cares to work.*

Whatever Johnny Dooit was singing he was certainly doing things, and they all stood by and watched him in amazement.

He seized an axe and in a couple of chops felled a tree. Next he took a saw and in a few minutes sawed the tree-trunk into broad long boards. He then nailed the boards together into the shape of a boat, about twelve feet long and four feet wide. He cut from another tree a long, slender pole which, when trimmed of its branches and fastened upright in the center of the boat, served as a mast. From the chest he drew a coil of rope and a big bundle of canvas, and with these—still humming his song—he rigged up a sail, arranging it so it could be raised or lowered upon the mast.

Dorothy fairly gasped with wonder to see the thing grow so speedily before her eyes, and both Button-Bright and Polly looked on with the same absorbed interest.

"It ought to be painted," said Johnny Dooit, tossing his tools back into the chest, "for that would make it look prettier.

But 'though I can paint it for you in three seconds it would take an hour to dry, and that's a waste of time."

"We don't care how it looks," said the shaggy man, "if only it will take us across the desert."

"It will do that," declared Johnny Dooit. "All you need worry about is tipping over. Did you ever sail a ship?"

"I've seen one sailed," said the shaggy man.

"Good. Sail this boat the way you've seen a ship sailed, and you'll be across the sands before you know it."

With this he slammed down the lid of the chest, and the noise made them all wink. While they were winking the workman disappeared, tools and all.

Chapter 12

The DEADLY DESERT CROSSED

O h, that's too bad!" cried Dorothy; "I wanted to thank Johnny Dooit for all his kindness to us."

"He hasn't time to listen to thanks," replied the shaggy man; "but I'm sure he knows we are grateful. I suppose he is already at work in some other part of the world."

They now looked more carefully at the sand-boat, and saw that the bottom was modelled with two sharp runners which would glide through the sand. The front of the sand-boat was pointed like the bow of a ship, and there was a rudder at the stern to steer by.

It had been built just at the edge of the desert, so that all its length lay upon the grey sand except the after part, which still rested on the strip of grass.

"Get in, my dears," said the shaggy man; "I'm sure I can manage this boat as well as any sailor. All you need do is sit still in your places."

Dorothy got in, Toto in her arms, and sat on the bottom of the boat just in front of the mast. Button-Bright sat in front of Dorothy, while Polly leaned over the bow. The shaggy man knelt behind the mast. When all were ready he raised the sail half way. The wind caught it. At once the sand-boat started forward—slowly at first, then with added speed. The shaggy man pulled the sail way up, and they flew so fast over the deadly desert that every one held fast to the sides of the boat and scarcely dared to breathe.

The sand lay in billows, and was in places very uneven, so that the boat rocked dangerously from side to side; but it never quite tipped over, and the speed was so great that the shaggy man himself became frightened and began to wonder how he could make the ship go slower.

"It we're spilled in this sand, in the middle of the desert," Dorothy thought to herself, "we'll be nothing but dust in a few minutes, and that will be the end of us."

But they were not spilled, and by-and-by Polychrome, who was clinging to the bow and looking straight ahead, saw a dark line before them and wondered what it was. It grew plainer every second, until she discovered it to be a row of jagged rocks at the end of the desert, while high above these rocks she could see a tableland of green grass and beautiful trees.

"Look out!" she screamed to the shaggy man. "Go slowly, or we shall smash into the rocks."

He heard her, and tried to pull down the sail; but the wind would not let go of the broad canvas and the ropes had become tangled.

Nearer and nearer they drew to the great rocks, and the shaggy man was in despair because he could do nothing to stop the wild rush of the sand-boat.

They reached the edge of the desert and bumped squarely into the rocks. There was a crash as Dorothy, Button-Bright, Toto and Polly flew up in the air in a curve like a skyrocket's, one after another landing high upon the grass, where they rolled and tumbled for a time before they could stop themselves.

The shaggy man flew after them, head first, and lighted in a heap beside Toto, who, being much excited at the time, seized one of the donkey ears between his teeth and shook and worried it as hard as he could, growling angrily. The shaggy man made the little dog let go, and sat up to look around him.

Dorothy was feeling one of her front teeth, which was loosened by knocking against her knee as she fell. Polly was looking sorrowfully at a rent in her pretty gauze gown, and Button-Bright's fox head had stuck fast in a gopher hole and he was wiggling his little fat legs frantically in an effort to get free.

Otherwise they were unhurt by the adventure; so the shaggy man stood up and pulled Button-Bright out of the hole and went to the edge of the desert to look at the sand-boat. It was a mere mass of splinters now, crushed out of shape against the rocks. The wind had torn away the sail and carried it to the top of a tall tree, where the fragments of it fluttered like a white flag.

"Well," he said, cheerfully, "we're here; but where the here is I don't know."

"It must be some part of the Land of Oz," observed Dorothy, coming to his side.

"Must it?"

"'Course it must. We're across the desert, aren't we? And somewhere in the middle of Oz is the Emerald City."

"To be sure," said the shaggy man, nodding. "Let's go there."

"But I don't see any people about, to show us the way," she continued.

"Let's hunt for them," he suggested. "There must be people somewhere; but perhaps they did not expect us, and so are not at hand to give us a welcome."

Chapter 13

The TRUTH POND

They now made a more careful examination of the country around them. All was fresh and beautiful after the sultriness of the desert, and the sunshine and sweet, crisp air were delightful to the wanderers. Little mounds of yellowish green were away at the right, while on the left waved a group of tall leafy trees bearing yellow blossoms that looked like tassels and pompoms. Among the grasses carpeting the ground were pretty buttercups and cowslips and marigolds. After looking at these a moment Dorothy said reflectively:

"We must be in the Country of the Winkies, for the color of that country is yellow, and you will notice that 'most everything here is yellow that has any color at all."

"But I thought this was the Land of Oz," replied the shaggy man, as if greatly disappointed.

"So it is," she declared; "but there are four parts to the Land of Oz. The North Country is purple, and it's the Country of the Gillikins. The East Country is blue, and that's the Country of the Munchkins. Down at the South is the red Country of the Quadlings, and here, in the West, the yellow Country of the Winkies. This is the part that is ruled by the Tin Woodman, you know."

"Who's he?" asked Button-Bright.

"Why, he's the tin man I told you about. His name is Nick Chopper, and he has a lovely heart given him by the wonderful Wizard."

"Where does *he* live?" asked the boy.

"The Wizard? Oh, he lives in the Emerald City, which is just in the middle of Oz, where the corners of the four countries meet."

"Oh," said Button-Bright, puzzled by this explanation.

"We must be some distance from the Emerald City," remarked the shaggy man.

"That's true," she replied; "so we'd better start on and see if we can find any of the Winkies. They're nice people," she continued, as the little party began walking toward the group of trees, "and I came here once with my friends the Scarecrow, and the Tin Woodman, and the Cowardly Lion, to fight a wicked witch who had made all the Winkies her slaves."

"Did you conquer her?" asked Polly.

"Why, I melted her with a bucket of water, and that was the end of her," replied Dorothy. "After that the people were free, you know, and they made Nick Chopper—that's the Tin Woodman—their Emp'ror."

"What's that?" asked Button-Bright.

"Emp'ror? Oh, it's something like an alderman, I guess."

"Oh," said the boy.

"But I thought Princess Ozma ruled Oz," said the shaggy man.

"So she does; she rules the Emerald City and all the four countries of Oz; but each country has another little Ruler, not so big as Ozma. It's like the officers of an army, you see; the little rulers are all captains, and Ozma's the general."

By this time they had reached the trees, which stood in a perfect circle and just far enough apart so that their thick branches touched—or "shook hands," as Button-Bright remarked. Under the shade of the trees they found, in the center of the circle, a crystal pool, its water as still as glass. It must have been deep, too, for when Polychrome bent over it she gave a little sigh of pleasure.

"Why, it's a mirror!" she cried; for she could see all her pretty face and fluffy, rainbow-tinted gown reflected in the pool, as natural as life.

Dorothy bent over, too, and began to arrange her hair,

blown by the desert wind into straggling tangles. Button-Bright leaned over the edge next, and then began to cry, for the sight of his fox head frightened the poor little fellow.

"I guess I won't look," remarked the shaggy man, sadly, for he didn't like his donkey head, either. While Polly and Dorothy tried to comfort Button-Bright, the shaggy man sat down near the edge of the pool, where his image could not be reflected, and stared at the water thoughtfully. As he did this he noticed a silver plate fastened to a rock just under the surface of the water, and on the silver plate was engraved these words:

THE TRUTH POND

"Ah!" cried the shaggy man, springing to his feet with eager joy; "we've found it at last."

"Found what?" asked Dorothy, running to him.

"The Truth Pond. Now, at last, I may get rid of this frightful head; for we were told, you remember, that only the Truth Pond could restore to me my proper face."

"Me, too!" shouted Button-Bright, trotting up to them.

"Of course," said Dorothy. "It will cure you both of your bad heads, I guess. Isn't it lucky we found it?"

"It is, indeed," replied the shaggy man. "I hated dreadfully to go to Princess Ozma looking like this; and she's to have a birthday celebration, too."

Just then a splash startled them, for Button-Bright, in his

anxiety to see the pool that would "cure" him, had stepped too near the edge and tumbled heels over head into the water. Down he went, out of sight entirely, so that only his sailor hat floated on the top of the Truth Pond.

He soon bobbed up, and the shaggy man seized him by his sailor collar and dragged him to the shore, dripping and gasping for breath. They all looked upon the boy wonderingly, for the fox head with its sharp nose and pointed ears was gone, and in its place appeared the chubby round face and blue eyes and pretty curls that had belonged to Button-Bright before King Dox of Foxville transformed him.

"Oh, what a darling!" cried Polly, and would have hugged the little one had he not been so wet.

Their joyful exclamations made the child rub the water out of his eyes and look at his friends questioningly.

"You're all right now, dear," said Dorothy. "Come and look at yourself." She led him to the pool, and although there were still a few ripples on the surface of the water he could see his reflection plainly.

"It's me!" he said, in a pleased yet awed whisper.

"'Course it is," replied the girl, "and we're all as glad as you are, Button-Bright."

"Well," announced the shaggy man, "it's my turn next." He took off his shaggy coat and laid it on the grass and dived head first into the Truth Pond.

When he came up the donkey head had disappeared, and

the shaggy man's own shaggy head was in its place, with the water dripping in little streams from his shaggy whiskers. He scrambled ashore and shook himself to get off some of the wet, and then leaned over the pool to look admiringly at his reflected face.

"I may not be strictly beautiful, even now," he said to his companions, who watched him with smiling faces; "but I'm so much handsomer than any donkey that I feel as proud as I can be."

"You're all right, Shaggy Man," declared Dorothy. "And Button-Bright is all right, too. So let's thank the Truth Pond for being so nice, and start on our journey to the Emerald City."

"I hate to leave it," murmured the shaggy man, with a sigh. "A truth pond wouldn't be a bad thing to carry around with us." But he put on his coat and started with the others in search of some one to direct them on their way.

Chapter 14

TIK-TOK and BILLINA

They had not walked far across the flower-strewn meadows when they came upon a fine road leading toward the northwest and winding gracefully among the pretty yellow hills.

"That way," said Dorothy, "must be the direction of the Emerald City. We'd better follow the road until we meet some one or come to a house."

The sun soon dried Button-Bright's sailor suit and the shaggy man's shaggy clothes, and so pleased were they at regaining their own heads that they did not mind at all the brief discomfort of getting wet.

"It's good to be able to whistle again," remarked the shaggy man, "for those donkey lips were so thick I could not whistle a note with them." He warbled a tune as merrily as any bird.

"You'll look more natural at the birthday celebration, too," said Dorothy, happy in seeing her friends so happy.

Polychrome was dancing ahead in her usual sprightly manner, whirling gaily along the smooth, level road, until she passed from sight around the curve of one of the mounds. Suddenly they heard her exclaim "Oh!" and she appeared again, running toward them at full speed.

"What's the matter, Polly?" asked Dorothy, perplexed.

There was no need for the Rainbow's Daughter to answer, for turning the bend in the road there came advancing slowly toward them a funny round man made of burnished copper, gleaming brightly in the sun. Perched on the copper man's shoulder sat a yellow hen, with fluffy feathers and a pearl necklace around her throat.

"Oh, Tik-Tok!" cried Dorothy, running forward. When she came to him, the copper man lifted the little girl in his copper arms and kissed her cheek with his copper lips.

"Oh, Billina!" cried Dorothy, in a glad voice, and the yellow hen flew to her arms, to be hugged and petted by turns.

The others were curiously crowding around the group, and the girl said to them:

"It's Tik-Tok and Billina; and oh! I'm so glad to see them again."

"Wel-come to Oz," said the copper man in a monotonous voice.

Dorothy sat right down in the road, the yellow hen in her arms, and began to stroke Billina's back. Said the hen:

"Dorothy, dear, I've got some wonderful news to tell you."

"Tell it quick, Billina!" said the girl.

Just then Toto, who had been growling to himself in a cross way, gave a sharp bark and flew at the yellow hen, who ruffled her feathers and let out such an angry screech that Dorothy was startled.

"Stop, Toto! Stop that this minute!" she commanded. "Can't you see that Billina is my friend?" In spite of this warning had she not grabbed Toto quickly by the neck the little dog would have done the yellow hen a mischief, and even now he struggled madly to escape Dorothy's grasp. She slapped his ears once or twice and told him to behave, and the yellow hen flew to Tik-Tok's shoulder again, where she was safe.

"What a brute!" croaked Billina, glaring down at the little dog.

"Toto isn't a brute," replied Dorothy, "but at home Uncle Henry has to whip him sometimes for chasing the chickens. Now, look here, Toto," she added, holding up her finger and speaking sternly to him, "you've got to understand that Billina is one of my dearest friends, and musn't be hurt—now or ever."

Toto wagged his tail as if he understood.

"The miserable thing can't talk," said Billina, with a sneer.

"Yes, he can," replied Dorothy; "he talks with his tail, and I know everything he says. If you could wag your tail, Billina, you wouldn't need words to talk with."

"Nonsense!" said Billina.

"It isn't nonsense at all. Just now Toto says he's sorry, and that he'll try to love you for my sake. Don't you, Toto?"

"Bow-wow!" said Toto, wagging his tail again.

"But I've such wonderful news for you, Dorothy," cried the yellow hen; "I've—"

"Wait a minute, dear," interrupted the little girl; "I've got to introduce you all, first. That's manners, Billina. This," turning to her traveling companions, "is Mr. Tik-Tok, who works by machinery, 'cause his thoughts wind up, and his talk winds up, and his action winds up—like a clock."

"Do they all wind up together?" asked the shaggy man.

"No; each one separate. But he works just lovely, and Tik-Tok was a good friend to me once, and saved my life—and Billina's life, too."

"Is he alive?" asked Button-Bright, looking hard at the copper man.

"Oh, no, but his machinery makes him just as good as alive." She turned to the copper man and said politely: "Mr. Tik-Tok, these are my new friends: the shaggy man, and Polly the Rainbow's Daughter, and Button-Bright, and Toto. Only Toto isn't a new friend, 'cause he's been to Oz before."

The copper man bowed low, removing his copper hat as he did so.

"I'm ve-ry pleased to meet Dor-o-thy's fr-r-r-r-r—" Here he stopped short.

"Oh, I guess his speech needs winding!" said the little girl, running behind the copper man to get the key off a hook at his back. She wound him up at a place under his right arm and he went on to say:

"Par-don me for run-ning down. I was a-bout to say I am pleased to meet Dor-o-thy's friends, who must be my friends." The words were somewhat jerky, but plain to understand.

"And this is Billina," continued Dorothy, introducing the yellow hen, and they all bowed to her in turn.

"I've such wonderful news," said the hen, turning her head so that one bright eye looked full at Dorothy.

"What is it, dear?" asked the girl.

"I've hatched out ten of the loveliest chicks you ever saw."

"Oh, how nice! And where are they, Billina?"

"I left them at home. But they're beauties, I assure you, and all wonderfully clever. I've named them Dorothy."

"Which one?" asked the girl.

"All of them," replied Billina.

"That's funny. Why did you name them all with the same name?"

"It was so hard to tell them apart," explained the hen. "Now, when I call 'Dorothy,' they all come running to me in a

bunch; it's much easier, after all, than having a separate name
for each."

"I'm just dying to see 'em, Billina," said Dorothy, eagerly.
"But tell me, my friends, how did you happen to be here, in the
Country of the Winkies, the first of all to meet us?"

"I'll tell you," answered Tik-Tok, in his monotonous voice,
all the sounds of his words being on one level— "Prin-cess
Oz-ma saw you in her mag-ic pic-ture, and knew you were
com-ing here; so she sent Bil-lin-a and me to wel-come you as
she could not come her-self; so that—fiz-i-dig-le cum-so-lut-
ing hy-ber-gob-ble in-tu-zib-ick—"

"Good gracious! Whatever's the matter now?" cried
Dorothy, as the copper man continued to babble these unmean-
ing words, which no one could understand at all because they
had no sense.

"Don't know," said Button-Bright, who was half scared.
Polly whirled away to a distance and turned to look at the
copper man in a fright.

"His thoughts have run down, this time," remarked Billina
composedly, as she sat on Tik-Tok's shoulder and pruned her
sleek feathers. "When he can't think, he can't talk properly,
any more than you can. You'll have to wind up his thoughts,
Dorothy, or else I'll have to finish his story myself."

Dorothy ran around and got the key again and wound up
Tik-Tok under his left arm, after which he could speak plainly
again.

"Par-don me," he said, "but when my thoughts run down, my speech has no mean-ing, for words are formed on-ly by thought. I was a-bout to say that Oz-ma sent us to wel-come you and in-vite you to come straight to the Em-er-ald Ci-ty. She was too bus-y to come her-self, for she is pre-par-ing for her birth-day cel-e-bra-tion, which is to be a grand af-fair."

"I've heard of it," said Dorothy, "and I'm glad we've come in time to attend. Is it far from here to the Emerald City?"

"Not ve-ry far," answered Tik-Tok, "and we have plen-ty of time. To-night we will stop at the pal-ace of the Tin Wood-man, and to-mor-row night we will ar-rive at the Em-er-ald Ci-ty."

"Goody!" cried Dorothy. "I'd like to see dear Nick Chopper again. How's his heart?"

"It's fine," said Billina; "the Tin Woodman says it gets softer and kindlier every day. He's waiting at his castle to welcome you, Dorothy; but he couldn't come with us because he's getting polished as bright as possible for Ozma's party."

"Well, then," said Dorothy, "let's start on, and we can talk more as we go."

They proceeded on their journey in a friendly group, for Polychrome had discovered that the copper man was harmless and was no longer afraid of him. Button-Bright was also reassured, and took quite a fancy to Tik-Tok. He wanted the clockwork man to open himself, so that he might see the wheels go round; but that was a thing Tik-Tok could not do.

Button-Bright then wanted to wind up the copper man, and Dorothy promised he should do so as soon as any part of the machinery ran down. This pleased Button-Bright, who held fast to one of Tik-Tok's copper hands as he trudged along the road, while Dorothy walked on the other side of her old friend and Billina perched by turns upon his shoulder or his copper hat. Polly once more joyously danced ahead and Toto ran after her, barking with glee. The shaggy man was left to walk behind; but he didn't seem to mind that a bit, and whistled merrily or looked curiously upon the pretty scenes they passed.

At last they came to a hilltop from which the tin castle of Nick Chopper could plainly be seen, its towers glistening magnificently under the rays of the declining sun.

"How pretty!" exclaimed Dorothy. "I've never seen the Emp'ror's new house before."

"He built it because the old castle was damp, and likely to rust his tin body," said Billina. "All those towers and steeples and domes and gables took a lot of tin, as you can see."

"Is it a toy?" asked Button-Bright softly.

"No, dear," answered Dorothy; "it's better than that. It's the fairy dwelling of a fairy prince."

Chapter 15

The EMPEROR'S TIN CASTLE

The grounds around Nick Chopper's new house were laid out in pretty flower-beds, with fountains of crystal water and statues of tin representing the Emperor's personal friends. Dorothy was astonished and delighted to find a tin statue of herself standing on a tin pedestal at a bend in the avenue leading up to the entrance. It was life-size and showed her in her sunbonnet with her basket on her arm, just as she had first appeared in the Land of Oz.

"Oh, Toto—you're there too!" she exclaimed; and sure enough there was the tin figure of Toto lying at the tin Dorothy's feet.

Also, Dorothy saw figures of the Scarecrow, and the Wizard, and Ozma, and of many others, including Tik-Tok. They reached the grand tin entrance to the tin castle, and the Tin Woodman himself came running out of the door to embrace little Dorothy and give her a glad welcome. He welcomed her friends as well, and the Rainbow's Daughter he declared to be the loveliest vision his tin eyes had ever beheld. He patted Button-Bright's curly head tenderly, for he was fond of children, and turned to the shaggy man and shook both his hands at the same time.

Nick Chopper, the Emperor of the Winkies, who was also known throughout the Land of Oz as the Tin Woodman, was certainly a remarkable person. He was neatly made, all of tin, nicely soldered at the joints, and his various limbs were cleverly hinged to his body so that he could use them nearly as well as if they had been common flesh. Once, he told the shaggy man, he had been made all of flesh and bones, as other people are, and then he chopped wood in the forests to earn his living. But the axe slipped so often and cut off parts of him—which he had replaced with tin—that finally there was no flesh left, nothing but tin; so he became a real tin woodman. The wonderful Wizard of Oz had given him an excellent heart to replace his old one, and he didn't at all mind being tin. Every one loved him, he loved every one; and he was therefore as happy as the day was long.

The Emperor was proud of his new tin castle, and showed

his visitors through all the rooms. Every bit of the furniture was made of brightly polished tin—the tables, chairs, beds, and all—even the floors and walls were of tin.

"I suppose," said he, "that there are no cleverer tinsmiths in all the world than the Winkies. It would be hard to match this castle in Kansas; wouldn't it, little Dorothy?"

"Very hard," replied the child, gravely.

"It must have cost a lot of money," remarked the shaggy man.

"Money! Money in Oz!" cried the Tin Woodman. "What a queer idea! Did you suppose we are so vulgar as to use money here?"

"Why not?" asked the shaggy man.

"If we used money to buy things with, instead of love and kindness and the desire to please one another, then we should be no better than the rest of the world," declared the Tin Woodman. "Fortunately money is not known in the Land of Oz at all. We have no rich, and no poor; for what one wishes the others all try to give him, in order to make him happy, and no one in all Oz cares to have more than he can use."

"Good!" cried the shaggy man, greatly pleased to hear this. "I also despise money—a man in Butterfield owes me fifteen cents, and I will not take it from him. The Land of Oz is surely the most favored land in all the world, and its people the happiest. I should like to live here always."

The Tin Woodman listened with respectful attention.

Already he loved the shaggy man, although he did not yet know of the Love Magnet. So he said:

"If you can prove to the Princess Ozma that you are honest and true and worthy of our friendship, you may indeed live here all your days, and be as happy as we are."

"I'll try to prove that," said the shaggy man, earnestly.

"And now," continued the Emperor, "you must all go to your rooms and prepare for dinner, which will presently be served in the grand tin dining-hall. I am sorry, Shaggy Man, that I can not offer you a change of clothing; but I dress only in tin, myself, and I suppose that would not suit you."

"I care little about dress," said the shaggy man, indifferently.

"So I should imagine," replied the Emperor, with true politeness.

They were shown to their rooms and permitted to make such toilets as they could, and soon they assembled again in the grand tin dining-hall, even Toto being present. For the Emperor was fond of Dorothy's little dog, and the girl explained to her friends that in Oz all animals were treated with as much consideration as the people—"if they behave themselves," she added.

Toto behaved himself, and sat in a tin high-chair beside Dorothy and ate his dinner from a tin platter.

Indeed, they all ate from tin dishes, but these were of pretty shapes and brightly polished; Dorothy thought they were just as good as silver.

Button-Bright looked curiously at the man who had "no appetite inside him," for the Tin Woodman, although he had prepared so fine a feast for his guests, ate not a mouthful himself, sitting patiently in his place to see that all built so they could eat were well and plentifully served.

What pleased Button-Bright most about the dinner was the tin orchestra that played sweet music while the company ate. The players were not tin, being just ordinary Winkies; but the instruments they played upon were all tin—tin trumpets, tin fiddles, tin drums and cymbals and flutes and horns and all. They played so nicely the "Shining Emperor Waltz," composed expressly in honor of the Tin Woodman by Mr. H. M. Woggle-Bug, T.E., that Polly could not resist dancing to it. After she had tasted a few dewdrops, freshly gathered for her, she danced gracefully to the music while the others finished their repast; and when she whirled until her fleecy draperies of rainbow hues enveloped her like a cloud, the Tin Woodman was so delighted that he clapped his tin hands until the noise of them drowned the sound of the cymbals.

Altogether it was a merry meal, although Polychrome ate little and the host nothing at all.

"I'm sorry the Rainbow's Daughter missed her mist-cakes," said the Tin Woodman to Dorothy; "but by a mistake Miss Polly's mist-cakes were mislaid and not missed until now. I'll try to have some for her breakfast."

They spent the evening telling stories, and the next morning left the splendid tin castle and set out upon the road to the Emerald City. The Tin Woodman went with them, of course, having by this time been so brightly polished that he sparkled like silver. His axe, which he always carried with him, had a steel blade that was tin plated and a handle covered with tin plate beautifully engraved and set with diamonds.

The Winkies assembled before the castle gates and cheered their Emperor as he marched away, and it was easy to see that they all loved him dearly.

Chapter 16

VISITING the PUMPKIN-FIELD

Dorothy let Button-Bright wind up the clock-work in the copper man this morning—his thinking machine first, then his speech, and finally his action; so he would doubt-less run perfectly until they had reached the Emerald City. The copper man and the tin man were good friends, and not so much alike as you might think. For one was alive and the other moved by means of machinery; one was tall and angular and the other short and round. You could love the Tin Woodman because he had a fine nature, kindly and simple; but the machine man you could only admire without loving, since to love such a thing as

he was as impossible as to love a sewing-machine or an auto-
mobile. Yet Tik-Tok was popular with the people of Oz because
he was so trustworthy, reliable and true; he was sure to do
exactly what he was wound up to do, at all times and in all circumstances. Perhaps it is better to be a machine that does its
duty than a flesh-and-blood person who will not, for a dead
truth is better than a live falsehood.

About noon the travelers reached a large field of pumpkins—a
vegetable quite appropriate to the yellow country of the Winkies—
and some of the pumpkins which grew there were of remarkable
size. Just before they entered upon this field they saw three little
mounds that looked like graves, with a pretty headstone to each
one of them.

"What is this?" asked Dorothy, in wonder.

"It's Jack Pumpkinhead's private graveyard," replied the
Tin Woodman.

"But I thought nobody ever died in Oz," she said.

"Nor do they; although if one is bad, he may be condemned
and killed by the good citizens," he answered.

Dorothy ran over to the little graves and read the words
engraved upon the tombstones. The first one said:

Here Lies the Mortal Part of
JACK PUMPKINHEAD
Which Spoiled April 9th.

She then went to the next stone, which read:

Here Lies the Mortal Part of
JACK PUMPKINHEAD
Which Spoiled October 2nd.

On the third stone were carved these words:

Here Lies the Mortal Part of
JACK PUMPKINHEAD
Which Spoiled January 24th.

"Poor Jack!" sighed Dorothy. "I'm sorry he had to die in three parts, for I hoped to see him again."

"So you shall," declared the Tin Woodman, "since he is still alive. Come with me to his house, for Jack is now a farmer and lives in this very pumpkin field."

They walked over to a monstrous big, hollow pumpkin which had a door and windows cut through the rind. There was a stovepipe running through the stem, and six steps had been built leading up to the front door.

They walked up to this door and looked in. Seated on a bench was a man clothed in a spotted shirt, a red vest, and faded blue trousers, whose body was merely sticks of wood, jointed clumsily together. On his neck was set a round, yellow pumpkin, with a face carved on it such as a boy often carves on a jack-lantern.

This queer man was engaged in snapping slippery pumpkin-seeds with his wooden fingers, trying to hit a target on the other side of the room with them. He did not know he had visitors until Dorothy exclaimed:

"Why, it's Jack Pumpkinhead himself!"

He turned and saw them, and at once came forward to greet the little Kansas girl and Nick Chopper, and to be introduced to their new friends.

Button-Bright was at first rather shy with the quaint Pumpkinhead, but Jack's face was so jolly and smiling—being carved that way—that the boy soon grew to like him.

"I thought a while ago that you were buried in three parts," said Dorothy, "but now I see you're just the same as ever."

"Not quite the same, my dear, for my mouth is a little more one-sided than it used to be; but pretty nearly the same. I've a new head, and this is the fourth one I've owned since Ozma first made me and brought me to life by sprinkling me with the Magic Powder."

"What became of the other heads, Jack?"

"They spoiled and I buried them, for they were not even fit for pies. Each time Ozma has carved me a new head just like the old one, and as my body is by far the largest part of me, I am still Jack Pumpkinhead, no matter how often I change my upper end. Once we had a dreadful time to find another pumpkin, as they were out of season, and so I was obliged to wear my old head a little longer than was strictly healthy. But after this sad experience I resolved to raise pumpkins myself, so as never to be caught again without one handy; and now I have this fine field that you see before you. Some grow pretty big—too big to be used for heads—so I dug out this one and use it for a house."

"Isn't it damp?" asked Dorothy.

"Not very. There isn't much left but the shell, you see, and it will last a long time yet."

"I think you are brighter than you used to be, Jack," said the Tin Woodman. "Your last head was a stupid one."

"The seeds in this one are better," was the reply.

"Are you going to Ozma's party?" asked Dorothy.

"Yes," said he, "I wouldn't miss it for anything. Ozma's my parent, you know, because she built my body and carved my pumpkin head. I'll follow you to the Emerald City to-morrow, where we shall meet again. I can't go to-day, because I have to plant fresh pumpkin-seeds and water the young vines. But give my love to Ozma, and tell her I'll be there in time for the jubilation."

"We will," she promised; and then they all left him and resumed their journey.

· Chapter 17 ·

The ROYAL CHARIOT ARRIVES

The neat yellow houses of the Winkies were now to be seen standing here and there along the roadway, giving the country a more cheerful and civilized look. They were farm-houses, though, and set far apart; for in the Land of Oz there were no towns or villages except the magnificent Emerald City in its center.

Hedges of evergreen or of yellow roses bordered the broad highway and the farms showed the care of their industrious inhabitants. The nearer the travelers came to the great city the more prosperous the country became, and they crossed many bridges over the sparkling streams and rivulets that watered the lands.

As they walked leisurely along the shaggy man said to the Tin Woodman:

"What sort of a Magic Powder was it, that made your friend the Pumpkinhead live?"

"It was called the Powder of Life," was the answer; "and it was invented by a crooked Sorcerer who lived in the mountains of the North Country. A Witch named Mombi got some of this powder from the crooked Sorcerer and took it home with her. Ozma lived with the Witch then, for it was before she became our Princess, while Mombi had transformed her into the shape of a boy. Well, while Mombi was gone to the crooked Sorcerer's, the boy made this pumpkin-headed man to amuse himself, and also with the hope of frightening the Witch with it when she returned. But Mombi was not scared, and she sprinkled the Pumpkinhead with her Magic Powder of Life, to see if the Powder would work. Ozma was watching, and saw the Pumpkinhead come to life; so that night she took the pepper-box containing the Powder and ran away with it and with Jack, in search of adventures.

"Next day they found a wooden Sawhorse standing by the roadside, and sprinkled it with the Powder. It came to life at once, and Jack Pumpkinhead rode the Sawhorse to the Emerald City."

"What became of the Sawhorse, afterward?" asked the shaggy man, much interested in this story.

"Oh, it's alive yet, and you will probably meet it presently in the Emerald City. Afterward Ozma used the last of the Powder to bring the Flying Gump to life; but as soon as it had carried her away from her enemies the Gump was taken apart, so it doesn't exist any more."

"It's too bad the Powder of Life was all used up," remarked the shaggy man; "it would be a handy thing to have around."

"I am not so sure of that, sir," answered the Tin Woodman. "A while ago the crooked Sorcerer who invented the magic Powder fell down a precipice and was killed. All his possessions went to a relative—an old woman named Dyna, who lives in the Emerald City. She went to the mountains where the Sorcerer had lived and brought away everything she thought of value. Among them was a small bottle of the Powder of Life; but of course Dyna didn't know it was a magic Powder, at all. It happened she had once had a big blue bear for a pet; but the bear choked to death on a fishbone one day, and she loved it so dearly that Dyna made a rug of its skin, leaving the head and four paws on the hide. She kept the rug on the floor of her front parlor."

"I've seen rugs like that," said the shaggy man, nodding, "but never one made from a blue bear."

"Well," continued the Tin Woodman, "the old woman had an idea that the Powder in the bottle must be moth-powder, because it smelled something like moth-powder; so one day she sprinkled it on her bear rug to keep the moths out of it. She said, looking lovingly at the skin: 'I wish my dear bear were alive again!' To her horror, the bear rug at once came to life, having been sprinkled with the magic Powder; and now this live bear rug is a great trial to her, and makes her a lot of trouble."

"Why?" asked the shaggy man.

"Well, it stands up on its four feet and walks all around, and gets in the way; and that spoils it for a rug. It can't speak, although it is alive; for, while its head might say words, it has no breath in a solid body to push the words out of its mouth. It's a very slimpsy affair altogether, that bear rug, and the old woman is sorry it came to life. Every day she has to scold it, and make it lie down flat on the parlor floor to be walked upon; but sometimes when she goes to market the rug will hump up its back skin, and stand on its four feet, and trot along after her."

"I should think Dyna would like that," said Dorothy.

"Well, she doesn't; because every one knows it isn't a real bear, but just a hollow skin, and so of no actual use in the world except for a rug," answered the Tin Woodman. "Therefore I believe it is a good thing that all the magic Powder of Life is now used up, as it cannot cause any more trouble."

"Perhaps you're right," said the shaggy man, thoughtfully.

At noon they stopped at a farm-house, where it delighted the farmer and his wife to be able to give them a good luncheon. The farm people knew Dorothy, having seen her when she was in the country before, and they treated the little girl with as much respect as they did the Emperor, because she was a friend of the powerful Princess Ozma.

They had not proceeded far after leaving this farm-house before coming to a high bridge over a broad river. This river, the Tin Woodman informed them, was the boundary between the Country of the Winkies and the territory of the Emerald City. The city itself was still a long way off, but all around it was a green meadow, as pretty as a well-kept lawn, and in this were neither houses nor farms to spoil the beauty of the scene.

From the top of the high bridge they could see far away the magnificent spires and splendid domes of the superb city, sparkling like brilliant jewels as they towered above the emerald walls. The shaggy man drew a deep breath of awe and amazement, for never had he dreamed that such a grand and beautiful place could exist—even in the fairyland of Oz.

Polly was so pleased that her violet eyes sparkled like amethysts, and she danced away from her companions across the bridge and into a group of feathery trees lining both the roadsides. These trees she stopped to look at with pleasure and surprise, for their leaves were shaped like ostrich plumes, their feather edges beautifully curled; and all the plumes were tinted in the same dainty rainbow hues that appeared in Polychrome's own pretty gauze gown.

"Father ought to see these trees," she murmured; "they are almost as lovely as his own rainbows."

Then she gave a start of terror, for beneath the trees came

stalking two great beasts, either one big enough to crush the little Daughter of the Rainbow with one blow of his paws, or to eat her up with one snap of his enormous jaws. One was a tawny lion, as tall as a horse, nearly; the other a striped tiger almost the same size.

Polly was too frightened to scream or to stir; she stood still with a wildly beating heart until Dorothy rushed past her and with a glad cry threw her arms around the huge lion's neck, hugging and kissing the beast with evident joy.

"Oh, I'm *so* glad to see you again!" cried the little Kansas girl. "And the Hungry Tiger, too! How fine you're both looking. Are you well and happy?"

"We certainly are, Dorothy," answered the Lion, in a deep voice that sounded pleasant and kind; "and we are greatly pleased that you have come to Ozma's party. It's going to be a grand affair, I promise you."

"There will be lots of fat babies at the celebration, I hear," remarked the Hungry Tiger, yawning so that his mouth opened dreadfully wide and showed all his big, sharp teeth; "but of course I can't eat any of 'em."

"Is your Conscience still in good order?" asked Dorothy, anxiously.

"Yes; it rules me like a tyrant," answered the Tiger, sorrowfully. "I can imagine nothing more unpleasant than to own a Conscience," and he winked slyly at his friend the Lion.

"You're fooling me!" said Dorothy, with a laugh. "I don't

b'lieve you'd eat a baby if you lost your Conscience. Come here, Polly," she called, "and be introduced to my friends."

Polly advanced rather shyly.

"You have some queer friends, Dorothy," she said.

"The queerness doesn't matter, so long as they're friends," was the answer. "This is the Cowardly Lion, who isn't a coward at all, but just thinks he is. The Wizard gave him some courage once, and he has part of it left."

The Lion bowed with great dignity to Polly.

"You are very lovely, my dear," said he. "I hope we shall be friends when we are better acquainted."

"And this is the Hungry Tiger," continued Dorothy. "He says he longs to eat fat babies; but the truth is he is never hungry at all, 'cause he gets plenty to eat; and I don't s'pose he'd hurt anybody even if he *was* hungry."

"Hush, Dorothy," whispered the Tiger; "you'll ruin my reputation if you are not more discreet. It isn't what we are, but what folks think we are, that counts in this world. And come to think of it Miss Polly would make a fine variegated breakfast, I'm sure."

Chapter 18

The EMERALD CITY

The others now came up, and the Tin Woodman greeted the Lion and the Tiger cordially. Button-Bright yelled with fear when Dorothy first took his hand and led him toward the great beasts; but the girl insisted they were kind and good, and so the boy mustered up courage enough to pat their heads; after they had spoken to him gently and he had looked into their intelligent eyes his fear vanished entirely and he was so delighted with the animals that he wanted to keep close to them and stroke their soft fur every minute.

As for the shaggy man, he might have been afraid if he had met the beasts alone, or in any other country; but so many were the marvels in the Land of Oz that he was no longer easily surprised, and Dorothy's friendship for the Lion and Tiger was enough to assure him they were safe companions. Toto barked at the Cowardly Lion in joyous greeting, for he knew the beast of old and loved him, and it was funny to see how gently the Lion raised his huge paw to pat Toto's head. The little dog smelled of the Tiger's nose and the Tiger politely shook paws with him; so they were quite likely to become firm friends.

Tik-Tok and Billina knew the beasts well, so merely bade them good day and asked after their healths and inquired about the Princess Ozma.

Now it was seen that the Cowardly Lion and the Hungry Tiger were drawing behind them a splendid golden chariot, to which they were harnessed by golden cords. The body of the chariot was decorated on the outside with designs in clusters of sparkling emeralds, while inside it was lined with a green and gold satin, and the cushions of the seats were of green plush embroidered in gold with a crown, underneath which was a monogram.

"Why, it's Ozma's own royal chariot!" exclaimed Dorothy.

"Yes," said the Cowardly Lion; "Ozma sent us to meet you here, for she feared you would be weary with your long walk and she wished you to enter the City in a style becoming your exalted rank."

"What!" cried Polly, looking at Dorothy curiously. "Do you belong to the nobility?"

"Just in Oz I do," said the child, "'cause Ozma made me a Princess, you know. But when I'm home in Kansas I'm only a country girl, and have to help with the churning and wipe the dishes while Aunt Em washes 'em. Do you have to help wash dishes on the rainbow, Polly?"

"No, dear," answered Polychrome, smiling.

"Well, I don't have to work any in Oz, either," said Dorothy. "It's kind of fun to be a Princess once in a while; don't you think so?"

"Dorothy and Polychrome and Button-Bright are all to ride in the chariot," said the Lion. "So get in, my dears, and be careful not to mar the gold or put your dusty feet on the embroidery."

Button-Bright was delighted to ride behind such a superb team, and he told Dorothy it made him feel like an actor in a circus. As the strides of the animals brought them nearer to the Emerald City every one bowed respectfully to the children, as well as to the Tin Woodman, Tik-Tok, and the shaggy man, who were following behind.

The Yellow Hen had perched upon the back of the chariot, where she could tell Dorothy more about her wonderful chickens as they rode. And so the grand chariot came finally to the high wall surrounding the City, and paused before the magnificent jewel-studded gates.

These were opened by a cheerful looking little man who wore green spectacles over his eyes. Dorothy introduced him to her friends as the Guardian of the Gates, and they noticed a big bunch of keys suspended on the golden chain that hung around his neck. The chariot passed through the outer gates into a fine arched chamber built in the thick wall, and through the inner gates into the streets of the Emerald City.

Polychrome exclaimed in rapture at the wondrous beauty that met her eyes on every side as they rode through this stately and imposing City, the equal of which has never been discovered, even in fairyland. Button-Bright could only say "My!" so amazing was the sight; but his eyes were wide open and he tried to look in every direction at the same time, so as not to miss anything.

The shaggy man was fairly astounded at what he saw, for the graceful and handsome buildings were covered with plates of gold and set with emeralds so splendid and valuable that in any other part of the world any one of them would have been worth a fortune to its owner. The sidewalks were superb marble slabs polished as smooth as glass, and the curbs that separated the walks from the broad street were also set thick with clustered emeralds. There were many people on these walks—men, women, and children—all dressed in handsome garments of silk or satin or velvet, with beautiful jewels. Better even than this: all seemed happy and contented, for their faces were smiling and free from care, and music and laughter might be heard on every side.

"Don't they work, at all?" asked the shaggy man.

"To be sure they work," replied the Tin Woodman; "this fair city could not be built or cared for without labor, nor could the fruit and vegetables and other food be provided for the inhabitants to eat. But no one works more than half his time, and the people of Oz enjoy their labors as much as they do their play."

"It's wonderful!" declared the shaggy man. "I do hope Ozma will let me live here."

The chariot, winding through many charming streets, paused before a building so vast and noble and elegant that even Button-Bright guessed at once that it was the royal palace. Its gardens and ample grounds were surrounded by a separate wall, not so high or thick as the wall around the City, but more daintily designed and built all of green marble. The gates flew open as the chariot appeared before them, and the Cowardly Lion and Hungry Tiger trotted up a jeweled driveway to the front door of the palace and stopped short.

"Here we are!" said Dorothy, gaily, and helped Button-Bright from the chariot. Polychrome leaped out lightly after them, and they were greeted by a crowd of gorgeously dressed servants who bowed low as the visitors mounted the marble steps. At their head was a pretty little maid with dark hair and eyes, dressed all in green embroidered with silver. Dorothy ran up to her with evident pleasure, and exclaimed:

"O, Jellia Jamb! I'm so glad to see you again. Where's Ozma?"

"In her room, your Highness," replied the little maid demurely, for this was Ozma's favorite attendant. "She wishes you to come to her as soon as you have rested and changed your dress, Princess Dorothy. And you and your friends are to dine with her this evening."

"When is her birthday, Jellia?" asked the girl.

"Day after to-morrow, your Highness."

"And where's the Scarecrow?"

"He's gone into the Munchkin country to get some fresh straw to stuff himself with, in honor of Ozma's celebration," replied the maid. "He returns to the Emerald City to-morrow, he said."

By this time, Tik-tok, the Tin Woodman, and the shaggy man had arrived and the chariot had gone around to the back of the palace, Billina going with the Lion and Tiger to see her chickens after her absence from them. But Toto stayed close beside Dorothy.

"Come in, please," said Jellia Jamb; "it shall be our pleasant duty to escort all of you to the rooms prepared for your use."

The shaggy man hesitated. Dorothy had never known him to be ashamed of his shaggy looks before, but now that he was surrounded by so much magnificence and splendor the shaggy man felt sadly out of place.

Dorothy assured him that all her friends were welcome at Ozma's palace, so he carefully dusted his shaggy shoes with his shaggy handkerchief and entered the grand hall after the others.

Tik-Tok lived at the royal palace and the Tin Woodman always had the same room whenever he visited Ozma, so these two went at once to remove the dust of the journey from their shining bodies. Dorothy also had a pretty suite of rooms which she always occupied when in the Emerald City; but several servants walked ahead politely to show the way, although she was quite sure she could find the rooms herself. She took Button-Bright with her, because he seemed too small to be left alone in such a big palace; but Jellia Jamb herself ushered the beautiful Daughter of the Rainbow to her apartments, because it was easy to see that Polychrome was used to splendid palaces and was therefore entitled to especial attention.

Chapter 19

The SHAGGY MAN'S WELCOME

The shaggy man stood in the great hall, his shaggy hat in his hands, wondering what would become of him. He had never been a guest in a fine palace before; perhaps he had never been a guest anywhere. In the big, cold, outside world people did not invite shaggy men to their homes, and this shaggy man of ours had slept more in hay-lofts and stables than in comfortable rooms. When the others left the great hall he eyed the splendidly dressed servants of the Princess Ozma as if he expected to be ordered out; but one of them bowed before him as respectfully as if he had been a prince, and said:

"Permit me, sir, to conduct you to your apartments."

The shaggy man drew a long breath and took courage.

"Very well," he answered. "I'm ready."

Through the big hall they went, up the grand staircase carpeted thick with velvet, and so along a wide corridor to a carved doorway. Here the servant paused, and opening the door said with polite deference:

"Be good enough to enter, sir, and make yourself at home in the rooms our Royal Ozma has ordered prepared for you. Whatever you see is for you to use and enjoy, as if your own. The Princess dines at seven, and I shall be here in time to lead you to the drawing-room, where you will be privileged to meet the lovely Ruler of Oz. Is there any command, in the meantime, with which you desire to honor me?"

"No," said the shaggy man; "but I'm much obliged."

He entered the room and shut the door, and for a time stood in bewilderment, admiring the grandeur before him.

He had been given one of the handsomest apartments in the most magnificent palace in the world, and you can not wonder that his good fortune astonished and awed him until he grew used to his surroundings.

The furniture was upholstered in cloth of gold, with the royal crown embroidered upon it in scarlet. The rug upon the marble floor was so thick and soft that he could not hear the sound of his own footsteps, and upon the walls were splendid tapestries woven with scenes from the Land of Oz. Books and ornaments were scattered about in profusion, and the shaggy man thought he had never seen so many pretty things in one place before. In one corner played a tinkling fountain of perfumed water, and in another was a table bearing a golden tray loaded with freshly gathered fruit, including several of the red-cheeked apples that the shaggy man loved.

At the farther end of this charming room was an open doorway, and he crossed over to find himself in a bedroom containing more comforts than the shaggy man had ever before imagined. The bedstead was of gold and set with many brilliant diamonds, and the coverlet had designs of pearls and rubies sewed upon it. At one side of the bedroom was a dainty dressing-room with closets containing a large assortment of fresh clothing; and beyond this was the bath—a large room having a marble pool big enough to swim in, with white marble steps leading down to the water. Around the edge of the pool were set rows of fine emeralds as large as door-knobs, while the water of the bath was clear as crystal.

For a time the shaggy man gazed upon all this luxury with silent amazement. Then he decided, being wise in his way, to take advantage of his good fortune. He removed his shaggy boots and his shaggy clothing, and bathed in the pool with rare enjoyment. After he had dried himself with the soft towels he went into the dressing-room and took fresh linen from the drawers and put it on, finding that everything fitted him exactly. He examined the contents of the closets and selected an elegant suit of clothing. Strangely enough, everything about it was shaggy, although so new and beautiful, and he sighed with contentment to realize that he could now be finely dressed and still be the Shaggy Man. His coat was of rose-colored velvet, trimmed with shags and bobtails, with buttons of blood-red rubies and golden shags around the edges. His vest was a shaggy satin of a delicate cream color, and his knee-breeches of rose velvet trimmed like the coat. Shaggy creamy stockings of silk, and shaggy slippers of rose leather with ruby buckles, completed his costume, and when he was thus attired the shaggy man looked at himself in a long mirror with great admiration. On a table he found a mother-of-pearl chest decorated with delicate silver vines and flowers of clustered rubies, and on the cover was a silver plate engraved with these words:

THE SHAGGY MAN:

HIS BOX OF ORNAMENTS

The chest was not locked, so he opened it and was almost dazzled by the brilliance of the rich jewels it contained. After admiring the pretty things, he took out a fine golden watch with a big chain, several handsome finger-rings, and an ornament of rubies to pin upon the breast of his shaggy shirt-bosom. Having carefully brushed his hair and whiskers all the wrong way, to make them look as shaggy as possible, the shaggy man breathed a deep sigh of joy and decided he was ready to meet the Royal Princess as soon as she sent for him. While he waited he returned to the beautiful sitting room and ate several of the red-cheeked apples to pass away the time.

Meanwhile, Dorothy had dressed herself in a pretty gown of soft grey embroidered with silver, and put a blue-and-gold suit of satin upon little Button-Bright, who looked as sweet as a cherub in it. Followed by the boy and Toto—the dog with a new green ribbon around his neck—she hastened down to the splendid drawing-room of the palace, where, seated upon an exquisite throne of carved malachite and nestled amongst its green satin cushions was the lovely Princess Ozma, waiting eagerly to welcome her friend.

Chapter 20

PRINCESS OZMA of OZ

The royal historians of Oz, who are fine writers and know any number of big words, have often tried to describe the rare beauty of Ozma and failed because the words were not good enough. So of course I cannot hope to tell you how great was the charm of this little Princess, or how her loveliness put to shame all the sparkling jewels and magnificent luxury that surrounded her in this her royal palace. Whatever else was beautiful or dainty or delightful of itself faded to dullness when contrasted with Ozma's bewitching face, and it has often been said by those who know that no other ruler in all the world can ever hope to equal the gracious charm of her manner.

Everything about Ozma attracted one, and she inspired love and the sweetest affection rather than awe or ordinary admiration. Dorothy threw her arms around her little friend and hugged and kissed her rapturously, and Toto barked joyfully and Button-Bright smiled a happy smile and consented to sit on the soft cushions close beside the Princess.

"Why didn't you send me word you were going to have a birthday party?" asked the little Kansas girl, when the first greetings were over.

"Didn't I?" asked Ozma, her pretty eyes dancing with merriment.

"Did you?" replied Dorothy, trying to think.

"Who do you imagine, dear, mixed up those roads, so as to start you wandering in the direction of Oz?" inquired the Princess.

"Oh! I never 'spected *you* of that," cried Dorothy.

"I've watched you in my Magic Picture all the way here," declared Ozma, "and twice I thought I should have to use the Magic Belt to save you and transport you to the Emerald City. Once was when the Scoodlers caught you, and again when you reached the deadly desert. But the shaggy man was able to help you out both times, so I did not interfere."

"Do you know who Button-Bright is?" asked Dorothy.

"No; I never saw him until you found him in the road, and then only in my Magic Picture."

"And did you send Polly to us?"

"No, dear; the Rainbow's Daughter slid from her father's pretty arch just in time to meet you."

"Well," said Dorothy, "I've promised King Dox of Foxville and King Kik-a-bray of Dunkiton that I'd ask you to invite them to your party."

"I have already done that," returned Ozma, "because I thought it would please you to favor them."

"Did you 'vite the Musicker?" asked Button-Bright.

"No; because he would be too noisy, and might interfere with the comfort of others. When music is not very good, and is indulged in all the time, it is better that the performer should be alone," said the Princess.

"I like the Musicker's music," declared the boy, gravely.

"But I don't," said Dorothy.

"Well, there will be plenty of music at my celebration," promised Ozma; "so I've an idea Button-Bright won't miss the Musicker at all."

Just then Polychrome danced in, and Ozma rose to greet the Rainbow's Daughter in her sweetest and most cordial manner.

Dorothy thought she had never seen two prettier creatures together than these lovely maidens; but Polly knew at once her own dainty beauty could not match that of Ozma, yet was not a bit jealous because this was so.

The Wizard of Oz was announced, and a dried-up, little, old man, clothed all in black, entered the drawing-room. His face was cheery and his eyes twinkling with humor, so Polly and Button-Bright were not at all afraid of the wonderful personage whose fame as a humbug magician had spread throughout the world. After greeting Dorothy with much affection, he stood modestly behind Ozma's throne and listened to the lively prattle of the young people.

Now the shaggy man appeared, and so startling was his appearance, all clad in shaggy new raiment, that Dorothy cried "Oh!" and clasped her hands impulsively as she examined her friend with pleased eyes.

"He's still shaggy, all right," remarked Button-Bright; and Ozma nodded brightly because she had meant the shaggy man to remain shaggy when she provided his new clothes for him.

Dorothy led him toward the throne, as he was shy in such fine company, and presented him gracefully to the Princess, saying:

"This, your Highness, is my friend, the shaggy man, who owns the Love Magnet."

"You are welcome to Oz," said the girl Ruler, in gracious accents. "But tell me, sir, where did you get the Love Magnet which you say you own?"

The shaggy man grew red and looked downcast, as he answered in a low voice:

"I stole it, your Majesty."

"Oh, Shaggy Man!" cried Dorothy. "How dreadful! And you told me the Eskimo gave you the Love Magnet."

He shuffled first on one foot and then on the other, much embarrassed.

"I told you a falsehood, Dorothy," he said; "but now, having bathed in the Truth Pond, I must tell nothing but the truth."

"Why did you steal it?" asked Ozma, gently.

"Because no one loved me, or cared for me," said the shaggy man, "and I wanted to be loved a great deal. It was owned by a girl in Butterfield who was loved too much, so that the young men quarreled over her, which made her unhappy. After I had stolen the Magnet from her, only one young man continued to love the girl, and she married him and regained her happiness."

"Are you sorry you stole it?" asked the Princess.

"No, your Highness; I'm glad," he answered; "for it has pleased me to be loved, and if Dorothy had not cared for me I could not have accompanied her to this beautiful Land of Oz, or met its kind-hearted Ruler. Now that I'm here, I hope to remain, and to become one of your Majesty's most faithful subjects."

"But in Oz we are loved for ourselves alone, and for our kindness to one another, and for our good deeds," she said.

"I'll give up the Love Magnet," said the shaggy man, eagerly; "Dorothy shall have it."

"But every one loves Dorothy already," declared the Wizard.

"Then Button-Bright shall have it."

"Don't want it," said the boy, promptly.

"Then I'll give it to the Wizard, for I'm sure the lovely Princess Ozma does not need it."

"All my people love the Wizard, too," announced the Princess, laughing; "so we will hang the Love Magnet over the gates of the Emerald City, that whoever shall enter or leave the gates may be loved and loving."

"That is a good idea," said the shaggy man; "I agree to it most willingly."

Those assembled now went in to dinner, which you may imagine was a grand affair; and afterward Ozma asked the Wizard to give them an exhibition of his magic.

The Wizard took eight tiny white piglets from an inside pocket and set them on the table. One was dressed like a clown, and performed funny antics, and the others leaped over the spoons and dishes and ran around the table like race-horses, and turned hand-springs and were so sprightly and amusing that they kept the company in one roar of merry laughter. The Wizard had trained these pets to do many curious things, and they were so little and so cunning and soft that Polychrome loved to pick them up as they passed near her place and fondle them as if they were kittens.

It was late when the entertainment ended, and they separated to go to their rooms.

"To-morrow," said Ozma, "my invited guests will arrive, and you will find among them some interesting and curious people, I promise you. The next day will be my birthday, and the festivities will be held on the broad green just outside the gates of the City, where all my people can assemble without being crowded."

"I hope the Scarecrow won't be late," said Dorothy, anxiously.

"Oh, he is sure to return to-morrow," answered Ozma. "He wanted new straw to stuff himself with, so he went to the Munchkin Country, where straw is plentiful."

With this the Princess bade her guests good night and went to her own room.

Chapter 21

DOROTHY RECEIVES the GUESTS

Next morning Dorothy's breakfast was served in her own pretty sitting room, and she sent to invite Polly and the shaggy man to join her and Button-Bright at the meal. They came gladly, and Toto also had breakfast with them, so that the little party that had traveled together to Oz was once more reunited.

No sooner had they finished eating than they heard the distant blast of many trumpets, and the sound of a brass band playing martial music; so they all went out upon the balcony. This was at the front of the palace and overlooked the streets of the City, being higher than the wall that shut in the palace grounds. They saw approaching down the street a band of musicians, playing as hard and loud as they could, while the people of the Emerald City crowded the sidewalks and cheered so lustily that they almost drowned the noise of the drums and horns.

Dorothy looked to see what they were cheering at, and discovered that behind the band was the famous Scarecrow, riding proudly upon the back of a wooden Sawhorse which pranced along the street almost as gracefully as if it had been made of flesh. Its hoofs, or rather the ends of its wooden legs, were shod with plates of solid gold, and the saddle strapped to the wooden body was richly embroidered and glittered with jewels.

As he reached the palace the Scarecrow looked up and saw Dorothy, and at once waved his peaked hat at her in greeting. He rode up to the front door and dismounted, and the band stopped playing and went away and the crowds of people returned to their dwellings.

By the time Dorothy and her friends had re-entered her room, the Scarecrow was there, and he gave the girl a hearty embrace and shook the hands of the others with his own squashy hands, which were white gloves filled with straw.

The shaggy man, Button-Bright, and Polychrome stared hard at this celebrated person, who was acknowledged to be the most popular and most beloved man in all the Land of Oz.

"Why, your face has been newly painted!" exclaimed Dorothy, when the first greetings were over.

"I had it touched up a bit by the Munchkin farmer who

first made me," answered the Scarecrow, pleasantly. "My complexion had become a bit grey and faded, you know, and the paint had peeled off one end of my mouth, so I couldn't talk quite straight. Now I feel like myself again, and I may say without immodesty that my body is stuffed with the loveliest oat-straw in all Oz." He pushed against his chest. "Hear me crunkle?" he asked.

"Yes," said Dorothy; "you sound fine."

Button-Bright was wonderfully attracted by the straw man, and so was Polly. The shaggy man treated him with great respect, because he was so queerly made.

Jellia Jamb now came to say that Ozma wanted Princess Dorothy to receive the invited guests in the Throne Room, as they arrived. The Ruler was herself busy ordering the preparations for the morrow's festivities, so she wished her friend to act in her place.

Dorothy willingly agreed, being the only other Princess in the Emerald City; so she went to the great Throne Room and sat in Ozma's seat, placing Polly on one side of her and Button-Bright on the other. The Scarecrow stood at the left of the throne and the Tin Woodman at the right, while the Wonderful Wizard and the shaggy man stood behind.

The Cowardly Lion and the Hungry Tiger came in, with bright new bows of ribbon on their collars and tails. After greeting Dorothy affectionately the huge beasts lay down at the foot of the throne.

While they waited, the Scarecrow, who was near the little boy, asked:

"Why are you called Button-Bright?"

"Don't know," was the answer.

"Oh yes, you do, dear," said Dorothy. "Tell the Scarecrow how you got your name."

"Papa always said I was bright as a button, so mama always called me Button-Bright," announced the boy.

"Where is your mama?" asked the Scarecrow.

"Don't know," said Button-Bright.

"Where is your home?" asked the Scarecrow.

"Don't know," said Button-Bright.

"Don't you want to find your mama again?" asked the Scarecrow.

"Don't know," said Button-Bright, calmly.

The Scarecrow looked thoughtful.

"Your papa may have been right," he observed; "but there are many kinds of buttons, you see. There are silver and gold buttons, which are highly polished and glitter brightly. There are pearl and rubber buttons, and other kinds, with surfaces more or less bright. But there is still another sort of button which is covered with dull cloth, and that must be the sort your papa meant when he said you were bright as a button. Don't you think so?"

"Don't know," said Button-Bright.

Jack Pumpkinhead arrived, wearing a pair of new white

kid gloves; and he brought a birthday present for Ozma consisting of a necklace of pumpkin-seeds. In each seed was set a sparkling carolite, which is considered the rarest and most beautiful gem that exists. The necklace was in a plush case and Jellia Jamb put it on a table with the Princess Ozma's other presents.

Next came a tall, beautiful woman clothed in a splendid trailing gown, trimmed with exquisite lace as fine as cobweb. This was the important Sorceress known as Glinda the Good, who had been of great assistance to both Ozma and Dorothy. There was no humbug about her magic, you may be sure, and Glinda was as kind as she was powerful. She greeted Dorothy most lovingly, and kissed Button-Bright and Polly, and smiled upon the shaggy man, after which Jellia Jamb led the Sorceress to one of the most magnificent rooms of the royal palace and appointed fifty servants to wait upon her.

The next arrival was Mr. H. M. Woggle-Bug, T.E.; the "H. M." meaning Highly Magnified and the "T.E." meaning Thoroughly Educated. The Woggle-Bug was head professor at the Royal College of Oz, and he had composed a fine Ode in honor of Ozma's birthday. This he wanted to read to them; but the Scarecrow wouldn't let him.

Soon they heard a clucking sound and a chorus of "cheep! cheep!" and a servant threw open the door to allow Billina and her ten fluffy chicks to enter the Throne Room. As the Yellow Hen marched proudly at the head of her family, Dorothy cried,

"Oh, you lovely things!" and ran down from her seat to pet the little yellow downy balls. Billina wore a pearl necklace, and around the neck of each chicken was a tiny gold chain holding a locket with the letter "D" engraved upon the outside.

"Open the lockets, Dorothy," said Billina. The girl obeyed and found a picture of herself in each locket. "They were named after you, my dear," continued the Yellow Hen, "so I wanted all my chickens to wear your picture. Cluck—cluck! come here, Dorothy—this minute!" she cried, for the chickens were scattered and wandering all around the big room.

They obeyed the call at once, and came running as fast as they could, fluttering their fluffy wings in a laughable way.

It was lucky that Billina gathered the little ones under her soft breast just then, for Tik-Tok came in and tramped up to the throne on his flat copper feet.

"I am all wound up and work-ing fine-ly," said the clock-work man to Dorothy.

"I can hear him tick," declared Button-Bright.

"You are quite the polished gentleman," said the Tin Woodman. "Stand up here beside the shaggy man, Tik-Tok, and help receive the company."

Dorothy placed soft cushions in a corner for Billina and her chicks, and had just returned to the throne and seated herself when the playing of the royal band outside the palace announced the approach of distinguished guests.

And my, how they did stare when the High Chamberlain

threw open the doors and the visitors entered the Throne Room!

First walked a gingerbread man neatly formed and baked to a lovely brown tint. He wore a silk hat and carried a candy cane prettily striped with red and yellow. His shirt-front and cuffs were white frosting, and the buttons on his coat were licorice drops.

Behind the gingerbread man came a child with flaxen hair and merry blue eyes, dressed in white pajamas, with sandals on the soles of its pretty bare feet. The child looked around smiling and thrust its hands into the pockets of the pajamas. Close after it came a big rubber bear, walking erect on its hind feet. The bear had twinkling black eyes and its body looked as if it had been pumped full of air.

Following these curious visitors were two tall, thin men and two short, fat men, all four dressed in gorgeous uniforms.

Ozma's High Chamberlain now hurried forward to announce the names of the new arrivals, calling out in a loud voice:

"His Gracious and Most Edible Majesty, King Dough the First, Ruler of the Two Kingdoms of Hiland and Loland. Also the Head Booleywag of his Majesty, known as Chick the Cherub, and their faithful friend Para Bruin, the rubber bear."

These great personages bowed low as their names were called, and Dorothy hastened to introduce them to the assembled company. They were the first foreign arrivals, and the friends of Princess Ozma were polite to them and tried to make them feel that they were welcome.

Chick the Cherub shook hands with every one, including Billina, and was so joyous and frank and full of good spirits that John Dough's Head Booleywag at once became a prime favorite.

"Is it a boy or a girl?" whispered Dorothy.

"Don't know," said Button-Bright.

"Goodness me! What a queer lot of people you are," exclaimed the rubber bear, looking at the assembled company.

"So're you," said Button-Bright, gravely. "Is King Dough good to eat?"

"He's too good to eat," laughed Chick the Cherub.

"I hope none of you are fond of gingerbread," said the King, rather anxiously.

"We should never think of eating our visitors, if we were," declared the Scarecrow; "so please do not worry, for you will be perfectly safe while you remain in Oz."

"Why do they call you Chick?" the Yellow Hen asked the child.

"Because I'm an Incubator Baby, and never had any parents," replied the Head Booleywag.

"My chicks have a parent, and I'm it," said Billina.

"I'm glad of that," answered the Cherub, "because they'll have more fun worrying you than if they were brought up in an Incubator. The Incubator never worries, you know."

King John Dough had brought for Ozma's birthday present a lovely gingerbread crown, with rows of small pearls
around it and a fine big pearl in each of its five points. After
this had been received by Dorothy with proper thanks and
placed on the table with the other presents, the visitors from
Hiland and Loland were escorted to their rooms by the High
Chamberlain.

They had no sooner departed than the band before the
palace began to play again, announcing more arrivals, and as
these were doubtless from foreign parts the High Chamberlain
hurried back to receive them in his most official manner.

IMPORTANT ARRIVALS

First entered a band of Ryls from the Happy Valley, all merry little sprites like fairy elves. A dozen crooked Knooks followed from the great Forest of Burzee. They had long whiskers and pointed caps and curling toes, yet were no taller than Button-Bright's shoulder. With this group came a man so easy to recognize and so important and dearly beloved throughout the known world, that all present rose to their feet and bowed their heads in respectful homage, even before the High Chamberlain knelt to announce his name.

"The most Mighty and Loyal Friend of Children, His

Supreme Highness—Santa Claus!" said the Chamberlain, in an awed voice.

"Well, well, well! Glad to see you—glad to meet you all!" cried Santa Claus, briskly, as he trotted up the long room.

He was round as an apple, with a fresh rosy face, laughing eyes, and a bushy beard as white as snow. A red cloak trimmed with beautiful ermine hung from his shoulders and upon his back was a basket filled with pretty presents for the Princess Ozma.

"Hello, Dorothy; still having adventures?" he asked in his jolly way, as he took the girl's hand in both his own.

"How did you know my name, Santa?" she replied, feeling more shy in the presence of this immortal saint than she ever had before in her young life.

"Why, don't I see you every Christmas Eve, when you're asleep?" he rejoined, pinching her blushing cheek.

"Oh, do you?"

"And here's Button-Bright, I declare!" cried Santa Claus, holding up the boy to kiss him. "What a long way from home you are; dear me!"

"Do you know Button-Bright, too?" questioned Dorothy, eagerly.

"Indeed I do. I've visited his home several Christmas Eves."

"And do you know his father?" asked the girl.

"Certainly, my dear. Who else do you suppose brings him

his Christmas neckties and stockings?" with a sly wink at the Wizard.

"Then where does he live? We're just crazy to know, 'cause Button-Bright's lost," she said.

Santa laughed and laid his finger aside of his nose as if thinking what to reply. He leaned over and whispered something in the Wizard's ear, at which the Wizard smiled and nodded as if he understood.

Now Santa Claus spied Polychrome, and trotted over to where she stood.

"Seems to me the Rainbow's Daughter is farther from home than any of you," he observed, looking at the pretty maiden admiringly. "I'll have to tell your father where you are, Polly, and send him to get you."

"Please do, dear Santa Claus," implored the little maid, beseechingly.

"But just now we must all have a jolly good time at Ozma's party," said the old gentleman, turning to put his presents on the table with the others already there. "It isn't often I find time to leave my castle, as you know; but Ozma invited me and I just couldn't help coming to celebrate the happy occasion."

"I'm so glad!" exclaimed Dorothy.

"These are my Ryls," pointing to the little sprites squatting around him. "Their business is to paint the colors of the flowers when they bud and bloom; but I brought the merry fellows along to see Oz, and they've left their paint-pots behind them. Also I brought these crooked Knooks, whom I love. My dears, the Knooks are much nicer than they look, for their duty is to water and care for the young trees of the forest, and they do their work faithfully and well. It's hard work, though, and it makes my Knooks crooked and gnarled, like the trees themselves; but their hearts are big and kind, as are the hearts of all who do good in our beautiful world."

"I've read of the Ryls and Knooks," said Dorothy, looking upon these little workers with interest.

Santa Claus turned to talk with the Scarecrow and the Tin Woodman, and he also said a kind word to the shaggy man, and afterward went away to ride the Sawhorse around the Emerald City. "For," said he, "I must see all the grand sights while I am here and have the chance, and Ozma has promised to let me ride the Sawhorse because I'm getting fat and short of breath."

"Where are your reindeer?" asked Polychrome.

"I left them at home, for it is too warm for them in this sunny country," he answered. "They're used to winter weather when they travel."

In a flash he was gone, and the Ryls and Knooks with him; but they could all hear the golden hoofs of the Sawhorse ringing on the marble pavement outside, as he pranced away with his noble rider.

Presently the band played again, and the High Chamberlain announced:

"Her Gracious Majesty, the Queen of Merryland."

They looked earnestly to discover whom this queen might be, and saw advancing up the room an exquisite wax doll dressed in dainty fluffs and ruffles and spangled gown. She was almost as big as Button-Bright, and her cheeks and mouth and eyebrow were prettily painted in delicate colors. Her blue eyes stared a bit, being of glass, yet the expression upon her Majesty's face was quite pleasant and decidedly winning. With the Queen of Merryland were four wooden soldiers, two stalking ahead of her with much dignity and two following behind, like a royal bodyguard. The soldiers were painted in bright colors and carried wooden guns, and after them came a fat little man who attracted attention at once, although he seemed modest and retiring. For he was made of candy, and carried a tin sugar-sifter filled with powdered sugar, with which he dusted himself frequently so that he wouldn't stick to things if he touched them. The High Chamberlain had called him "The Candy Man of Merryland," and Dorothy saw that one of his thumbs looked as if it had been bitten off by some one who was fond of candy and couldn't resist the temptation.

The wax doll Queen spoke prettily to Dorothy and the others, and sent her loving greetings to Ozma before she retired to the rooms prepared for her. She had brought a birthday present wrapped in tissue paper and tied with pink and blue ribbons, and one of the wooden soldiers placed it on the table with the other gifts. But the Candy Man did not go to his room, because he said he preferred to stay and talk with

the Scarecrow and Tik-Tok and the Wizard and Tin Woodman, whom he declared the queerest people he had ever met.
Button-Bright was glad the Candy Man stayed in the Throne
Room, because the boy thought this guest smelled deliciously
of wintergreen and maple sugar.

The braided man now entered the room, having been fortunate enough to receive an invitation to the Princess Ozma's
party. He was from a cave halfway between the Invisible Valley and the Country of the Gargoyles, and his hair and whiskers were so long that he was obliged to plait them into many
braids that hung to his feet, and every braid was tied with a
bow of colored ribbon.

"I've brought Princess Ozma a box of flutters for her
birthday," said the braided man, earnestly; "and I hope she
will like them, for they are the finest quality I have ever made."

"I'm sure she will be greatly pleased," said Dorothy, who
remembered the braided man well; and the Wizard introduced the guest to the rest of the company and made him sit
down in a chair and keep quiet, for, if allowed, he would talk
continually about his flutters.

The band then played a welcome to another set of guests,
and into the Throne Room swept the handsome and stately
Queen of Ev. Beside her was young King Evardo, and following
them came the entire royal family of five Princesses and four
Princes of Ev. The Kingdom of Ev lay just across the deadly
desert to the North of Oz, and once Ozma and her people had

rescued the Queen of Ev and her ten children from the Nome King, who had enslaved them. Dorothy had been present on this adventure, so she greeted the royal family cordially; and all the visitors were delighted to meet the little Kansas girl again. They knew Tik-Tok and Billina, too, and the Scarecrow and Tin Woodman, as well as the Lion and Tiger; so there was a joyful reunion, as you may imagine, and it was fully an hour before the Queen and her train retired to their rooms. Perhaps they would not have gone then had not the band begun to play to announce new arrivals; but before they left the great Throne Room King Evardo added to Ozma's birthday presents a diadem of diamonds set in radium.

The next comer proved to be King Renard of Foxville; or King Dox, as he preferred to be called. He was magnificently dressed in a new feather costume and wore white kid mittens over his paws and a flower in his button-hole and had his hair parted in the middle.

King Dox thanked Dorothy fervently for getting him the invitation to come to Oz, which he had all his life longed to visit. He strutted around rather absurdly as he was introduced to all the famous people assembled in the Throne Room, and when he learned that Dorothy was a Princess of Oz the Fox King insisted on kneeling at her feet and afterward retired backward—a dangerous thing to do, as he might have stubbed his paw and tumbled over.

No sooner was he gone than the blasts of bugles and

clatter of drums and cymbals announced important visitors, and the High Chamberlain assumed his most dignified tone as he threw open the door and said proudly:

"Her Sublime and Resplendent Majesty, Queen Zixi of Ix! His Serene and Tremendous Majesty, King Bud of Noland. Her Royal Highness, the Princess Fluff."

That three such high and mighty royal personages should arrive at once was enough to make Dorothy and her companions grow solemn and assume their best company manners; but when the exquisite beauty of Queen Zixi met their eyes they thought they had never beheld anything so charming. Dorothy decided that Zixi must be about sixteen years old, but the Wizard whispered to her that this wonderful queen had lived thousands of years, but knew the secret of remaining always fresh and beautiful.

King Bud of Noland and his dainty fair-haired sister, the Princess Fluff, were friends of Zixi, as their kingdoms were adjoining, so they had traveled together from their far-off domains to do honor to Ozma of Oz on the occasion of her birthday. They brought many splendid gifts; so the table was now fairly loaded down with presents.

Dorothy and Polly loved the Princess Fluff the moment they saw her, and little King Bud was so frank and boyish that Button-Bright accepted him as a chum at once and did not want him to go away. But it was after noon now, and the royal guests must prepare their toilets for the grand banquet at which they were to assemble that evening to meet the reigning Princess of this fairyland; so Queen Zixi was shown to her room by a troop of maidens led by Jellia Jamb, and Bud and Fluff presently withdrew to their own apartments.

"My! what a big party Ozma is going to have," exclaimed Dorothy. "I guess the palace will be chock full, Button-Bright; don't you think so?"

"Don't know," said the boy.

"But we must go to our rooms, pretty soon, to dress for the banquet," continued the girl.

"I don't have to dress," said the Candy Man from Merryland. "All I need do is to dust myself with fresh sugar."

"Tik-Tok always wears the same suits of clothes," said the Tin Woodman; "and so does our friend the Scarecrow."

"My feathers are good enough for any occasion," cried Billina, from her corner.

"Then I shall leave you four to welcome any new guests that come," said Dorothy; "for Button-Bright and I must look our very best at Ozma's banquet."

"Who is still to come?" asked the Scarecrow.

"Well, there's King Kik-a-bray of Dunkiton, and Johnny Dooit, and the Good Witch of the North. But Johnny Dooit may not get here until late, he's so very busy."

"We will receive them and give them a proper welcome," promised the Scarecrow. "So run along, little Dorothy, and get yourself dressed."

···—···◁ Chapter 23 ▷···—···

The GRAND BANQUET

I wish I could tell you how fine the company was that assembled that evening at Ozma's royal banquet. A long table was spread in the center of the great dining-hall of the palace and the splendor of the decorations and the blaze of lights and jewels was acknowledged to be the most magnificent sight that any of the guests had ever seen.

The jolliest person present, as well as the most important, was of course, old Santa Claus; so he was given the seat of honor at one end of the table while at the other end sat Princess Ozma, the hostess.

John Dough, Queen Zixi, King Bud, the Queen of Ev

and her son Evardo, and the Queen of Merryland had golden thrones to sit in, while the others were supplied with beautiful chairs.

At the upper end of the banquet room was a separate table provided for the animals. Toto sat at one end of this table, with a bib tied around his neck and a silver platter to eat from. At the other end was placed a small stand, with a low rail around the edge of it, for Billina and her chicks. The rail kept the ten little Dorothys from falling off the stand, while the Yellow Hen could easily reach over and take her food from her tray upon the table. At other places sat the Hungry Tiger, the Cowardly Lion, the Sawhorse, the Rubber Bear, the Fox King and the Donkey King; they made quite a company of animals.

At the lower end of the great room was another table, at which sat the Ryls and Knooks who had come with Santa Claus, the wooden soldiers who had come with the Queen of Merryland, and the Hilanders and Lolanders who had come with John Dough. Here were also seated the officers of the royal palace and of Ozma's army.

The splendid costumes of those at the three tables made a gorgeous and glittering display that no one present was ever likely to forget; perhaps there has never been in any part of the world at any time another assemblage of such wonderful people as that which gathered this evening to honor the birthday of the Ruler of Oz.

When all members of the company were in their places

an orchestra of five hundred pieces, in a balcony overlooking the banquet room, began to play sweet and delightful music. Then a door draped with royal green opened, and in came the fair and girlish Princess Ozma, who now greeted her guests in person for the first time.

As she stood by her throne at the head of the banquet table every eye was turned eagerly upon the lovely Princess, who was as dignified as she was bewitching, and who smiled upon all her old and new friends in a way that touched their hearts and brought an answering smile to every face.

Each guest had been served with a crystal goblet filled with lacasa, which is a sort of nectar famous in Oz and nicer to drink than soda-water or lemonade. Santa now made a pretty speech in verse, congratulating Ozma on having a birthday, and asking every one present to drink to the health and happiness of their dearly beloved hostess. This was done with great enthusiasm by those who were made so they could drink at all, and those who could not drink politely touched the rims of their goblets to their lips. All seated themselves at the tables and the servants of the Princess began serving the feast.

I am quite sure that only in fairyland could such a delicious repast be prepared. The dishes were of precious metals set with brilliant jewels and the good things to eat which were placed upon them were countless in number and of exquisite flavor. Several present, such as the Candy Man, the Rubber Bear,

Tik-Tok, and the Scarecrow, were not made so they could eat, and the Queen of Merryland contented herself with a small dish of sawdust; but these enjoyed the pomp and glitter of the gorgeous scene as much as did those who feasted.

The Woggle-Bug read his "Ode to Ozma," which was written in very good rhythm and was well received by the company. The Wizard added to the entertainment by making a big pie appear before Dorothy, and when the little girl cut the pie the nine tiny piglets leaped out of it and danced around the table, while the orchestra played a merry tune. This amused the company very much, but they were even more pleased when Polychrome, whose hunger had been easily satisfied, rose from the table and performed her graceful and bewildering Rainbow Dance for them. When it was ended the people clapped their hands and the animals clapped their paws, while Billina cackled and the Donkey King brayed approval.

Johnny Dooit was present, and of course he proved he could do wonders in the way of eating, as well as in everything else that he undertook to do; the Tin Woodman sang a love song, every one joining in the chorus; and the wooden soldiers from Merryland gave an exhibition of a lightning drill with their wooden muskets; the Ryls and Knooks danced the Fairy Circle; and the Rubber Bear bounced himself all around the room. There was laughter and merriment on every side, and everybody was having a royal good time. Button-Bright was so excited and interested that he paid little attention to his fine dinner and a great deal of attention to his queer companions; and perhaps he was wise to do this, because he could eat at any other time.

The feasting and merrymaking continued until late in the evening, when they separated to meet again the next morning and take part in the birthday celebration, to which this royal banquet was merely the introduction.

Chapter 24

The BIRTHDAY CELEBRATION

clear, perfect day, with a gentle breeze and a sunny sky, greeted Princess Ozma as she wakened next morning, the anniversary of her birth. While it was yet early all the city was astir and crowds of people came from all parts of the Land of Oz to witness the festivities in honor of their girl Ruler's birthday.

The noted visitors from foreign countries, who had all been transported to the Emerald City by means of the Magic Belt, were as much a show to the Ozites as were their own familiar celebrities, and the streets leading from the royal palace to the jeweled gates were thronged with men, women, and children to see the procession as it passed out to the green fields where the ceremonies were to take place.

And what a great procession it was!

First came a thousand young girls—the prettiest in the land—dressed in white muslin, with green sashes and hair ribbons, bearing green baskets of red roses. As they walked they scattered these flowers upon the marble pavements, so that the way was carpeted thick with roses for the procession to walk upon.

Then came the Rulers of the four Kingdoms of Oz: the Emperor of the Winkies, the Monarch of the Munchkins, the King of the Quadlings and the Sovereign of the Gillikins, each wearing a long chain of emeralds around his neck to show that he was a vassal of the Ruler of the Emerald City.

Next marched the Emerald City Cornet Band, clothed in green-and-gold uniforms and playing the "Ozma Two-Step." The Royal Army of Oz followed, consisting of twenty-seven officers, from the Captain-General down to the Lieutenants. There were no privates in Ozma's army because soldiers were not needed to fight battles, but only to look important, and an officer always looks more imposing than a private.

While the people cheered and waved their hats and hand-kerchiefs, there came walking the Royal Princess Ozma, looking so pretty and sweet that it is no wonder her people love her so dearly. She had decided she would not ride in her chariot that day, as she preferred to walk in the procession with her favored subjects and her guests. Just in front of her trotted the living Blue Bear Rug owned by old Dyna, which wobbled clumsily on its four feet because there was nothing but the skin to support them, with a stuffed head at one end and a stubby tail at the other. But whenever Ozma paused in her walk the Bear Rug would flop down flat upon the ground for the princess to stand upon until she resumed her progress.

Following the Princess stalked her two enormous beasts, the Cowardly Lion and the Hungry Tiger, and even if the army had not been there these two would have been powerful enough to guard their mistress from any harm.

Next marched the invited guests, who were loudly cheered by the people of Oz along the road, and were therefore obliged to bow to right and left almost every step of the way. First was Santa Claus, who, because he was fat and not used to walking, rode the wonderful Sawhorse. The merry old gentleman had a basket of small toys with him, and he tossed the toys one by one to the children as he passed by. His Ryls and Knooks marched close behind him.

Queen Zixi of Ix came after; then John Dough and the Cherub, with the rubber bear named Para Bruin strutting between them on its hind legs; then the Queen of Merryland, escorted by her wooden soldiers; then King Bud of Noland and his sister, the Princess Fluff; then the Queen of Ev and her ten royal children; then the braided man and the Candy Man, side by side; then King Dox of Foxville and King Kik-a-bray of

Dunkiton, who by this time had become good friends; and finally Johnny Dooit, in his leather apron, smoking his long pipe.

These wonderful personages were not more heartily cheered by the people than were those who followed after them in the procession. Dorothy was a general favorite, and she walked arm in arm with the Scarecrow, who was beloved by all. Then came Polychrome and Button-Bright, and the people loved the Rainbow's pretty Daughter and the beautiful blue-eyed boy as soon as they saw them. The shaggy man in his shaggy new suit attracted much attention because he was such a novelty. With regular steps tramped the machineman Tik-Tok, and there was more cheering when the Wizard of Oz followed in the procession. The Woggle-Bug and Jack Pumpkinhead were next, and behind them Glinda the Sorceress and the Good Witch of the North. Finally came Billina, with her brood of chickens to whom she clucked anxiously to keep them together and to hasten them along so they would not delay the procession.

Another band followed, this time the Tin Band of the Emperor of the Winkies, playing a beautiful march called, "There's No Plate Like Tin." Then came the servants of the royal palace, in a long line, and behind them all the people joined the procession and marched away through the emerald gates and out upon the broad green.

Here had been erected a splendid pavilion, with a grandstand big enough to seat all the royal party and those who had taken part in the procession. Over the pavilion, which was of green silk and cloth of gold, countless banners waved in the breeze. Just in front of this, and connected with it by a runway had been built a broad platform, so that all the spectators could see plainly the entertainment provided for them.

The Wizard now became Master of Ceremonies, as Ozma had placed the conduct of the performance in his hands. After the people had all congregated about the platform and the royal party and the visitors were seated in the grandstand, the Wizard skillfully performed some feats of juggling glass balls and lighted candles. He tossed a dozen or so of them high in the air and caught them one by one as they came down, without missing any.

Then he introduced the Scarecrow, who did a sword-swallowing act that aroused much interest. After this the Tin Woodman gave an exhibition of Swinging the Axe, which he made to whirl around him so rapidly that the eye could scarcely follow the motion of the gleaming blade. Glinda the Sorceress then stepped upon the platform, and by her magic made a big tree grow in the middle of the space, made blossoms appear upon the tree, and made the blossoms become delicious fruit called tamornas; and so great was the quantity of fruit produced that when the servants climbed the tree and tossed it down to the crowd, there was enough to satisfy every person present.

Para Bruin, the rubber bear, climbed to a limb of the big tree, rolled himself into a ball, and dropped to the platform, whence he bounded up again to the limb. He repeated this bouncing act several times, to the great delight of all the children present. After he had finished, and bowed, and returned to his seat, Glinda waved her wand and the tree disappeared; but its fruit still remained to be eaten.

The Good Witch of the North amused the people by transforming ten stones into ten birds, the ten birds into ten lambs, and the ten lambs into ten little girls, who gave a pretty dance and were then transformed into ten stones again, just as they were in the beginning.

Johnny Dooit next came on the platform with his tool-chest, and in a few minutes built a great flying machine; then put his chest in the machine and the whole thing flew away together—Johnny and all—after he had bid good-bye to those present and thanked the Princess for her hospitality.

The Wizard then announced the last act of all, which was considered really wonderful. He had invented a machine to blow huge soap-bubbles, as big as balloons, and this machine was hidden under the platform so that only the rim of the big clay pipe to produce the bubbles showed above the flooring. The tank of soap-suds, and the air-pumps to inflate the bubbles, were out of sight beneath, so that when the bubbles began to grow upon the floor of the platform it really seemed like magic to the people of Oz, who knew nothing about even the common soap-bubbles that our children blow with a penny clay pipe and a basin of soap-and-water.

The Wizard had invented another thing. Usually soap-bubbles are frail and burst easily, lasting only a few moments as they float in the air; but the Wizard added a sort of glue to his soap-suds, which made his bubbles tough; and, as the glue dried rapidly when exposed to the air, the Wizard's bubbles were strong enough to float for hours without breaking.

He began by blowing—by means of his machinery and air-pumps—several large bubbles which he allowed to float upward into the sky, where the sunshine fell upon them and gave them iridescent hues that were most beautiful. This aroused much wonder and delight because it was a new amusement to every one present—except perhaps Dorothy and Button-Bright, and even they had never seen such big, strong bubbles before.

The Wizard then blew a bunch of small bubbles and after-ward blew a big bubble around them so they were left in the center of it; then he allowed the whole mass of pretty globes to float into the air and disappear in the far distant sky.

"That is really fine!" declared Santa Claus, who loved toys and pretty things. "I think, Mr. Wizard, I shall have you blow a bubble around me; then I can float away home and see the country spread out beneath me as I travel. There isn't a spot on earth that I haven't visited, but I usually go in the night-time, riding behind my swift reindeer. Here is a good chance to observe the country by daylight, while I am riding slowly and at my ease."

"Do you think you will be able to guide the bubble?" asked the Wizard.

"Oh yes; I know enough magic to do that," replied Santa Claus. "You blow the bubble, with me inside of it, and I'll be sure to get home in safety."

"Please send me home in a bubble, too!" begged the Queen of Merryland.

"Very well, madam; you shall try the journey first," politely answered old Santa.

The pretty wax doll bade good-bye to the Princess Ozma and the others and stood on the platform while the Wizard blew a big soap-bubble around her. When completed, he allowed the bubble to float slowly upward, and there could be seen the little Queen of Merryland standing in the middle of it and blowing kisses from her fingers to those below. The bubble took a southerly direction, quickly floating out of sight.

"That's a very nice way to travel," said Princess Fluff. "I'd like to go home in a bubble, too."

So the Wizard blew a big bubble around Princess Fluff, and another around King Bud, her brother, and a third one around Queen Zixi; and soon these three bubbles had mounted into the sky and were floating off in a group in the direction of the kingdom of Noland.

The success of these ventures induced the other guests from foreign lands to undertake bubble journeys, also; so the Wizard put them one by one inside his bubbles, and Santa Claus directed the way they should go, because he knew exactly where everybody lived.

Finally, Button-Bright said:

"I want to go home, too."

"Why, so you shall!" cried Santa; "for I'm sure your father and mother will be glad to see you again. Mr. Wizard, please blow a big, fine bubble for Button-Bright to ride in, and I'll agree to send him home to his family as safe as safe can be."

"I'm sorry," said Dorothy with a sigh, for she was fond of her little comrade; "but p'raps it's best for Button-Bright to get home; 'cause his folks must be worrying just dreadful."

She kissed the boy, and Ozma kissed him, too, and all the others waved their hands and said good-bye and wished him a pleasant journey.

"Are you glad to leave us, dear?" asked Dorothy, a little wistfully.

"Don't know," said Button-Bright.

He sat down cross-legged on the platform, with his sailor hat tipped back on his head, and the Wizard blew a beautiful bubble all around him.

A minute later it had mounted into the sky, sailing toward the west, and the last they saw of Button-Bright he was still sitting in the middle of the shining globe and waving his sailor hat at those below.

"Will you ride in a bubble, or shall I send you and Toto home by means of the Magic Belt?" the Princess asked Dorothy.

"Guess I'll use the Belt," replied the little girl. "I'm sort of 'fraid of those bubbles."

"Bow-wow!" said Toto, approvingly. He loved to bark at the bubbles as they sailed away, but he didn't care to ride in one.

Santa Claus decided to go next. He thanked Ozma for her hospitality and wished her many happy returns of the day. Then the Wizard blew a bubble around his chubby little body and smaller bubbles around each of his Ryls and Knooks.

As the kind and generous friend of children mounted into the air the people all cheered at the top of their voices, for they loved Santa Claus dearly; and the little man heard them through the walls of his bubble and waved his hands in return as he smiled down upon them. The band played bravely while every one watched the bubble until it was completely out of sight.

"How 'bout you, Polly?" Dorothy asked her friend. "Are you 'fraid of bubbles, too?"

"No," answered Polychrome, smiling; "but Santa Claus promised to speak to my father as he passed through the sky. So perhaps I shall get home an easier way."

Indeed, the little maid had scarcely made this speech when a sudden radiance filled the air, and while the people looked on in wonder the end of a gorgeous rainbow slowly settled down upon the platform.

With a glad cry, the Rainbow's Daughter sprang from her seat and danced along the curve of the bow, mounting gradually upward, while the folds of her gauzy gown whirled and floated around her like a cloud and blended with the colors of the rainbow itself.

"Good-bye, Ozma! Good-bye, Dorothy!" cried a voice they knew belonged to Polychrome; but now the little maiden's form had melted wholly into the rainbow, and their eyes could no longer see her.

Suddenly, the end of the rainbow lifted and its colors slowly faded like mist before a breeze. Dorothy sighed deeply and turned to Ozma.

"I'm sorry to lose Polly," she said; "but I guess she's better off with her father, 'cause even the Land of Oz couldn't be like home to a Cloud Fairy."

"No indeed," replied the Princess; "but it has been delightful for us to know Polychrome for a little while, and—who knows?—perhaps we may meet the Rainbow's daughter again, some day."

The entertainment being now ended, all left the pavilion and formed their gay procession back to the Emerald City again. Of Dorothy's recent traveling companions only Toto and the shaggy man remained, and Ozma had decided to allow the latter to live in Oz for a time, at least. If he proved honest and true she promised to let him live there always, and the shaggy man was anxious to earn this reward.

They had a nice quiet dinner together and passed a pleasant evening with the Scarecrow, the Tin Woodman, Tik-Tok, and the Yellow Hen for company.

When Dorothy bade them good-night, she kissed them all good-bye at the same time. For Ozma had agreed that while Dorothy slept she and Toto should be transported by means of the Magic Belt to her own little bed in the Kansas farm-house and the little girl laughed as she thought how astonished Uncle Henry and Aunt Em would be when she came down to breakfast with them next morning.

Quite content to have had so pleasant an adventure, and a little tired by all the day's busy scenes, Dorothy clasped Toto in her arms and lay down upon the pretty white bed in her room in Ozma's royal palace.

Presently she was sound asleep.

The

Emerald

City

—·· ·—◄ of ►—·· ·—

OZ

To Her Royal Highness Cynthia II of Syracuse;
and to each and every one of the children whose
loyal appreciation has encouraged me to write the Oz books,
this volume is affectionately dedicated.

Perhaps I should admit on the title page that this book is "By L. Frank Baum and his correspondents," for I have used many suggestions conveyed to me in letters from children. Once on a time I really imagined myself "an author of fairy tales," but now I am merely an editor or private secretary for a host of youngsters whose ideas I am requested to weave into the thread of my stories.

These ideas are often clever. They are also logical and interesting. So I have used them whenever I could find an opportunity, and it is but just that I acknowledge my indebtedness to my little friends.

My, what imaginations these children have developed! Sometimes I am fairly astounded by their daring and genius. There will be no lack of fairy-tale authors in the future, I am sure. My readers have told me what to do with Dorothy, and

Aunt Em and Uncle Henry, and I have obeyed their mandates. They have also given me a variety of subjects to write about in the future: enough, in fact, to keep me busy for some time. I am very proud of this alliance. Children love these stories because children have helped to create them. My readers know what they want and realize that I try to please them. The result is very satisfactory to the publishers, to me, and (I am quite sure) to the children.

I hope, my dears, it will be a long time before we are obliged to dissolve partnership.

L. Frank Baum

Coronado, 1910

Chapter 1

HOW the NOME KING BECAME ANGRY

The Nome King was in an angry mood, and at such times he was very disagreeable. Every one kept away from him, even his Chief Steward Kaliko.

Therefore the King stormed and raved all by himself, walking up and down in his jewel-studded cavern and getting angrier all the time. Then he remembered that it was no fun being angry unless he had some one to frighten and make miserable, and he rushed to his big gong and made it clatter as loud as he could.

In came the Chief Steward, trying not to show the Nome King how frightened he was.

"Send the Chief Counselor here!" shouted the angry monarch.

Kaliko ran out as fast as his spindle legs could carry his fat round body, and soon the Chief Counselor entered the cavern. The King scowled and said to him:

"I'm in great trouble over the loss of my Magic Belt. Every little while I want to do something magical, and find I can't because the Belt is gone. That makes me angry, and when I'm angry I can't have a good time. Now, what do you advise?"

"Some people," said the Chief Counselor, "enjoy getting angry."

"But not all the time," declared the King. "To be angry once in a while is really good fun, because it makes others so miserable. But to be angry morning, noon and night, as I am, grows monotonous and prevents my gaining any other pleasure in life. Now, what do you advise?"

"Why, if you are angry because you want to do magical things and can't, and if you don't want to get angry at all, my advice is not to want to do magical things."

Hearing this, the King glared at his Counselor with a furious expression and tugged at his own long white whiskers until he pulled them so hard that he yelled with pain.

"You are a fool!" he exclaimed.

"I share that honor with your Majesty," said the Chief Counselor.

The King roared with rage and stamped his foot.

"Ho, there, my guards!" he cried. "Ho" is a royal way of saying, "Come here." So, when the guards had hoed, the King said to them:

"Take this Chief Counselor and throw him away."

Then the guards took the Chief Counselor, and bound him with chains to prevent his struggling, and threw him away. And the King paced up and down his cavern more angry than before.

Finally he rushed to his big gong and made it clatter like a fire-alarm. Kaliko appeared again, trembling and white with fear.

"Fetch my pipe!" yelled the King.

"Your pipe is already here, your Majesty," replied Kaliko.

"Then get my tobacco!" roared the King.

"The tobacco is in your pipe, your Majesty," returned the Steward.

"Then bring a live coal from the furnace!" commanded the King.

"The tobacco is lighted, and your Majesty is already smoking your pipe," answered the Steward.

"Why, so I am!" said the King, who had forgotten this fact; "but you are very rude to remind me of it."

"I am a lowborn, miserable villain," declared the Chief Steward, humbly.

The Nome King could think of nothing to say next, so he puffed away at his pipe and paced up and down the room. Finally he remembered how angry he was, and cried out:

"What do you mean, Kaliko, by being so contented when your monarch is unhappy?"

"What makes you unhappy?" asked the Steward.

"I've lost my Magic Belt. A little girl named Dorothy, who was here with Ozma of Oz, stole my Belt and carried it away with her," said the King, grinding his teeth with rage.

"She captured it in a fair fight," Kaliko ventured to say.

"But I want it! I must have it! Half my power is gone with that Belt!" roared the King.

"You will have to go to the Land of Oz to recover it, and your Majesty can't get to the Land of Oz in any possible way," said the Steward, yawning because he had been on duty ninety-six hours, and was sleepy.

"Why not?" asked the King.

"Because there is a deadly desert all around that fairy country, which no one is able to cross. You know that fact as well as I do, your Majesty. Never mind the lost Belt. You have plenty of power left, for you rule this underground kingdom like a tyrant, and thousands of Nomes obey your commands. I advise you to drink a glass of melted silver, to quiet your nerves, and then go to bed."

The King grabbed a big ruby and threw it at Kaliko's head. The Steward ducked to escape the heavy jewel, which crashed against the door just over his left ear.

"Get out of my sight! Vanish! Go away—and send General Blug here," screamed the Nome King.

Kaliko hastily withdrew, and the Nome King stamped up and down until the General of his armies appeared.

This Nome was known far and wide as a terrible fighter and a cruel, desperate commander. He had fifty thousand Nome soldiers, all well drilled, who feared nothing but their stern master. Yet General Blug was a trifle uneasy when he arrived and saw how angry the Nome King was.

"Ha! So you're here!" cried the King.

"So I am," said the General.

"March your army at once to the Land of Oz, capture and destroy the Emerald City, and bring back to me my Magic Belt!" roared the King.

"You're crazy," calmly remarked the General.

"What's that? What's that? What's that?" And the Nome King danced around on his pointed toes, he was so enraged.

"You don't know what you're talking about," continued the General, seating himself upon a large cut diamond. "I advise you to stand in a corner and count sixty before you speak again. By that time you may be more sensible."

The King looked around for something to throw at General Blug, but as nothing was handy he began to consider that perhaps the man was right and he had been talking foolishly. So he merely threw himself into his glittering throne and tipped his crown over his ear and curled his feet up under him and glared wickedly at Blug.

"In the first place," said the General, "we cannot march

across the deadly desert to the Land of Oz; and, if we could, the Ruler of that country, Princess Ozma, has certain fairy powers that would render my army helpless. Had you not lost your Magic Belt we might have some chance of defeating Ozma; but the Belt is gone."

"I want it!" screamed the King. "I must have it."

"Well, then, let us try in a sensible way to get it," replied the General. "The Belt was captured by a little girl named Dorothy, who lives in Kansas, in the United States of America."

"But she left it in the Emerald City, with Ozma," declared the King.

"How do you know that?" asked the General.

"One of my spies, who is a Blackbird, flew over the desert to the Land of Oz, and saw the Magic Belt in Ozma's palace," replied the King with a groan.

"Now that gives me an idea," said General Blug, thoughtfully. "There are two ways to get to the Land of Oz without traveling across the sandy desert."

"What are they?" demanded the King, eagerly.

"One way is *over* the desert, through the air; and the other way is *under* the desert, through the earth."

Hearing this the Nome King uttered a yell of joy and leaped from his throne, to resume his wild walk up and down the cavern.

"That's it, Blug!" he shouted. "That's the idea, General! I'm King of the Under World, and my subjects are all miners.

I'll make a secret tunnel under the desert to the Land of Oz—
yes! right up to the Emerald City—and you will march your
armies there and capture the whole country!"

"Softly, softly, your Majesty. Don't go too fast," warned
the General. "My Nomes are good fighters, but they are not
strong enough to conquer the Emerald City."

"Are you sure?" asked the King.

"Absolutely certain, your Majesty."

"Then what am I to do?"

"Give up the idea and mind your own business," advised
the General. "You have plenty to do trying to rule your underground kingdom."

"But I want the Magic Belt—and I'm going to have it!"
roared the Nome King.

"I'd like to see you get it," replied the General, laughing
maliciously.

The King was by this time so exasperated that he picked
up his scepter, which had a heavy ball, made from a sapphire,
at the end of it, and threw it with all his force at General Blug.
The sapphire hit the General upon his forehead and knocked
him flat upon the ground, where he lay motionless. Then the
King rang his gong and told his guards to drag out the General
and throw him away; which they did.

This Nome King was named Roquat the Red, and no one
loved him. He was a bad man and a powerful monarch, and
he had resolved to destroy the Land of Oz and its magnificent

Emerald City, to enslave Princess Ozma and little Dorothy and all the Oz people, and recover his Magic Belt. This same Belt had once enabled Roquat the Red to carry out many wicked plans; but that was before Ozma and her people marched to the underground cavern and captured it. The Nome King could not forgive Dorothy or Princess Ozma, and he had determined to be revenged upon them.

But they, for their part, did not know they had so dangerous an enemy. Indeed, Ozma and Dorothy had both almost forgotten that such a person as the Nome King yet lived under the mountains of the Land of Ev—which lay just across the deadly desert to the south of the Land of Oz.

An unsuspected enemy is doubly dangerous.

Chapter 2

HOW UNCLE HENRY GOT
into TROUBLE

Dorothy Gale lived on a farm in Kansas, with her Aunt Em and her Uncle Henry. It was not a big farm, nor a very good one, because sometimes the rain did not come when the crops needed it, and then everything withered and dried up. Once a cyclone had carried away Uncle Henry's house, so that he was obliged to build another; and as he was a poor man he had to mortgage his farm to get the money to pay for the new house. Then his health became bad and he was too feeble to work. The doctor ordered him to take a sea voyage and he went to Australia and took Dorothy with him. That cost a lot of money, too.

Uncle Henry grew poorer every year, and the crops raised on the farm only bought food for the family. Therefore the mortgage could not be paid. At last the banker who had loaned him the money said that if he did not pay on a certain day, his farm would be taken away from him.

This worried Uncle Henry a good deal, for without the farm he would have no way to earn a living. He was a good man, and worked in the field as hard as he could; and Aunt Em did all the housework, with Dorothy's help. Yet they did not seem to get along.

This little girl, Dorothy, was like dozens of little girls you know. She was loving and usually sweet-tempered, and had a round rosy face and earnest eyes. Life was a serious thing to Dorothy, and a wonderful thing, too, for she had encountered more strange adventures in her short life than many other girls of her age.

Aunt Em once said she thought the fairies must have marked Dorothy at her birth, because she had wandered into strange places and had always been protected by some unseen power. As for Uncle Henry, he thought his little niece merely a dreamer, as her dead mother had been, for he could not quite believe all the curious stories Dorothy told them of the Land of Oz, which she had several times visited. He did not think that she tried to deceive her uncle and aunt, but he imagined that she had dreamed all of those astonishing adventures, and that the dreams had been so real to her that she had come to believe them true.

Whatever the explanation might be, it was certain that Dorothy had been absent from her Kansas home for several long periods, always disappearing unexpectedly, yet always coming back safe and sound, with amazing tales of where she had been and the unusual people she had met. Her uncle and aunt listened to her stories eagerly and in spite of their doubts began to feel that the little girl had gained a lot of experience and wisdom that were unaccountable in this age, when fairies are supposed no longer to exist.

Most of Dorothy's stories were about the Land of Oz, with its beautiful Emerald City and a lovely girl Ruler named Ozma, who was the most faithful friend of the little Kansas girl. When Dorothy told about the riches of this fairy country Uncle Henry would sigh, for he knew that a single one of the great emeralds that were so common there would pay all his debts and leave his farm free. But Dorothy never brought any jewels home with her, so their poverty became greater every year.

When the banker told Uncle Henry that he must pay the money in thirty days or leave the farm, the poor man was in despair, as he knew he could not possibly get the money. So he told his wife, Aunt Em, of his trouble, and she first cried a little and then said that they must be brave and do the best they could, and go away somewhere and try to earn an honest living. But they were getting old and feeble and she feared that they could not take care of Dorothy as well as they had formerly done. Probably the little girl would also be obliged to go to work.

They did not tell their niece the sad news for several days, not wishing to make her unhappy; but one morning the little girl found Aunt Em softly crying while Uncle Henry tried to comfort her. Then Dorothy asked them to tell her what was the matter.

"We must give up the farm, my dear," replied her uncle sadly, "and wander away into the world to work for our living."

The girl listened quite seriously, for she had not known before how desperately poor they were.

"We don't mind for ourselves," said her aunt, stroking the little girl's head tenderly; "but we love you as if you were our own child, and we are heart-broken to think that you must also endure poverty, and work for a living before you have grown big and strong."

"What could I do to earn money?" asked Dorothy.

"You might do housework for some one, dear, you are so handy; or perhaps you could be a nurse-maid to little children. I'm sure I don't know exactly what you *can* do to earn money, but if your uncle and I are able to support you we will do it willingly, and send you to school. We fear, though, that we shall have much trouble in earning a living for ourselves. No one wants to employ old people who are broken down in health, as we are."

Dorothy smiled.

"Wouldn't it be funny," she said, "for me to do housework in Kansas, when I'm a Princess in the Land of Oz?"

"A Princess!" they both exclaimed, astonished.

"Yes; Ozma made me a Princess some time ago, and she has often begged me to come and live always in the Emerald City," said the child.

Her uncle and aunt looked at her in amazement. Then the man said:

"Do you suppose you could manage to return to your fairyland, my dear?"

"Oh yes," replied Dorothy; "I could do that easily."

"How?" asked Aunt Em.

"Ozma sees me every day at four o'clock, in her Magic Picture. She can see me wherever I am, no matter what I am doing. And at that time, if I make a certain secret sign, she will send for me by means of the Magic Belt, which I once captured from the Nome King. Then, in the wink of an eye, I shall be with Ozma in her palace."

The elder people remained silent for some time after Dorothy had spoken. Finally, Aunt Em said, with another sigh of regret:

"If that is the case, Dorothy, perhaps you'd better go and live in the Emerald City. It will break our hearts to lose you from our lives, but you will be so much better off with your fairy friends that it seems wisest and best for you to go."

"I'm not so sure about that," remarked Uncle Henry, shaking his grey head doubtfully. "These things all seem real to Dorothy, I know; but I'm afraid our little girl won't find her fairyland just what she had dreamed it to be. It would make me very unhappy to think that she was wandering among strangers who might be unkind to her."

Dorothy laughed merrily at this speech, and then she became very sober again, for she could see how all this trouble was worrying her aunt and uncle, and knew that unless she found a way to help them their future lives would be quite miserable and unhappy. She knew that she *could* help them. She had thought of a way already. Yet she did not tell them at once what it was, because she must ask Ozma's consent before she would be able to carry out her plans.

So she only said:

"If you will promise not to worry a bit about me, I'll go to the Land of Oz this very afternoon. And I'll make a promise, too; that you shall both see me again before the day comes when you must leave this farm."

"The day isn't far away, now," her uncle sadly replied. "I did not tell you of our trouble until I was obliged to, dear Dorothy, so the evil time is near at hand. But if you are quite sure your fairy friends will give you a home, it will be best for you to go to them, as your aunt says."

That was why Dorothy went to her little room in the attic that afternoon, taking with her a small dog named Toto. The dog had curly black hair and big brown eyes and loved Dorothy very dearly.

The child had kissed her uncle and aunt affectionately before she went upstairs, and now she looked around her little room rather wistfully, gazing at the simple trinkets and worn calico and gingham dresses, as if they were old friends. She was tempted at first to make a bundle of them, yet she knew very well that they would be of no use to her in her future life.

She sat down upon a broken-backed chair—the only one the room contained—and holding Toto in her arms waited patiently until the clock struck four.

Then she made the secret signal that had been agreed upon between her and Ozma.

Uncle Henry and Aunt Em waited downstairs. They were uneasy and a good deal excited, for this is a practical hum-drum world, and it seemed to them quite impossible that their little niece could vanish from her home and travel instantly to fairyland.

So they watched the stairs, which seemed to be the only way that Dorothy could get out of the farm-house, and they watched them a long time. They heard the clock strike four but there was no sound from above.

Half-past four came, and now they were too impatient to wait any longer. Softly, they crept up the stairs to the door of the little girl's room.

"Dorothy! Dorothy!" they called.

There was no answer.

They opened the door and looked in.

The room was empty.

Chapter 3

HOW OZMA GRANTED
DOROTHY'S REQUEST

I suppose you have read so much about the magnificent Emerald City that there is little need for me to describe it here. It is the Capital City of the Land of Oz, which is justly considered the most attractive and delightful fairyland in all the world.

The Emerald City is built all of beautiful marbles in which are set a profusion of emeralds, every one exquisitely cut and of very great size. There are other jewels used in the decorations inside the houses and palaces, such as rubies, diamonds, sapphires, amethysts and turquoises. But in the streets and upon the outside of the buildings only emeralds appear, from which circumstance the place is named the Emerald City

of Oz. It has nine thousand, six hundred and fifty-four buildings, in which lived fifty-seven thousand three hundred and
eighteen people, up to the time my story opens.

All the surrounding country, extending to the borders of
the desert which enclosed it upon every side, was full of pretty
and comfortable farm-houses, in which resided those inhabitants of Oz who preferred country to city life.

Altogether there were more than half a million people
in the Land of Oz—although some of them, as you will soon
learn, were not made of flesh and blood as we are—and every
inhabitant of that favored country was happy and prosperous.

No disease of any sort was ever known among the Ozites,
and so no one ever died unless he met with an accident that
prevented him from living. This happened very seldom, indeed.
There were no poor people in the Land of Oz, because there
was no such thing as money, and all property of every sort
belonged to the Ruler. The people were her children, and she
cared for them. Each person was given freely by his neighbors
whatever he required for his use, which is as much as any one
may reasonably desire. Some tilled the lands and raised great
crops of grain, which was divided equally among the entire
population, so that all had enough. There were many tailors
and dressmakers and shoemakers and the like, who made
things that any who desired them might wear. Likewise there
were jewelers who made ornaments for the person, which
pleased and beautified the people, and these ornaments also

were free to those who asked for them. Each man and woman, no matter what he or she produced for the good of the community, was supplied by the neighbors with food and clothing and a house and furniture and ornaments and games. If by chance the supply ever ran short, more was taken from the great storehouses of the Ruler, which were afterward filled up again when there was more of any article than the people needed.

Every one worked half the time and played half the time, and the people enjoyed the work as much as they did the play, because it is good to be occupied and to have something to do. There were no cruel overseers set to watch them, and no one to rebuke them or to find fault with them. So each one was proud to do all he could for his friends and neighbors, and was glad when they would accept the things he produced.

You will know, by what I have here told you, that the Land of Oz was a remarkable country. I do not suppose such an arrangement would be practical with us, but Dorothy assures me that it works finely with the Oz people.

Oz being a fairy country, the people were, of course, fairy people; but that does not mean that all of them were very unlike the people of our own world. There were all sorts of queer characters among them, but not a single one who was evil, or who possessed a selfish or violent nature. They were peaceful, kind-hearted, loving and merry, and every inhabitant adored the beautiful girl who ruled them, and delighted to obey her every command.

In spite of all I have said in a general way, there were some parts of the Land of Oz not quite so pleasant as the farming country and the Emerald City which was its center. Far away in the South Country there lived in the mountains a band of strange people called Hammer-Heads, because they had no arms and used their flat heads to pound any one who came near them. Their necks were like rubber, so that they could shoot out their heads to quite a distance, and afterward draw them back again to their shoulders. The Hammer-Heads were called the "Wild People," but never harmed any but those who disturbed them in the mountains where they lived.

In some of the dense forests there lived great beasts of every sort; yet these were for the most part harmless and even sociable, and conversed agreeably with those who visited their haunts. The Kalidahs—beasts with bodies like bears and heads like tigers—had once been fierce and bloodthirsty, but even they were now nearly all tamed, although at times one or another of them would get cross and disagreeable.

Not so tame were the Fighting Trees, which had a forest of their own. If any one approached them these curious trees would bend down their branches, twine them around the intruders, and hurl them away.

But these unpleasant things existed only in a few remote parts of the Land of Oz. I suppose every country has some drawbacks, so even this almost perfect fairyland could not be quite perfect. Once there had been wicked witches in the land, too; but now these had all been destroyed; so, as I said, only peace and happiness reigned in Oz.

For some time Ozma had ruled over this fair country, and never was Ruler more popular or beloved. She is said to be the most beautiful girl the world has ever known, and her heart and mind are as lovely as her person.

Dorothy Gale had several times visited the Emerald City and experienced adventures in the Land of Oz, so that she and Ozma had now become firm friends. The girl Ruler had even made Dorothy a Princess of Oz, and had often implored her to come to Ozma's stately palace and live there always; but Dorothy had been loyal to her Aunt Em and Uncle Henry, who had cared for her since she was a baby, and she had refused to leave them because she knew they would be lonely without her.

However, Dorothy now realized that things were going to be different with her uncle and aunt from this time forth, so after giving the matter deep thought she decided to ask Ozma to grant her a very great favor.

A few seconds after she had made the secret signal in her little bedchamber, the Kansas girl was seated in a lovely room in Ozma's palace in the Emerald City of Oz. When the first loving kisses and embraces had been exchanged, the fair Ruler inquired:

"What is the matter, dear? I know something unpleasant

has happened to you, for your face was very sober when I saw it in my Magic Picture. And whenever you signal me to transport you to this safe place, where you are always welcome, I know you are in danger or in trouble."

Dorothy sighed.

"This time, Ozma, it isn't I," she replied. "But it's worse, I guess, for Uncle Henry and Aunt Em are in a heap of trouble, and there seems no way for them to get out of it—anyhow, not while they live in Kansas."

"Tell me about it, Dorothy," said Ozma, with ready sympathy.

"Why, you see Uncle Henry is poor; for the farm in Kansas doesn't 'mount to much, as farms go. So one day Uncle Henry borrowed some money, and wrote a letter saying that if he didn't pay the money back they could take his farm for pay. Course he 'spected to pay by making money from the farm; but he just couldn't. An' so they're going to take the farm, and Uncle Henry and Aunt Em won't have any place to live. They're pretty old to do much hard work, Ozma; so I'll have to work for them, unless—"

Ozma had been thoughtful during the story, but now she smiled and pressed her little friend's hand.

"Unless what, dear?" she asked.

Dorothy hesitated, because her request meant so much to them all.

"Well," said she, "I'd like to live here in the Land of Oz,

where you've often 'vited me to live. But I can't, you know, unless Uncle Henry and Aunt Em could live here too."

"Of course not," exclaimed the Ruler of Oz, laughing gaily. "So, in order to get you, little friend, we must invite your Uncle and Aunt to live in Oz, also."

"Oh, will you, Ozma?" cried Dorothy, clasping her chubby little hands eagerly. "Will you bring them here with the Magic Belt, and give them a nice little farm in the Munchkin Country, or the Winkie Country—or some other place?"

"To be sure," answered Ozma, full of joy at the chance to please her little friend. "I have long been thinking of this very thing, Dorothy dear, and often I have had it in my mind to propose it to you. I am sure your uncle and aunt must be good and worthy people, or you would not love them so much; and for *your* friends, Princess, there is always room in the Land of Oz."

Dorothy was delighted, yet not altogether surprised, for she had clung to the hope that Ozma would be kind enough to grant her request. When, indeed, had her powerful and faithful friend refused her anything?

"But you must not call me 'Princess,'" she said; "for after this I shall live on the little farm with Uncle Henry and Aunt Em, and princesses ought not to live on farms."

"Princess Dorothy will not," replied Ozma with her sweet smile. "You are going to live in your own rooms in this palace, and be my constant companion."

"But Uncle Henry—" began Dorothy.

"Oh, he is old, and has worked enough in his lifetime," interrupted the girl Ruler; "so we must find a place for your uncle and aunt where they will be comfortable and happy and need not work more than they care to. When shall we transport them here, Dorothy?"

"I promised to go and see them again before they were turned out of the farm-house," answered Dorothy; "so— perhaps next Saturday—"

"But why wait so long?" asked Ozma. "And why make the journey back to Kansas again? Let us surprise them, and bring them here without any warning."

"I'm not sure that they believe in the Land of Oz," said Dorothy, "though I've told 'em 'bout it lots of times."

"They'll believe when they see it," declared Ozma; "and if they are told they are to make a magical journey to our fairyland, it may make them nervous. I think the best way will be to use the Magic Belt without warning them, and when they have arrived you can explain to them whatever they do not understand."

"Perhaps that's best," decided Dorothy. "There isn't much use in their staying at the farm until they are put out, 'cause it's much nicer here."

"Then to-morrow morning they shall come here," said Princess Ozma. "I will order Jellia Jamb, who is the palace housekeeper, to have rooms all prepared for them, and after breakfast we will get the Magic Belt and by its aid transport your uncle and aunt to the Emerald City."

"Thank you, Ozma!" cried Dorothy, kissing her friend gratefully.

"And now," Ozma proposed, "let us take a walk in the gardens before we dress for dinner. Come, Dorothy dear!"

Chapter 4

HOW the NOME KING
PLANNED REVENGE

The reason most people are bad is because they do not try to be good. Now, the Nome King had never tried to be good, so he was very bad indeed. Having decided to conquer the Land of Oz and to destroy the Emerald City and enslave all its people, King Roquat the Red kept planning ways to do this dreadful thing, and the more he planned the more he believed he would be able to accomplish it.

About the time Dorothy went to Ozma the Nome King called his Chief Steward to him and said:

"Kaliko, I think I shall make you the General of my armies."

"I think you won't," replied Kaliko, positively.

"Why not?" inquired the King, reaching for his scepter with the big sapphire.

"Because I'm your Chief Steward and know nothing of warfare," said Kaliko, preparing to dodge if anything were thrown at him. "I manage all the affairs of your kingdom better than you could yourself, and you'll never find another Steward as good as I am. But there are a hundred Nomes better fitted to command your army, and your Generals get thrown away so often that I have no desire to be one of them."

"Ah, there is some truth in your remarks, Kaliko," remarked the King, deciding not to throw the scepter. "Summon my army to assemble in the Great Cavern."

Kaliko bowed and retired, and in a few minutes returned to say that the army was assembled. So the King went out upon a balcony that overlooked the Great Cavern, where fifty thousand Nomes, all armed with swords and pikes, stood marshaled in military array.

When they were not required as soldiers all these Nomes were metal workers and miners, and they had hammered so much at the forges and dug so hard with pick and shovel that they had acquired great muscular strength. They were strangely formed creatures, rather round and not very tall. Their toes were curly and their ears broad and flat.

In time of war every Nome left his forge or mine and became part of the great army of King Roquat. The soldiers wore rock-colored uniforms and were excellently drilled.

The King looked upon this tremendous army, which stood silently arrayed before him, and a cruel smile curled the corners of his mouth, for he saw that his legions were very powerful. Then he addressed them from the balcony, saying:

"I have thrown away General Blug, because he did not please me. So I want another General to command this army. Who is next in command?"

"I am," replied Colonel Crinkle, a dapper-looking Nome, as he stepped forward to salute his monarch.

The King looked at him carefully and said:

"I want you to march this army through an underground tunnel, which I am going to bore, to the Emerald City of Oz. When you get there I want you to conquer the Oz people, destroy them and their city, and bring all their gold and silver and precious stones back to my cavern. Also you are to recapture my Magic Belt and return it to me. Will you do this, General Crinkle?"

"No, your Majesty," replied the Nome; "for it can't be done."

"Oh indeed!" exclaimed the King. Then he turned to his servants and said: "Please take General Crinkle to the torture chamber. There you will kindly slice him into thin slices. Afterward you may feed him to the seven-headed dogs."

"Anything to oblige your Majesty," replied the servants, politely, and led the condemned man away.

When they had gone, the King addressed the army again.

"Listen!" said he. "The General who is to command my armies must promise to carry out my orders. If he fails he will share the fate of poor Crinkle. Now, then, who will volunteer to lead my hosts to the Emerald City?"

For a time no one moved and all were silent. Then an old Nome with white whiskers so long that they were tied around his waist to prevent their tripping him up, stepped out of the ranks and saluted the King.

"I'd like to ask a few questions, your Majesty," he said.

"Go ahead," replied the King.

"These Oz people are quite good, are they not?"

"As good as apple-pie," said the King.

"And they are happy, I suppose?" continued the old Nome.

"Happy as the day is long," said the King.

"And contented and prosperous?" inquired the Nome.

"Very much so," said the King.

"Well, your Majesty," remarked he of the white whiskers, "I think I should like to undertake the job, so I'll be your General. I hate good people; I detest happy people; I'm opposed to any one who is contented and prosperous. That is why I am so fond of your Majesty. Make me your General and I'll promise to conquer and destroy the Oz people. If I fail I'm ready to be sliced thin and fed to the seven-headed dogs."

"Very good! Very good, indeed! That's the way to talk!" cried Roquat the Red, who was greatly pleased. "What is your name, General?"

"I'm called Guph, your Majesty."

"Well, Guph, come with me to my private cave and we'll talk it over." Then he turned to the army. "Nomes and soldiers," said he, "you are to obey the commands of General Guph until he becomes dog-feed. Any man who fails to obey his new General will be promptly thrown away. You are now dismissed."

Guph went to the King's private cave and sat down upon an amethyst chair and put his feet on the arm of the King's ruby throne. Then he lighted his pipe and threw the live coal he had taken from his pocket upon the King's left foot and puffed the smoke into the King's eyes and made himself comfortable. For he was a wise old Nome, and he knew that the best way to get along with Roquat the Red was to show that he was not afraid of him.

"I'm ready for the talk, your Majesty," he said.

The King coughed and looked at his new General fiercely.

"Do you not tremble to take such liberties with your monarch?" he asked.

"Oh, no," replied Guph, calmly, and he blew a wreath of smoke that curled around the King's nose and made him sneeze. "You want to conquer the Emerald City, and I'm the only Nome in all your dominions who can conquer it. So you will be very careful not to hurt me until I have carried out your wishes. After that—"

"Well, what then?" inquired the King.

"Then you will be so grateful to me that you won't care to hurt me," replied the General.

"That is a very good argument," said Roquat. "But suppose you fail?"

"Then it's the slicing machine. I agree to that," announced Guph. "But if you do as I tell you there will be no failure. The trouble with you, Roquat, is that you don't think carefully enough. I do. You would go ahead and march through your tunnel into Oz, and get defeated and driven back. I won't. And the reason I won't is because when I march I'll have all my plans made, and a host of allies to assist my Nomes."

"What do you mean by that?" asked the King.

"I'll explain, King Roquat. You're going to attack a fairy country, and a mighty fairy country, too. They haven't much of an army in Oz, but the Princess who rules them has a fairy wand; and the little girl Dorothy has your Magic Belt; and at the North of the Emerald City lives a clever sorceress called Glinda the Good, who commands the spirits of the air. Also I have heard that there is a wonderful Wizard in Ozma's palace, who is so skillful that people used to pay him money in America to see him perform. So you see it will be no easy thing to overcome all this magic."

"We have fifty thousand soldiers!" cried the King proudly.

"Yes; but they are Nomes," remarked Guph, taking a silk handkerchief from the King's pocket and wiping his own pointed shoes with it. "Nomes are immortals, but they are not strong on magic. When you lost your famous Belt the greater part of your own power was gone from you. Against Ozma you and your Nomes would have no show at all."

Roquat's eyes flashed angrily.

"Then away you go to the slicing machine!" he cried.

"Not yet," said the General, filling his pipe from the King's private tobacco pouch.

"What do you propose to do?" asked the monarch.

"I propose to obtain the power we need," answered Guph. "There are a good many evil creatures who have magic powers sufficient to destroy and conquer the Land of Oz. We will get them on our side, band them all together, and then take Ozma and her people by surprise. It's all very simple and easy when you know how. Alone, we should be helpless to injure the Ruler of Oz, but with the aid of the evil powers we can summon we shall easily succeed."

King Roquat was delighted with this idea, for he realized how clever it was.

"Surely, Guph, you are the greatest General I have ever had!" he exclaimed, his eyes sparkling with joy. "You must go at once and make arrangements with the evil powers to assist us, and meantime I'll begin to dig the tunnel."

"I thought you'd agree with me, Roquat," replied the new General. "I'll start this very afternoon to visit the Chief of the Whimsies."

Chapter 5

How Dorothy Became a Princess

When the people of the Emerald City heard that Dorothy had returned to them every one was eager to see her, for the little girl was a general favorite in the Land of Oz. From time to time some of the folk from the great outside world had found their way into this fairyland, but all except one had been companions of Dorothy and had turned out to be very agreeable people. The exception I speak of was the wonderful Wizard of Oz, a sleight-of-hand performer from Omaha who went up in a balloon and was carried by a current of air to the Emerald City. His queer and puzzling tricks made the people of Oz believe him a great wizard for a time, and he ruled over them until Dorothy arrived on her first visit and showed the Wizard to be a mere humbug. He was a gentle, kindly-hearted little man, and Dorothy grew to like him afterward. When, after an absence, the Wizard returned to the Land of Oz, Ozma received him graciously and gave him a home in a part of the palace.

In addition to the Wizard two other personages from the outside world had been allowed to make their home in the Emerald City. The first was a quaint Shaggy Man, whom Ozma had made the Governor of the Royal Storehouses, and the second a Yellow Hen named Billina, who had a fine house in the gardens back of the palace, where she looked after a large family. Both these had been old comrades of Dorothy, so you see the little girl was quite an important personage in Oz, and the people thought she had brought them good luck, and loved her next best to Ozma. During her several visits this little girl had been the means of destroying two wicked witches who oppressed the people, and she had discovered a live scarecrow who was now one of the most popular personages in all the fairy country. With the Scarecrow's help she had rescued Nick Chopper, a Tin Woodman, who had rusted in a lonely forest, and the tin man was now the Emperor of the Country of the Winkies and much beloved because of his kind heart. No wonder the people thought Dorothy had brought them good luck! Yet, strange as it may seem, she had accomplished all these wonders not because she was a fairy or had any magical powers whatever, but because she was a simple, sweet and true little girl who was honest to herself and to all whom she met. In this world in which we live simplicity and kindness are the only magic wands that work wonders, and in the Land of Oz Dorothy found these same qualities had won for her the love and admiration of the people. Indeed, the little girl had made many warm friends in the fairy country, and the only real grief the Ozites had ever experienced was when Dorothy left them and returned to her Kansas home.

Now she received a joyful welcome, although no one except Ozma knew at first that she had finally come to stay for good and all.

That evening Dorothy had many callers, and among them were such important people as Tiktok, a machine man who thought and spoke and moved by clockwork; her old companion the genial Shaggy Man; Jack Pumpkinhead, whose body was brush-wood and whose head was a ripe pumpkin with a face carved upon it; the Cowardly Lion and the Hungry Tiger, two great beasts from the forest, who served Princess Ozma, and Professor H. M. Woggle-Bug, T.E. This woggle-bug was a remarkable creature. He had once been a tiny little bug, crawling around in a school-room, but he was discovered and highly magnified so that he could be seen more plainly, and while in this magnified condition he had escaped. He had always remained big, and he dressed like a dandy and was so full of knowledge and information (which are distinct acquirements), that he had been made a Professor and the head of the Royal College.

Dorothy had a nice visit with these old friends, and also talked a long time with the Wizard, who was little and old and withered and dried up, but as merry and active as a child. Afterward, she went to see Billina's fast growing family of chicks.

Toto, Dorothy's little black dog, also met with a cordial reception. Toto was an especial friend of the Shaggy Man, and he knew every one else. Being the only dog in the Land of Oz, he was highly respected by the people, who believed animals entitled to every consideration if they behaved themselves properly.

Dorothy had four lovely rooms in the palace, which were always reserved for her use and were called "Dorothy's rooms." These consisted of a beautiful sitting room, a dressing room, a dainty bedchamber and a big marble bathroom. And in these rooms were everything that heart could desire, placed there with loving thoughtfulness by Ozma for her little friend's use. The royal dressmakers had the little girl's measure, so they kept the closets in her dressing room filled with lovely dresses of every description and suitable for every occasion. No wonder Dorothy had refrained from bringing with her her old calico and gingham dresses! Here everything that was dear to a little girl's heart was supplied in profusion, and nothing so rich and beautiful could ever have been found in the biggest department stores in America. Of course Dorothy enjoyed all

these luxuries, and the only reason she had heretofore preferred to live in Kansas was because her uncle and aunt loved
her and needed her with them.

Now, however, all was to be changed, and Dorothy was
really more delighted to know that her dear relatives were to
share in her good fortune and enjoy the delights of the Land of
Oz, than she was to possess such luxury for herself.

Next morning, at Ozma's request, Dorothy dressed herself in a pretty sky-blue gown of rich silk, trimmed with real
pearls. The buckles of her shoes were set with pearls, too, and
more of these priceless gems were on a lovely coronet which
she wore upon her forehead. "For," said her friend Ozma,
"from this time forth, my dear, you must assume your rightful
rank as a Princess of Oz, and being my chosen companion you
must dress in a way befitting the dignity of your position."

Dorothy agreed to this, although she knew that neither
gowns nor jewels could make her anything else than the
simple, unaffected little girl she had always been.

As soon as they had breakfasted—the girls eating together
in Ozma's pretty boudoir—the Ruler of Oz said:

"Now, dear friend, we will use the Magic Belt to transport
your uncle and aunt from Kansas to the Emerald City. But
I think it would be fitting, in receiving such distinguished
guests, for us to sit in my Throne Room."

"Oh, they're not very 'stinguished, Ozma," said Dorothy.
"They're just plain people, like me."

"Being your friends and relatives, Princess Dorothy, they are certainly distinguished," replied the Ruler, with a smile.

"They—they won't hardly know what to make of all your splendid furniture and things," protested Dorothy, gravely. "It may scare 'em to see your grand Throne Room, an' p'raps we'd better go into the back yard, Ozma, where the cabbages grow an' the chickens are playing. Then it would seem more natural to Uncle Henry and Aunt Em."

"No; they shall first see me in my Throne Room," replied Ozma, decidedly; and when she spoke in that tone Dorothy knew it was not wise to oppose her, for Ozma was accustomed to having her own way.

So together they went to the Throne Room, an immense domed chamber in the center of the palace. Here stood the royal throne, made of solid gold and encrusted with enough precious stones to stock a dozen jewelry stores in our country.

Ozma, who was wearing the Magic Belt, seated herself in the throne, and Dorothy sat at her feet. In the room were assembled many ladies and gentlemen of the court, clothed in rich apparel and wearing fine jewelry. Two immense animals squatted, one on each side of the throne—the Cowardly Lion and the Hungry Tiger. In a balcony high up in the dome an orchestra played sweet music, and beneath the dome two electric fountains sent sprays of colored perfumed water shooting up nearly as high as the arched ceiling.

"Are you ready, Dorothy?" asked the Ruler.

"I am," replied Dorothy; "but I don't know whether Aunt Em and Uncle Henry are ready."

"That won't matter," declared Ozma. "The old life can have very little to interest them, and the sooner they begin the new life here the happier they will be. Here they come, my dear!"

As she spoke, there before the throne appeared Uncle Henry and Aunt Em, who for a moment stood motionless, glaring with white and startled faces at the scene that confronted them. If the ladies and gentlemen present had not been so polite I am sure they would have laughed at the two strangers.

Aunt Em had her calico dress skirt "tucked up," and she wore a faded, blue-checked apron. Her hair was rather straggly and she had on a pair of Uncle Henry's old slippers. In one hand she held a dish-towel and in the other a cracked earthenware plate, which she had been engaged in wiping when so suddenly transported to the Land of Oz.

Uncle Henry, when the summons came, had been out in the barn "doin' chores." He wore a ragged and much soiled straw hat, a checked shirt without any collar and blue overalls tucked into the tops of his old cowhide boots.

"By gum!" gasped Uncle Henry, looking around as if bewildered.

"Well, I swan!" gurgled Aunt Em in a hoarse, frightened voice. Then her eyes fell upon Dorothy, and she said: "D-d-d-don't that look like our little girl—our Dorothy, Henry?"

"Hi, there—look out, Em!" exclaimed the old man, as Aunt Em advanced a step; "take care o' the wild beastses, or you're a goner!"

But now Dorothy sprang forward and embraced and kissed her aunt and uncle affectionately, afterward taking their hands in her own.

"Don't be afraid," she said to them. "You are now in the Land of Oz, where you are to live always, and be comfer'ble an' happy. You'll never have to worry over anything again, 'cause there won't be anything to worry about. And you owe it all to the kindness of my friend Princess Ozma."

Here she led them before the throne and continued:

"Your Highness, this is Uncle Henry. And this is Aunt Em. They want to thank you for bringing them here from Kansas."

Aunt Em tried to "slick" her hair, and she hid the dish-towel and dish under her apron while she bowed to the lovely Ozma. Uncle Henry took off his straw hat and held it awkwardly in his hands.

But the Ruler of Oz rose and came from her throne to greet her newly arrived guests, and she smiled as sweetly upon them as if they had been a king and queen.

"You are very welcome here, where I have brought you for Princess Dorothy's sake," she said, graciously, "and I hope you will be quite happy in your new home." Then she turned to her courtiers, who were silently and gravely regarding the scene, and added: "I present to my people our Princess Dorothy's beloved Uncle Henry and Aunt Em, who will hereafter be subjects of our kingdom. It will please me to have you show them every kindness and honor in your power, and to join me in making them happy and contented."

Hearing this, all those assembled bowed low and respectfully to the old farmer and his wife, who bobbed their own heads in return.

"And now," said Ozma to them, "Dorothy will show you the rooms prepared for you. I hope you will like them, and shall expect you to join me at luncheon."

So Dorothy led her relatives away, and as soon as they were out of the Throne Room and alone in the corridor, Aunt Em squeezed Dorothy's hand and said:

"Child, child! How in the world did we ever get here so quick? And is it all real? And are we to stay here, as she says? And what does it all mean, anyhow?"

Dorothy laughed.

"Why didn't you tell us what you were goin' to do?" inquired Uncle Henry, reproachfully. "If I'd known about it, I'd 'a put on my Sunday clothes."

"I'll 'splain ever'thing as soon as we get to your rooms," promised Dorothy. "You're in great luck, Uncle Henry and Aunt Em; an' so am I! And oh! I'm so happy to have got you here, at last!"

As he walked by the little girl's side Uncle Henry stroked his whiskers thoughtfully.

"'Pears to me, Dorothy, we won't make bang-up fairies," he remarked.

"An' my back hair looks like a fright!" wailed Aunt Em.

"Never mind," returned the little girl, reassuringly. "You won't have anything to do now but to look pretty, Aunt Em; an' Uncle Henry won't have to work till his back aches, that's certain."

"Sure?" they asked, wonderingly, and in the same breath.

"Course I'm sure," said Dorothy. "You're in the fairyland of Oz, now; an' what's more, you belong to it!"

Chapter 6

How Guph Visited the Whimsies

The new General of the Nome King's army knew perfectly well that to fail in his plans meant death for him. Yet he was not at all anxious or worried. He hated every one who was good and longed to make all who were happy unhappy. Therefore he had accepted this dangerous position as General quite willingly, feeling sure in his evil mind that he would be able to do a lot of mischief and finally conquer the Land of Oz.

Yet Guph determined to be careful, and to lay his plans well, so as not to fail. He argued that only careless people fail in what they attempt to do.

The mountains underneath which the Nome King's extensive caverns were located lay grouped just north of the Land of Ev, which lay directly across the deadly desert to the east of the Land of Oz. As the mountains were also on the edge of the desert the Nome King found that he had only to tunnel underneath the desert to reach Ozma's dominions. He did not wish his armies to appear above ground in the Country of the Winkies, which was the part of the Land of Oz nearest to King Roquat's own country, as then the people would give the alarm and enable Ozma to fortify the Emerald City and assemble an army. He wanted to take all the Oz people by surprise; so he decided to run the tunnel clear through to the Emerald City, where he and his hosts could break through the ground without warning and conquer the people before they had time to defend themselves.

Roquat the Red began work at once upon his tunnel, setting a thousand miners at the task and building it high and broad enough for his armies to march through it with ease. The Nomes were used to making tunnels, as all the kingdom in which they lived was underground; so they made rapid progress.

While this work was going on General Guph started out alone to visit the Chief of the Whimsies.

These Whimsies were curious people who lived in a retired country of their own. They had large, strong bodies, but heads so small that they were no bigger than door-knobs. Of course, such tiny heads could not contain any great amount of brains, and the Whimsies were so ashamed of their personal appearance and lack of commonsense that they wore big heads made of pasteboard, which they fastened over their own little heads. On these pasteboard heads they sewed sheep's wool for hair, and the wool was colored many tints—pink, green and lavender being the favorite colors.

The faces of these false heads were painted in many ridiculous ways, according to the whims of the owners, and these big, burly creatures looked so whimsical and absurd in their queer masks that they were called "Whimsies." They foolishly imagined that no one would suspect the little heads that were inside the imitation ones, not knowing that it is folly to try to appear otherwise than as nature has made us.

The Chief of the Whimsies had as little wisdom as the others, and had been chosen chief merely because none among them was any wiser or more capable of ruling. The Whimsies were evil spirits and could not be killed. They were hated and feared by every one and were known as terrible fighters because they were so strong and muscular and had not sense enough to know when they were defeated.

General Guph thought the Whimsies would be a great help to the Nomes in the conquest of Oz, for under his leadership they could be induced to fight so long as they could stand up. So he traveled to their country and asked to see the Chief, who lived in a house that had a picture of his grotesque false head painted over the doorway.

The Chief's false head had blue hair, a turned-up nose, and a mouth that stretched half across the face. Big green eyes had been painted upon it, but in the center of the chin were two small holes made in the pasteboard, so that the Chief could see through them with his own tiny eyes; for when the big head was fastened upon his shoulders the eyes in his own natural head were on a level with the false chin.

Said General Guph to the Chief of the Whimsies:

"We Nomes are going to conquer the Land of Oz and capture our King's Magic Belt, which the Oz people stole from him. Then we are going to plunder and destroy the whole country. And we want the Whimsies to help us."

"Will there be any fighting?" asked the Chief.

"Plenty," replied Guph.

That must have pleased the Chief, for he got up and danced around the room three times. Then he seated himself again, adjusted his false head, and said:

"We have no quarrel with Ozma of Oz."

"But you Whimsies love to fight, and here is a splendid chance to do so," urged Guph.

"Wait till I sing a song," said the Chief. Then he lay back in his chair and sang a foolish song that did not seem to the General to mean anything, although he listened carefully. When he had finished, the Chief Whimsie looked at him through the holes in his chin and asked:

"What reward will you give us if we help you?"

The General was prepared for this question, for he had been thinking the matter over on his journey. People often do a good deed without hope of reward, but for an evil deed they always demand payment.

"When we get our Magic Belt," he made reply, "our King, Roquat the Red, will use its power to give every Whimsie a natural head as big and fine as the false head he now wears. Then you will no longer be ashamed because your big strong bodies have such teeny-weenty heads."

"Oh! Will you do that?" asked the Chief, eagerly.

"We surely will," promised the General.

"I'll talk to my people," said the Chief.

So he called a meeting of all the Whimsies and told them of the offer made by the Nomes. The creatures were delighted with the bargain, and at once agreed to fight for the Nome King and help him to conquer Oz.

One Whimsie alone seemed to have a glimmer of sense, for he asked:

"Suppose we fail to capture the Magic Belt? What will happen then, and what good will all our fighting do?"

But they threw him into the river for asking foolish questions, and laughed when the water ruined his pasteboard head before he could swim out again.

So the compact was made and General Guph was delighted with his success in gaining such powerful allies.

But there were other people, too, just as important as the Whimsies, whom the clever old Nome had determined to win to his side.

Chapter 7

How Aunt Em
Conquered the Lion

These are your rooms," said Dorothy, opening a door.

Aunt Em drew back at the sight of the splendid furniture and draperies.

"Ain't there any place to wipe my feet?" she asked.

"You will soon change your slippers for new shoes," replied Dorothy. "Don't be afraid, Aunt Em. Here is where you are to live, so walk right in and make yourself at home."

Aunt Em advanced hesitatingly.

"It beats the Topeka Hotel!" she cried admiringly. "But this place is too grand for us, child. Can't we have some back room in the attic, that's more in our class?"

"No," said Dorothy. "You've got to live here, 'cause Ozma says so. And all the rooms in this palace are just as fine as these, and some are better. It won't do any good to fuss, Aunt Em. You've got to be swell and high-toned in the Land of Oz, whether you want to or not; so you may as well make up your mind to it."

"It's hard luck," replied her aunt, looking around with an awed expression; "but folks can get used to anything, if they try. Eh, Henry?"

"Why, as to that," said Uncle Henry, slowly, "I b'lieve in takin' what's pervided us, an' askin' no questions. I've traveled some, Em, in my time, and you hain't; an' that makes a difference atween us."

Then Dorothy showed them through the rooms. The first was a handsome sitting-room, with windows opening upon the rose gardens. Then came separate bedrooms for Aunt Em and Uncle Henry, with a fine bathroom between them. Aunt Em had a pretty dressing room, besides, and Dorothy opened the closets and showed several exquisite costumes that had been provided for her aunt by the royal dressmakers, who had worked all night to get them ready. Everything that Aunt Em could possibly need was in the drawers and closets, and her dressing-table was covered with engraved gold toilet articles.

Uncle Henry had nine suits of clothes, cut in the popular Munchkin fashion, with knee-breeches, silk stockings and low shoes with jeweled buckles. The hats to match these costumes had pointed tops and wide brims with small gold bells around the edges. His shirts were of fine linen with frilled bosoms, and his vests were richly embroidered with colored silks.

Uncle Henry decided that he would first take a bath and then dress himself in a blue satin suit that had caught his fancy. He accepted his good fortune with calm composure and refused to have a servant to assist him. But Aunt Em was "all of a flutter," as she said, and it took Dorothy and Jellia Jamb, the housekeeper, and two maids a long time to dress her and do up her hair and get her "rigged like a popinjay," as she quaintly expressed it. She wanted to stop and admire everything that caught her eye, and she sighed continually and declared that such finery was too good for an old country woman, and that she never thought she would have to "put on airs" at her time of life.

Finally she was dressed, and when they went into the sitting-room there was Uncle Henry in his blue satin, walking gravely up and down the room. He had trimmed his beard and mustache and looked very dignified and respectable.

"Tell me, Dorothy," he said; "do all the men here wear duds like these?"

"Yes," she replied; "all 'cept the Scarecrow and the Shaggy Man—and of course the Tin Woodman and Tiktok, who are made of metal. You'll find all the men at Ozma's court dressed just as you are—only perhaps a little finer."

"Henry, you look like a play-actor," announced Aunt Em, looking at her husband critically.

"An' you, Em, look more highfalutin' than a peacock," he replied.

"I guess you're right," she said regretfully; "but we're helpless victims of high-toned royalty."

Dorothy was much amused.

"Come with me," she said, "and I'll show you 'round the palace."

She took them through the beautiful rooms and introduced them to all the people they chanced to meet. Also she showed them her own pretty rooms, which were not far from their own.

"So it's all true," said Aunt Em, wide-eyed with amazement, "and what Dorothy told us of this fairy country was plain facts instead of dreams! But where are all the strange creatures you used to know here?"

"Yes, where's the Scarecrow?" inquired Uncle Henry.

"Why, he's just now away on a visit to the Tin Woodman, who is Emp'ror of the Winkie Country," answered the little girl. "You'll see him when he comes back, and you're sure to like him."

"And where's the Wonderful Wizard?" asked Aunt Em.

"You'll see him at Ozma's luncheon, for he lives here in this palace," was the reply.

"And Jack Pumpkinhead?"

"Oh, he lives a little way out of town, in his own pumpkin

field. We'll go there some time and see him, and we'll call on Professor Woggle-Bug, too. The Shaggy Man will be at the luncheon, I guess, and Tiktok. And now I'll take you out to see Billina, who has a house of her own."

So they went into the back yard, and after walking along winding paths some distance through the beautiful gardens they came to an attractive little house where the Yellow Hen sat on the front porch sunning herself.

"Good morning, my dear Mistress," called Billina, fluttering down to meet them. "I was expecting you to call, for I heard you had come back and brought your uncle and aunt with you."

"We're here for good and all, this time, Billina," cried Dorothy, joyfully. "Uncle Henry and Aunt Em belong to Oz now as much as I do!"

"Then they are very lucky people," declared Billina; "for there couldn't be a nicer place to live. But come, my dear; I must show you all my Dorothys. Nine are living and have grown up to be very respectable hens; but one took cold at Ozma's birthday party and died of the pip, and the other two turned out to be horrid roosters, so I had to change their names from Dorothy to Daniel. They all had the letter 'D' engraved upon their gold lockets, you remember, with your picture inside, and 'D' stands for Daniel as well as for Dorothy."

"Did you call both the roosters Daniel?" asked Uncle Henry.

"Yes, indeed. I've nine Dorothys and two Daniels; and the

nine Dorothys have eighty-six sons and daughters and over three hundred grandchildren," said Billina, proudly.

"What names do you give 'em all, dear?" inquired the little girl.

"Oh, they are all Dorothys and Daniels, some being Juniors and some Double-Juniors. Dorothy and Daniel are two good names, and I see no object in hunting for others," declared the Yellow Hen. "But just think, Dorothy, what a big chicken family we've grown to be, and our numbers increase nearly every day! Ozma doesn't know what to do with all the eggs we lay, and we are never eaten or harmed in any way, as chickens are in your country. They give us everything to make us contented and happy, and I, my dear, am the acknowledged Queen and Governor of every chicken in Oz, because I'm the eldest and started the whole colony."

"You ought to be very proud, ma'am," said Uncle Henry, who was astonished to hear a hen talk so sensibly.

"Oh, I am," she replied. "I've the loveliest pearl necklace you ever saw. Come in the house and I'll show it to you. And I've nine leg bracelets and a diamond pin for each wing. But I only wear them on state occasions."

They followed the Yellow Hen into the house, which Aunt Em declared was neat as a pin. They could not sit down, because all Billina's chairs were roosting-poles made of silver; so they had to stand while the hen fussily showed them her treasures.

Then they had to go into the back rooms occupied by

Billina's nine Dorothys and two Daniels, who were all plump yellow chickens and greeted the visitors very politely. It was easy to see that they were well bred and that Billina had looked after their education.

In the yards were all the children and grandchildren of these eleven elders and they were of all sizes, from well-grown hens to tiny chickens just out of the shell. About fifty fluffy yellow youngsters were at school, being taught good manners and good grammar by a young hen who wore spectacles. They sang in chorus a patriotic song of the Land of Oz, in honor of their visitors, and Aunt Em was much impressed by these talking chickens.

Dorothy wanted to stay and play with the young chickens for awhile, but Uncle Henry and Aunt Em had not seen the palace grounds and gardens yet and were eager to get better acquainted with the marvelous and delightful land in which they were to live.

"I'll stay here, and you can go for a walk," said Dorothy. "You'll be perfec'ly safe anywhere, and may do whatever you want to. When you get tired, go back to the palace and find your rooms, and I'll come to you before luncheon is ready."

So Uncle Henry and Aunt Em started out alone to explore the grounds, and Dorothy knew that they couldn't get lost, because all the palace grounds were enclosed by a high wall of green marble set with emeralds.

It was a rare treat to these simple folk, who had lived in the country all their lives and known little enjoyment of any sort, to wear beautiful clothes and live in a palace and be treated with respect and consideration by all around them. They were very happy indeed as they strolled up the shady walks and looked upon the gorgeous flowers and shrubs, feeling that their new home was more beautiful than any tongue could describe.

Suddenly, as they turned a corner and walked through a gap in a high hedge, they came face to face with an enormous Lion, which crouched upon the green lawn and seemed surprised by their appearance.

They stopped short, Uncle Henry trembling with horror and Aunt Em too terrified to scream. Next moment the poor woman clasped her husband around the neck and cried:

"Save me, Henry, save me!"

"Can't even save myself, Em," he returned, in a husky voice, "for the animile looks as if it could eat both of us, an' lick its chops for more! If I only had a gun—"

"Haven't you, Henry? Haven't you?" she asked anxiously.

"Nary gun, Em. So let's die as brave an' graceful as we can. I knew our luck couldn't last!"

"I won't die. I won't be eaten by a lion!" wailed Aunt Em, glaring upon the huge beast. Then a thought struck her, and she whispered, "Henry, I've heard as savage beastses can be conquered by the human eye. I'll eye that lion out o' countenance an' save our lives."

"Try it, Em," he returned, also in a whisper. "Look at him as you do at me when I'm late to dinner."

Aunt Em turned upon the Lion a determined countenance and a wild dilated eye. She glared at the immense beast steadily, and the Lion, who had been quietly blinking at them, began to appear uneasy and disturbed.

"Is anything the matter, ma'am?" he asked, in a mild voice.

At this speech from the terrible beast Aunt Em and Uncle Henry both were startled, and then Uncle Henry remembered that this must be the Lion they had seen in Ozma's Throne Room.

"Hold on, Em!" he exclaimed. "Quit the eagle eye conquest an' take courage. I guess this is the same Cowardly Lion Dorothy has told us about."

"Oh, is it?" she cried, much relieved.

"When he spoke, I got the idea; and when he looked so 'shamed like, I was sure of it," Uncle Henry continued.

Aunt Em regarded the animal with new interest.

"Are you the Cowardly Lion?" she inquired. "Are you Dorothy's friend?"

"Yes'm," answered the Lion, meekly. "Dorothy and I are old chums and are very fond of each other. I'm the King of Beasts, you know, and the Hungry Tiger and I serve Princess Ozma as her body guards."

"To be sure," said Aunt Em, nodding. "But the King of Beasts shouldn't be cowardly."

"I've heard that said before," remarked the Lion, yawning till he showed two great rows of sharp white teeth; "but that does not keep me from being frightened whenever I go into battle."

"What do you do, run?" asked Uncle Henry.

"No; that would be foolish, for the enemy would run after me," declared the Lion. "So I tremble with fear and pitch in as hard as I can; and so far I have always won my fight."

"Ah, I begin to understand," said Uncle Henry.

"Were you scared when I looked at you just now?" inquired Aunt Em.

"Terribly scared, madam," answered the Lion, "for at first I thought you were going to have a fit. Then I noticed you were trying to overcome me by the power of your eye, and your glance was so fierce and penetrating that I shook with fear."

This greatly pleased the lady, and she said quite cheerfully:

"Well, I won't hurt you, so don't be scared any more. I just wanted to see what the human eye was good for."

"The human eye is a fearful weapon," remarked the Lion, scratching his nose softly with his paw to hide a smile. "Had I not known you were Dorothy's friends I might have torn you both into shreds in order to escape your terrible gaze."

Aunt Em shuddered at hearing this, and Uncle Henry said hastily:

"I'm glad you knew us. Good morning, Mr. Lion; we'll hope to see you again—by and by—some time in the future."

"Good morning," replied the Lion, squatting down upon the lawn again. "You are likely to see a good deal of me, if you live in the Land of Oz."

Chapter 8

HOW the GRAND GALLIPOOT JOINED the NOMES

fter leaving the Whimsies, Guph contin-
ued on his journey and penetrated far into
the Northwest. He wanted to get to the
Country of the Growleywogs, and in order
to do that he must cross the Ripple Land, which was a hard
thing to do. For the Ripple Land was a succession of hills and
valleys, all very steep and rocky, and they changed places constantly by rippling. While Guph was climbing a hill it sank
down under him and became a valley, and while he was
descending into a valley it rose up and carried him to the top of
a hill. This was very perplexing to the traveler, and a stranger
might have thought he could never cross the Ripple Land at

all. But Guph knew that if he kept steadily on he would get to the end at last; so he paid no attention to the changing hills and valleys and plodded along as calmly as if walking upon the level ground.

The result of this wise persistence was that the General finally reached firmer soil and, after penetrating a dense forest, came to the Dominion of the Growleywogs.

No sooner had he crossed the border of this domain when two guards seized him and carried him before the Grand Gallipoot of the Growleywogs, who scowled upon him ferociously and asked him why he dared intrude upon his territory.

"I'm the Lord High General of the Invincible Army of the Nomes, and my name is Guph," was the reply. "All the world trembles when that name is mentioned."

The Growleywogs gave a shout of jeering laughter at this, and one of them caught the Nome in his strong arms and tossed him high into the air. Guph was considerably shaken when he fell upon the hard ground, but he appeared to take no notice of the impertinence and composed himself to speak again to the Grand Gallipoot.

"My master, King Roquat the Red, has sent me here to confer with you. He wishes your assistance to conquer the Land of Oz."

Here the General paused, and the Grand Gallipoot scowled upon him more terribly than ever and said:

"Go on!"

The voice of the Grand Gallipoot was partly a roar and partly a growl. He mumbled his words badly and Guph had to listen carefully in order to understand him.

These Growleywogs were certainly remarkable creatures. They were of gigantic size, yet were all bone and skin and muscle, there being no meat or fat upon their bodies at all. Their powerful muscles lay just underneath their skins, like bunches of tough rope, and the weakest Growleywog was so strong that he could pick up an elephant and toss it seven miles away.

It seems unfortunate that strong people are usually so disagreeable and overbearing that no one cares for them. In fact, to be different from your fellow creatures is always a misfortune. The Growleywogs knew that they were disliked and avoided by every one, so they had become surly and unsociable even among themselves. Guph knew that they hated all people, including the Nomes; but he hoped to win them over, nevertheless, and knew that if he succeeded they would afford him very powerful assistance.

"The Land of Oz is ruled by a namby-pamby girl who is disgustingly kind and good," he continued. "Her people are all happy and contented and have no care or worries whatever."

"Go on!" growled the Grand Gallipoot.

"Once the Nome King enslaved the Royal Family of Ev— another goody-goody lot that we detest," said the General. "But Ozma interfered, although it was none of her business, and marched her army against us. With her was a Kansas girl named Dorothy, and a Yellow Hen, and they marched directly into the Nome King's cavern. There they liberated our slaves from Ev and stole King Roquat's Magic Belt, which they carried away with them. So now our King is making a tunnel under the deadly desert, so we can march through it to the Emerald City. When we get there we mean to conquer and destroy all the land and recapture the Magic Belt."

Again he paused, and again the Grand Gallipoot growled: "Go on!"

Guph tried to think what to say next, and a happy thought soon occurred to him.

"We want you to help us in this conquest," he announced, "for we need the mighty aid of the Growleywogs in order to make sure that we shall not be defeated. You are the strongest people in all the world, and you hate good and happy creatures as much as we Nomes do. I am sure it will be a real pleasure to you to tear down the beautiful Emerald City, and in return for your valuable assistance we will allow you to bring back to your country ten thousand people of Oz, to be your slaves."

"Twenty thousand!" growled the Grand Gallipoot.

"All right, we promise you twenty thousand," agreed the General.

The Gallipoot made a signal and at once his attendants picked up General Guph and carried him away to a prison, where the jailer amused himself by sticking pins in the round fat body of the old Nome, to see him jump and hear him yell.

But while this was going on the Grand Gallipoot was talking with his counselors, who were the most important officials of the Growleywogs. When he had stated to them the proposition of the Nome King, he said:

"My advice is to offer to help them. Then, when we have conquered the Land of Oz, we will take not only our twenty thousand prisoners but all the gold and jewels we want."

"Let us take the Magic Belt, too," suggested one counselor.

"And rob the Nome King and make him our slave," said another.

"That is a good idea," declared the Grand Gallipoot. "I'd like King Roquat for my own slave. He could black my boots and bring me my porridge every morning while I am in bed."

"There is a famous Scarecrow in Oz. I'll take him for my slave," said a counselor.

"I'll take Tiktok, the machine man," said another.

"Give me the Tin Woodman," said a third.

They went on for some time, dividing up the people and the treasure of Oz in advance of the conquest. For they had no doubt at all that they would be able to destroy Ozma's domain. Were they not the strongest people in all the world?

"The deadly desert has kept us out of Oz before," remarked the Grand Gallipoot, "but now that the Nome King is building a tunnel we shall get into the Emerald City very easily. So let us send the little fat General back to his King with our promise to assist him. We will not say that we intend to conquer the Nomes after we have conquered Oz, but we will do so, just the same."

This plan being agreed upon, they all went home to dinner, leaving General Guph still in prison. The Nome had no idea that he had succeeded in his mission, for finding himself in prison he feared the Growleywogs intended to put him to death.

By this time the jailer had tired of sticking pins in the General, and was amusing himself by carefully pulling the Nome's whiskers out by the roots, one at a time. This enjoyment was interrupted by the Grand Gallipoot sending for the prisoner.

"Wait a few hours," begged the jailer. "I haven't pulled out a quarter of his whiskers yet."

"If you keep the Grand Gallipoot waiting, he'll break your back," declared the messenger.

"Perhaps you're right," sighed the jailer. "Take the prisoner away, if you will, but I advise you to kick him at every step he takes. It will be good fun, for he is as soft as a ripe peach."

So Guph was led away to the royal castle, where the Grand Gallipoot told him that the Growleywogs had decided to assist the Nomes in conquering the Land of Oz.

"Whenever you are ready," he added, "send me word and I will march with eighteen thousand of my most powerful warriors to your aid."

Guph was so delighted that he forgot all the smarting caused by the pins and the pulling of whiskers. He did not even complain of the treatment he had received, but thanked the Grand Gallipoot and hurried away upon his journey.

He had now secured the assistance of the Whimsies and the Growleywogs; but his success made him long for still more allies. His own life depended upon his conquering Oz, and he said to himself:

"I'll take no chances. I'll be certain of success. Then, when Oz is destroyed, perhaps I shall be a greater man than old Roquat, and I can throw him away and be King of the Nomes myself. Why not? The Whimsies are stronger than the Nomes, and they also are my friends. There are some people still stronger than the Growleywogs, and if I can but induce them to aid me I shall have nothing more to fear."

Chapter 9

HOW the WOGGLE-BUG
TAUGHT ATHLETICS

It did not take Dorothy long to establish herself in her new home, for she knew the people and the manners and customs of the Emerald City just as well as she knew the old Kansas farm.

But Uncle Henry and Aunt Em had some trouble in getting used to the finery and pomp and ceremony of Ozma's palace, and felt uneasy because they were obliged to be "dressed up" all the time. Yet every one was very courteous and kind to them and endeavored to make them happy. Ozma, especially, made much of Dorothy's relatives, for her little friend's sake, and she well knew that the awkwardness and strangeness of their new mode of life would all wear off in time.

The old people were chiefly troubled by the fact that there was no work for them to do.

"Ev'ry day is like Sunday, now," declared Aunt Em, solemnly, "and I can't say I like it. If they'd only let me do up the dishes after meals, or even sweep an' dust my own rooms, I'd be a deal happier. Henry don't know what to do with himself either, and once when he stole out an' fed the chickens Billina scolded him for letting 'em eat between meals. I never knew before what a hardship it is to be rich and have everything you want."

These complaints began to worry Dorothy; so she had a long talk with Ozma upon the subject.

"I see I must find them something to do," said the girlish Ruler of Oz, seriously. "I have been watching your uncle and aunt, and I believe they will be more contented if occupied with some light tasks. While I am considering this matter, Dorothy, you might make a trip with them through the Land of Oz, visiting some of the odd corners and introducing your relatives to some of our curious people."

"Oh, that would be fine!" exclaimed Dorothy, eagerly.

"I will give you an escort befitting your rank as a Princess," continued Ozma; "and you may go to some of the places you have not yet visited yourself, as well as some others that you know. I will mark out a plan of the trip for you and have everything in readiness for you to start to-morrow morning. Take your time, dear, and be gone as long as you wish. By the time you return I shall have found some occupation for Uncle Henry and Aunt Em that will keep them from being restless and dissatisfied."

Dorothy thanked her good friend and kissed the lovely Ruler gratefully. Then she ran to tell the joyful news to her uncle and aunt.

Next morning, after breakfast, everything was found ready for their departure.

The escort included Omby Amby, the Captain General of Ozma's army, which consisted merely of twenty-seven officers besides the Captain General. Once Omby Amby had been a private soldier—the only private in the army—but as there was never any fighting to do Ozma saw no need of a private, so she made Omby Amby the highest officer of them all. He was very tall and slim and wore a gay uniform and a fierce mustache. Yet the mustache was the only fierce thing about Omby Amby, whose nature was as gentle as that of a child.

The wonderful Wizard had asked to join the party, and with him came his friend the Shaggy Man, who was shaggy but not ragged, being dressed in fine silks with satin shags and bobtails. The Shaggy Man had shaggy whiskers and hair, but a sweet disposition and a soft, pleasant voice.

There was an open wagon, with three seats for the passengers, and the wagon was drawn by the famous wooden Sawhorse which had once been brought to life by Ozma by means of a magic powder. The Sawhorse wore golden shoes to keep his wooden legs from wearing away, and he was strong and swift. As this curious creature was Ozma's own favorite steed, and very popular with all the people of the Emerald City, Dorothy knew that she had been highly favored by being permitted to use the Sawhorse on her journey.

In the front seat of the wagon sat Dorothy and the Wizard. Uncle Henry and Aunt Em sat in the next seat and the Shaggy Man and Omby Amby in the third seat. Of course Toto was with the party, curled up at Dorothy's feet, and just as they were about to start Billina came fluttering along the path and begged to be taken with them. Dorothy readily agreed, so the Yellow Hen flew up and perched herself upon the dashboard. She wore her pearl necklace and three bracelets upon each leg, in honor of the occasion.

Dorothy kissed Ozma good-bye, and all the people standing around waved their handkerchiefs, and the band in an upper balcony struck up a military march. Then the Wizard clucked to the Sawhorse and said: "Gid-dap!" and the wooden animal pranced away and drew behind him the big red wagon and all the passengers, without any effort at all. A servant threw open a gate of the palace enclosure, that they might pass out; and so, with music and shouts following them, the journey was begun.

"It's almost like a circus," said Aunt Em, proudly. "I can't help feelin' high an' mighty in this kind of a turn-out."

Indeed, as they passed down the street, all the people

cheered them lustily, and the Shaggy Man and the Wizard and the Captain General all took off their hats and bowed politely in acknowledgment.

When they came to the great wall of the Emerald City the gates were opened by the Guardian who always tended them. Over the gateway hung a dull-colored metal magnet shaped like a horse-shoe, placed against a shield of polished gold.

"That," said the Shaggy Man, impressively, "is the wonderful Love Magnet. I brought it to the Emerald City myself, and all who pass beneath this gateway are both loving and beloved."

"It's a fine thing," declared Aunt Em, admiringly. "If we'd had it in Kansas I guess the man who held a mortgage on the farm wouldn't have turned us out."

"Then I'm glad we didn't have it," returned Uncle Henry. "I like Oz better than Kansas, even; an' this little wood Sawhorse beats all the critters I ever saw. He don't have to be curried, or fed, or watered, an' he's strong as an ox. Can he talk, Dorothy?"

"Yes, Uncle," replied the child. "But the Sawhorse never says much. He told me once that he can't talk and think at the same time, so he prefers to think."

"Which is very sensible," declared the Wizard, nodding approvingly. "Which way do we go, Dorothy?"

"Straight ahead into the Quadling Country," she answered. "I've got a letter of interduction to Miss Cuttenclip."

"Oh!" exclaimed the Wizard, much interested. "Are we going there? Then I'm glad I came, for I've always wanted to meet the Cuttenclips."

"Who are they?" inquired Aunt Em.

"Wait till we get there," replied Dorothy, with a laugh; "then you'll see for yourself. I've never seen the Cuttenclips, you know, so I can't 'zactly 'splain 'em to you."

Once free of the Emerald City the Sawhorse dashed away at tremendous speed. Indeed, he went so fast that Aunt Em had hard work to catch her breath, and Uncle Henry held fast to the seat of the red wagon.

"Gently—gently, my boy!" called the Wizard, and at this the Sawhorse slackened his speed.

"What's wrong?" asked the animal, slightly turning his wooden head to look at the party with one eye, which was a knot of wood.

"Why, we wish to admire the scenery, that's all," answered the Wizard.

"Some of your passengers," added the Shaggy Man, "have never been out of the Emerald City before, and the country is all new to them."

"If you go too fast you'll spoil all the fun," said Dorothy. "There's no hurry."

"Very well; it is all the same to me," observed the Sawhorse; and after that he went at a more moderate pace.

Uncle Henry was astonished.

"How can a wooden thing be so intelligent?" he asked.

"Why, I gave him some sawdust brains the last time I fitted his head with new ears," explained the Wizard. "The sawdust was made from hard knots, and now the Sawhorse is able to think out any knotty problem he meets with."

"I see," said Uncle Henry.

"I don't," remarked Aunt Em; but no one paid any attention to this statement.

Before long they came to a stately building that stood upon a green plain with handsome shade trees grouped here and there.

"What is that?" asked Uncle Henry.

"That," replied the Wizard, "is the Royal Athletic College of Oz, which is directed by Professor H. M. Woggle-Bug, T.E."

"Let's stop and make a call," suggested Dorothy.

So the Sawhorse drew up in front of the great building and they were met at the door by the learned Woggle-Bug himself. He seemed fully as tall as the Wizard, and was dressed in a red and white checked vest and a blue swallow-tailed coat, and had yellow knee breeches and purple silk stockings upon his slender legs. A tall hat was jauntily set upon his head and he wore spectacles over his big bright eyes.

"Welcome, Dorothy," said the Woggle-Bug; "and welcome to all your friends. We are indeed pleased to receive you at this great Temple of Learning."

"I thought it was an Athletic College," said the Shaggy Man.

"It is, my dear sir," answered the Woggle-Bug, proudly. "Here it is that we teach the youth of our great land scientific College Athletics—in all their purity."

"Don't you teach them anything else?" asked Dorothy. "Don't they get any reading, writing and 'rithmetic?"

"Oh, yes; of course. They get all those, and more," returned the Professor. "But such things occupy little of their time. Please follow me and I will show you how my scholars are usually occupied. This is a class hour and they are all busy."

They followed him to a big field back of the college building, where several hundred young Ozites were at their classes. In one place they played football, in another baseball. Some played tennis, some golf; some were swimming in a big pool. Upon a river which wound through the grounds several crews in racing boats were rowing with great enthusiasm. Other groups of students played basketball and cricket, while in one place a ring was roped in to permit boxing and wrestling by the energetic youths. All the collegians seemed busy and there was much laughter and shouting.

"This college," said Professor Woggle-Bug, complacently, "is a great success. Its educational value is undisputed, and we are turning out many great and valuable citizens every year."

"But when do they study?" asked Dorothy.

"Study?" said the Woggle-Bug, looking perplexed at the question.

"Yes; when do they get their 'rithmetic, and jogerfy, and such things?"

"Oh, they take doses of those every night and morning," was the reply.

"What do you mean by doses?" Dorothy inquired, wonderingly.

"Why, we use the newly invented School Pills, made by your friend the Wizard. These pills we have found to be very effective, and they save a lot of time. Please step this way and I will show you our Laboratory of Learning."

He led them to a room in the building where many large bottles were standing in rows upon shelves.

"These are the Algebra Pills," said the Professor, taking down one of the bottles. "One at night, on retiring, is equal to four hours of study. Here are the Geography Pills—one at night and one in the morning. In this next bottle are the Latin Pills—one three times a day. Then we have the Grammar Pills—one before each meal—and the Spelling Pills, which are taken whenever needed."

"Your scholars must have to take a lot of pills," remarked Dorothy, thoughtfully. "How do they take 'em, in apple-sauce?"

"No, my dear. They are sugar-coated and are quickly and easily swallowed. I believe the students would rather take the pills than study, and certainly the pills are a more effective method. You see, until these School Pills were invented we wasted a lot of time in study that may now be better employed in practising athletics."

"Seems to me the pills are a good thing," said Omby Amby, who remembered how it used to make his head ache as a boy to study arithmetic.

"They are, sir," declared the Woggle-Bug, earnestly. "They give us an advantage over all other colleges, because at no loss of time our boys become thoroughly conversant with Greek and Latin, Mathematics and Geography, Grammar and Literature. You see they are never obliged to interrupt their games to acquire the lesser branches of learning."

"It's a great invention, I'm sure," said Dorothy, looking admiringly at the Wizard, who blushed modestly at this praise.

"We live in an age of progress," announced Professor Woggle-Bug, pompously. "It is easier to swallow knowledge than to acquire it laboriously from books. Is it not so, my friends?"

"Some folks can swallow anything," said Aunt Em, "but to me this seems too much like taking medicine."

"Young men in college always have to take their medicine, one way or another," observed the Wizard, with a smile; "and, as our Professor says, these School Pills have proved to be a great success. One day while I was making them I happened to drop one of them, and one of Billina's chickens gobbled it up. A few minutes afterward this chick got upon a roost and recited 'The Boy Stood on the Burning Deck' without making a single mistake. Then it recited 'The Charge of the Light Brigade' and afterwards 'Excelsior.' You see, the chicken had eaten an Elocution Pill."

They now bade good-bye to the Professor, and thanking him for his kind reception mounted again into the red wagon and continued their journey.

Chapter 10

HOW the CUTTENCLIPS LIVED

The travelers had taken no provisions with them because they knew that they would be welcomed wherever they might go in the Land of Oz, and that the people would feed and lodge them with genuine hospitality. So about noon they stopped at a farm-house and were given a delicious luncheon of bread and milk, fruits and wheat cakes with maple syrup. After resting a while and strolling through the orchards with their host—a round, jolly farmer—they got into the wagon and again started the Sawhorse along the pretty, winding road.

There were sign-posts at all the corners, and finally they came to one which read:

TAKE THIS ROAD TO THE CUTTENCLIPS

There was also a hand pointing in the right direction, so they turned the Sawhorse that way and found it a very good road, but seemingly little traveled.

"I've never seen the Cuttenclips before," remarked Dorothy.

"Nor I," said the Captain General.

"Nor I," said the Wizard.

"Nor I," said Billina.

"I've hardly been out of the Emerald City since I arrived in this country," added the Shaggy Man.

"Why, none of us has been there, then," exclaimed the little girl. "I wonder what the Cuttenclips are like."

"We shall soon find out," said the Wizard, with a sly laugh. "I've heard they are rather flimsy things."

The farm-houses became fewer as they proceeded, and the path was at times so faint that the Sawhorse had hard work to keep in the road. The wagon began to jounce, too; so they were obliged to go slowly.

After a somewhat wearisome journey they came in sight of a high wall, painted blue with pink ornaments. This wall was circular, and seemed to enclose a large space. It was so high that only the tops of the trees could be seen above it.

The path led up to a small door in the wall, which was closed and latched. Upon the door was a sign in gold letters reading as follows:

VISITORS are requested to MOVE SLOWLY
and CAREFULLY, and to avoid COUGHING
or making any BREEZE or DRAUGHT

"That's strange," said the Shaggy Man, reading the sign aloud. "Who *are* the Cuttenclips, anyhow?"

"Why, they're paper dolls," answered Dorothy. "Didn't you know that?"

"Paper dolls! Then let's go somewhere else," said Uncle Henry. "We're all too old to play with dolls, Dorothy."

"But these are different," declared the girl. "They're alive."

"Alive!" gasped Aunt Em, in amazement.

"Yes. Let's go in," said Dorothy.

So they all got out of the wagon, since the door in the wall was not big enough for them to drive the Sawhorse and wagon through it.

"You stay here, Toto!" commanded Dorothy, shaking her finger at the little dog. "You're so careless that you might make a breeze if I let you inside."

Toto wagged his tail as if disappointed at being left behind; but he made no effort to follow them. The Wizard unlatched the door, which opened outward, and they all looked eagerly inside.

Just before the entrance was drawn up a line of tiny soldiers, with uniforms brightly painted and paper guns upon their shoulders. They were exactly alike, from one end of the line to the other, and all were cut out of paper and joined together in the centers of their bodies.

As the visitors entered the enclosure the Wizard let the door swing back into place, and at once the line of soldiers tumbled over, fell flat upon their backs, and lay fluttering upon the ground.

"Hi, there!" called one of them; "what do you mean by slamming the door and blowing us over?"

"I beg your pardon, I'm sure," said the Wizard, regretfully. "I didn't know you were so delicate."

"We're not delicate!" retorted another soldier, raising his head from the ground. "We are strong and healthy; but we can't stand draughts."

"May I help you up?" asked Dorothy.

"If you please," replied the end soldier. "But do it gently, little girl."

Dorothy carefully stood up the line of soldiers, who first dusted their painted clothes and then saluted the visitors with their paper muskets. From the end it was easy to see that the entire line had been cut out of paper, although from the front the soldiers looked rather solid and imposing.

"I've a letter of introduction from Princess Ozma to Miss Cuttenclip," announced Dorothy.

"Very well," said the end soldier, and blew upon a paper whistle that hung around his neck. At once a paper soldier in a Captain's uniform came out of a paper house near by and approached the group at the entrance. He was not very big, and he walked rather stiffly and uncertainly on his paper legs; but he had a pleasant face, with very red cheeks and very blue eyes, and he bowed so low to the strangers that Dorothy laughed, and the breeze from her mouth nearly blew the Captain over. He wavered and struggled and finally managed to remain upon his feet.

"Take care, Miss!" he said, warningly. "You're breaking the rules, you know, by laughing."

"Oh, I didn't know that," she replied.

"To laugh in this place is nearly as dangerous as to cough," said the Captain. "You'll have to breathe very quietly, I assure you."

"We'll try to," promised the girl. "May we see Miss Cuttenclip, please?"

"You may," promptly returned the Captain. "This is one of her reception days. Be good enough to follow me."

He turned and led the way up a path, and as they followed slowly, because the paper Captain did not move very swiftly, they took the opportunity to gaze around them at this strange paper country.

Beside the path were paper trees, all cut out very neatly and painted a brilliant green color. And back of the trees were rows of cardboard houses, painted in various colors but most of them having green blinds. Some were large and some small, and in the front yards were beds of paper flowers quite natural in appearance. Over some of the porches paper vines were twined, giving them a cozy and shady look.

As the visitors passed along the street a good many paper dolls came to the doors and windows of their houses to look at them curiously. These dolls were nearly all the same height, but were cut into various shapes, some being fat and some lean. The girl dolls wore many beautiful costumes of tissue paper, making them quite fluffy; but their heads and hands were no thicker than the paper of which they were made.

Some of the paper people were on the street, walking along or congregated in groups and talking together; but as soon as they saw the strangers they all fluttered into the houses as fast as they could go, so as to be out of danger.

"Excuse me if I go edgewise," remarked the Captain as they came to a slight hill. "I can get along faster that way and not flutter so much."

"That's all right," said Dorothy. "We don't mind how you go, I'm sure."

At one side of the street was a paper pump, and a paper boy was pumping paper water into a paper pail. The Yellow Hen happened to brush against this boy with her wing, and he flew into the air and fell into a paper tree, where he stuck until the Wizard gently pulled him out. At the same time, the pail went into the air, spilling the paper water, while the paper pump bent nearly double.

"Goodness me!" said the Hen. "If I should flop my wings I believe I'd knock over the whole village!"

"Then don't flop them—please don't!" entreated the Captain. "Miss Cuttenclip would be very much distressed if her village was spoiled."

"Oh, I'll be careful," promised Billina.

"Are not all these paper girls and women named Miss Cuttenclips?" inquired Omby Amby.

"No, indeed," answered the Captain, who was walking better since he began to move edgewise. "There is but one Miss Cuttenclip, who is our Queen, because she made us all. These girls are Cuttenclips, to be sure, but their names are Emily and Polly and Sue and Betty and such things. Only the Queen is called Miss Cuttenclip."

"I must say that this place beats anything I ever heard of," observed Aunt Em. "I used to play with paper dolls myself, an' cut 'em out; but I never thought I'd ever see such things alive."

"I don't see as it's any more curious than hearing hens talk," returned Uncle Henry.

"You're likely to see many queer things in the Land of Oz, sir," said the Wizard. "But a fairy country is extremely interesting when you get used to being surprised."

"Here we are!" called the Captain, stopping before a cottage.

This house was made of wood, and was remarkably pretty in design. In the Emerald City it would have been considered a tiny dwelling, indeed; but in the midst of this paper village it seemed immense. Real flowers were in the garden and real trees grew beside it. Upon the front door was a sign reading:

MISS CUTTENCLIP

Just as they reached the porch the front door opened and a little girl stood before them. She appeared to be about the same age as Dorothy, and smiling upon her visitors she said, sweetly:

"You are welcome."

All the party seemed relieved to find that here was a real girl, of flesh and blood. She was very dainty and pretty as she stood there welcoming them. Her hair was a golden blonde and her eyes turquoise blue. She had rosy cheeks and lovely white teeth. Over her simple white lawn dress she wore an apron with pink and white checks, and in one hand she held a pair of scissors.

"May we see Miss Cuttenclip, please?" asked Dorothy.

"I am Miss Cuttenclip," was the reply. "Won't you come in?"

She held the door open while they all entered a pretty sitting-room that was littered with all sorts of paper—some stiff, some thin, and some tissue. The sheets and scraps were of all colors. Upon a table were paints and brushes, while several pair of scissors, of different sizes, were lying about.

"Sit down, please," said Miss Cuttenclip, clearing the paper scraps off some of the chairs. "It is so long since I have had any visitors that I am not properly prepared to receive them. But I'm sure you will pardon my untidy room, for this is my workshop."

"Do you make all the paper dolls?" inquired Dorothy.

"Yes; I cut them out with my scissors, and paint the faces and some of the costumes. It is very pleasant work, and I am happy making my paper village grow."

"But how do the paper dolls happen to be alive?" asked Aunt Em.

"The first dolls I made were not alive," said Miss Cuttenclip. "I used to live near the castle of a great Sorceress named Glinda the Good, and she saw my dolls and said they were very pretty. I told her I thought I would like them better if they were alive, and the next day the Sorceress brought me a lot of magic paper. 'This is live paper,' she said, 'and all the dolls you cut out of it will be alive, and able to think and to talk. When you have used it all up, come to me and I will give you more.'

"Of course I was delighted with this present," continued Miss Cuttenclip, "and at once set to work and made several paper dolls, which, as soon as they were cut out, began to walk around and talk to me. But they were so thin that I found that any breeze would blow them over and scatter them dreadfully; so Glinda found this lonely place for me, where few people ever come. She built the wall to keep any wind from blowing away my people, and told me I could build a paper village here and be its Queen. That is why I came here and settled down to work and started the village you now see. It was many years ago that I built the first houses, and I've kept pretty busy and made my village grow finely; and I need not tell you that I am very happy in my work."

"Many years ago!" exclaimed Aunt Em. "Why, how old are you, child?"

"I never keep track of the years," said Miss Cuttenclip, laughing. "You see, I don't grow up at all, but stay just the same as I was when first I came here. Perhaps I'm older even than you are, madam; but I couldn't say for sure."

They looked at the lovely little girl wonderingly, and the Wizard asked:

"What happens to your paper village when it rains?"

"It does not rain here," replied Miss Cuttenclip. "Glinda keeps all the rain storms away; so I never worry about my dolls getting wet. But now, if you will come with me, it will give me pleasure to show you over my paper kingdom. Of course you must go slowly and carefully, and avoid making any breeze."

They left the cottage and followed their guide through the various streets of the village. It was indeed an amazing place, when one considered that it was all made with scissors, and the visitors were not only greatly interested but full of admiration for the skill of little Miss Cuttenclip.

In one place a large group of especially nice paper dolls assembled to greet their Queen, whom it was easy to see they loved dearly. These dolls marched and danced before the visitors, and then they all waved their paper handkerchiefs and sang in a sweet chorus a song called "The Flag of Our Native Land."

At the conclusion of the song they ran up a handsome paper flag on a tall flagpole, and all of the people of the village gathered around to cheer as loudly as they could—although, of course, their voices were not especially strong.

Miss Cuttenclip was about to make her subjects a speech in reply to this patriotic song, when the Shaggy Man happened to sneeze.

He was a very loud and powerful sneezer at any time, and he had tried so hard to hold in this sneeze that when it suddenly exploded the result was terrible.

The paper dolls were mowed down by dozens, and flew and fluttered in wild confusion in every direction, tumbling this way and that and getting more or less wrinkled and bent.

A wail of terror and grief came from the scattered throng, and Miss Cuttenclip exclaimed:

"Dear me! dear me!" and hurried at once to the rescue of her overturned people.

"Oh, Shaggy Man! How could you?" asked Dorothy, reproachfully.

"I couldn't help it—really I couldn't," protested the Shaggy Man, looking quite ashamed. "And I had no idea it took so little to upset these paper dolls."

"So little!" said Dorothy. "Why, it was 'most as bad as a Kansas cyclone." And then she helped Miss Cuttenclip rescue the paper folk and stand them on their feet again. Two of the cardboard houses had also tumbled over, and the little Queen said she would have to repair them and paste them together before they could be lived in again.

And now, fearing they might do more damage to the flimsy paper people, they decided to go away. But first they thanked Miss Cuttenclip very warmly for her courtesy and kindness to them.

"Any friend of Princess Ozma is always welcome here—unless he sneezes," said the Queen with a rather severe look at the Shaggy Man, who hung his head. "I like to have visitors admire my wonderful village, and I hope you will call again."

Miss Cuttenclip herself led them to the door in the wall, and as they passed along the street the paper dolls peeped at them half fearfully from the doors and windows. Perhaps they will never forget the Shaggy Man's awful sneeze, and I am sure they were all glad to see the meat people go away.

Chapter 11

HOW the GENERAL MET
the FIRST and FOREMOST

O n leaving the Growleywogs General Guph had to recross the Ripple Lands, and he did not find it a pleasant thing to do. Perhaps having his whiskers pulled out one by one and being used as a pin-cushion for the innocent amusement of a good natured jailer had not improved the quality of Guph's temper, for the old Nome raved and raged at the recollection of the wrongs he had suffered, and vowed to take vengeance upon the Growleywogs after he had used them for his purposes and Oz had been conquered. He went on in this furious way until he was half across the Ripple Land. Then he became seasick, and the rest of the way this naughty Nome was almost as miserable as he deserved to be.

But when he reached the plains again and the ground was firm under his feet he began to feel better, and instead of going back home he turned directly west. A squirrel, perched in a tree, saw him take this road and called to him warningly: "Look out!" But he paid no attention. An eagle paused in its flight through the air to look at him wonderingly and say: "Look out!" But on he went.

No one can say that Guph was not brave, for he had determined to visit those dangerous creatures the Phanfasms, who resided upon the very top of the dread Mountain of Phantastico. The Phanfasms were Erbs, and so dreaded by mortals and immortals alike that no one had been near their mountain home for several thousand years. Yet General Guph hoped to induce them to join in his proposed warfare against the good and happy Oz people.

Guph knew very well that the Phanfasms would be almost as dangerous to the Nomes as they would to the Ozites, but he thought himself so clever that he believed he could manage these strange creatures and make them obey him. And there was no doubt at all that if he could enlist the services of the Phanfasms, their tremendous power, united to the strength of the Growleywogs and the cunning of the Whimsies would doom the Land of Oz to absolute destruction.

So the old Nome climbed the foothills and trudged along the wild mountain paths until he came to a big gully that encircled the Mountain of Phantastico and marked the boundary line of the dominion of the Phanfasms. This gully was about a third of the way up the mountain, and it was filled to the brim with red-hot molten lava in which swam fire-serpents and poisonous salamanders. The heat from this mass and its poisonous smell were both so unbearable that even birds hesitated to fly over the gully, but circled around it. All living things kept away from the mountain.

Now Guph had heard, during his long lifetime, many tales of these dreaded Phanfasms; so he had heard of this barrier of melted lava, and also he had been told that there was a narrow bridge that spanned it in one place. So he walked along the edge until he found the bridge. It was a single arch of grey stone, and lying flat upon the bridge was a scarlet alligator, seemingly fast asleep.

When Guph stumbled over the rocks in approaching the bridge the creature opened its eyes, from which tiny flames shot in all directions, and after looking at the intruder very wickedly the scarlet alligator closed its eyelids again and lay still.

Guph saw there was no room for him to pass the alligator on the narrow bridge, so he called out to it:

"Good morning, friend. I don't wish to hurry you, but please tell me if you are coming down, or going up?"

"Neither," snapped the alligator, clicking its cruel jaws together.

The General hesitated.

"Are you likely to stay there long?" he asked.

"A few hundred years or so," said the alligator.

Guph softly rubbed the end of his nose and tried to think what to do.

"Do you know whether the First and Foremost Phanfasm of Phantastico is at home or not?" he presently inquired.

"I expect he is, seeing he is always at home," replied the alligator.

"Ah; who is that coming down the mountain?" asked the Nome, gazing upward.

The alligator turned to look over its shoulder, and at once Guph ran to the bridge and leaped over the sentinel's back before it could turn back again. The scarlet monster made a snap at the Nome's left foot, but missed it by fully an inch.

"Ah ha!" laughed the General, who was now on the mountain path. "I fooled you that time."

"So you did; and perhaps you fooled yourself," retorted the alligator. "Go up the mountain, if you dare, and find out what the First and Foremost will do to you!"

"I will," declared Guph, boldly; and on he went up the path.

At first the scene was wild enough, but gradually it grew more and more awful in appearance. All the rocks had the shapes of frightful beings and even the tree trunks were gnarled and twisted like serpents.

Suddenly there appeared before the Nome a man with the

head of an owl. His body was hairy like that of an ape, and his only clothing was a scarlet scarf twisted around his waist. He bore a huge club in his hand and his round owl eyes blinked fiercely upon the intruder.

"What are you doing here?" he demanded, threatening Guph with his club.

"I've come to see the First and Foremost Phanfasm of Phantastico," replied the General, who did not like the way this creature looked at him, but still was not afraid.

"Ah; you shall see him!" the man said, with a sneering laugh. "The First and Foremost shall decide upon the best way to punish you."

"He will not punish me," returned Guph, calmly, "for I have come here to do him and his people a rare favor. Lead on, fellow, and take me directly to your master."

The owl-man raised his club with a threatening gesture.

"If you try to escape," he said, "beware—"

But here the General interrupted him.

"Spare your threats," said he, "and do not be impertinent, or I will have you severely punished. Lead on, and keep silent!"

This Guph was really a clever rascal, and it seems a pity he was so bad, for in a good cause he might have accomplished much. He realized that he had put himself into a dangerous position by coming to this dreadful mountain, but he also knew that if he showed fear he was lost. So he adopted a bold manner as his best defense. The wisdom of this plan was soon evident, for the Phanfasm with the owl's head turned and led the way up the mountain.

At the very top was a level plain upon which were heaps of rock that at first glance seemed solid. But on looking closer Guph discovered that these rock heaps were dwellings, for each had an opening.

Not a person was to be seen outside the rock huts. All was silent.

The owl-man led the way among the groups of dwellings to one standing in the center. It seemed no better and no worse than any of the others. Outside the entrance to this rock heap the guide gave a low wail that sounded like "Lee-ow-ah!"

Suddenly there bounded from the opening another hairy man. This one wore the head of a bear. In his hand he bore a brass hoop. He glared at the stranger in evident surprise.

"Why have you captured this foolish wanderer and brought him here?" he demanded, addressing the owl-man.

"I did not capture him," was the answer. "He passed the scarlet alligator and came here of his own free will and accord."

The First and Foremost looked at the General.

"Have you tired of life, then?" he asked.

"No, indeed," answered Guph. "I am a Nome, and the Chief General of King Roquat the Red's great army of Nomes. I come of a long-lived race, and I may say that I expect to live a long time yet. Sit down, you Phanfasms—if you can find a seat in this wild haunt—and listen to what I have to say."

With all his knowledge and bravery General Guph did not know that the steady glare from the bear eyes was reading his inmost thoughts as surely as if they had been put into words. He did not know that these despised rock heaps of the Phanfasms were merely deceptions to his own eyes, nor could he guess that he was standing in the midst of one of the most splendid and luxurious cities ever built by magic power. All that he saw was a barren waste of rock heaps, a hairy man with an owl's head and another with a bear's head. The sorcery of the Phanfasms permitted him to see no more.

Suddenly the First and Foremost swung his brass hoop and caught Guph around the neck with it. The next instant, before the General could think what had happened to him, he was dragged inside the rock hut. Here, his eyes still blinded to realities, he perceived only a dim light, by which the hut seemed as rough and rude inside as it was outside. Yet he had a strange feeling that many bright eyes were fastened upon him and that he stood in a vast and extensive hall.

The First and Foremost now laughed grimly and released his prisoner.

"If you have anything to say that is interesting," he remarked, "speak out, before I strangle you."

So Guph spoke out. He tried not to pay any attention to a strange rustling sound that he heard, as of an unseen multitude drawing near to listen to his words. His eyes could see only the fierce bear-man, and to him he addressed his speech. First he told of his plan to conquer the Land of Oz and plunder the country of its riches and enslave its people, who, being fairies, could not be killed. After relating all this, and telling of the tunnel the Nome King was building, he said he had come to ask the First and Foremost to join the Nomes, with his band of terrible warriors, and help them to defeat the Oz people.

The General spoke very earnestly and impressively, but when he had finished the bear-man began to laugh as if much amused, and his laughter seemed to be echoed by a chorus of merriment from an unseen multitude. Then, for the first time, Guph began to feel a trifle worried.

"Who else has promised to help you?" finally asked the First and Foremost.

"The Whimsies," replied the General.

Again the bear-headed Phanfasm laughed.

"Any others?" he inquired.

"Only the Growleywogs," said Guph.

This answer set the First and Foremost laughing anew.

"What share of the spoils am I to have?" was the next question.

"Anything you like, except King Roquat's Magic Belt," replied Guph.

At this the Phanfasm set up a roar of laughter, which had its echo in the unseen chorus, and the bear-man seemed so amused that he actually rolled upon the ground and shouted with merriment.

"Oh, these blind and foolish Nomes!" he said. "How big they seem to themselves and how small they really are!"

Suddenly he arose and seized Guph's neck with one hairy paw, dragging him out of the hut into the open.

Here he gave a curious wailing cry, and, as if in answer, from all the rocky huts on the mountain-top came flocking a horde of Phanfasms, all with hairy bodies, but wearing heads of various animals, birds and reptiles. All were ferocious and repulsive-looking to the deceived eyes of the Nome, and Guph could not repress a shudder of disgust as he looked upon them.

The First and Foremost slowly raised his arms, and in a twinkling his hairy skin fell from him and he appeared before the astonished Nome as a beautiful woman, clothed in a flowing gown of pink gauze. In her dark hair flowers were entwined, and her face was noble and calm.

At the same instant the entire band of Phanfasms was transformed into a pack of howling wolves, running here and there as they snarled and showed their ugly yellow fangs.

The woman now raised her arms, even as the man-bear had done, and in a twinkling the wolves became crawling lizards, while she herself changed into a huge butterfly.

Guph had only time to cry out in fear and take a step backward to avoid the lizards when another transformation occurred, and all returned instantly to the forms they had originally worn.

Then the First and Foremost, who had resumed his hairy

body and bear head, turned to the Nome and asked:

"Do you still demand our assistance?"

"More than ever," answered the General, firmly.

"Then tell me: what can you offer the Phanfasms that they have not already?" inquired the First and Foremost.

Guph hesitated. He really did not know what to say. The Nome King's vaunted Magic Belt seemed a poor thing compared to the astonishing magical powers of these people. Gold, jewels and slaves they might secure in any quantity without especial effort. He felt that he was dealing with powers greatly beyond him. There was but one argument that might influence the Phanfasms, who were creatures of evil.

"Permit me to call your attention to the exquisite joy of making the happy unhappy," said he at last. "Consider the pleasure of destroying innocent and harmless people."

"Ah! you have answered me," cried the First and Foremost. "For that reason alone we will aid you. Go home, and tell your bandy-legged king that as soon as his tunnel is finished the Phanfasms will be with him and lead his legions to the conquest of Oz. The deadly desert alone has kept us from destroying Oz long ago, and your underground tunnel is a clever thought. Go home, and prepare for our coming!"

Guph was very glad to be permitted to go with this promise. The owl-man led him back down the mountain path and ordered the scarlet alligator to crawl away and allow the Nome to cross the bridge in safety.

After the visitor had gone a brilliant and gorgeous city appeared upon the mountain top, clearly visible to the eyes of the gaily dressed multitude of Phanfasms that lived there. And the First and Foremost, beautifully arrayed, addressed the others in these words:

"It is time we went into the world and brought sorrow and dismay to its people. Too long have we remained by ourselves upon this mountain top, for while we are thus secluded many nations have grown happy and prosperous, and the chief joy of the race of Phanfasms is to destroy happiness. So I think it is lucky that this messenger from the Nomes arrived among us just now, to remind us that the opportunity has come for us to make trouble. We will use King Roquat's tunnel to conquer the Land of Oz. Then we will destroy the Whimsies, the Growleywogs and the Nomes, and afterward go out to ravage and annoy and grieve the whole world."

The multitude of evil Phanfasms eagerly applauded this plan, which they fully approved.

I am told that the Erbs are the most powerful and merciless of all the evil spirits, and the Phanfasms of Phantastico belong to the race of Erbs.

Chapter 12

How They Matched the Fuddles

Dorothy and her fellow travelers rode away from the Cuttenclip village and followed the indistinct path as far as the sign-post. Here they took the main road again and proceeded pleasantly through the pretty farming country. When evening came they stopped at a dwelling and were joyfully welcomed and given plenty to eat and good beds for the night.

Early next morning, however, they were up and eager to start, and after a good breakfast they bade their host good-bye and climbed into the red wagon, to which the Sawhorse had been hitched all night. Being made of wood, this horse never got tired nor cared to lie down. Dorothy was not quite sure whether he ever slept or not, but it was certain that he never did when anybody was around.

The weather is always beautiful in Oz, and this morning the air was cool and refreshing and the sunshine brilliant and delightful.

In about an hour they came to a place where another road branched off. There was a sign-post here which read:

THIS WAY TO FUDDLECUMJIG

"Oh, here is where we turn," said Dorothy, observing the sign.

"What! Are we going to Fuddlecumjig?" asked the Captain General.

"Yes; Ozma thought we might enjoy the Fuddles. They are said to be very interesting," she replied.

"No one would suspect it from their name," said Aunt Em. "Who are they, anyhow? More paper things?"

"I think not," answered Dorothy, laughing; "but I can't say 'zactly, Aunt Em, what they are. We'll find out when we get there."

"Perhaps the Wizard knows," suggested Uncle Henry.

"No; I've never been there before," said the Wizard. "But I've often heard of Fuddlecumjig and the Fuddles, who are said to be the most peculiar people in all the Land of Oz."

"In what way?" asked the Shaggy Man.

"I don't know, I'm sure," said the Wizard.

Just then, as they rode along the pretty green lane toward Fuddlecumjig, they espied a kangaroo sitting by the roadside. The poor animal had its face covered with both its front paws and was crying so bitterly that the tears coursed down its cheeks in two tiny streams and trickled across the road, where they formed a pool in a small hollow.

The Sawhorse stopped short at this pitiful sight, and Dorothy cried out, with ready sympathy:

"What's the matter, Kangaroo?"

"Boo-hoo! Boo-hoo!" wailed the Kangaroo; "I've lost my mi—mi—mi—Oh, boo-hoo! Boo-hoo!"—

"Poor thing," said the Wizard, "she's lost her mister. It's probably her husband, and he's dead."

"No, no, no!" sobbed the kangaroo. "It—it isn't that. I've lost my mi—mi—Oh, boo, boo-hoo!"

"I know," said the Shaggy Man; "she's lost her mirror."

"No; it's my mi—mi—mi—Boo-hoo! My mi—Oh, Boo-hoo!" and the kangaroo cried harder than ever.

"It must be her mince-pie," suggested Aunt Em.

"Or her milk-toast," proposed Uncle Henry.

"I've lost my mi—mi—mittens!" said the kangaroo, getting it out at last.

"Oh!" cried the Yellow Hen, with a cackle of relief. "Why didn't you say so before?"

"Boo-hoo! I—I—couldn't," answered the kangaroo.

"But, see here," said Dorothy, "you don't need mittens in this warm weather."

"Yes, indeed I do," replied the animal, stopping her sobs and removing her paws from her face to look at the little girl reproachfully. "My hands will get all sunburned and tanned without my mittens, and I've worn them so long that I'll probably catch cold without them."

"Nonsense!" said Dorothy. "I never heard of any kangaroo wearing mittens."

"Didn't you?" asked the animal, as if surprised.

"Never!" repeated the girl. "And you'll probably make yourself sick if you don't stop crying. Where do you live?"

"About two miles beyond Fuddlecumjig," was the answer. "Grandmother Gnit made me the mittens, and she's one of the Fuddles."

"Well, you'd better go home now, and perhaps the old lady will make you another pair," suggested Dorothy. "We're on our way to Fuddlecumjig, and you may hop along beside us."

So they rode on, and the kangaroo hopped beside the red wagon and seemed quickly to have forgotten her loss. By and by the Wizard said to the animal:

"Are the Fuddles nice people?"

"Oh, very nice," answered the kangaroo; "that is, when they're properly put together. But they get dreadfully scattered and mixed up, at times, and then you can't do anything with them."

"What do you mean by their getting scattered?" inquired Dorothy.

"Why, they're made in a good many small pieces," explained the kangaroo; "and whenever any stranger comes near them they have a habit of falling apart and scattering themselves around. That's when they get so dreadfully mixed, and it's a hard puzzle to put them together again."

"Who usually puts them together?" asked Omby Amby.

"Any one who is able to match the pieces. I sometimes put Grandmother Gnit together myself, because I know her so well I can tell every piece that belongs to her. Then, when she's all matched, she knits for me, and that's how she made my mittens. But it took a good many days hard knitting, and I had to put Grandmother together a good many times, because every time I came near, she'd scatter herself."

"I should think she would get used to your coming, and not be afraid," said Dorothy.

"It isn't that," replied the kangaroo. "They're not a bit afraid, when they're put together, and usually they're very jolly and pleasant. It's just a habit they have, to scatter themselves, and if they didn't do it they wouldn't be Fuddles."

The travelers thought upon this quite seriously for a time, while the Sawhorse continued to carry them rapidly forward. Then Aunt Em remarked:

"I don't see much use our visitin' these Fuddles. If we find them scattered, all we can do is to sweep 'em up, and then go about our business."

"Oh, I b'lieve we'd better go on," replied Dorothy. "I'm getting hungry, and we must try to get some luncheon at Fuddlecumjig. Perhaps the food won't be scattered as badly as the people."

"You'll find plenty to eat there," declared the kangaroo, hopping along in big bounds because the Sawhorse was going so fast; "and they have a fine cook, too, if you can manage to put him together. There's the town now—just ahead of us!"

They looked ahead and saw a group of very pretty houses standing in a green field a little apart from the main road.

"Some Munchkins came here a few days ago and matched a lot of people together," said the kangaroo. "I think they are together yet, and if you go softly, without making any noise, perhaps they won't scatter."

"Let's try it," suggested the Wizard.

So they stopped the Sawhorse and got out of the wagon, and, after bidding good-bye to the kangaroo, who hopped away home, they entered the field and very cautiously approached the group of houses.

So silently did they move that soon they saw through the

windows of the houses, people moving around, while others were passing to and fro in the yards between the buildings. They seemed much like other people, from a distance, and apparently they did not notice the little party so quietly approaching.

They had almost reached the nearest house when Toto saw a large beetle crossing the path and barked loudly at it. Instantly a wild clatter was heard from the houses and yards. Dorothy thought it sounded like a sudden hailstorm, and the visitors, knowing that caution was no longer necessary, hurried forward to see what had happened.

After the clatter an intense stillness reigned in the town. The strangers entered the first house they came to, which was also the largest, and found the floor strewn with pieces of the people who lived there. They looked much like fragments of wood neatly painted, and were of all sorts of curious and fantastic shapes, no two pieces being in any way alike.

They picked up some of these pieces and looked at them carefully. On one which Dorothy held was an eye, which looked at her pleasantly but with an interested expression, as if it wondered what she was going to do with it. Quite near by she discovered and picked up a nose, and by matching the two pieces together found that they were part of a face.

"If I could find the mouth," she said, "this Fuddle might be able to talk, and tell us what to do next."

"Then let us find it," replied the Wizard, and so all got down on their hands and knees and began examining the scattered pieces.

"I've found it!" cried the Shaggy Man, and ran to Dorothy with a queer-shaped piece that had a mouth on it. But when they tried to fit it to the eye and nose they found the parts wouldn't match together.

"That mouth belongs to some other person," said Dorothy. "You see we need a curve here and a point there, to make it fit the face."

"Well, it must be here some place," declared the Wizard; "so if we search long enough we shall find it."

Dorothy fitted an ear on next, and the ear had a little patch of red hair above it. So while the others were searching for the mouth she hunted for pieces with red hair, and found several of them which, when matched to the other pieces, formed the top of a man's head. She had also found the other eye and the ear by the time Omby Amby in a far corner discovered the mouth. When the face was thus completed all the parts joined together with a nicety that was astonishing.

"Why, it's like a picture puzzle!" exclaimed the little girl. "Let's find the rest of him, and get him all together."

"What's the rest of him like?" asked the Wizard. "Here are some pieces of blue legs and green arms, but I don't know whether they are his or not."

"Look for a white shirt and a white apron," said the head

which had been put together, speaking in a rather faint voice. "I'm the cook."

"Oh, thank you," said Dorothy. "It's lucky we started you first, for I'm hungry, and you can be cooking something for us to eat while we match the other folks together."

It was not so very difficult, now that they had a hint as to how the man was dressed, to find the other pieces belonging to him, and as all of them now worked on the cook, trying piece after piece to see if it would fit, they finally had the cook set up complete.

When he was finished he made them a low bow and said:

"I will go at once to the kitchen to prepare your dinner. You will find it something of a job to get all the Fuddles together, so I advise you to begin on the Lord High Chiggle-witz, whose first name is Larry. He's a bald-headed fat man and is dressed in a blue coat with brass buttons, a pink vest and drab breeches. A piece of his left knee is missing, having been lost years ago when he scattered himself too carelessly. That makes him limp a little, but he gets along very well with half a knee. As he is the chief personage in this town of Fuddlecumjig, he will be able to welcome you and assist you with the others. So it will be best to work on him while I'm getting your dinner."

"We will," said the Wizard; "and thank you very much, Cook, for the suggestion."

Aunt Em was the first to discover a piece of the Lord High Chigglewitz.

"It seems to me like a fool business, this matching folks together," she remarked; "but as we haven't anything to do till dinner's ready, we may as well get rid of some of this rubbish. Here, Henry, get busy and look for Larry's bald head. I've got his pink vest, all right."

They worked with eager interest, and Billina proved a great help to them. The Yellow Hen had sharp eyes and could put her head close to the various pieces that lay scattered around. She would examine the Lord High Chigglewitz and see which piece of him was next needed, and then hunt around until she found it. So before an hour had passed old Larry was standing complete before them.

"I congratulate you, my friends," he said, speaking in a cheerful voice. "You are certainly the cleverest people who ever visited us. I was never matched together so quickly in my life. I'm considered a great puzzle, usually."

"Well," said Dorothy, "there used to be a picture puzzle craze in Kansas, and so I've had some 'sperience matching puzzles. But the pictures were flat, while you are round, and that makes you harder to figure out."

"Thank you, my dear," replied old Larry, greatly pleased. "I feel highly complimented. Were I not a really good puzzle there would be no object in my scattering myself."

"Why do you do it?" asked Aunt Em, severely. "Why

don't you behave yourself, and stay put together?"

The Lord High Chigglewitz seemed annoyed by this speech; but he replied, politely:

"Madam, you have perhaps noticed that every person has some peculiarity. Mine is to scatter myself. What your own peculiarity is I will not venture to say; but I shall never find fault with you, whatever you do."

"Now you've got your diploma, Em," said Uncle Henry, with a laugh, "and I'm glad of it. This is a queer country, and we may as well take people as we find them."

"If we did, we'd leave these folks scattered," she returned, and this retort made everybody laugh good-naturedly.

Just then Omby Amby found a hand with a knitting needle in it, and they decided to put Grandmother Gnit together. She proved an easier puzzle than old Larry, and when she was completed they found her a pleasant old lady who welcomed them cordially. Dorothy told her how the kangaroo had lost her mittens, and Grandmother Gnit promised to set to work at once and make the poor animal another pair.

Then the cook came to call them to dinner, and they found an inviting meal prepared for them. The Lord High Chigglewitz sat at the head of the table and Grandmother Gnit at the foot, and the guests had a merry time and thoroughly enjoyed themselves.

After dinner they went out into the yard and matched several other people together, and this work was so interesting that they might have spent the entire day at Fuddlecumjig had not the Wizard suggested that they resume their journey.

"But I don't like to leave all these poor people scattered," said Dorothy, undecided what to do.

"Oh, don't mind us, my dear," returned old Larry. "Every day or so some of the Gillikins, or Munchkins, or Winkies come here to amuse themselves by matching us together, so there will be no harm in leaving these pieces where they are for a time. But I hope you will visit us again, and if you do you will always be welcome, I assure you."

"Don't you ever match each other?" she inquired.

"Never; for we are no puzzles to ourselves, and so there wouldn't be any fun in it."

They now said good-bye to the queer Fuddles and got into their wagon to continue their journey.

"Those are certainly strange people," remarked Aunt Em, thoughtfully, as they drove away from Fuddlecumjig, "but I really can't see what use they are, at all."

"Why, they amused us all for several hours," replied the Wizard. "That is being of use to us, I'm sure."

"I think they're more fun than playing solitaire or mumble-typeg," declared Uncle Henry, soberly. "For my part, I'm glad we visited the Fuddles."

Chapter 13

HOW the GENERAL TALKED to the KING

When General Guph returned to the cavern of the Nome King his Majesty asked:

"Well, what luck? Will the Whimsies join us?"

"They will," answered the General. "They will fight for us with all their strength and cunning."

"Good!" exclaimed the King. "What reward did you promise them?"

"Your Majesty is to use the Magic Belt to give each Whimsie a large, fine head, in place of the small one he is now obliged to wear."

"I agree to that," said the King. "This is good news, Guph,

and it makes me feel more certain of the conquest of Oz."

"But I have other news for you," announced the General.

"Good or bad?"

"Good, your Majesty."

"Then I will hear it," said the King, with interest.

"The Growleywogs will join us."

"No!" cried the astonished King.

"Yes, indeed," said the General. "I have their promise."

"But what reward do they demand?" inquired the King, suspiciously, for he knew how greedy the Growleywogs were.

"They are to take a few of the Oz people for their slaves," replied Guph. He did not think it necessary to tell Roquat that the Growleywogs demanded twenty thousand slaves. It would be time enough for that when Oz was conquered.

"A very reasonable request, I'm sure," remarked the King. "I must congratulate you, Guph, upon the wonderful success of your journey."

"But that is not all," said the General, proudly.

The King seemed astonished.

"Speak out, sir!" he commanded.

"I have seen the First and Foremost Phanfasm of the Mountain of Phantastico, and he will bring his people to assist us."

"What!" cried the King. "The Phanfasms! You don't mean it, Guph!"

"It is true," declared the General, proudly.

The King became thoughtful, and his brows wrinkled.

"I'm afraid, Guph," he said rather anxiously, "that the First and Foremost may prove as dangerous to us as to the Oz people. If he and his terrible band come down from the mountain they may take the notion to conquer the Nomes!"

"Pah! That is a foolish idea," retorted Guph, irritably, but he knew in his heart that the King was right. "The First and Foremost is a particular friend of mine, and will do us no harm. Why, when I was there, he even invited me into his house."

The General neglected to tell the King how he had been jerked into the hut of the First and Foremost by means of the brass hoop. So Roquat the Red looked at his General admiringly and said:

"You are a wonderful Nome, Guph. I'm sorry I did not make you my General before. But what reward did the First and Foremost demand?"

"Nothing at all," answered Guph. "Even the Magic Belt itself could not add to his powers of sorcery. All the Phanfasms wish is to destroy the Oz people, who are good and happy. This pleasure will amply repay them for assisting us."

"When will they come?" asked Roquat, half fearfully.

"When the tunnel is completed," said the General.

"We are nearly halfway under the desert now," announced the King; "and that is fast work, because the tunnel has to be drilled through solid rock. But after we have passed the desert it will not take us long to extend the tunnel to the walls of the Emerald City."

"Well, whenever you are ready, we shall be joined by the Whimsies, the Growleywogs and the Phanfasms," said Guph; "so the conquest of Oz is assured without a doubt."

Again, the King seemed thoughtful.

"I'm almost sorry we did not undertake the conquest alone," said he. "All of these allies are dangerous people, and they may demand more than you have promised them. It might have been better to have conquered Oz without any outside assistance."

"We could not do it," said the General, positively.

"Why not, Guph?"

"You know very well. You have had one experience with the Oz people, and they defeated you."

"That was because they rolled eggs at us," replied the King, with a shudder. "My Nomes cannot stand eggs, any more than I can myself. They are poison to all who live underground."

"That is true enough," agreed Guph.

"But we might have taken the Oz people by surprise, and conquered them before they had a chance to get any eggs. Our former defeat was due to the fact that the girl Dorothy had a Yellow Hen with her. I do not know what ever became of that hen, but I believe there are no hens at all in the Land of Oz, and so there could be no eggs there."

"On the contrary," said Guph, "there are now hundreds of chickens in Oz, and they lay heaps of those dangerous eggs.

I met a goshawk on my way home, and the bird informed me that he had lately been to Oz to capture and devour some of the young chickens. But they are protected by magic, so the hawk did not get a single one of them."

"That is a very bad report," said the King, nervously. "Very bad, indeed. My Nomes are willing to fight, but they simply can't face hen's eggs—and I don't blame them."

"They won't need to face them," replied Guph. "I'm afraid of eggs myself, and don't propose to take any chances of being poisoned by them. My plan is to send the Whimsies through the tunnel first, and then the Growleywogs and the Phanfasms. By the time we Nomes get there the eggs will all be used up, and we may then pursue and capture the inhabitants at our leisure."

"Perhaps you are right," returned the King, with a dismal sigh. "But I want it distinctly understood that I claim Ozma and Dorothy as my own prisoners. They are rather nice girls, and I do not intend to let any of those dreadful creatures hurt them, or make them their slaves. When I have captured them I will bring them here and transform them into china ornaments to stand on my mantle. They will look very pretty—Dorothy on one end of the mantle and Ozma on the other—and I shall take great care to see they are not broken when the maids dust them."

"Very well, your Majesty. Do what you will with the girls for all I care. Now that our plans are arranged, and we have the three most powerful bands of evil spirits in the world to assist us, let us make haste to get the tunnel finished as soon as possible."

"It will be ready in three days," promised the King, and hurried away to inspect the work and see that the Nomes kept busy.

Chapter 14

HOW the WIZARD PRACTICED SORCERY

Where next?" asked the Wizard when they had left the town of Fuddlecumjig and the Sawhorse had started back along the road.

"Why, Ozma laid out this trip," replied Dorothy, "and she 'vised us to see the Rigmaroles next, and then visit the Tin Woodman."

"That sounds good," said the Wizard. "But what road do we take to get to the Rigmaroles?"

"I don't know, 'zactly," returned the little girl; "but it must be somewhere just southwest from here."

"Then why need we go way back to the crossroads?" asked

the Shaggy Man. "We might save a lot of time by branching off here."

"There isn't any path," asserted Uncle Henry.

"Then we'd better go back to the signposts, and make sure of our way," decided Dorothy.

But after they had gone a short distance farther the Saw-horse, who had overheard their conversation, stopped and said:

"Here is a path."

Sure enough, a dim path seemed to branch off from the road they were on, and it led across pretty green meadows and past leafy groves, straight toward the southwest.

"That looks like a good path," said Omby Amby. "Why not try it?"

"All right," answered Dorothy. "I'm anxious to see what the Rigmaroles are like, and this path ought to take us there the quickest way."

No one made any objection to this plan, so the Sawhorse turned into the path, which proved to be nearly as good as the one they had taken to get to the Fuddles. As first they passed a few retired farm-houses, but soon these scattered dwellings were left behind and only the meadows and the trees were before them. But they rode along in cheerful contentment, and Aunt Em got into an argument with Billina about the proper way to raise chickens.

"I do not care to contradict you," said the Yellow Hen,

with dignity, "but I have an idea I know more about chickens than human beings do."

"Pshaw!" replied Aunt Em. "I've raised chickens for nearly forty years, Billina, and I know you've got to starve 'em to make 'em lay lots of eggs, and stuff 'em if you want good broilers."

"Broilers!" exclaimed Billina, in horror. "Broil my chickens!"

"Why, that's what they're for, ain't it?" asked Aunt Em, astonished.

"No, Aunt, not in Oz," said Dorothy. "People do not eat chickens here. You see, Billina was the first hen that was ever seen in this country, and I brought her here myself. Everybody liked her an' respected her, so the Oz people wouldn't any more eat her chickens than they would eat Billina."

"Well, I declare," gasped Aunt Em. "How about the eggs?"

"Oh, if we have more eggs than we want to hatch, we allow people to eat them," said Billina. "Indeed, I am very glad the Oz folks like our eggs, for otherwise they would spoil."

"This certainly is a queer country," sighed Aunt Em.

"Excuse me," called the Sawhorse, "the path has ended and I'd like to know which way to go."

They looked around and, sure enough, there was no path to be seen.

"Well," said Dorothy, "we're going southwest, and it seems just as easy to follow that direction without a path as with one."

"Certainly," answered the Sawhorse. "It is not hard to draw the wagon over the meadow. I only want to know where to go."

"There's a forest over there across the prairie," said the Wizard, "and it lies in the direction we are going. Make straight for the forest, Sawhorse, and you're bound to go right."

So the wooden animal trotted on again and the meadow grass was so soft under the wheels that it made easy riding. But Dorothy was a little uneasy at losing the path, because now there was nothing to guide them.

No houses were to be seen at all, so they could not ask their way of any farmer; and although the Land of Oz was always beautiful, wherever one might go, this part of the country was strange to all the party.

"Perhaps we're lost," suggested Aunt Em, after they had proceeded quite a way in silence.

"Never mind," said the Shaggy Man; "I've been lost many a time—and so has Dorothy—and we've always been found again."

"But we may get hungry," remarked Omby Amby. "That is the worst of getting lost in a place where there are no houses near."

"We had a good dinner at the Fuddle town," said Uncle Henry, "and that will keep us from starving to death for a long time."

"No one ever starved to death in Oz," declared Dorothy, positively; "but people may get pretty hungry sometimes."

The Wizard said nothing, and he did not seem especially anxious. The Sawhorse was trotting along briskly, yet the forest seemed farther away than they had thought when they first saw it. So it was nearly sundown when they finally came to the trees; but now they found themselves in a most beautiful spot, the wide-spreading trees being covered with flowering vines and having soft mosses underneath them.

"This will be a good place to camp," said the Wizard, as the Sawhorse stopped for further instructions.

"Camp!" they all echoed.

"Certainly," asserted the Wizard. "It will be dark before very long and we cannot travel through this forest at night. So let us make a camp here, and have some supper, and sleep until daylight comes again."

They all looked at the little man in astonishment, and Aunt Em said, with a sniff:

"A pretty camp we'll have, I must say! I suppose you intend us to sleep under the wagon."

"And chew grass for our supper," added the Shaggy Man, laughing.

But Dorothy seemed to have no doubts and was quite cheerful.

"It's lucky we have the wonderful Wizard with us," she said; "because he can do 'most anything he wants to."

"Oh, yes; I forgot we had a Wizard," said Uncle Henry, looking at the little man curiously.

"I didn't," chirped Billina, contentedly.

The Wizard smiled and climbed out of the wagon, and all the others followed him.

"In order to camp," said he, "the first thing we need is tents. Will some one please lend me a handkerchief?"

The Shaggy Man offered him one, and Aunt Em another. He took them both and laid them carefully upon the grass near to the edge of the forest. Then he laid his own handkerchief down, too, and standing a little back from them he waved his left hand toward the handkerchiefs and said:

> *"Tents of canvas, white as snow,*
> *Let me see how fast you grow!"*

Then, lo and behold! the handkerchiefs became tiny tents, and as the travelers looked at them the tents grew bigger and bigger until in a few minutes each one was large enough to contain the entire party.

"This," said the Wizard, pointing to the first tent, "is for the accommodation of the ladies. Dorothy, you and your Aunt may step inside and take off your things."

Every one ran to look inside the tent, and they saw two pretty white beds, all ready for Dorothy and Aunt Em, and a silver roost for Billina. Rugs were spread upon the grassy floor and some camp chairs and a table completed the furniture.

"Well, well, well! This beats anything I ever saw or heard of!" exclaimed Aunt Em, and she glanced at the Wizard almost fearfully, as if he might be dangerous because of his great powers.

"Oh, Mr. Wizard! How did you manage to do it?" asked Dorothy.

"It's a trick Glinda the Sorceress taught me, and it is much better magic than I used to practice in Omaha, or when I first came to Oz," he answered. "When the good Glinda found I was to live in the Emerald City always, she promised to help me, because she said the Wizard of Oz ought really to be a clever Wizard, and not a humbug. So we have been much together and I am learning so fast that I expect to be able to accomplish some really wonderful things in time."

"You've done it now!" declared Dorothy. "These tents are just wonderful!"

"But come and see the men's tent," said the Wizard. So they went to the second tent, which had shaggy edges because it had been made from the Shaggy Man's handkerchief, and found that completely furnished also. It contained four neat beds for Uncle Henry, Omby Amby, the Shaggy Man and the Wizard. Also there was a soft rug for Toto to lie upon.

"The third tent," explained the Wizard, "is our dining room and kitchen."

They visited that next, and found a table and dishes in

the dining tent, with plenty of those things necessary to use in cooking. The Wizard carried out a big kettle and set it swinging on a crossbar before the tent. While he was doing this Omby Amby and the Shaggy Man brought a supply of twigs from the forest and then they built a fire underneath the kettle.

"Now, Dorothy," said the Wizard, smiling, "I expect you to cook our supper."

"But there is nothing in the kettle," she cried.

"Are you sure?" inquired the Wizard.

"I didn't see anything put in, and I'm almost sure it was empty when you brought it out," she replied.

"Nevertheless," said the little man, winking slyly at Uncle Henry, "you will do well to watch our supper, my dear, and see that it doesn't boil over."

Then the men took some pails and went into the forest to search for a spring of water, and while they were gone Aunt Em said to Dorothy:

"I believe the Wizard is fooling us. I saw the kettle myself, and when he hung it over the fire there wasn't a thing in it but air."

"Don't worry," remarked Billina, confidently, as she nestled in the grass before the fire. "You'll find something in the kettle when it's taken off—and it won't be poor, innocent chickens, either."

"Your hen has very bad manners, Dorothy," said Aunt Em,

looking somewhat disdainfully at Billina. "It seems too bad she ever learned how to talk."

There might have been another unpleasant quarrel between Aunt Em and Billina had not the men returned just then with their pails filled with clear, sparkling water. The Wizard told Dorothy that she was a good cook and he believed their supper was ready.

So Uncle Henry lifted the kettle from the fire and poured its contents into a big platter which the Wizard held for him. The platter was fairly heaped with a fine stew, smoking hot, with many kinds of vegetables and dumplings and a rich, delicious gravy.

The Wizard triumphantly placed the platter upon the table in the dining tent and then they all sat down in camp chairs to the feast.

There were several other dishes on the table, all carefully covered, and when the time came to remove these covers they found bread and butter, cakes, cheese, pickles and fruits— including some of the luscious strawberries of Oz.

No one ventured to ask a question as to how these things came there. They contented themselves by eating heartily the good things provided, and Toto and Billina had their full share, you may be sure. After the meal was over, Aunt Em whispered to Dorothy:

"That may have been magic food, my dear, and for that reason perhaps it won't be very nourishing; but I'm willing to say it tasted as good as anything I ever et." Then she added, in a louder voice: "Who's going to do the dishes?"

"No one, madam," answered the Wizard. "The dishes have 'done' themselves."

"La sakes!" ejaculated the good lady, holding up her hands in amazement. For, sure enough, when she looked at the dishes they had a moment before left upon the table, she found them all washed and dried and piled up into neat stacks.

Chapter 15

HOW DOROTHY
HAPPENED to GET LOST

It was a beautiful evening, so they drew their camp chairs in a circle before one of the tents and began to tell stories to amuse themselves and pass away the time before they went to bed.

Pretty soon a zebra was seen coming out of the forest, and he trotted straight up to them and said politely:

"Good evening, people."

The zebra was a sleek little animal and had a slender head, a stubby mane and a paint-brush tail—very like a donkey's. His neatly shaped white body was covered with regular bars of dark brown, and his hoofs were delicate as those of a deer.

"Good evening, friend Zebra," said Omby Amby, in reply to the creature's greeting. "Can we do anything for you?"

"Yes," answered the zebra. "I should like you to settle a dispute that has long been a bother to me, as to whether there is more water or land in the world."

"Who are you disputing with?" asked the Wizard.

"With a soft-shell crab," said the zebra. "He lives in a pool where I go to drink every day, and he is a very impertinent crab, I assure you. I have told him many times that the land is much greater in extent than the water, but he will not be convinced. Even this very evening, when I told him he was an insignificant creature who lived in a small pool, he asserted that the water was greater and more important than the land. So, seeing your camp, I decided to ask you to settle the dispute for once and all, that I may not be further annoyed by this ignorant crab."

When they had listened to this explanation Dorothy inquired:

"Where is the soft-shell crab?"

"Not far away," replied the zebra. "If you will agree to judge between us I will run and get him."

"Run along, then," said the little girl.

So the animal pranced into the forest and soon came trotting back to them. When he drew near they found a soft-shell crab clinging fast to the stiff hair of the zebra's head, where it held on by one claw.

"Now then, Mr. Crab," said the zebra, "here are the people I told you about; and they know more than you do, who lives in a pool, and more than I do, who lives in a forest. For they have been travelers all over the world, and know every part of it."

"There is more of the world than Oz," declared the crab, in a stubborn voice.

"That is true," said Dorothy; "but I used to live in Kansas, in the United States, and I've been to California and to Australia—and so has Uncle Henry."

"For my part," added the Shaggy Man, "I've been to Mexico and Boston and many other foreign countries."

"And I," said the Wizard, "have been to Europe and Ireland."

"So you see," continued the zebra, addressing the crab, "here are people of real consequence, who know what they are talking about."

"Then they know there's more water in the world than there is land," asserted the crab, in a shrill, petulant voice.

"They know you are wrong to make such an absurd statement, and they will probably think you are a lobster instead of a crab," retorted the animal.

At this taunt the crab reached out its other claw and seized the zebra's ear, and the creature gave a cry of pain and began prancing up and down, trying to shake off the crab, which clung fast.

"Stop pinching!" cried the zebra. "You promised not to pinch if I would carry you here!"

"And you promised to treat me respectfully," said the crab, letting go the ear.

"Well, haven't I?" demanded the zebra.

"No; you called me a lobster," said the crab.

"Ladies and gentlemen," continued the zebra, "please pardon my poor friend, because he is ignorant and stupid, and does not understand. Also the pinch of his claw is very annoying. So pray tell him that the world contains more land than water, and when he has heard your judgment I will carry him back and dump him into his pool, where I hope he will be more modest in the future."

"But we cannot tell him that," said Dorothy, gravely, "because it would not be true."

"What!" exclaimed the zebra, in astonishment; "do I hear you aright?"

"The soft-shell crab is correct," declared the Wizard. "There is considerably more water than there is land in the world."

"Impossible!" protested the zebra. "Why, I can run for days upon the land, and find but little water."

"Did you ever see an ocean?" asked Dorothy.

"Never," admitted the zebra. "There is no such thing as an ocean in the Land of Oz."

"Well, there are several oceans in the world," said Dorothy, "and people sail in ships upon these oceans for weeks and weeks, and never see a bit of land at all. And the joggerfys will tell you that all the oceans put together are bigger than all the land put together."

At this the crab began laughing in queer chuckles that reminded Dorothy of the way Billina sometimes cackled.

"*Now* will you give up, Mr. Zebra?" it cried, jeeringly; "now will you give up?"

The zebra seemed much humbled.

"Of course I cannot read geographys," he said.

"You could take one of the Wizard's School Pills," suggested Billina, "and that would make you learned and wise without studying."

The crab began laughing again, which so provoked the zebra that he tried to shake the little creature off. This resulted in more ear-pinching, and finally Dorothy told them that if they could not behave they must go back to the forest.

"I'm sorry I asked you to decide this question," said the zebra, crossly. "So long as neither of us could prove we were right we quite enjoyed the dispute; but now I can never drink at that pool again without the soft-shell crab laughing at me. So I must find another drinking place."

"Do! Do, you ignoramus!" shouted the crab, as loudly as his little voice would carry. "Rile some other pool with your clumsy hoofs, and let your betters alone after this!"

Then the zebra trotted back to the forest, bearing the crab

with him, and disappeared amid the gloom of the trees. And as it was now getting dark the travelers said good night to one another and went to bed.

Dorothy awoke just as the light was beginning to get strong next morning, and not caring to sleep any later she quietly got out of bed, dressed herself, and left the tent where Aunt Em was yet peacefully slumbering.

Outside she noticed Billina busily pecking around to secure bugs or other food for breakfast, but none of the men in the other tent seemed awake. So the little girl decided to take a walk in the woods and try to discover some path or road that they might follow when they again started upon their journey.

She had reached the edge of the forest when the Yellow Hen came fluttering along and asked where she was going.

"Just to take a walk, Billina; and maybe I'll find some path," said Dorothy.

"Then I'll go along," decided Billina, and scarcely had she spoken when Toto ran up and joined them.

Toto and the Yellow Hen had become quite friendly by this time, although at first they did not get along well together. Billina had been rather suspicious of dogs, and Toto had had an idea that it was every dog's duty to chase a hen on sight. But Dorothy had talked to them and scolded them for not being agreeable to one another until they grew better acquainted and became friends.

I won't say they loved each other dearly, but at least they had stopped quarreling and now managed to get on together very well.

The day was growing lighter every minute and driving the black shadows out of the forest; so Dorothy found it very pleasant walking under the trees. She went some distance in one direction, but not finding a path, presently turned in a different direction. There was no path here, either, although she advanced quite a way into the forest, winding here and there among the trees and peering through the bushes in an endeavor to find some beaten track.

"I think we'd better go back," suggested the Yellow Hen, after a time. "The people will all be up by this time and breakfast will be ready."

"Very well," agreed Dorothy. "Let's see—the camp must be over this way."

She had probably made a mistake about that, for after they had gone far enough to have reached the camp they still found themselves in the thick of the woods. So the little girl stopped short and looked around her, and Toto glanced up into her face with his bright little eyes and wagged his tail as if he knew something was wrong. He couldn't tell much about direction himself, because he had spent his time prowling among the bushes and running here and there; nor had Billina paid much attention to where they were going, being interested in picking bugs from the moss as they passed along.

The Yellow Hen now turned one eye up toward the little girl and asked:

"Have you forgotten where the camp is, Dorothy?"

"Yes," she admitted; "have you, Billina?"

"I didn't try to remember," returned Billina. "I'd no idea you would get lost, Dorothy."

"It's the thing we don't expect, Billina, that usually happens," observed the girl, thoughtfully. "But it's no use standing here. Let's go in that direction," pointing a finger at random. "It may be we'll get out of the forest over there."

So on they went again, but this way the trees were closer together, and the vines were so tangled that often they tripped Dorothy up.

Suddenly a voice cried sharply:

"Halt!"

At first, Dorothy could see nothing, although she looked around very carefully. But Billina exclaimed:

"Well, I declare!"

"What is it?" asked the little girl: for Toto began barking at something, and following his gaze she discovered what it was.

A row of spoons had surrounded the three, and these spoons stood straight up on their handles and carried swords and muskets. Their faces were outlined in the polished bowls and they looked very stern and severe.

Dorothy laughed at the queer things.

"Who are you?" she asked.

"We're the Spoon Brigade," said one.

"In the service of his Majesty King Kleaver," said another.

"And you are our prisoners," said a third.

Dorothy sat down on an old stump and looked at them, her eyes twinkling with amusement.

"What would happen," she inquired, "if I should set my dog on your Brigade?"

"He would die," replied one of the spoons, sharply. "One shot from our deadly muskets would kill him, big as he is."

"Don't risk it, Dorothy," advised the Yellow Hen. "Remember this is a fairy country, yet none of us three happens to be a fairy."

Dorothy grew sober at this.

"P'raps you're right, Billina," she answered. "But how funny it is, to be captured by a lot of spoons!"

"I do not see anything very funny about it," declared a spoon. "We're the regular military brigade of the kingdom."

"What kingdom?" she asked.

"Utensia," said he.

"I never heard of it before," asserted Dorothy. Then she added, thoughtfully, "I don't believe Ozma ever heard of Utensia, either. Tell me, are you not subjects of Ozma of Oz?"

"We have never heard of her," retorted a spoon. "We are subjects of King Kleaver, and obey only his orders, which are to bring all prisoners to him as soon as they are captured. So step lively, my girl, and march with us, or we may be tempted to cut off a few of your toes with our swords."

This threat made Dorothy laugh again. She did not believe she was in any danger; but here was a new and interesting adventure, so she was willing to be taken to Utensia that she might see what King Kleaver's kingdom was like.

How Dorothy Visited
Utensia

There must have been from six to eight dozen
spoons in the Brigade, and they marched
away in the shape of a hollow square, with
Dorothy, Billina and Toto in the center of the
square. Before they had gone very far Toto knocked over one
of the spoons by wagging his tail, and then the Captain of the
Spoons told the little dog to be more careful, or he would be
punished. So Toto was careful, and the Spoon Brigade moved
along with astonishing swiftness, while Dorothy really had to
walk fast to keep up with it.

By and by they left the woods and entered a big clearing,
in which was the Kingdom of Utensia.

Standing all around the clearing were a good many cook-stoves, ranges and grills, of all sizes and shapes, and besides these there were several kitchen cabinets and cupboards and a few kitchen tables. These things were crowded with utensils of all sorts: frying pans, sauce pans, kettles, forks, knives, basting and soup spoons, nutmeg graters, sifters, colanders, meat saws, flat irons, rolling pins and many other things of a like nature.

When the Spoon Brigade appeared with the prisoners a wild shout arose and many of the utensils hopped off their stoves or their benches and ran crowding around Dorothy and the hen and the dog.

"Stand back!" cried the Captain, sternly, and he led his captives through the curious throng until they came before a big range that stood in the center of the clearing. Beside this range was a butcher's block upon which lay a great cleaver with a keen edge. It rested upon the flat of its back, its legs were crossed and it was smoking a long pipe.

"Wake up, your Majesty," said the Captain. "Here are prisoners."

Hearing this, King Kleaver sat up and looked at Dorothy sharply.

"Gristle and fat!" he cried. "Where did this girl come from?"

"I found her in the forest and brought her here a prisoner," replied the Captain.

"Why did you do that?" inquired the King, puffing his pipe lazily.

"To create some excitement," the Captain answered. "It is so quiet here that we are all getting rusty for want of amusement. For my part, I prefer to see stirring times."

"Naturally," returned the cleaver, with a nod. "I have always said, Captain, without a bit of irony, that you are a sterling officer and a solid citizen, bowled and polished to a degree. But what do you expect me to do with these prisoners?"

"That is for you to decide," declared the Captain. "You are the King."

"To be sure; to be sure," muttered the cleaver, musingly. "As you say, we have had dull times since the steel and grindstone eloped and left us. Command my Counselors and the Royal Courtiers to attend me, as well as the High Priest and the Judge. We'll then decide what can be done."

The Captain saluted and retired and Dorothy sat down on an overturned kettle and asked:

"Have you anything to eat in your kingdom?"

"Here! Get up! Get off from me!" cried a faint voice, at which his Majesty the cleaver said:

"Excuse me, but you're sitting on my friend the Ten-quart Kettle."

Dorothy at once arose, and the kettle turned right side up and looked at her reproachfully.

"I'm a friend of the King, so no one dares sit on me," said he.

"I'd prefer a chair, anyway," she replied.

"Sit on that hearth," commanded the King.

So Dorothy sat on the hearth-shelf of the big range, and the subjects of Utensia began to gather around in a large and inquisitive throng. Toto lay at Dorothy's feet and Billina flew upon the range, which had no fire in it, and perched there as comfortably as she could.

When all the Counselors and Courtiers had assembled— and these seemed to include most of the inhabitants of the kingdom—the King rapped on the block for order and said:

"Friends and Fellow Utensils! Our worthy Commander of the Spoon Brigade, Captain Dipp, has captured the three prisoners you see before you and brought them here for— for—I don't know what for. So I ask your advice how to act in this matter, and what fate I should mete out to these captives. Judge Sifter, stand on my right. It is your business to sift this affair to the bottom. High Priest Colander, stand on my left and see that no one testifies falsely in this matter."

As these two officials took their places, Dorothy asked:

"Why is the colander the High Priest?"

"He's the holiest thing we have in the kingdom," replied King Kleaver.

"Except me," said a sieve. "I'm the whole thing when it comes to holes."

"What we need," remarked the King, rebukingly, "is a wireless sieve. I must speak to Marconi about it. These old-fashioned sieves talk too much. Now, it is the duty of the King's Counselors to counsel the King at all times of emergency, so I beg you to speak out and advise me what to do with these prisoners."

"I demand that they be killed several times, until they are dead!" shouted a pepperbox, hopping around very excitedly.

"Compose yourself, Mr. Paprica," advised the King. "Your remarks are piquant and highly-seasoned, but you need a scattering of commonsense. It is only necessary to kill a person once to make him dead; but I do not see that it is necessary to kill this little girl at all."

"I don't, either," said Dorothy.

"Pardon me, but you are not expected to advise me in this matter," replied King Kleaver.

"Why not?" asked Dorothy.

"You might be prejudiced in your own favor, and so mislead us," he said. "Now then, good subjects, who speaks next?"

"I'd like to smooth this thing over, in some way," said a flatiron, earnestly. "We are supposed to be useful to mankind, you know."

"But the girl isn't mankind! She's womankind!" yelled a corkscrew.

"What do you know about it?" inquired the King.

"I'm a lawyer," said the corkscrew, proudly. "I am accustomed to appear at the bar."

"But you're crooked," retorted the King, "and that debars

you. You may be a corking good lawyer, Mr. Popp, but I must ask you to withdraw your remarks."

"Very well," said the corkscrew, sadly; "I see I haven't any pull at this court."

"Permit me," continued the flatiron, "to press my suit, your Majesty. I do not wish to gloss over any fault the prisoner may have committed, if such a fault exists; but we owe her some consideration, and that's flat!"

"I'd like to hear from Prince Karver," said the King.

At this a stately carvingknife stepped forward and bowed.

"The Captain was wrong to bring this girl here, and she was wrong to come," he said. "But now that the foolish deed is done let us all prove our mettle and have a slashing good time."

"That's it! that's it!" screamed a fat choppingknife. "We'll make mincemeat of the girl and hash of the chicken and sausage of the dog!"

There was a shout of approval at this and the King had to rap again for order.

"Gentlemen, gentlemen!" he said, "your remarks are somewhat cutting and rather disjointed, as might be expected from such acute intellects. But you give me no reasons for your demands."

"See here, Kleaver; you make me tired," said a saucepan, strutting before the King very impudently. "You're about the worst King that ever reigned in Utensia, and that's saying a good deal. Why don't you run things yourself, instead of asking everybody's advice, like the big, clumsy idiot you are?"

The King sighed.

"I wish there wasn't a saucepan in my kingdom," he said. "You fellows are always stewing, over something, and every once in a while you slop over and make a mess of it. Go hang yourself, sir—by the handle—and don't let me hear from you again."

Dorothy was much shocked by the dreadful language the utensils employed, and she thought that they must have had very little proper training. So she said, addressing the King, who seemed very unfit to rule his turbulent subjects:

"I wish you'd decide my fate right away. I can't stay here all day, trying to find out what you're going to do with me."

"This thing is becoming a regular broil, and it's time I took part in it," observed a big gridiron, coming forward.

"What I'd like to know," said a can-opener, in a shrill voice, "is why the little girl came to our forest, anyhow, and why she intruded upon Captain Dipp—who ought to be called Dippy—and who she is, and where she came from, and where she is going, and why and wherefore and therefore and when."

"I'm sorry to see, Sir Jabber," remarked the King to the can-opener, "that you have such a prying disposition. As a matter of fact, all the things you mention are none of our business."

Having said this the King relighted his pipe, which had gone out.

"Tell me, please, what *is* our business?" inquired a potato-masher, winking at Dorothy somewhat impertinently. "I'm fond of little girls, myself, and it seems to me she has as much right to wander in the forest as we have."

"Who accuses the little girl, anyway?" inquired a rolling-pin. "What has she done?"

"I don't know," said the King. "What has she done, Captain Dipp?"

"That's the trouble, your Majesty. She hasn't done anything," replied the Captain.

"What do you want me to do?" asked Dorothy.

This question seemed to puzzle them all. Finally, a chafing-dish, exclaimed irritably:

"If no one can throw any light on this subject you must excuse me if I go out."

At this, a big kitchen fork pricked up its ears and said in a tiny voice:

"Let's hear from Judge Sifter."

"That's proper," returned the King.

So Judge Sifter turned around slowly several times and then said:

"We have nothing against the girl except the stove-hearth upon which she sits. Therefore I order her instantly discharged."

"Discharged!" cried Dorothy. "Why, I never was discharged in my life, and I don't intend to be. If it's all the same to you, I'll resign."

"It's all the same," declared the King. "You are free—you and your companions—and may go wherever you like."

"Thank you," said the little girl. "But haven't you anything to eat in your kingdom? I'm hungry."

"Go into the woods and pick blackberries," advised the King, lying down upon his back again and preparing to go to sleep. "There isn't a morsel to eat in all Utensia, that I know of."

So Dorothy jumped up and said:

"Come on, Toto and Billina. If we can't find the camp, we may find some blackberries."

The utensils drew back and allowed them to pass without protest, although Captain Dipp marched the Spoon Brigade in close order after them until they had reached the edge of the clearing.

There the spoons halted; but Dorothy and her companions entered the forest again and began searching diligently for a way back to the camp, that they might rejoin their party.

Chapter 17

How They Came to Bunbury

Wandering through the woods, without knowing where you are going or what adventure you are about to meet next, is not as pleasant as one might think. The woods are always beautiful and impressive, and if you are not worried or hungry you may enjoy them immensely; but Dorothy was worried and hungry that morning, so she paid little attention to the beauties of the forest, and hurried along as fast as she could go. She tried to keep in one direction and not circle around, but she was not at all sure that the direction she had chosen would lead her to the camp.

By and by, to her great joy, she came upon a path. It ran to the right and to the left, being lost in the trees in both directions, and just before her, upon a big oak, were fastened two signs, with arms pointing both ways. One sign read:

TAKE THE OTHER ROAD TO BUNBURY

and the second sign read:

TAKE THE OTHER ROAD TO BUNNYBURY

"Well!" exclaimed Billina, eyeing the signs, "this looks as if we were getting back to civilization again."

"I'm not sure about the civil'zation, dear," replied the little girl; "but it looks as if we might get *somewhere*, and that's a big relief, anyhow."

"Which path shall we take?" inquired the Yellow Hen.

Dorothy stared at the signs thoughtfully.

"Bunbury sounds like something to eat," she said. "Let's go there."

"It's all the same to me," replied Billina. She had picked up enough bugs and insects from the moss as she went along to satisfy her own hunger, but the hen knew Dorothy could not eat bugs; nor could Toto.

The path to Bunbury seemed little traveled, but it was distinct enough and ran through the trees in a zigzag course until it finally led them to an open space filled with the queerest houses Dorothy had ever seen. They were all made of crackers laid out in tiny squares, and were of many pretty and ornamental shapes, having balconies and porches with posts of bread-sticks and roofs shingled with wafer-crackers.

There were walks of bread-crusts leading from house to house and forming streets, and the place seemed to have many inhabitants.

When Dorothy, followed by Billina and Toto, entered the place, they found people walking the streets or assembled in groups talking together, or sitting upon the porches and balconies.

And what funny people they were!

Men, women and children were all made of buns and bread. Some were thin and others fat; some were white, some light brown and some very dark of complexion. A few of the buns, which seemed to form the more important class of the people, were neatly frosted. Some had raisins for eyes and currant buttons on their clothes; others had eyes of cloves and legs of stick cinnamon, and many wore hats and bonnets frosted pink and green.

There was something of a commotion in Bunbury when the strangers suddenly appeared among them. Women caught up their children and hurried into their houses, shutting the cracker doors carefully behind them. Some men ran so hastily that they tumbled over one another, while others, more brave, assembled in a group and faced the intruders defiantly.

Dorothy at once realized that she must act with caution in order not to frighten these shy people, who were evidently unused to the presence of strangers. There was a delightful fragrant odor of fresh bread in the town, and this made the little girl more hungry than ever. She told Toto and Billina to stay back while she slowly advanced toward the group that stood silently awaiting her.

"You must 'scuse me for coming unexpected," she said, softly, "but I really didn't know I was coming here until I arrived. I was lost in the woods, you know, and I'm as hungry as anything."

"Hungry!" they murmured, in a horrified chorus.

"Yes; I haven't had anything to eat since last night's supper," she exclaimed. "Are there any eatables in Bunbury?"

They looked at one another undecidedly, and then one portly bun man, who seemed a person of consequence, stepped forward and said:

"Little girl, to be frank with you, we are all eatables. Everything in Bunbury is eatable to ravenous human creatures like you. But it is to escape being eaten and destroyed that we have secluded ourselves in this out-of-the-way place, and there is neither right nor justice in your coming here to feed upon us."

Dorothy looked at him longingly.

"You're bread, aren't you?" she asked.

"Yes; bread and butter. The butter is inside me, so it won't melt and run. I do the running myself."

At this joke all the others burst into a chorus of laughter, and Dorothy thought they couldn't be much afraid if they could laugh like that.

"Couldn't I eat something besides people?" she asked. "Couldn't I eat just one house, or a side-walk or something? I wouldn't mind much what it was, you know."

"This is not a public bakery, child," replied the man, sternly. "It's private property."

"I know Mr.—Mr.—"

"My name is C. Bunn, Esquire," said the man. "C stands for Cinnamon, and this place is called after my family, which is the most aristocratic in the town."

"Oh, I don't know about that," objected another of the queer people. "The Grahams and the Browns and Whites are all excellent families, and there is none better of their kind. I'm a Boston Brown, myself."

"I admit you are all desirable citizens," said Mr. Bunn, rather stiffly; "but the fact remains that our town is called Bunbury."

"'Scuse me," interrupted Dorothy; "but I'm getting hungrier every minute. Now, if you're polite and kind, as I'm sure you ought to be, you'll let me eat *something*. There's so much to eat here that you will never miss it."

Then a big, puffed-up man, of a delicate brown color, stepped forward and said:

"I think it would be a shame to send this child away hungry, especially as she agrees to eat whatever we can spare and not touch our people."

"So do I, Pop," replied a Roll who stood near.

"What, then, do you suggest, Mr. Over?" inquired Mr. Bunn.

"Why, I'll let her eat my back fence, if she wants to. It's made of waffles, and they're very crisp and nice."

"She may also eat my wheelbarrow," added a pleasant looking Muffin. "It's made of nabiscos with a zuzu wheel."

"Very good; very good," remarked Mr. Bunn. "That is certainly very kind of you. Go with Pop Over and Mr. Muffin, little girl, and they will feed you."

"Thank you very much," said Dorothy, gratefully. "May I bring my dog Toto, and the Yellow Hen? They're hungry, too."

"Will you make them behave?" asked the Muffin.

"Of course," promised Dorothy.

"Then come along," said Pop Over.

So Dorothy and Billina and Toto walked up the street and the people seemed no longer to be at all afraid of them. Mr. Muffin's house came first, and as his wheelbarrow stood in the front yard the little girl ate that first. It didn't seem very fresh, but she was so hungry that she was not particular. Toto ate some, too, while Billina picked up the crumbs.

While the strangers were engaged in eating, many of the people came and stood in the street curiously watching them. Dorothy noticed six roguish looking brown children standing all in a row, and she asked:

"Who are you, little ones?"

"We're the Graham Gems," replied one; "and we're all twins."

"I wonder if your mother could spare one or two of you?" asked Billina, who decided that they were fresh baked; but at this dangerous question the six little gems ran away as fast as they could go.

"You musn't say such things, Billina," said Dorothy, reprovingly. "Now let's go into Pop Over's back yard and get the waffles."

"I sort of hate to let that fence go," remarked Mr. Over, nervously, as they walked toward his house. "The neighbors back of us are Soda Biscuits, and I don't care to mix with them."

"But I'm hungry yet," declared the girl. "That wheelbarrow wasn't very big."

"I've got a shortcake piano, but none of my family can play on it," he said, reflectively. "Suppose you eat that."

"All right," said Dorothy; "I don't mind. Anything to be accommodating."

So Mr. Over led her into the house, where she ate the piano, which was of an excellent flavor.

"Is there anything to drink here?" she asked.

"Yes; I've a milk pump and a water pump; which will you have?" he asked.

"I guess I'll try 'em both," said Dorothy.

So Mr. Over called to his wife, who brought into the yard a

pail made of some kind of baked dough, and Dorothy pumped the pail full of cool, sweet milk and drank it eagerly.

The wife of Pop Over was several shades darker than her husband.

"Aren't you overdone?" the little girl asked her.

"No indeed," answered the woman. "I'm neither overdone nor done over; I'm just Mrs. Over, and I'm the President of the Bunbury Breakfast Band."

Dorothy thanked them for their hospitality and went away. At the gate Mr. Cinnamon Bunn met her and said he would show her around the town.

"We have some very interesting inhabitants," he remarked, walking stiffly beside her on his stick-cinnamon legs; "and all of us who are in good health are well bred. If you are no longer hungry we will call upon a few of the most important citizens."

Toto and Billina followed behind them, behaving very well, and a little way down the street they came to a handsome residence where Aunt Sally Lunn lived. The old lady was glad to meet the little girl and gave her a slice of white bread and butter which had been used as a door-mat. It was almost fresh and tasted better than anything Dorothy had eaten in the town.

"Where do you get the butter?" she inquired.

"We dig it out of the ground, which, as you may have observed, is all flour and meal," replied Mr. Bunn. "There is a butter mine just at the opposite side of the village. The trees which you see here are all doughleanders and doughderas, and in the season we get quite a crop of dough-nuts off them."

"I should think the flour would blow around and get into your eyes," said Dorothy.

"No," said he; "we are bothered with cracker dust sometimes, but never with flour."

Then he took her to see Johnny Cake, a cheerful old gentleman who lived near by.

"I suppose you've heard of me," said old Johnny, with an air of pride. "I'm a great favorite all over the world."

"Aren't you rather yellow?" asked Dorothy, looking at him critically.

"Maybe, child. But don't think I'm bilious, for I was never in better health in my life," replied the old gentleman. "If anything ailed me, I'd willingly acknowledge the corn."

"Johnny's a trifle stale," said Mr. Bunn, as they went away; "but he's a good mixer and never gets cross-grained. I will now take you to call upon some of my own relatives."

They visited the Sugar Bunns, the Currant Bunns and the Spanish Bunns, the latter having a decidedly foreign appearance. Then they saw the French Rolls, who were very polite to them, and made a brief call upon the Parker H. Rolls, who seemed a bit proud and overbearing.

"But they're not as stuck up as the Frosted Jumbles," declared Mr. Bunn, "who are people I really can't abide. I don't like to be suspicious or talk scandal, but sometimes I think the Jumbles have too much baking powder in them."

Just then a dreadful scream was heard, and Dorothy turned hastily around to find a scene of great excitement a little way down the street. The people were crowding around Toto and throwing at him everything they could find at hand. They pelted the little dog with hard-tack, crackers, and even articles of furniture which were hard baked and heavy enough for missiles.

Toto howled a little as the assortment of bake stuff struck him; but he stood still, with head bowed and tail between his legs, until Dorothy ran up and inquired what the matter was.

"Matter!" cried a rye loafer, indignantly, "why the horrid beast has eaten three of our dear Crumpets, and is now devouring a Salt-rising Biscuit!"

"Oh, Toto! How could you?" exclaimed Dorothy, much distressed.

Toto's mouth was full of his salt-rising victim; so he only whined and wagged his tail. But Billina, who had flown to the top of a cracker house to be in a safe place, called out:

"Don't blame him, Dorothy; the Crumpets dared him to do it."

"Yes, and you pecked out the eyes of a Raisin Bunn—one of our best citizens!" shouted a bread pudding, shaking its fist at the Yellow Hen.

"What's that! What's that?" wailed Mr. Cinnamon Bunn, who had now joined them. "Oh, what a misfortune—what a terrible misfortune!"

"See here," said Dorothy, determined to defend her pets, "I think we've treated you all pretty well, seeing you're eatables, an' reg'lar food for us. I've been kind to you and eaten your old wheelbarrows and pianos and rubbish, an' not said a word. But Toto and Billina can't be 'spected to go hungry when the town's full of good things they like to eat, 'cause they can't understand your stingy ways as I do."

"You must leave here at once!" said Mr. Bunn, sternly.

"Suppose we won't go?" said Dorothy, who was now much provoked.

"Then," said he, "we will put you into the great ovens where we are made, and bake you."

Dorothy gazed around and saw threatening looks upon the faces of all. She had not noticed any ovens in the town, but they might be there, nevertheless, for some of the inhabitants seemed very fresh. So she decided to go, and calling to Toto and Billina to follow her she marched up the street with as much dignity as possible, considering that she was followed by the hoots and cries of the buns and biscuits and other bake stuff.

Chapter 18

HOW OZMA LOOKED into the MAGIC PICTURE

Princess Ozma was a very busy little ruler, for she looked carefully after the comfort and welfare of her people and tried to make them happy. If any quarrels arose she decided them justly; if any one needed counsel or advice she was ready and willing to listen to them.

For a day or two after Dorothy and her companions had started on their trip, Ozma was occupied with the affairs of her kingdom. Then she began to think of some manner of occupation for Uncle Henry and Aunt Em that would be light and easy and yet give the old people something to do.

She soon decided to make Uncle Henry the Keeper of

the Jewels, for some one really was needed to count and look after the bins and barrels of emeralds, diamonds, rubies and other precious stones that were in the Royal Storehouses. That would keep Uncle Henry busy enough, but it was harder to find something for Aunt Em to do. The palace was full of servants, so there was no detail of housework that Aunt Em could look after.

While Ozma sat in her pretty room engaged in thought she happened to glance at her Magic Picture.

This was one of the most important treasures in all the Land of Oz. It was a large picture, set in a beautiful gold frame, and it hung in a prominent place upon a wall of Ozma's private room.

Usually this picture seemed merely a country scene, but whenever Ozma looked at it and wished to know what any of her friends or acquaintances were doing, the magic of this wonderful picture was straightway disclosed. For the country scene would gradually fade away and in its place would appear the likeness of the person or persons Ozma might wish to see, surrounded by the actual scenes in which they were then placed. In this way the Princess could view any part of the world she wished, and watch the actions of any one in whom she was interested.

Ozma had often seen Dorothy in her Kansas home by this means, and now, having a little leisure, she expressed a desire to see her little friend again. It was while the travelers were at Fuddlecumjig, and Ozma laughed merrily as she watched in the picture her friends trying to match the pieces of Grandmother Gnit.

"They seem happy and are doubtless having a good time," the girl Ruler said to herself; and then she began to think of the many adventures she herself had encountered with Dorothy.

The image of her friends now faded from the Magic Picture and the old landscape slowly reappeared.

Ozma was thinking of the time when with Dorothy and her army she marched to the Nome King's underground cavern, beyond the Land of Ev, and forced the old monarch to liberate his captives, who belonged to the Royal Family of Ev. That was the time when the Scarecrow nearly frightened the Nome King into fits by throwing one of Billina's eggs at him, and Dorothy had captured King Roquat's Magic Belt and brought it away with her to the Land of Oz.

The pretty Princess smiled at the recollection of this adventure, and then she wondered what had become of the Nome King since then. Merely because she was curious and had nothing better to do, Ozma glanced at the Magic Picture and wished to see in it the King of the Nomes.

Roquat the Red went every day into his tunnel to see how the work was getting along and to hurry his workmen as much as possible. He was there now, and Ozma saw him plainly in the Magic Picture.

She saw the underground tunnel, reaching far underneath

the deadly desert which separated the Land of Oz from the mountains beneath which the Nome King had his extensive caverns. She saw that the tunnel was being made in the direction of the Emerald City, and knew at once it was being dug so that the army of Nomes could march through it and attack her own beautiful and peaceful country.

"I suppose King Roquat is planning revenge against us," she said, musingly, "and thinks he can surprise us and make us his captives and slaves. How sad it is that any one can have such wicked thoughts! But I must not blame King Roquat too severely, for he is a Nome, and his nature is not so gentle as my own."

Then she dismissed from her mind further thought of the tunnel, for that time, and began to wonder if Aunt Em would not be happy as Royal Mender of the Stockings of the Ruler of Oz. Ozma wore few holes in her stockings; still, they sometimes needed mending. Aunt Em ought to be able to do that very nicely.

Next day the Princess watched the tunnel again in her Magic Picture, and every day afterward she devoted a few minutes to inspecting the work. It was not especially interesting, but she felt that it was her duty.

Slowly but surely the big arched hole crept through the rocks underneath the deadly desert, and day by day it drew nearer and nearer to the Emerald City.

Chapter 19

HOW BUNNYBURY WELCOMED
the STRANGERS

Dorothy left Bunbury the same way she had entered it and when they were in the forest again she said to Billina:

"I never thought that things good to eat could be so dis'gree'ble."

"Often I've eaten things that tasted good but were disagreeable afterward," returned the Yellow Hen. "I think, Dorothy, if eatables are going to act badly, it's better before than after you eat them."

"P'raps you're right," said the little girl, with a sigh. "But what shall we do now?"

"Let us follow the path back to the signpost," suggested

Billina. "That will be better than getting lost again."

"Why, we're lost anyhow," declared Dorothy; "but I guess you're right about going back to that signpost, Billina."

They returned along the path to the place where they had first found it, and at once took "the other road" to Bunnybury. This road was a mere narrow strip, worn hard and smooth but not wide enough for Dorothy's feet to tread. Still, it was a guide, and the walking through the forest was not at all difficult.

Before long they reached a high wall of solid white marble, and the path came to an end at this wall.

At first Dorothy thought there was no opening at all in the marble, but on looking closely she discovered a small square door about on a level with her head, and underneath this closed door was a bell-push. Near the bell-push a sign was painted in neat letters upon the marble, and the sign read:

NO ADMITTANCE

EXCEPT ON BUSINESS

This did not discourage Dorothy, however, and she rang the bell.

Pretty soon a bolt was cautiously withdrawn and the marble door swung slowly open. Then she saw it was not really a door, but a window, for several brass bars were placed across it, being set fast in the marble and so close together that the little girl's fingers might barely go between them. Back of the bars appeared the face of a white rabbit—a very sober and sedate face—with an eye-glass held in his left eye and attached to a cord in his button-hole.

"Well! what is it?" asked the rabbit, sharply.

"I'm Dorothy," said the girl, "and I'm lost, and—"

"State your business, please," interrupted the rabbit.

"My business," she replied, "is to find out where I am, and to—"

"No one is allowed in Bunnybury without an order or a letter of introduction from either Ozma of Oz or Glinda the Good," announced the rabbit; "so that settles the matter," and he started to close the window.

"Wait a minute!" cried Dorothy. "I've got a letter from Ozma."

"From the Ruler of Oz?" asked the rabbit, doubtingly.

"Of course. Ozma's my best friend, you know; and I'm a Princess myself," she announced, earnestly.

"Hum—ha! Let me see your letter," returned the rabbit, as if he still doubted her.

So she hunted in her pocket and found the letter Ozma had given her. Then she handed it through the bars to the rabbit, who took it in his paws and opened it. He read it aloud in a pompous voice, as if to let Dorothy and Billina see that he was educated and could read writing. The letter was as follows:

"It will please me to have my subjects greet Princess Dorothy, the bearer of this royal missive, with the same courtesy and consideration they would extend to me."

"Ha—hum! It is signed 'Ozma of Oz,'" continued the rabbit, "and is sealed with the Great Seal of the Emerald City. Well, well, well! How strange! How remarkable!"

"What are you going to do about it?" inquired Dorothy, impatiently.

"We must obey the royal mandate," replied the rabbit. "We are subjects of Ozma of Oz, and we live in her country. Also we are under the protection of the great Sorceress Glinda the Good, who made us promise to respect Ozma's commands."

"Then may I come in?" she asked.

"I'll open the door," said the rabbit. He shut the window and disappeared, but a moment afterward a big door in the wall opened and admitted Dorothy to a small room, which seemed to be a part of the wall and built into it.

Here stood the rabbit she had been talking with, and now that she could see all of him, she gazed at the creature in surprise. He was a good sized white rabbit with pink eyes, much like all other white rabbits. But the astonishing thing about him was the manner in which he was dressed. He wore a white satin jacket embroidered with gold, and having diamond buttons. His vest was rose-colored satin, with tourmaline buttons. His trousers were white, to correspond with the jacket, and they were baggy at the knees—like those of a zouave—being tied with knots of rose ribbons. His shoes were of white plush with diamond buckles, and his stockings were rose silk.

The richness and even magnificence of the rabbit's clothing made Dorothy stare at the little creature wonderingly. Toto and Billina had followed her into the room and when he saw them the rabbit ran to a table and sprang upon it nimbly. Then he looked at the three through his monocle and said:

"These companions, Princess, cannot enter Bunnybury with you."

"Why not?" asked Dorothy.

"In the first place they would frighten our people, who dislike dogs above all things on earth; and, secondly, the letter of the Royal Ozma does not mention them."

"But they're my friends," persisted Dorothy, "and go wherever I go."

"Not this time," said the rabbit, decidedly. "You, yourself, Princess, are a welcome visitor, since you come so highly recommended; but unless you consent to leave the dog and the hen in this room I cannot permit you to enter the town."

"Never mind us, Dorothy," said Billina. "Go inside and see what the place is like. You can tell us about it afterward, and Toto and I will rest comfortably here until you return."

This seemed the best thing to do, for Dorothy was curious to see how the rabbit people lived and she was aware of the fact that her friends might frighten the timid little creatures.

She had not forgotten how Toto and Billina had misbehaved in Bunbury, and perhaps the rabbit was wise to insist on their staying outside the town.

"Very well," she said, "I'll go in alone. I s'pose you're the King of this town, aren't you?"

"No," answered the rabbit, "I'm merely the Keeper of the Wicket, and a person of little importance, although I try to do my duty. I must now inform you, Princess, that before you enter our town you must consent to reduce."

"Reduce what?" asked Dorothy.

"Your size. You must become the size of the rabbits, although you may retain your own form."

"Wouldn't my clothes be too big for me?" she inquired.

"No; they will reduce when your body does."

"Can *you* make me smaller?" asked the girl.

"Easily," returned the rabbit.

"And will you make me big again, when I'm ready to go away?"

"I will," said he.

"All right, then; I'm willing," she announced.

The rabbit jumped from the table and ran—or rather hopped—to the further wall, where he opened a door so tiny that even Toto could scarcely have crawled through it.

"Follow me," he said.

Now, almost any other little girl would have declared that she could not get through so small a door; but Dorothy had already encountered so many fairy adventures that she believed nothing was impossible in the Land of Oz. So she quietly walked toward the door, and at every step she grew smaller and smaller until, by the time the opening was reached, she could pass through it with ease. Indeed, as she stood beside the rabbit, who sat upon his hind legs and used his paws as hands, her head was just about as high as his own.

Then the Keeper of the Wicket passed through and she followed, after which the door swung shut and locked itself with a sharp click.

Dorothy now found herself in a city so strange and beautiful that she gave a gasp of surprise. The high marble wall extended all around the place and shut out all the rest of the world. And here were marble houses of curious forms, most of them resembling overturned kettles but with delicate slender spires and minarets running far up into the sky. The streets were paved with white marble and in front of each house was a lawn of rich green clover. Everything was as neat as wax, the green and white contrasting prettily together.

But the rabbit people were, after all, the most amazing things Dorothy saw. The streets were full of them, and their costumes were so splendid that the rich dress of the Keeper of the Wicket was commonplace when compared with the others. Silks and satins of delicate hues seemed always used for material, and nearly every costume sparkled with exquisite gems.

But the lady rabbits outshone the gentlemen rabbits in

splendor, and the cut of their gowns was really wonderful. They wore bonnets, too, with feathers and jewels in them, and some wheeled baby carriages in which the girl could see wee bunnies. Some were lying asleep while others lay sucking their paws and looking around them with big pink eyes.

As Dorothy was no bigger in size than the grown-up rabbits she had a chance to observe them closely before they noticed her presence. Then they did not seem at all alarmed, although the little girl naturally became the center of attraction and all regarded her with great curiosity.

"Make way!" cried the Keeper of the Wicket, in a pompous voice; "make way for Princess Dorothy, who comes from Ozma of Oz."

Hearing this announcement, the throng of rabbits gave place to them on the walks, and as Dorothy passed along they all bowed their heads respectfully.

Walking thus through several handsome streets they came to a square in the center of the City. In this square were some pretty trees and a statue in bronze of Glinda the Good, while beyond it were the portals of the royal palace— an extensive and imposing building of white marble covered with a filigree of frosted gold.

Chapter 20

HOW DOROTHY LUNCHED
with a KING

line of rabbit soldiers was drawn up before the palace entrance, and they wore green and gold uniforms with high shakos upon their heads and held tiny spears in their hands. The Captain had a sword and a white plume in his shako.

"Salute!" called the Keeper of the Wicket. "Salute Princess Dorothy, who comes from Ozma of Oz!"

"Salute!" yelled the Captain, and all the soldiers promptly saluted.

They now entered the great hall of the palace, where they met a gaily dressed attendant, from whom the Keeper of the Wicket inquired if the King were at leisure.

"I think so," was the reply. "I heard his Majesty blubbering and wailing as usual only a few minutes ago. If he doesn't stop acting like a cry-baby I'm going to resign my position here and go to work."

"What's the matter with your King?" asked Dorothy, surprised to hear the rabbit attendant speak so disrespectfully of his monarch.

"Oh, he doesn't want to be King, that's all; and he simply *has* to," was the reply.

"Come!" said the Keeper of the Wicket, sternly; "lead us to his Majesty; and do not air our troubles before strangers, I beg of you."

"Why, if this girl is going to see the King, he'll air his own troubles," returned the attendant.

"That is his royal privilege," declared the Keeper.

So the attendant led them into a room all draped with cloth-of-gold and furnished with satin-covered gold furniture. There was a throne in this room, set on a dais and having a big, cushioned seat, and on this seat reclined the Rabbit King. He was lying on his back, with his paws in the air, and whining very like a puppy-dog.

"Your Majesty! your Majesty! Get up. Here's a visitor," called out the attendant.

The King rolled over and looked at Dorothy with one watery pink eye. Then he sat up and wiped his eyes carefully with a silk handkerchief and put on his jeweled crown, which had fallen off.

"Excuse my grief, fair stranger," he said, in a sad voice. "You behold in me the most miserable monarch in all the world. What time is it, Blinkem?"

"One o'clock, your Majesty," replied the attendant to whom the question was addressed.

"Serve luncheon at once!" commanded the King. "Luncheon for two—that's for my visitor and me—and see that the human has some sort of food she's accustomed to."

"Yes, your Majesty," answered the attendant, and went away.

"Tie my shoe, Bristle," said the King to the Keeper of the Wicket. "Ah me! how unhappy I am!"

"What seems to be worrying your Majesty?" asked Dorothy.

"Why, it's this king business, of course," he returned, while the Keeper tied his shoe. "I didn't want to be King of Bunnybury at all, and the rabbits all knew it. So they elected me—to save themselves from such a dreadful fate, I suppose—and here I am, shut up in a palace, when I might be free and happy."

"Seems to me," said Dorothy, "it's a great thing to be a King."

"Were you ever a King?" inquired the monarch.

"No," she answered, laughing.

"Then you know nothing about it," he said. "I haven't inquired who you are, but it doesn't matter. While we're at luncheon, I'll tell you all my troubles. They're a great deal more interesting than anything you can say about yourself."

"Perhaps they are, to you," replied Dorothy.

"Luncheon is served!" cried Blinkem, throwing open the door, and in came a dozen rabbits in livery, all bearing trays which they placed upon the table, where they arranged the dishes in an orderly manner.

"Now clear out—all of you!" exclaimed the King. "Bristle, you may wait outside, in case I want you."

When they had gone and the King was alone with Dorothy he came down from his throne, tossed his crown into a corner and kicked his ermine robe under the table.

"Sit down," he said, "and try to be happy. It's useless for me to try, because I'm always wretched and miserable. But I'm hungry, and I hope you are."

"I am," said Dorothy. "I've only eaten a wheelbarrow and a piano to-day—oh, yes! and a slice of bread and butter that used to be a door-mat."

"That sounds like a square meal," remarked the King, seating himself opposite her; "but perhaps it wasn't a square piano. Eh?"

Dorothy laughed.

"You don't seem so very unhappy now," she said.

"But I am," protested the King, fresh tears gathering in his eyes. "Even my jokes are miserable. I'm wretched, woeful, afflicted, distressed and dismal as an individual can be. Are you not sorry for me?"

"No," answered Dorothy, honestly, "I can't say I am. Seems

to me that for a rabbit you're right in clover. This is the prettiest little city I ever saw."

"Oh, the city is good enough," he admitted. "Glinda, the Good Sorceress, made it for us because she was fond of rabbits. I don't mind the City so much, although I wouldn't live here if I had my choice. It is being King that has absolutely ruined my happiness."

"Why wouldn't you live here by choice?" she asked.

"Because it is all unnatural, my dear. Rabbits are out of place in such luxury. When I was young I lived in a burrow in the forest. I was surrounded by enemies and often had to run for my life. It was hard getting enough to eat, at times, and when I found a bunch of clover I had to listen and look for danger while I ate it. Wolves prowled around the hole in which I lived and sometimes I didn't dare stir out for days at a time. Oh, how happy and contented I was then! I was a real rabbit, as nature made me—wild and free!—and I even enjoyed listening to the startled throbbing of my own heart!"

"I've often thought," said Dorothy, who was busily eating, "that it would be fun to be a rabbit."

"It *is* fun—when you're the genuine article," agreed his Majesty. "But look at me now! I live in a marble palace instead of a hole in the ground. I have all I want to eat, without the joy of hunting for it. Every day I must dress in fine clothes and wear that horrible crown till it makes my head ache. Rabbits come to me with all sorts of troubles, when my own troubles are the only ones I care about. When I walk out I can't hop and run; I must strut on my rear legs and wear an ermine robe! And the soldiers salute me and the band plays and the other rabbits laugh and clap their paws and cry out: 'Hail to the King!' Now let me ask you, as a friend and a young lady of good judgment: isn't all this pomp and foolishness enough to make a decent rabbit miserable?"

"Once," said Dorothy, reflectively, "men were wild and unclothed and lived in caves and hunted for food as wild beasts do. But they got civ'lized, in time, and now they'd hate to go back to the old days."

"That is an entirely different case," replied the King. "None of you Humans were civilized in one lifetime. It came to you by degrees. But I have known the forest and the free life, and that is why I resent being civilized all at once, against my will, and being made a King with a crown and an ermine robe. Pah!"

"If you don't like it, why don't you resign?" she asked.

"Impossible!" wailed the Rabbit, wiping his eyes again with his handkerchief. "There's a beastly law in this town that forbids it. When one is elected a King, there's no getting out of it."

"Who made the laws?" inquired Dorothy.

"The same Sorceress who made the town—Glinda the Good. She built the wall, and fixed up the City, and gave us several valuable enchantments, and made the laws. Then she invited all the pink-eyed white rabbits of the forest to come here, after which she left us to our fate."

"What made you 'cept the invitation, and come here?" asked the child.

"I didn't know how dreadful city life was, and I'd no idea I would be elected King," said he, sobbing bitterly. "And—and—now I'm It—with a capital I—and can't escape!"

"I know Glinda," remarked Dorothy, eating for dessert a dish of charlotte russe, "and when I see her again, I'll ask her to put another King in your place."

"Will you? Will you, indeed?" asked the King, joyfully.

"I will if you want me to," she replied.

"Hurroo—hurray!" shouted the King; and then he jumped up from the table and danced wildly about the room, waving his napkin like a flag and laughing with glee.

After a time he managed to control his delight and returned to the table.

"When are you likely to see Glinda?" he inquired.

"Oh, p'raps in a few days," said Dorothy.

"And you won't forget to ask her?"

"Of course not."

"Princess," said the Rabbit King, earnestly, "you have relieved me of a great unhappiness, and I am very grateful. Therefore I propose to entertain you, since you are my guest and I am the King, as a slight mark of my appreciation. Come with me to my reception hall."

He then summoned Bristle and said to him: "Assemble all the nobility in the great reception hall, and also tell Blinkem that I want him immediately."

The Keeper of the Wicket bowed and hurried away, and his Majesty turned to Dorothy and continued: "We'll have time for a walk in the gardens before the people get here."

The gardens were back of the palace and were filled with beautiful flowers and fragrant shrubs, with many shade and fruit trees and marble paved walks running in every direction. As they entered this place Blinkem came running to the King, who gave him several orders in a low voice. Then his Majesty rejoined Dorothy and led her through the gardens, which she admired very much.

"What lovely clothes your Majesty wears!" she said, glancing at the rich blue satin costume, embroidered with pearls, in which the King was dressed.

"Yes," he returned, with an air of pride, "this is one of my favorite suits; but I have a good many that are even more elaborate. We have excellent tailors in Bunnybury, and Glinda supplies all the material. By the way, you might ask the Sorceress, when you see her, to permit me to keep my wardrobe."

"But if you go back to the forest you will not need clothes," she said.

"N—o!" he faltered; "that may be so. But I've dressed up so long that I'm used to it, and I don't imagine I'd care to run around naked again. So perhaps the Good Glinda will let me keep the costumes."

"I'll ask her," agreed Dorothy.

Then they left the gardens and went into a fine, big reception hall, where rich rugs were spread upon the tiled floors and the furniture was exquisitely carved and studded with jewels. The King's chair was an especially pretty piece of furniture, being in the shape of a silver lily with one leaf bent over to form the seat. The silver was everywhere thickly encrusted with diamonds and the seat was upholstered in white satin.

"Oh, what a splendid chair!" cried Dorothy, clasping her hands admiringly.

"Isn't it?" answered the King, proudly. "It is my favorite seat, and I think it especially becoming to my complexion. While I think of it, I wish you'd ask Glinda to let me keep this lily chair when I go away."

"It wouldn't look very well in a hole in the ground, would it?" she suggested.

"Maybe not; but I'm used to sitting in it and I'd like to take it with me," he answered. "But here come the ladies and gentlemen of the court; so please sit beside me and be presented."

Chapter 21

HOW the KING
CHANGED HIS MIND

J ust then a rabbit band of nearly fifty pieces marched
in, playing upon golden instruments and dressed in
neat uniforms. Following the band came the nobility
of Bunnybury, all richly dressed and hopping along
on their rear legs. Both the ladies and the gentlemen wore
white gloves upon their paws, with their rings on the outside of
the gloves, as this seemed to be the fashion here. Some of the
lady rabbits carried lorgnettes, while many of the gentlemen
rabbits wore monocles in their left eyes.

The courtiers and their ladies paraded past the King, who
introduced Princess Dorothy to each couple in a very graceful

manner. Then the company seated themselves in chairs and on sofas and looked expectantly at their monarch.

"It is our royal duty, as well as our royal pleasure," he said, "to provide fitting entertainment for our distinguished guest. We will now present the Royal Band of Whiskered Friskers."

As he spoke the musicians, who had arranged themselves in a corner, struck up a dance melody while into the room pranced the Whiskered Friskers. They were eight pretty rabbits dressed only in gauzy purple skirts fastened around their waists with diamond bands. Their whiskers were colored a rich purple, but otherwise they were pure white.

After bowing before the King and Dorothy the Friskers began their pranks, and these were so comical that Dorothy laughed with real enjoyment. They not only danced together, whirling and gyrating around the room, but they leaped over one another, stood upon their heads and hopped and skipped here and there so nimbly that it was hard work to keep track of them. Finally, they all made double somersaults and turned handsprings out of the room.

The nobility enthusiastically applauded, and Dorothy applauded with them.

"They're fine!" she said to the King.

"Yes, the Whiskered Friskers are really very clever," he replied. "I shall hate to part with them when I go away, for they have often amused me when I was very miserable. I wonder if you would ask Glinda—"

"No, it wouldn't do at all," declared Dorothy, positively. "There wouldn't be room in your hole in the ground for so many rabbits, 'spec'ly when you get the lily chair and your clothes there. Don't think of such a thing, your Majesty."

The King sighed. Then he stood up and announced to the company:

"We will now hold a military drill by my picked Bodyguard of Royal Pikemen."

Now the band played a march and a company of rabbit soldiers came in. They wore green and gold uniforms and marched very stiffly but in perfect time. Their spears, or pikes, had slender shafts of polished silver with golden heads, and during the drill they handled these weapons with wonderful dexterity.

"I should think you'd feel pretty safe with such a fine Bodyguard," remarked Dorothy.

"I do," said the King. "They protect me from every harm. I suppose Glinda wouldn't—"

"No," interrupted the girl; "I'm sure she wouldn't. It's the King's own Bodyguard, and when you are no longer King you can't have 'em."

The King did not reply, but he looked rather sorrowful for a time.

When the soldiers had marched out he said to the company:

"The Royal Jugglers will now appear."

Dorothy had seen many jugglers in her lifetime, but never any so interesting as these. There were six of them, dressed in black satin embroidered with queer symbols in silver—a costume which contrasted strongly with their snow-white fur.

First, they pushed in a big red ball and three of the rabbit jugglers stood upon its top and made it roll. Then two of them caught up a third and tossed him into the air, all vanishing, until only the two were left. Then one of these tossed the other upward and remained alone of all his fellows. This last juggler now touched the red ball, which fell apart, being hollow, and the five rabbits who had disappeared in the air scrambled out of the hollow ball.

Next they all clung together and rolled swiftly upon the floor. When they came to a stop only one fat rabbit juggler was seen, the others seeming to be inside him. This one leaped lightly into the air and when he came down he exploded and separated into the original six. Then four of them rolled them-selves into round balls and the other two tossed them around and played ball with them.

These were but a few of the tricks the rabbit jugglers performed, and they were so skillful that all the nobility and even the King applauded as loudly as did Dorothy.

"I suppose there are no rabbit jugglers in all the world to compare with these," remarked the King. "And since I may not have the Whiskers Friskers or my Bodyguard, you might ask Glinda to let me take away just two or three of these jugglers. Will you?"

"I'll ask her," replied Dorothy, doubtfully.

"Thank you," said the King; "thank you very much. And now you shall listen to the Winsome Waggish Warblers, who have often cheered me in my moments of anguish."

The Winsome Waggish Warblers proved to be a quartette of rabbit singers, two gentlemen and two lady rabbits. The gentlemen Warblers wore full-dress swallow-tailed suits of white satin, with pearls for buttons, while the lady Warblers were gowned in white satin dresses with long trails.

The first song they sang began in this way:

> *"When a rabbit gets a habit*
> *Of living in a city*
> *And wearing clothes and furbelows*
> *And jewels rare and pretty,*
> *He scorns the Bun who has to run*
> *And burrow in the ground*
> *And pities those whose watchful foes*
> *Are man and gun and hound."*

Dorothy looked at the King when she heard this song and noticed that he seemed disturbed and ill at ease.

"I don't like that song," he said to the Warblers. "Give us something jolly and rollicking."

So they sang to a joyous, tinkling melody as follows:

"Bunnies gay
Delight to play
In their fairy town secure;
Ev'ry frisker
Flirts his whisker
At a pink-eyed girl demure.
Ev'ry maid
In silk arrayed
At her partner shyly glances,
Paws are grasped,
Waists are clasped
As they whirl in giddy dances.
Then together
Through the heather
'Neath the moonlight soft they stroll;
Each is very
Blithe and merry,
Gamboling with laughter droll.
Life is fun
To ev'ry one
Guarded by our magic charm

For to dangers
We are strangers,
Safe from any thought of harm."

"You see," said Dorothy to the King, when the song ended, "the rabbits all seem to like Bunnybury except you. And I guess you're the only one that ever has cried or was unhappy and wanted to get back to your muddy hole in the ground."

His Majesty seemed thoughtful, and while the servants passed around glasses of nectar and plates of frosted cakes their King was silent and a bit nervous.

When the refreshments had been enjoyed by all and the servants had retired Dorothy said:

"I must go now, for it's getting late and I'm lost. I've got to find the Wizard and Aunt Em and Uncle Henry and all the rest sometime before night comes, if I poss'bly can."

"Won't you stay with us?" asked the King. "You will be very welcome."

"No, thank you," she replied. "I must get back to my friends. And I want to see Glinda just as soon as I can, you know."

So the King dismissed his court and said he would himself walk with Dorothy to the gate. He did not weep nor groan any more, but his long face was quite solemn and his big ears hung dejectedly on each side of it. He still wore his crown and his ermine and walked with a handsome gold-headed cane.

When they arrived at the room in the wall the little girl

found Toto and Billina waiting for her very patiently. They had been liberally fed by some of the attendants and were in no hurry to leave such comfortable quarters.

The Keeper of the Wicket was by this time back in his old place, but he kept a safe distance from Toto. Dorothy bade good-bye to the King as they stood just inside the wall.

"You've been good to me," she said, "and I thank you ever so much. As soon as poss'ble I'll see Glinda and ask her to put another King in your place and send you back into the wild forest. And I'll ask her to let you keep some of your clothes and the lily chair and one or two jugglers to amuse you. I'm sure she will do it, 'cause she's so kind she doesn't like any one to be unhappy."

"Ahem!" said the King, looking rather downcast. "I don't like to trouble you with my misery; so you needn't see Glinda."

"Oh, yes I will," she replied. "It won't be any trouble at all."

"But, my dear," continued the King, in an embarrassed way, "I've been thinking the subject over carefully, and I find there are a lot of pleasant things here in Bunnybury that I would miss if I went away. So perhaps I'd better stay."

Dorothy laughed. Then she looked grave.

"It won't do for you to be a King and a cry-baby at the same time," she said. "You've been making all the other rabbits unhappy and discontented with your howls about being so miserable. So I guess it's better to have another King."

"Oh, no indeed!" exclaimed the King, earnestly. "If you

won't say anything to Glinda I'll promise to be merry and gay all the time, and never cry or wail again."

"Honor bright?" she asked.

"On the royal word of a King I promise it!" he answered.

"All right," said Dorothy. "You'd be a reg'lar lunatic to want to leave Bunnybury for a wild life in the forest, and I'm sure any rabbit outside the city would be glad to take your place."

"Forget it, my dear; forget all my foolishness," pleaded the King, earnestly. "Hereafter I'll try to enjoy myself and do my duty by my subjects."

So then she left him and entered through the little door into the room in the wall, where she grew gradually bigger and bigger until she had resumed her natural size.

The Keeper of the Wicket let them out into the forest and told Dorothy that she had been of great service to Bunnybury because she had brought their dismal King to a realization of the pleasure of ruling so beautiful a city.

"I shall start a petition to have your statue erected beside Glinda's in the public square," said the Keeper. "I hope you will come again, some day, and see it."

"Perhaps I shall," she replied.

Then, followed by Toto and Billina, she walked away from the high marble wall and started back along the narrow path toward the sign-post.

HOW the WIZARD FOUND
DOROTHY

When they came to the signpost, there, to their joy, were the tents of the Wizard pitched beside the path and the kettle bubbling merrily over the fire. The Shaggy Man and Omby Amby were gathering firewood while Uncle Henry and Aunt Em sat in their camp chairs talking with the Wizard.

They all ran forward to greet Dorothy, as she approached, and Aunt Em exclaimed: "Goodness gracious, child! Where have you been?"

"You've played hookey the whole day," added the Shaggy Man, reproachfully.

"Well, you see, I've been lost," explained the little girl,

"and I've tried awful hard to find the way back to you, but just couldn't do it."

"Did you wander in the forest all day?" asked Uncle Henry.

"You must be a'most starved!" said Aunt Em.

"No," said Dorothy, "I'm not hungry. I had a wheelbarrow and a piano for breakfast, and lunched with a King."

"Ah!" exclaimed the Wizard, nodding with a bright smile. "So you've been having adventures again."

"She's stark crazy!" cried Aunt Em. "Whoever heard of eating a wheelbarrow?"

"It wasn't very big," said Dorothy; "and it had a zuzu wheel."

"And I ate the crumbs," said Billina, soberly.

"Sit down and tell us about it," begged the Wizard. "We've hunted for you all day, and at last I noticed your footsteps in this path—and the tracks of Billina. We found the path by accident, and seeing it only led to two places I decided you were at either one or the other of those places. So we made camp and waited for you to return. And now, Dorothy, tell us where you have been—to Bunbury or to Bunnybury?"

"Why, I've been to both," she replied; "but first I went to Utensia, which isn't on any path at all."

She then sat down and related the day's adventures, and you may be sure Aunt Em and Uncle Henry were much astonished at the story.

"But after seeing the Cuttenclips and the Fuddles," remarked her uncle, "we ought not to wonder at anything in this strange country."

"Seems like the only common and ordinary folks here are ourselves," rejoined Aunt Em, diffidently.

"Now that we're together again, and one reunited party," observed the Shaggy Man, "what are we to do next?"

"Have some supper and a night's rest," answered the Wizard promptly, "and then proceed upon our journey."

"Where to?" asked the Captain General.

"We haven't visited the Rigmaroles or the Flutterbudgets yet," said Dorothy. "I'd like to see them—wouldn't you?"

"They don't sound very interesting," objected Aunt Em. "But perhaps they are."

"And then," continued the little Wizard, "we will call upon the Tin Woodman and Jack Pumpkinhead and our old friend the Scarecrow, on our way home."

"That will be nice!" cried Dorothy, eagerly.

"Can't say *they* sound very interesting, either," remarked Aunt Em.

"Why, they're the best friends I have!" asserted the little girl, "and you're sure to like them, Aunt Em, 'cause *ever*'body likes them."

By this time twilight was approaching, so they ate the fine supper which the Wizard magically produced from the kettle and then went to bed in the cozy tents.

They were all up bright and early next morning, but Dorothy

didn't venture to wander from the camp again for fear of more accidents.

"Do you know where there's a road?" she asked the little man.

"No, my dear," replied the Wizard; "but I'll find one."

After breakfast he waved his hand toward the tents and they became handkerchiefs again, which were at once returned to the pockets of their owners. Then they all climbed into the red wagon and the Sawhorse inquired:

"Which way?"

"Never mind which way," replied the Wizard. "Just go as you please and you're sure to be right. I've enchanted the wheels of the wagon, and they will roll in the right direction, never fear."

As the Sawhorse started away through the trees Dorothy said:

"If we had one of those new-fashioned airships we could float away over the top of the forest, and look down and find just the places we want."

"Airship? Pah!" retorted the little man, scornfully. "I hate those things, Dorothy, although they are nothing new to either you or me. I was a balloonist for many years, and once my balloon carried me to the Land of Oz, and once to the Vegetable Kingdom. And once Ozma had a Gump that flew all over this kingdom and had sense enough to go where it was told to—which airships won't do. The house which the cyclone brought to Oz all the way from Kansas, with you and Toto in it—was a real airship at the time; so you see we've got plenty of experience flying with the birds."

"Airships are not so bad, after all," declared Dorothy. "Some day they'll fly all over the world, and perhaps bring people even to the Land of Oz."

"I must speak to Ozma about that," said the Wizard, with a slight frown. "It wouldn't do at all, you know, for the Emerald City to become a way-station on an airship line."

"No," said Dorothy, "I don't s'pose it would. But what can we do to prevent it?"

"I'm working out a magic recipe to fuddle men's brains, so they'll never make an airship that will go where they want it to go," the Wizard confided to her. "That won't keep the things from flying, now and then, but it'll keep them from flying to the Land of Oz."

Just then the Sawhorse drew the wagon out of the forest and a beautiful landscape lay spread before the travelers' eyes. Moreover, right before them was a good road that wound away through the hills and valleys.

"Now," said the Wizard, with evident delight, "we are on the right track again, and there is nothing more to worry about."

"It's a foolish thing to take chances in a strange country," observed the Shaggy Man. "Had we kept to the roads we never would have been lost. Roads always lead to some place, else they wouldn't be roads."

"This road," added the Wizard, "leads to Rigmarole Town.

I'm sure of that because I enchanted the wagon wheels."

Sure enough, after riding along the road for an hour or two they entered a pretty valley where a village was nestled among the hills. The houses were Munchkin shaped, for they were all domes, with windows wider than they were high, and pretty balconies over the front doors.

Aunt Em was greatly relieved to find this town "neither paper nor patch-work," and the only surprising thing about it was that it was so far distant from all other towns.

As the Sawhorse drew the wagon into the main street the travelers noticed that the place was filled with people, standing in groups and seeming to be engaged in earnest conversation. So occupied with themselves were the inhabitants that they scarcely noticed the strangers at all. So the Wizard stopped a boy and asked:

"Is this Rigmarole Town?"

"Sir," replied the boy, "if you have traveled very much you will have noticed that every town differs from every other town in one way or another and so by observing the methods of the people and the way they live as well as the style of their dwelling places it ought not to be a difficult thing to make up your mind without the trouble of asking questions whether the town bears the appearance of the one you intended to visit or whether perhaps having taken a different road from the one you should have taken you have made an error in your way and arrived at some point where—"

"Land sakes!" cried Aunt Em, impatiently; "what's all this rigmarole about?"

"That's it!" said the Wizard, laughing merrily. "It's a rigmarole because the boy is a Rigmarole and we've come to Rigmarole Town."

"Do they all talk like that?" asked Dorothy, wonderingly.

"He might have said 'yes' or 'no' and settled the question," observed Uncle Henry.

"Not here," said Omby Amby. "I don't believe the Rigmaroles know what 'yes' or 'no' means."

While the boy had been talking several other people had approached the wagon and listened intently to his speech. Then they began talking to one another in long, deliberate speeches, where many words were used but little was said. But when the strangers criticized them so frankly one of the women, who had no one else to talk to, began an address to them, saying:

"It is the easiest thing in the world for a person to say 'yes' or 'no' when a question that is asked for the purpose of gaining information or satisfying the curiosity of the one who has given expression to the inquiry has attracted the attention of an individual who may be competent either from personal experience or the experience of others to answer it with more or less correctness or at least an attempt to satisfy the desire for information on the part of the one who has made the inquiry by—"

"Dear me!" exclaimed Dorothy, interrupting the speech. "I've lost all track of what you are saying."

"Don't let her begin over again, for goodness sake!" cried Aunt Em.

But the woman did not begin again. She did not even stop talking, but went right on as she had begun, the words flowing from her mouth in a stream.

"I'm quite sure that if we waited long enough and listened carefully, some of these people might be able to tell us something, in time," said the Wizard.

"Let's don't wait," returned Dorothy. "I've heard of the Rigmaroles, and wondered what they were like; but now I know, and I'm ready to move on."

"So am I," declared Uncle Henry; "we're wasting time here."

"Why, we're all ready to go," said the Shaggy Man, putting his fingers to his ears to shut out the monotonous babble of those around the wagon.

So the Wizard spoke to the Sawhorse, who trotted nimbly through the village and soon gained the open country on the other side of it. Dorothy looked back, as they rode away, and noticed that the woman had not yet finished her speech but was talking as glibly as ever, although no one was near to hear her.

"If those people wrote books," Omby Amby remarked with a smile, "it would take a whole library to say the cow jumped over the moon."

"Perhaps some of 'em do write books," asserted the little Wizard. "I've read a few rigmaroles that might have come from this very town."

"Some of the college lecturers and ministers are certainly related to these people," observed the Shaggy Man; "and it seems to me the Land of Oz is a little ahead of the United States in some of its laws. For here, if one can't talk clearly, and straight to the point, they send him to Rigmarole Town; while Uncle Sam lets him roam around wild and free, to torture innocent people."

Dorothy was thoughtful. The Rigmaroles had made a strong impression upon her. She decided that whenever she spoke, after this, she would use only enough words to express what she wanted to say.

Chapter 23

How They Encountered the Flutterbudgets

They were soon among the pretty hills and valleys again, and the Sawhorse sped up hill and down at a fast and easy pace, the roads being hard and smooth. Mile after mile was speedily covered, and before the ride had grown at all tiresome they sighted another village. The place seemed even larger than Rigmarole Town, but was not so attractive in appearance.

"This must be Flutterbudget Center," declared the Wizard. "You see, it's no trouble at all to find places if you keep to the right road."

"What are the Flutterbudgets like?" inquired Dorothy.

"I do not know, my dear. But Ozma has given them a town

all their own, and I've heard that whenever one of the people becomes a Flutterbudget he is sent to this place to live."

"That is true," Omby Amby added; "Flutterbudget Center and Rigmarole Town are called 'the Defensive Settlements of Oz.'"

The village they now approached was not built in a valley, but on top of a hill, and the road they followed wound around the hill like a corkscrew, ascending the hill easily until it came to the town.

"Look out!" screamed a voice. "Look out, or you'll run over my child!"

They gazed around and saw a woman standing upon the sidewalk nervously wringing her hands as she gazed at them appealingly.

"Where is your child?" asked the Sawhorse.

"In the house," said the woman, bursting into tears; "but if it should happen to be in the road, and you ran over it, those great wheels would crush my darling to jelly. Oh dear! oh dear! Think of my darling child being crushed into jelly by those great wheels!"

"Gid-dap!" said the Wizard sharply, and the Sawhorse started on.

They had not gone far before a man ran out of a house shouting wildly, "Help! Help!"

The Sawhorse stopped short and the Wizard and Uncle Henry and the Shaggy Man and Omby Amby jumped out of the wagon and ran to the poor man's assistance. Dorothy followed them as quickly as she could.

"What's the matter?" asked the Wizard.

"Help! Help!" screamed the man; "my wife has cut her finger off and she's bleeding to death!"

Then he turned and rushed back to the house, and all the party went with him. They found a woman in the front dooryard moaning and groaning as if in great pain.

"Be brave, madam!" said the Wizard, consolingly. "You won't die just because you have cut off a finger, you may be sure."

"But I haven't cut off a finger!" she sobbed.

"Then what *has* happened?" asked Dorothy.

"I—I pricked my finger with a needle while I was sewing, and—and the blood came!" she replied. "And now I'll have blood-poisoning, and the doctors will cut off my finger, and that will give me a fever and I shall die!"

"Pshaw!" said Dorothy; "I've pricked my finger many a time, and nothing happened."

"Really?" asked the woman, brightening and wiping her eyes upon her apron.

"Why, it's nothing at all," declared the girl. "You're more scared than hurt."

"Ah, that's because she's a Flutterbudget," said the Wizard, nodding wisely. "I think I know now what these people are like."

"So do I," announced Dorothy.

"Oh, boo-hoo-hoo!" sobbed the woman, giving way to a fresh burst of grief.

"What's wrong now?" asked the Shaggy Man.

"Oh, suppose I had pricked my foot!" she wailed. "Then the doctors would have cut my foot off, and I'd be lamed for life!"

"Surely, ma'am," replied the Wizard, "and if you'd pricked your nose they might cut your head off. But you see you didn't."

"But I might have!" she exclaimed, and began to cry again. So they left her and drove away in their wagon. And her husband came out and began calling "Help!" as he had before; but no one seemed to pay any attention to him.

As the travelers turned into another street they found a man walking excitedly up and down the pavement. He appeared to be in a very nervous condition and the Wizard stopped him to ask:

"Is anything wrong, sir?"

"Everything is wrong," answered the man, dismally. "I can't sleep."

"Why not?" inquired Omby Amby.

"If I go to sleep I'll have to shut my eyes," he explained; "and if I shut my eyes they may grow together, and then I'd be blind for life!"

"Did you ever hear of any one's eyes growing together?" asked Dorothy.

"No," said the man, "I never did. But it would be a dreadful thing, wouldn't it? And the thought of it makes me so nervous I'm afraid to go to sleep."

"There's no help for this case," declared the Wizard; and they went on.

At the next street corner a woman rushed up to them crying:

"Save my baby! Oh, good, kind people, save my baby!"

"Is it in danger?" asked Dorothy, noticing that the child was clasped in her arms and seemed sleeping peacefully.

"Yes, indeed," said the woman, nervously. "If I should go into the house and throw my child out of the window, it would roll way down to the bottom of the hill; and then if there were a lot of tigers and bears down there, they would tear my darling babe to pieces and eat it up!"

"Are there any tigers and bears in this neighborhood?" the Wizard asked.

"I've never heard of any," admitted the woman, "but if there were—"

"Have you any idea of throwing your baby out of the window?" questioned the little man.

"None at all," she said; "but if—"

"All your troubles are due to those 'ifs,'" declared the Wizard. "If you were not a Flutterbudget you wouldn't worry."

"There's another 'if,'" replied the woman. "Are you a Flutterbudget, too?"

"I will be, if I stay here long," exclaimed the Wizard, nervously.

"Another 'if'!" cried the woman.

But the Wizard did not stop to argue with her. He made the Sawhorse canter all the way down the hill, and only breathed easily when they were miles away from the village.

After they had ridden in silence for a while Dorothy turned to the little man and asked:

"Do 'ifs' really make Flutterbudgets?"

"I think the 'ifs' help," he answered seriously. "Foolish fears, and worries over nothing, with a mixture of nerves and ifs, will soon make a Flutterbudget of any one."

Then there was another long silence, for all the travelers were thinking over this statement, and nearly all decided it must be true.

The country they were now passing through was everywhere tinted purple, the prevailing color of the Gillikin Country; but as the Sawhorse ascended a hill they found that upon the other side everything was of a rich yellow hue.

"Aha!" cried the Captain General; "here is the Country of the Winkies. We are just crossing the boundary line."

"Then we may be able to lunch with the Tin Woodman," announced the Wizard, joyfully.

"Must we lunch on tin?" asked Aunt Em.

"Oh, no;" replied Dorothy. "Nick Chopper knows how to feed meat people, and he will give us plenty of good things to eat, never fear. I've been to his castle before."

"Is Nick Chopper the Tin Woodman's name?" asked Uncle Henry.

"Yes; that's one of his names," answered the little girl; "and another of his names is 'Emp'ror of the Winkies.' He's the King of this country, you know, but Ozma rules over all the countries of Oz."

"Does the Tin Woodman keep any Flutterbudgets or Rigmaroles at his castle?" inquired Aunt Em, uneasily.

"No indeed," said Dorothy, positively. "He lives in a new tin castle, all full of lovely things."

"I should think it would rust," said Uncle Henry.

"He has thousands of Winkies to keep it polished for him," explained the Wizard. "His people love to do anything in their power for their beloved Emperor, so there isn't a particle of rust on all the big castle."

"I suppose they polish their Emperor, too," said Aunt Em.

"Why, some time ago he had himself nickel-plated," the Wizard answered; "so he only needs rubbing up once in a while. He's the brightest man in all the world, is dear Nick Chopper; and the kindest-hearted."

"I helped find him," said Dorothy, reflectively. "Once the Scarecrow and I found the Tin Woodman in the woods, and he was just rusted still, that time, an' no mistake. But we oiled his joints, an' got 'em good and slippery, and after that he went with us to visit the Wizard at the Em'rald City."

"Was that the time the Wizard scared you?" asked Aunt Em.

"He didn't treat us well, at first," acknowledged Dorothy; "for he made us go away and destroy the Wicked Witch. But after we found out he was only a humbug wizard we were not afraid of him."

The Wizard sighed and looked a little ashamed.

"When we try to deceive people we always make mistakes," he said. "But I'm getting to be a real wizard now, and Glinda the Good's magic, that I am trying to practice, can never harm any one."

"You were always a good man," declared Dorothy, "even when you were a bad wizard."

"He's a good wizard now," asserted Aunt Em, looking at the little man admiringly. "The way he made those tents grow out of handkerchiefs was just wonderful! And didn't he enchant the wagon wheels so they'd find the road?"

"All the people of Oz," said the Captain General, "are very proud of their Wizard. He once made some soap-bubbles that astonished the world."

The Wizard blushed at this praise, yet it pleased him. He no longer looked sad, but seemed to have recovered his usual good humor.

The country through which they now rode was thickly dotted with farm-houses, and yellow grain waved in all the fields. Many of the Winkies could be seen working on their farms and the wild and unsettled parts of Oz were by this time left far behind.

These Winkies appeared to be happy, light-hearted folk, and all removed their caps and bowed low when the red wagon with its load of travelers passed by.

It was not long before they saw something glittering in the sunshine far ahead.

"See!" cried Dorothy; "that's the Tin Castle, Aunt Em!"

And the Sawhorse, knowing his passengers were eager to arrive, broke into a swift trot that soon brought them to their destination.

Chapter 24

HOW the TIN WOODMAN
TOLD the SAD NEWS

The Tin Woodman received Princess Dorothy's party with much grace and cordiality, yet the little girl decided that something must be worrying her old friend, because he was not so merry as usual.

But at first she said nothing about this, for Uncle Henry and Aunt Em were fairly bubbling over with admiration for the beautiful tin castle and its polished tin owner. So her suspicion that something unpleasant had happened was for a time forgotten.

"Where is the Scarecrow?" she asked, when they had all been ushered into the big tin drawing-room of the castle, the

Sawhorse being led around to the tin stable in the rear.

"Why, our old friend has just moved into his new mansion," explained the Tin Woodman. "It has been a long time in building, although my Winkies and many other people from all parts of the country have been busily working upon it. At last, however, it is completed, and the Scarecrow took possession of his new home just two days ago."

"I hadn't heard that he wanted a home of his own," said Dorothy. "Why doesn't he live with Ozma in the Emerald City? He used to, you know; and I thought he was happy there."

"It seems," said the Tin Woodman, "that our dear Scarecrow cannot be contented with city life, however beautiful his surroundings might be. Originally he was a farmer, for he passed his early life in a cornfield, where he was supposed to frighten away the crows."

"I know," said Dorothy, nodding. "I found him, and lifted him down from his pole."

"So now, after a long residence in the Emerald City, his tastes have turned to farm life again," continued the Tin Man. "He feels that he cannot be happy without a farm of his own, so Ozma gave him some land and every one helped him build his mansion, and now he is settled there for good."

"Who designed his house?" asked the Shaggy Man.

"I believe it was Jack Pumpkinhead, who is also a farmer," was the reply.

They were now invited to enter the tin dining room, where luncheon was served.

Aunt Em found, to her satisfaction, that Dorothy's promise was more than fulfilled; for, although the Tin Woodman had no appetite of his own, he respected the appetites of his guests and saw that they were bountifully fed.

They passed the afternoon in wandering through the beautiful gardens and grounds of the palace. The walks were all paved with sheets of tin, brightly polished, and there were tin fountains and tin statues here and there among the trees. The flowers were mostly natural flowers and grew in the regular way; but their host showed them one flower bed which was his especial pride.

"You see, all common flowers fade and die in time," he explained, "and so there are seasons when the pretty blooms are scarce. Therefore I decided to make one tin flower bed all of tin flowers, and my workmen have created them with rare skill. Here you see tin camelias, tin marigolds, tin carnations, tin poppies and tin hollyhocks growing as naturally as if they were real."

Indeed, they were a pretty sight, and glistened under the sunlight like spun silver.

"Isn't this tin hollyhock going to seed?" asked the Wizard, bending over the flowers.

"Why, I believe it is!" exclaimed the Tin Woodman, as if surprised. "I hadn't noticed that before. But I shall plant the tin seeds and raise another bed of tin hollyhocks."

In one corner of the gardens Nick Chopper had established a fish-pond in which they saw swimming and disporting themselves many pretty tin fishes.

"Would they bite on hooks?" asked Aunt Em, curiously.

The Tin Woodman seemed hurt at this question.

"Madam," said he, "do you suppose I would allow anyone to catch my beautiful fishes, even if they were foolish enough to bite on hooks? No, indeed! Every created thing is safe from harm in my domain, and I would as soon think of killing my little friend Dorothy as killing one of my tin fishes."

"The Emperor is very kind-hearted, ma'am," explained the Wizard. "If a fly happens to light upon his tin body he doesn't rudely brush it off, as some people might do; he asks it politely to find some other resting place."

"What does the fly do then?" enquired Aunt Em.

"Usually it begs his pardon and goes away," said the Wizard, gravely. "Flies like to be treated politely as well as other creatures, and here in Oz they understand what we say to them, and behave very nicely."

"Well," said Aunt Em, "the flies in Kansas, where I came from, don't understand anything but a swat. You have to smash 'em to make 'em behave; and it's the same way with 'skeeters. Do you have 'skeeters in Oz?"

"We have some very large mosquitoes here, which sing as beautifully as song birds," replied the Tin Woodman. "But they never bite or annoy our people, because they are well fed and taken care of. The reason they bite people in your country is because they are hungry—poor things!"

"Yes," agreed Aunt Em; "they're hungry, all right. An' they ain't very particular who they feed on. I'm glad you've got the 'skeeters educated in Oz."

That evening after dinner they were entertained by the Emperor's Tin Cornet Band, which played for them several sweet melodies. Also the Wizard did a few sleight-of-hand tricks to amuse the company; after which they all retired to their cozy tin bedrooms and slept soundly until morning.

After breakfast Dorothy said to the Tin Woodman:

"If you'll tell us which way to go we'll visit the Scarecrow on our way home."

"I will go with you, and show you the way," replied the Emperor; "for I must journey to-day to the Emerald City."

He looked so anxious, as he said this, that the little girl asked:

"There isn't anything wrong with Ozma, is there?"

"Not yet," said he; "but I'm afraid the time has come when I must tell you some very bad news, little friend."

"Oh, what is it?" cried Dorothy.

"Do you remember the Nome King?" asked the Tin Woodman.

"I remember him very well," she replied.

"The Nome King has not a kind heart," said the Emperor, sadly, "and he has been harboring wicked thoughts of revenge, because we once defeated him and liberated his slaves and you took away his Magic Belt. So he has ordered his Nomes to dig a long tunnel underneath the deadly desert, so that he may march his hosts right into the Emerald City. When he gets there he intends to destroy our beautiful country."

Dorothy was much surprised to hear this.

"How did Ozma find out about the tunnel?" she asked.

"She saw it in her Magic Picture."

"Of course," said Dorothy; "I might have known that. And what is she going to do?"

"I cannot tell," was the reply.

"Pooh!" cried the Yellow Hen. "We're not afraid of the Nomes. If we roll a few of our eggs down the tunnel they'll run away back home as fast as they can go."

"Why, that's true enough!" exclaimed Dorothy. "The Scarecrow once conquered all the Nome King's army with some of Billina's eggs."

"But you do not understand all of the dreadful plot," continued the Tin Woodman. "The Nome King is clever, and he knows his Nomes would run from eggs; so he has bargained with many terrible creatures to help him. These evil spirits are not afraid of eggs or anything else, and they are very powerful. So the Nome King will send them through the tunnel first, to conquer and destroy, and then the Nomes will follow after to get their share of the plunder and slaves."

They were all startled to hear this, and every face wore a troubled look.

"Is the tunnel all ready?" asked Dorothy.

"Ozma sent me word yesterday that the tunnel was all completed except for a thin crust of earth at the end. When our enemies break through this crust, they will be in the gardens of the royal palace, in the heart of the Emerald City. I offered to arm all my Winkies and march to Ozma's assistance; but she said no."

"I wonder why?" asked Dorothy.

"She answered that all the inhabitants of Oz, gathered together, were not powerful enough to fight and overcome the evil forces of the Nome King. Therefore she refuses to fight at all."

"But they will capture and enslave us, and plunder and ruin all our lovely land!" exclaimed the Wizard, greatly disturbed by this statement.

"I fear they will," said the Tin Woodman, sorrowfully. "And I also fear that those who are not fairies, such as the Wizard, and Dorothy, and her uncle and aunt, as well as Toto and Billina, will be speedily put to death by the conquerors."

"What can be done?" asked Dorothy, shuddering a little at the prospect of this awful fate.

"Nothing can be done!" gloomily replied the Emperor of the Winkies. "But since Ozma refuses my army I will go myself to the Emerald City. The least I may do is to perish beside my beloved Ruler."

Chapter 25

HOW the SCARECROW
DISPLAYED HIS WISDOM

This amazing news had saddened every heart and all were now anxious to return to the Emerald City and share Ozma's fate. So they started without loss of time, and as the road led past the Scarecrow's new mansion they determined to make a brief halt there and confer with him.

"The Scarecrow is probably the wisest man in all Oz," remarked the Tin Woodman, when they had started upon their journey. "His brains are plentiful and of excellent quality, and often he has told me things I might never have thought of myself. I must say I rely a great deal upon the Scarecrow's brains in this emergency."

The Tin Woodman rode on the front seat of the wagon, where Dorothy sat between him and the Wizard.

"Has the Scarecrow heard of Ozma's trouble?" asked the Captain General.

"I do not know, sir," was the reply.

"When I was a private," said Omby Amby, "I was an excellent army, as I fully proved in our war against the Nomes. But now there is not a single private left in our army, since Ozma made me the Captain General, so there is no one to fight and defend our lovely Ruler."

"True," said the Wizard. "The present army is composed only of officers, and the business of an officer is to order his men to fight. Since there are no men there can be no fighting."

"Poor Ozma!" whispered Dorothy, with tears in her sweet eyes. "It's dreadful to think of all her lovely fairy country being destroyed. I wonder if we couldn't manage to escape and get back to Kansas by means of the Magic Belt? And we might take Ozma with us and all work hard to get money for her, so she wouldn't be so *very* lonely and unhappy about the loss of her fairyland."

"Do you think there would be any work for *me* in Kansas?" asked the Tin Woodman.

"If you are hollow, they might use you in a canning factory," suggested Uncle Henry. "But I can't see the use of your working for a living. You never eat or sleep or need a new suit of clothes."

"I was not thinking of myself," replied the Emperor, with dignity. "I merely wondered if I could not help to support Dorothy and Ozma."

As they indulged in these sad plans for the future they journeyed in sight of the Scarecrow's new mansion, and even though filled with care and worry over the impending fate of Oz, Dorothy couldn't help a feeling of wonder at the sight she saw.

The Scarecrow's new house was shaped like an immense ear of corn. The rows of kernels were made of solid gold, and the green upon which the ear stood upright was a mass of sparkling emeralds. Upon the very top of the structure was perched a figure representing the Scarecrow himself, and upon his extended arms, as well as upon his head, were several crows carved out of ebony and having ruby eyes. You may imagine how big this ear of corn was when I tell you that a single gold kernel formed a window, swinging outward upon hinges, while a row of four kernels opened to make the front entrance. Inside there were five stories, each story being a single room.

The gardens around the mansion consisted of cornfields, and Dorothy acknowledged that the place was in all respects a very appropriate home for her good friend the Scarecrow.

"He would have been very happy here, I'm sure," she said, "if only the Nome King had left us alone. But if Oz is destroyed of course this place will be destroyed too."

"Yes," replied the Tin Woodman, "and also my beautiful tin castle, that has been my joy and pride."

"Jack Pumpkinhead's house will go too," remarked the Wizard, "as well as Professor Woggle-Bug's Athletic College, and Ozma's royal palace, and all our other handsome buildings."

"Yes, Oz will indeed become a desert when the Nome King gets through with it," sighed Omby Amby.

The Scarecrow came out to meet them and gave them all a hearty welcome.

"I hear you have decided always to live in the Land of Oz, after this," he said to Dorothy; "and that will delight my heart, for I have greatly disliked our frequent partings. But why are you all so downcast?"

"Have you heard the news?" asked the Tin Woodman.

"No news to make me sad," replied the Scarecrow.

Then Nick Chopper told his friend of the Nome King's tunnel, and how the evil creatures of the North had allied themselves with the underground monarch for the purpose of conquering and destroying Oz. "Well," said the Scarecrow, "it certainly looks bad for Ozma, and all of us. But I believe it is wrong to worry over anything before it happens. It is surely time enough to be sad when our country is despoiled and our people made slaves. So let us not deprive ourselves of the few happy hours remaining to us."

"Ah! that is real wisdom," declared the Shaggy Man, approvingly. "After we become really unhappy we shall regret these few hours that are left to us, unless we enjoy them to the utmost."

"Nevertheless," said the Scarecrow, "I shall go with you to the Emerald City and offer Ozma my services."

"She says we can do nothing to oppose our enemies," announced the Tin Woodman.

"And doubtless she is right, sir," answered the Scarecrow. "Still, she will appreciate our sympathy, and it is the duty of Ozma's friends to stand by her side when the final disaster occurs."

He then led them into his queer mansion and showed them the beautiful rooms in all the five stories. The lower room was a grand reception hall, with a hand-organ in one corner. This instrument the Scarecrow, when alone, could turn to amuse himself, as he was very fond of music. The walls were hung with white silk, upon which flocks of black crows were embroidered in black diamonds. Some of the chairs were made in the shape of big crows and upholstered with cushions of corn-colored silk.

The second story contained a fine banquet room, where the Scarecrow might entertain his guests, and the three stories above that were bed-chambers exquisitely furnished and decorated.

"From these rooms," said the Scarecrow, proudly, "one may obtain fine views of the surrounding cornfields. The corn I grow is always husky, and I call the ears my regiments, because they have so many kernels. Of course I cannot ride my cobs, but I really don't care shucks about that. Taken altogether, my farm will stack up with any in the neighborhood."

The visitors partook of some light refreshment and then hurried away to resume the road to the Emerald City. The Scarecrow found a seat in the wagon between Omby Amby and the Shaggy Man, and his weight did not add much to the load because he was stuffed with straw.

"You will notice I have one oat-field on my property," he remarked, as they drove away. "Oat-straw is, I have found, the best of all straws to re-stuff myself with when my interior gets musty or out of shape."

"Are you able to re-stuff yourself without help?" asked Aunt Em. "I should think that after the straw was taken out of you there wouldn't be anything left but your clothes."

"You are almost correct, madam," he answered. "My servants do the stuffing, under my direction. For my head, in which are my excellent brains, is a bag tied at the bottom. My face is neatly painted upon one side of the bag, as you may see. My head does not need re-stuffing, as my body does, for all that it requires is to have the face touched up with fresh paint occasionally."

It was not far from the Scarecrow's mansion to the farm of Jack Pumpkinhead, and when they arrived there both Uncle Henry and Aunt Em were much impressed. The farm was one vast pumpkin field, and some of the pumpkins were of enormous size. In one of them, which had been neatly hollowed out, Jack himself lived, and he declared that it was a very comfortable residence. The reason he grew so many pumpkins was in order that he might change his head as often as it became wrinkled or threatened to spoil.

The pumpkin-headed man welcomed his visitors joyfully and offered them several delicious pumpkin pies to eat.

"I don't indulge in pumpkin pies myself, for two reasons," he said. "One reason is that were I to eat pumpkins I would become a cannibal, and the other reason is that I never eat, not being hollow inside."

"Very good reasons," agreed the Scarecrow.

They told Jack Pumpkinhead of the dreadful news about the Nome King, and he decided to go with them to the Emerald City and help comfort Ozma.

"I had expected to live here in ease and comfort for many centuries," said Jack, dolefully; "but of course if the Nome King destroys everything in Oz I shall be destroyed too. Really, it seems too bad, doesn't it?"

They were soon on their journey again, and so swiftly did the Sawhorse draw the wagon over the smooth roads that before twilight fell they had reached the royal palace in the Emerald City, and were at their journey's end.

How Ozma Refused to Fight for Her Kingdom

zma was in her rose garden picking a bouquet when the party arrived, and she greeted all her old and new friends as smilingly and sweetly as ever.

Dorothy's eyes were full of tears as she kissed the lovely Ruler of Oz, and she whispered to her:

"Oh, Ozma, Ozma! I'm *so* sorry!"

Ozma seemed surprised.

"Sorry for what, Dorothy?" she asked.

"For all your trouble about the Nome King," was the reply.

Ozma laughed with genuine amusement.

"Why, that has not troubled me a bit, dear Princess," she

replied. Then, looking around at the sad faces of her friends, she added: "Have you all been worrying about this tunnel?"

"We have!" they exclaimed in a chorus.

"Well, perhaps it is more serious than I imagined," admitted the fair Ruler; "but I haven't given the matter much thought. After dinner we will all meet together and talk it over."

So they went to their rooms and prepared for dinner, and Dorothy dressed herself in her prettiest gown and put on her coronet, for she thought that this might be the last time she would ever appear as a Princess of Oz.

The Scarecrow, the Tin Woodman and Jack Pumpkinhead all sat at the dinner table, although none of them was made so he could eat. Usually they served to enliven the meal with their merry talk, but to-night all seemed strangely silent and uneasy.

As soon as the dinner was finished Ozma led the company to her own private room in which hung the Magic Picture. When they had seated themselves the Scarecrow was the first to speak.

"Is the Nome King's tunnel finished, Ozma?" he asked.

"It was completed to-day," she replied. "They have built it right under my palace grounds, and it ends in front of the Forbidden Fountain. Nothing but a crust of earth remains to separate our enemies from us, and when they march here they will easily break through this crust and rush upon us."

"Who will assist the Nome King?" inquired the Scarecrow.

"The Whimsies, the Growleywogs and the Phanfasms," she replied. "I watched to-day in my Magic Picture the messengers whom the Nome King sent to all these people to summon them to assemble in his great caverns."

"Let us see what they are doing now," suggested the Tin Woodman.

So Ozma wished to see the Nome King's cavern, and at once the landscape faded from the Magic Picture and was replaced by the scene then being enacted in the jeweled cavern of King Roquat.

A wild and startling scene it was which the Oz people beheld.

Before the Nome King stood the Chief of the Whimsies and the Grand Gallipoot of the Growleywogs, surrounded by their most skillful generals. Very fierce and powerful they looked, so that even the Nome King and General Guph, who stood beside his master, seemed a bit fearful in the presence of their allies.

Now a still more formidable creature entered the cavern. It was the First and Foremost of the Phanfasms and he proudly sat down in King Roquat's own throne and demanded the right to lead his forces through the tunnel in advance of all the others. The First and Foremost now appeared to all eyes in his hairy skin and the bear's head. What his real form was even Roquat did not know.

Through the arches leading into the vast series of caverns

that lay beyond the throne room of King Roquat could be seen ranks upon ranks of the invaders—thousands of Phanfasms, Growleywogs and Whimsies standing in serried lines, while behind them were massed the thousands upon thousands of General Guph's own army of Nomes.

"Listen!" whispered Ozma. "I think we can hear what they are saying."

So they kept still and listened.

"Is all ready?" demanded the First and Foremost, haughtily.

"The tunnel is finally completed," replied General Guph.

"How long will it take us to march to the Emerald City?" asked the Grand Gallipoot of the Growleywogs.

"If we start at midnight," replied the Nome King, "we shall arrive at the Emerald City by daybreak. Then, while all the Oz people are sleeping, we will capture them and make them our slaves. After that we will destroy the city itself and march through the Land of Oz, burning and devastating as we go."

"Good!" cried the First and Foremost. "When we get through with Oz it will be a desert wilderness. Ozma shall be my slave."

"She shall be *my* slave!" shouted the Grand Gallipoot, angrily.

"We'll decide that by and by," said King Roquat hastily. "Don't let us quarrel now, friends. First let us conquer Oz, and then we will divide the spoils of war in a satisfactory manner."

The First and Foremost smiled wickedly; but he only said:

"I and my Phanfasms go first, for nothing on earth can oppose our power."

They all agreed to that, knowing the Phanfasms to be the mightiest of the combined forces. King Roquat now invited them to attend a banquet he had prepared, where they might occupy themselves in eating and drinking until midnight arrived.

As they had now seen and heard all of the plot against them that they cared to, Ozma allowed her Magic Pictur~ fade away. Then she turned to her friends and said:

"Our enemies will be here sooner than I expect~ do you advise me to do?"

"It is now too late to assemble our people," sai~ Woodman, despondently. "If you had allowed me t~ and drill my Winkies we might have put up a good fight and destroyed many of our enemies before we were conquered."

"The Munchkins are good fighters, too," said Omby Amby; "and so are the Gillikins."

"But I do not wish to fight," declared Ozma, firmly. "No one has the right to destroy any living creatures, however evil they may be, or to hurt them or make them unhappy. I will not fight—even to save my kingdom."

"The Nome King is not so particular," remarked the Scarecrow. "He intends to destroy us all and ruin our beautiful country."

"Because the Nome King intends to do evil is no excuse for my doing the same," replied Ozma.

"Self-preservation is the first law of nature," quoted the Shaggy Man.

"True," she said, readily. "I would like to discover a plan to save ourselves without fighting."

That seemed a hopeless task to them, but realizing that Ozma was determined not to fight, they tried to think of some means that might promise escape.

"Couldn't we bribe our enemies, by giving them a lot of emeralds and gold?" asked Jack Pumpkinhead.

"No, because they believe they are able to take everything we have," replied the Ruler.

"I have thought of something," said Dorothy.

"What is it, dear?" asked Ozma.

"Let us use the Magic Belt to wish all of us in Kansas. We will put some emeralds in our pockets, and can sell them in Topeka for enough to pay off the mortgage on Uncle Henry's farm. Then we can all live together and be happy."

"A clever idea!" exclaimed the Scarecrow.

"Kansas is a very good country. I've been there," said the Shaggy Man.

"That seems to me an excellent plan," approved the Tin Woodman.

"No!" said Ozma, decidedly. "Never will I desert my people and leave them to so cruel a fate. I will use the Magic Belt to send the rest of you to Kansas, if you wish, but if my beloved country must be destroyed and my people enslaved I will remain and share their fate."

"Quite right," asserted the Scarecrow, sighing. "I will remain with you."

"And so will I," declared the Tin Woodman and the Shaggy Man and Jack Pumpkinhead, in turn. Tiktok, the machine man, also said he intended to stand by Ozma. "For," said he, "I should be of no use at all in Kansas."

"For my part," announced Dorothy, gravely, "if the Ruler of Oz must not desert her people, a Princess of Oz has no right to run away, either. I'm willing to become a slave with the rest of you; so all we can do with the Magic Belt is to use it to send Uncle Henry and Aunt Em back to Kansas."

"I've been a slave all my life," Aunt Em replied, with considerable cheerfulness, "and so has Henry. I guess we won't go back to Kansas, anyway. I'd rather take my chances with the rest of you."

Ozma smiled upon them all gratefully.

"There is no need to despair just yet," she said. "I'll get up early to-morrow morning and be at the Forbidden Fountain when the fierce warriors break through the crust of the earth. I will speak to them pleasantly and perhaps they won't be so very bad, after all."

"Why do they call it the Forbidden Fountain?" asked Dorothy, thoughtfully.

"Don't you know, dear?" returned Ozma, surprised.

"No," said Dorothy. "Of course I've seen the fountain in the palace grounds, ever since I first came to Oz; and I've read the sign which says: 'All Persons are Forbidden to Drink at this Fountain.' But I never knew *why* they were forbidden. The water seems clear and sparkling and it bubbles up in a golden basin all the time."

"That water," declared Ozma, gravely, "is the most dangerous thing in all the Land of Oz. It is the Water of Oblivion."

"What does that mean?" asked Dorothy.

"Whoever drinks at the Forbidden Fountain at once forgets everything he has ever known," Ozma asserted.

"It wouldn't be a bad way to forget our troubles," suggested Uncle Henry.

"That is true; but you would forget everything else, and become as ignorant as a baby," returned Ozma.

"Does it make one crazy?" asked Dorothy.

"No; it only makes one forget," replied the girl Ruler. "It is said that once—long, long ago—a wicked King ruled Oz, and made himself and all his people very miserable and unhappy. So Glinda, the Good Sorceress, placed this fountain here, and the King drank of its water and forgot all his wickedness. His mind became innocent and vacant, and when he learned the things of life again they were all good things. But the people remembered how wicked their King had been, and were still afraid of him. Therefore he made them all drink of the Water of Oblivion and forget everything they had known, so that they became as simple and innocent as their King. After that they all grew wise together, and their wisdom was good, so that peace and happiness reigned in the land. But for fear some one might drink of the water again, and in an instant forget all he had learned, the King put that sign upon the fountain, where it has remained for many centuries up to this very day."

They had all listened intently to Ozma's story, and when she finished speaking there was a long period of silence while all thought upon the curious magical power of the Water of Oblivion.

Finally the Scarecrow's painted face took on a broad smile that stretched the cloth as far as it would go.

"How thankful I am," he said, "that I have such an excellent assortment of brains!"

"I gave you the best brains I ever mixed," declared the Wizard, with an air of pride.

"You did, indeed!" agreed the Scarecrow, "and they work so splendidly that they have found a way to save Oz—to save us all!"

"I'm glad to hear that," said the Wizard. "We never needed saving more than we do just now."

"Do you mean to say you can save us from those awful Phanfasms, and Growleywogs and Whimsies?" asked Dorothy eagerly.

"I'm sure of it, my dear," asserted the Scarecrow, still smiling genially.

"Tell us how!" cried the Tin Woodman.

"Not now," said the Scarecrow. "You may all go to bed, and I advise you to forget your worries just as completely as if you had drunk of the Water of Oblivion in the Forbidden Fountain. I'm going to stay here and tell my plan to Ozma alone, but if you will all be at the Forbidden Fountain at day-break, you'll see how easily we will save the kingdom when our enemies break through the crust of earth and come from the tunnel."

So they went away and let the Scarecrow and Ozma alone; but Dorothy could not sleep a wink all night.

"He is only a Scarecrow," she said to herself, "and I'm not sure that his mixed brains are as clever as he thinks they are."

But she knew that if the Scarecrow's plan failed they were all lost; so she tried to have faith in him.

Chapter 27

HOW the FIERCE WARRIORS INVADED OZ

The Nome King and his terrible allies sat at the banquet table until midnight. There was much quarreling between the Growleywogs and Phanfasms, and one of the wee-headed Whimsies got angry at General Guph and choked him until he nearly stopped breathing. Yet no one was seriously hurt, and the Nome King felt much relieved when the clock struck twelve and they all sprang up and seized their weapons.

"Aha!" shouted the First and Foremost. "Now to conquer the Land of Oz!"

He marshaled his Phanfasms in battle array and at his word of command they marched into the tunnel and began the long journey through it to the Emerald City. The First and Foremost intended to take all the treasures of Oz for himself; to kill all who could be killed and enslave the rest; to destroy and lay waste the whole country, and afterward to conquer and enslave the Nomes, the Growleywogs and the Whimsies. And he knew his power was sufficient to enable him to do all these things easily.

Next marched into the tunnel the army of gigantic Growleywogs, with their Grand Gallipoot at their head. They were dreadful beings, indeed, and longed to get to Oz that they might begin to pilfer and destroy. The Grand Gallipoot was a little afraid of the First and Foremost, but had a cunning plan to murder or destroy that powerful being and secure the wealth of Oz for himself. Mighty little of the plunder would the Nome King get, thought the Grand Gallipoot.

The Chief of the Whimsies now marched his false-headed forces into the tunnel. In his wicked little head was a plot to destroy both the First and Foremost and the Grand Gallipoot. He intended to let them conquer Oz, since they insisted on going first; but he would afterward treacherously destroy them, as well as King Roquat, and keep all the slaves and treasure of Ozma's kingdom for himself.

After all his dangerous allies had marched into the tunnel the Nome King and General Guph started to follow them, at the head of fifty thousand Nomes, all fully armed.

"Guph," said the King, "those creatures ahead of us mean mischief. They intend to get everything for themselves and leave us nothing."

"I know," replied the General; "but they are not as clever as they think they are. When you get the Magic Belt you must at once wish the Whimsies and Growleywogs and Phanfasms all back into their own countries—and the Belt will surely take them there."

"Good!" cried the King. "An excellent plan, Guph. I'll do it. While they are conquering Oz I'll get the Magic Belt, and then only the Nomes will remain to ravage the country."

So you see there was only one thing that all were agreed upon—that Oz should be destroyed.

On, on, on the vast ranks of invaders marched, filling the tunnel from side to side. With a steady tramp, tramp, they advanced, every step taking them nearer to the beautiful Emerald City.

"Nothing can save the Land of Oz!" thought the First and Foremost, scowling until his bear face was as black as the tunnel.

"The Emerald City is as good as destroyed already!" muttered the Grand Gallipoot, shaking his war club fiercely.

"In a few hours Oz will be a desert!" said the Chief of the Whimsies, with an evil laugh.

"My dear Guph," remarked the Nome King to his General,

"at last my vengeance upon Ozma of Oz and her people is about to be accomplished."

"You are right!" declared the General. "Ozma is surely lost."

And now the First and Foremost, who was in advance and nearing the Emerald City, began to cough and to sneeze.

"This tunnel is terribly dusty," he growled, angrily. "I'll punish that Nome King for not having it swept clean. My throat and eyes are getting full of dust and I'm as thirsty as a fish!"

The Grand Gallipoot was coughing too, and his throat was parched and dry.

"What a dusty place!" he cried. "I'll be glad when we reach Oz, where we can get a drink."

"Who has any water?" asked the Whimsie Chief, gasping and choking. But none of his followers carried a drop of water, so he hastened on to get through the dusty tunnel to the Land of Oz.

"Where did all this dust come from?" demanded General Guph, trying hard to swallow but finding his throat so dry he couldn't.

"I don't know," answered the Nome King. "I've been in the tunnel every day while it was being built, but I never noticed any dust before."

"Let's hurry!" cried the General. "I'd give half the gold in Oz for a drink of water."

The dust grew thicker and thicker, and the throats and eyes and noses of the invaders were filled with it. But not one halted or turned back. They hurried forward more fierce and vengeful than ever.

HOW THEY DRANK at the FORBIDDEN FOUNTAIN

T he Scarecrow had no need to sleep; neither had the Tin Woodman or Tiktok or Jack Pumpkinhead. So they all wandered out into the palace grounds and stood beside the sparkling water of the Forbidden Fountain until daybreak. During this time they indulged in occasional conversation.

"Nothing could make me forget what I know," remarked the Scarecrow, gazing into the fountain, "for I cannot drink the Water of Oblivion or water of any kind. And I am glad that this is so, for I consider my wisdom unexcelled."

"You are cer-tain-ly ve-ry wise," agreed Tiktok. "For my

part, I can on-ly think by ma-chin-er-y, so I do not pre-tend to know as much as you do."

"My tin brains are very bright, but that is all I claim for them," said Nick Chopper, modestly. "Yet I do not aspire to being very wise, for I have noticed that the happiest people are those who do not let their brains oppress them."

"Mine never worry me," Jack Pumpkinhead acknowl-edged. "There are many seeds of thought in my head, but they do not sprout easily. I am glad that it is so, for if I occu-pied my days in thinking I should have no time for anything else."

In this cheery mood they passed the hours until the first golden streaks of dawn appeared in the sky. Then Ozma joined them, as fresh and lovely as ever and robed in one of her prettiest gowns.

"Our enemies have not yet arrived," said the Scarecrow, after greeting affectionately the sweet and girlish Ruler.

"They will soon be here," she said, "for I have just glanced at my Magic Picture, and have seen them coughing and chok-ing with the dust in the tunnel."

"Oh, is there dust in the tunnel?" asked the Tin Wood-man.

"Yes; Ozma placed it there by means of the Magic Belt," explained the Scarecrow, with one of his broad smiles.

Then Dorothy came to them, Uncle Henry and Aunt Em following close after her. The little girl's eyes were heavy because she had had a sleepless and anxious night. Toto walked by her side, but the little dog's spirits were very much subdued. Billina, who was always up by daybreak, was not long in joining the group by the fountain.

The Wizard and the Shaggy Man next arrived, and soon after appeared Omby Amby, dressed in his best uniform.

"There lies the tunnel," said Ozma, pointing to a part of the ground just before the Forbidden Fountain, "and in a few moments the dreadful invaders will break through the earth and swarm over the land. Let us all stand on the other side of the Fountain and watch to see what happens."

At once they followed her suggestion and moved around the fountain of the Water of Oblivion. There they stood silent and expectant until the earth beyond gave way with a sudden crash and up leaped the powerful form of the First and Foremost, followed by all his grim warriors.

As the leader sprang forward his gleaming eyes caught the play of the fountain and he rushed toward it and drank eagerly of the sparkling water. Many of the other Phanfasms drank, too, in order to clear their dry and dusty throats. Then they stood around and looked at one another with simple, wondering smiles.

The First and Foremost saw Ozma and her companions beyond the fountain, but instead of making an effort to capture her he merely stared at her in pleased admiration of her beauty—for he had forgotten where he was and why he had come there.

But now the Grand Gallipoot arrived, rushing from the tunnel with a hoarse cry of mingled rage and thirst. He too saw the fountain and hastened to drink of its forbidden waters. The other Growleywogs were not slow to follow suit, and even before they had finished drinking the Chief of the Whimsies and his people came to push them away, while they one and all cast off their false heads that they might slake their thirst at the fountain.

When the Nome King and General Guph arrived they both made a dash to drink, but the General was so mad with thirst that he knocked his King over, and while Roquat lay sprawling upon the ground the General drank heartily of the Water of Oblivion.

This rude act of his General made the Nome King so angry that for a moment he forgot he was thirsty and rose to his feet to glare upon the group of terrible warriors he had brought here to assist him. He saw Ozma and her people, too, and yelled out:

"Why don't you capture them? Why don't you conquer Oz, you idiots? Why do you stand there like a lot of dummies?"

But the great warriors had become like little children. They had forgotten all their enmity against Ozma and against Oz. They had even forgotten who they themselves were, or why they were in this strange and beautiful country. As for the Nome King, they did not recognize him, and wondered who he was.

The sun came up and sent its flood of silver rays to light the faces of the invaders. The frowns and scowls and evil looks were all gone. Even the most monstrous of the creatures there assembled smiled innocently and seemed light-hearted and content merely to be alive.

Not so with Roquat, the Nome King. He had not drunk from the Forbidden Fountain and all his former rage against Ozma and Dorothy now inflamed him as fiercely as ever. The sight of General Guph babbling like a happy child and playing with his hands in the cool waters of the fountain astonished and maddened Red Roquat. Seeing that his terrible allies and his own General refused to act, the Nome King turned to order his great army of Nomes to advance from the tunnel and seize the helpless Oz people.

But the Scarecrow suspected what was in the King's mind and spoke a word to the Tin Woodman. Together they ran at Roquat and grabbing him up tossed him into the great basin of the fountain.

The Nome King's body was round as a ball, and it bobbed up and down in the Water of Oblivion while he spluttered and screamed with fear lest he should drown. And when he cried out, his mouth filled with water, which ran down his throat, so that straightway he forgot all he had formerly known just as completely as had all the other invaders.

Ozma and Dorothy could not refrain from laughing to see their dreaded enemies become as harmless as babies. There was no danger now that Oz would be destroyed. The only question remaining to solve was how to get rid of this horde of intruders.

The Shaggy Man kindly pulled the Nome King out of the fountain and set him upon his thin legs. Roquat was dripping wet, but he chattered and laughed and wanted to drink more of the water. No thought of injuring any person was now in his mind.

Before he left the tunnel he had commanded his fifty thousand Nomes to remain there until he ordered them to advance, as he wished to give his allies time to conquer Oz before he appeared with his own army. Ozma did not wish all these Nomes to overrun her land, so she advanced to King Roquat and taking his hand in her own said gently:

"Who are you? What is your name?"

"I don't know," he replied, smiling at her. "Who are you, my dear?"

"My name is Ozma," she said; "and your name is Roquat."

"Oh, is it?" he replied, seeming pleased.

"Yes; you are King of the Nomes," she said.

"Ah; I wonder what the Nomes are!" returned the King, as if puzzled.

"They are underground elves, and that tunnel over there is full of them," she answered. "You have a beautiful cavern at the other end of the tunnel, so you must go to your Nomes and say: 'March home!' Then follow after them and in time you will reach the pretty cavern where you live."

The Nome King was much pleased to learn this, for he had forgotten he had a cavern. So he went to the tunnel and said to his army: 'March home!' At once the Nomes turned and marched back through the tunnel, and the King followed after them, laughing with delight to find his orders so readily obeyed.

The Wizard went to General Guph, who was trying to count his fingers, and told him to follow the Nome King, who was his master. Guph meekly obeyed, and so all the Nomes quitted the Land of Oz forever.

But there were still the Phanfasms and Whimsies and Growleywogs standing around in groups, and they were so many that they filled the gardens and trampled upon the flowers and grass because they did not know that the tender plants would be injured by their clumsy feet. But in all other respects they were perfectly harmless and played together like children or gazed with pleasure upon the pretty sights of the royal gardens.

After counseling with the Scarecrow Ozma sent Omby Amby to the palace for the Magic Belt, and when the Captain General returned with it the Ruler of Oz at once clasped the precious Belt around her waist.

"I wish all these strange people—the Whimsies and the Growleywogs and the Phanfasms—safe back in their own homes!" she said.

It all happened in a twinkling, for of course the wish was no sooner spoken than it was granted.

All the hosts of the invaders were gone, and only the trampled grass showed that they had ever been in the Land of Oz.

How Glinda Worked
a Magic Spell

That was better than fighting," said Ozma, when all our friends were assembled in the palace after the exciting events of the morning; and each and every one agreed with her.

"No one was hurt," said the Wizard, delightedly.

"And no one hurt us," added Aunt Em.

"But, best of all," said Dorothy, "the wicked people have all forgotten their wickedness, and will not wish to hurt any one after this."

"True, Princess," declared the Shaggy Man. "It seems to me that to have reformed all those evil characters is more important than to have saved Oz."

"Nevertheless," remarked the Scarecrow, "I am glad Oz is saved. I can now go back to my new mansion and live happily."

"And I am glad and grateful that my pumpkin farm is saved," said Jack.

"For my part," added the Tin Woodman, "I cannot express my joy that my lovely tin castle is not to be demolished by wicked enemies."

"Still," said Tiktok, "o-ther en-e-mies may come to Oz some day."

"Why do you allow your clock-work brains to interrupt our joy?" asked Omby Amby, frowning at the machine man.

"I say what I am wound up to say," answered Tiktok.

"And you are right," declared Ozma. "I myself have been thinking of this very idea, and it seems to me there are entirely too many ways for people to get to the Land of Oz. We used to think the deadly desert that surrounds us was enough protection; but that is no longer the case. The Wizard and Dorothy have both come here through the air, and I am told the earth people have invented airships that can fly anywhere they wish them to go."

"Why, sometimes they do, and sometimes they don't," asserted Dorothy.

"But in time the airships may cause us trouble," continued Ozma, "for if the earth folk learn how to manage them we would be overrun with visitors who would ruin our lovely, secluded fairyland."

"That is true enough," agreed the Wizard.

"Also the desert fails to protect us in other ways," Ozma went on, thoughtfully. "Johnny Dooit once made a sand-boat that sailed across it, and the Nome King made a tunnel under it. So I believe something ought to be done to cut us off from the rest of the world entirely, so that no one in the future will ever be able to intrude upon us."

"How will you do that?" asked the Scarecrow.

"I do not know; but in some way I am sure it can be accomplished. To-morrow I will make a journey to the castle of Glinda the Good, and ask her advice."

"May I go with you?" asked Dorothy, eagerly.

"Of course, my dear Princess; and I also invite any of our friends here who would like to undertake the journey."

They all declared they wished to accompany their girl Ruler, for this was indeed an important mission, since the future of the Land of Oz to a great extent depended upon it. So Ozma gave orders to her servants to prepare for the journey on the morrow.

That day she watched her Magic Picture, and when it showed her that all the Nomes had returned through the tunnel to their underground caverns, Ozma used the Magic Belt to close up the tunnel, so that the earth underneath the desert sands became as solid as it was before the Nomes began to dig.

Early the following morning a gay cavalcade set out to visit the famous Sorceress, Glinda the Good. Ozma and Dorothy rode in a chariot drawn by the Cowardly Lion and the Hungry Tiger, while the Sawhorse drew the red wagon in which rode the rest of the party.

With hearts light and free from care they traveled merrily along through the lovely and fascinating Land of Oz, and in good season reached the stately castle in which resided the Sorceress.

Glinda knew that they were coming.

"I have been reading about you in my Magic Book," she said, as she greeted them in her gracious way.

"What is your Magic Book like?" inquired Aunt Em, curiously.

"It is a record of everything that happens," replied the Sorceress. "As soon as an event takes place, anywhere in the world, it is immediately found printed in my Magic Book. So when I read its pages I am well informed."

"Did it tell you how our enemies drank the Water of 'Blivion?" asked Dorothy.

"Yes, my dear; it told all about it. And also it told me you were all coming to my castle, and why."

"Then," said Ozma, "I suppose you know what is in my mind, and that I am seeking a way to prevent any one in the future from discovering the Land of Oz."

"Yes; I know that. And while you were on your journey I have thought of a way to accomplish your desire. For it seems to me unwise to allow too many outside people to come here. Dorothy, with her uncle and aunt, has now returned to Oz to live always, and there is no reason why we should leave any way open for others to travel uninvited to our fairyland. Let us make it impossible for any one ever to communicate with us in any way, after this. Then we may live peacefully and contentedly."

"Your advice is wise," returned Ozma. "I thank you, Glinda, for your promise to assist me."

"But how can you do it?" asked Dorothy. "How can you keep every one from ever finding Oz?"

"By making our country invisible to all eyes but our own," replied the Sorceress, smiling. "I have a magic charm powerful enough to accomplish that wonderful feat, and now that we have been warned of our danger by the Nome King's invasion, I believe we must not hesitate to separate ourselves forever from all the rest of the world."

"I agree with you," said the Ruler of Oz.

"Won't it make any difference to us?" asked Dorothy, doubtfully.

"No, my dear," Glinda answered, assuringly. "We shall still be able to see each other and everything in the Land of Oz. It won't affect us at all; but those who fly through the air over our country will look down and see nothing at all. Those who come to the edge of the desert, or try to cross it, will catch no glimpse of Oz, or know in what direction it lies. No one will try to tunnel to us again because we cannot be seen and therefore cannot be found. In other words, the Land of Oz will entirely disappear from the knowledge of the rest of the world."

"That's all right," said Dorothy, cheerfully. "You may make Oz invis'ble as soon as you please, for all I care."

"It is already invisible," Glinda stated. "I knew Ozma's wishes, and performed the Magic Spell before you arrived."

Ozma seized the hand of the Sorceress and pressed it gratefully.

"Thank you!" she said.

Chapter 30

HOW the STORY of OZ
CAME to an END

The writer of these Oz stories has received a little note from Princess Dorothy of Oz which, for a time, has made him feel rather disconcerted. The note was written on a broad, white feather from a stork's wing, and it said:

"You will never hear anything more about Oz, because we are now cut off forever from the rest of the world. But Toto and I will always love you and all the other children who love us.

"DOROTHY GALE."

This seemed to me too bad, at first, for Oz is a very interesting fairyland. Still, we have no right to feel grieved, for we have had enough of the history of the Land of Oz to fill six story books, and from its quaint people and their strange adventures we have been able to learn many useful and amusing things.

So good luck to little Dorothy and her companions. May they live long in their invisible country and be very happy!

EXPLORE the WORLD of OZ.

EXPLORE the WORLD of OZ.